Hip to be Square

Joan —
Thanks for the workout
spirit of
encouragement!

Hope Lyda

Hope Lyda

HARVEST HOUSE PUBLISHERS

EUGENE, OREGON

Cover by Left Coast Design, Portland, Oregon

Cover illustration by Krieg Barrie Illustrations, Hoquiam, Washington

HIP TO BE SQUARE
Copyright © 2005 by Hope Lyda
Published by Harvest House Publishers
Eugene, Oregon 97402
www.harvesthousepublishers.com

Library of Congress Cataloging-in-Publication Data
Lyda, Hope.
    Hip to be square / Hope Lyda.
        p. cm.
    ISBN-13: 978-0-7369-1589-2
    ISBN-10: 0-7369-1589-3 (pbk.)
    1. Women social workers—Fiction.   2. Old age homes—Employees—Fiction.   3 Physical fitness
    centers—Employees—Fiction.   I. Title.
    PS3612.Y35H57 2005
    813'.6—dc22   2005003040

Printed in the United States of America

05 06 07 08 09 10 11 12 13 / BP-MS / 10 9 8 7 6 5 4 3 2 1

This book is dedicated to my husband, Marc—
my champion, my home, and my pilgrimage partner
for fifteen years. Thank you for "getting me"
...and for loving me unconditionally.

And to my sister, Dawn,
who not only shares a childhood with me
but also joins me in the pursuit of purpose,
the examination of life's mysteries,
and the belief that when we finally pay attention,
we can hear that still, small voice.

Acknowledgments

Thanks to...

My parents, Dwaine and Jean Flora, who continue to say they are proud of their girls (and mean it).

Carolyn McCready and LaRae Weikert, for kicking me into gear on this (lovingly and with treats, of course).

Barb Sherrill, Betty Fletcher, Terry Glaspey, and Julie McKinney, for the support and encouragement throughout the process.

Bob Hawkins Jr., for taking a chance on a new voice in fiction.

The cheerleaders who inspire me to find my way, including: Jackie, who shared her own "Golden Horizons" stories and many encouraging words; Kari, for clever notes and chicken soup; my walking buddies—Christy, Abby, Andrea, and Shana—our conversations helped me shape my next step; Dawn R., for sweet friendship and belief; Nancy, for life discussions and walkie-talkies; Kimberly, for embracing the discipline and joy of writing.

Theos coffee shop, for providing me with a perfect setting to dream, write, and sip gallons of cold water extract coffee for hours on end.

Kim Moore, who is an empathetic reader, a dynamic editor, and a very kind soul. Thank you for taking care of my story and for shaping it into a stronger, tighter tale.

With gratitude for those who believe in the wonder and gift of books.

The Start of a Good Joke

Parents' Night Talent Show—Emerson Grade School
Washington, D.C.
1985

I cracked my knuckles and nervously awaited my chance to perform the finale. It was an honor to be last. I had barely beaten out Mick Bederstat for the coveted closing act. Actually, I had beaten him up, and he feigned the flu.

The velvet curtain, the color of red licorice, brushed against my skin and caused goose bumps to form. It wasn't nerves. That just wasn't my disposition…or whatever word Mrs. Engleman had used the day I offered to sing the Pledge of Allegiance as a solo because I tired of her monotone performance each morning.

I had no talent. Nothing to single out, anyway. So I decided to fall back on my natural wit.

Mrs. Engleman approached the adult-level mic. Her corduroy skirt bunched in the back and made the sound of a muted kazoo as she walked. "Ladies and gentleman, parents, grandparents, and supportive friends and family…I am pleased to introduce third grader Mari Hamilton. Her comedy act will be tonight's finale. Let's welcome Mari." Her clap pounded in the mic as I made my way around her to the lower mic.

I cleared my throat, looked at the seats reserved for my mom and dad, and took a leap into celebrity. "Parents (pause, one, two, three), can't live with them and we're too young to leave 'em."

Silence. Cough. Polite chuckle from the far corner.

"Parents (pause, one, two), can't live with them and until we can drive, we're stuck."

Nervous laughter from stepparents.

The audience was tough to crack, but I knew my next joke would win them over.

"Parents (pause, one), can't live with them…arrgghh."

I tell you the truth. I actually made a comic strip "arrrgggh" sound as Engleman yanked on my orange vest and pulled me behind the curtain.

Personal rights against censorship do not exist in the third grade. Still, I was quick to protest. "But my next line was really sweet. Sentimental even."

The old woman in front of me—who was probably no more than thirty years into her life—closed her eyes to count her way to patience. Meanwhile, her hand motioned for Tommy Lesburg to do another horrific drum solo.

"Just listen." I refused to give in easily. I had, after all, just been warming up the crowd. "Parents. Can't live with them…wouldn't be alive without them."

Pause.

"Sweet, right? It is saying we owe our lives to our parents. See?" My father always said I should teach debate at the college level. Not because I was good necessarily, but because I certainly favored practicing this discipline. Mrs. Engleman was not as impressed.

"Better. But, Mari, parents' night is not the place to voice such…

frustrations. I apologize for not taking the time to hear your comedy material prior to your performance. And I will take responsibility when I explain to your parents. Where are they seated?"

"Front row."

She poked her Ronald McDonald hair between the frayed panels to search the crowd.

I reeled her back in. "Front row of city hall. They are petitioning the city's new zoning law, which would force our…their…youth shelter out of the neighborhood." The next year I would discover that we lived in an "undesirable part of town" because Cynthia Louise Cantwell announces this to me and all of my other hard-earned friends at a birthday party held in the Smithsonian.

The red fluff was pushed back, and I watched brown eyes disappear behind blue-shadowed lids. Counting again, I assumed.

"Honest," I reiterated.

She released the hold of my vest in empathy. "I see. I'm sorry, honey." She smoothed an imaginary wrinkle in my green blouse. "Why don't I have Mr. and Mrs. Rochester drive you home now? They were here to help set up for the show. I don't think they'd mind. Is that okay?" She is not used to passing people off. "Can you wait in the foyer or do you want to stay with me?"

"Foyer." I turned to make my way down the back steps so I wouldn't have to face any of the uncensored performers.

"Mari…" My unrelenting teacher called after me.

My shoulders and sigh asked, "What?"

"The work your parents do is very important. Very important. Just think of all the children they help. You should feel honored. It's noble."

"Yep." I slouched my way to the so-called foyer, which consisted of a concrete bench and a plastic yucca.

When the glittery beige Cadillac pulled up, I slipped my hands further up into the tunnel of my sleeves, wishing I could disappear altogether. Mrs. Engleman opened the back door for me and gave the Rochesters directions to the shelter. Upon hearing the address, the couple sighed and grew teary. Old folks.

"This is a pretty car, all sparkly," I say, trying to distract them.

"They call it champagne."

In my world it was oatmeal, oatmeal with sugar sprinkles if you were lucky.

"I hear the young couple who runs the shelter is so kind. It's such noble work. The...what is their name, Fred?"

"Hammel? ...Hamlin? Oh, yes...Hamilton."

I didn't try to explain that I was not a resident of the facility but rather a captive by birth. I liked the idea of their misunderstanding. After all, I felt like an orphan most days...Mom and Dad spent so much of their time meeting the needs of fifteen live-in kids and countless other day charges. I was number eight in our dinner line. I was part of the Blue Team on the chore chart. I was the recipient of the "It is important to share" speech which was given by parent A while parent B pried a toy, a piece of candy, or a Schwinn handlebar from my grip.

This case of mistaken identity started me wondering what life would be like without parents. The wisdom of my comedy act returned to me... "And we're too young to leave 'em." Right then and there I vowed to become an adult as soon as possible. And when I could finally shed my childhood like an outgrown, hand-me-down sateen jacket, I would do wildly exciting things, like vacation in Mexico, drive a champagne-colored convertible, donate lots of money to good causes, but never, ever volunteer in a soup kitchen.

And the thought that delighted me most: I would celebrate a life free of my parents' opinions and their very oatmeal way of life.

God's Punch Line

Golden Horizons Retirement Center
Tucson, Arizona
Present Day

Honey, your bosom is very nice. You shouldn't wear such a terrible trench coat. You'll never find a man that way...or a man will never find you...under all that." Mrs. Sally Jenkins adjusts her wig in the mirror; I straighten her collar from behind her wheelchair.

"As you well know, Sally, this is not a trench coat. It is the official uniform for Golden Horizons Retirement Center, and I think it is quite stylish." I strike a pose that she ignores because she is putting large butterfly-shaped earrings onto her drooping lobes.

"You could try to be a bit more...available, you know." She points a press-on nail in my general direction. I duck in time to save an eye.

I believe God is fond of irony and humor. I believe he listens to the vow of a third grader and sets it aside for future material. He does not need to close his eyes and count because he is a God of abundant patience. He merely waited for the perfect rebuttal to my youthful self-promise and placed me here, in Tucson, as the activities director who serves not two, but two hundred controlling, opinionated surrogate parents among oatmeal-colored walls.

"Start getting out more, that's all I'm saying. I date more than you do." Sally tries to roll her eyes, but her mascara has just about welded the upper and lower lids together. She rotates her face and contorts her expression to test the elasticity of today's mask.

"I am not looking for a man," I say defensively.

Sally adjusts her hair one more time and tries to peak it to a mountainous crest and is displeased. "You sure don't do hair like Beau. Have I ever told you about…"

"Yes. Yes. The amazing chignon of 1998. Sally, if I have to hear about Beau the beautician one more time, I will never shave the back of your neck again."

Beau…my activities director predecessor and apparently a man who could do anything except fail. Even the most disgruntled residents reminisce about the days of Beau. I cannot stand the guy. We've never met. But I think that if I ran into a guy named Beau in a dark alley, I could take him at any challenge…chignons, sponge cake, karaoke, you name it. In fact, I look forward to the day I run across the boy named Beau.

My somewhat idle threat has worked for now. Sally returns to her original complaint. "If you take your own sweet time, you will run out of it. Don't wait until you are eighty. It's slim pickins at this age." She pauses only long enough to check her profile in the mirror. The orange foundation line across her chin does not faze her. Beneath wands of lashes, her eyes brighten with discovery. "Hey, where's the goat?"

"Excuse me?" I gather the makeup brushes and shove them back into plastic stackable cubbyholes, the kind used to store socks and underwear in dorm rooms.

"The painting…with the goat?" Her mass of orchestrated tangles leans toward the wall opposite the vanity.

"It's a Chagall print," I say without looking. I know its every brilliant hue and offbeat shape by heart. "It is one of my favorites. Though I really love his series housed at the Museum of the Biblical Message in Nice. I've only seen it in books, of course, but he painted scenes from—"

"Okay, show-off. Whatever it is, it is missing. Don't make me late for the reading group." Sally has little tolerance for new knowledge that does not relate to hair, George Clooney, or dating. As if on cue, she returns to this latter topic. "You know, my nephew Roger owns a much more respectable print of a Monet. Do you know the one that has the bridge and the faded flowers?" She unnecessarily describes the most overly reproduced art image in the history of museum gift shops. "My Roger is a catch by any standards. You two should— "

I pop a wheelie to throw Sally's last words back down her throat and to stop the image of Roger sitting on a pleather couch, offering me tap water from an emerald green Perrier bottle and fancy French cookies bought in bulk at the local supermarket while discussing the benefits of "art" collecting ad nauseum.

Only recently did I find out that my love life was fodder for more than Parcheesi gossip. My romantic endeavors, or lack of them, was the subject of the longest running bet ever to exist in the hallowed halls of Golden Horizons. Running so long, in fact, that seven residents had their bets redistributed after they…moved on.

The path from the salon to the commons room is scattered with other residents who are heading our way. They file in to the large multipurpose room and look for places to sit in the semicircle of metal chairs. I survey the octogenarian crowd waiting to discuss chapter 2 of Nicholas Sparks' *The Notebook* and am most certain that my Mr. Right will not be found among their spawn. God willing.

The gray-and-blue tiled area looks like a showroom for Deluxe Wheels and Regal-Rotary wheelchair models with an entire back section of reading group participants parked in orderly rows. They WD-40'd their wheels days in advance.

This latest book evokes very tender memories. While Stan Sherman discusses how his wife died of cancer ten years ago, I wipe away a few tears. His frayed baseball cap and oversized Yankees sweatshirt are endearing. I want to take him home. This, my friend Angelica would say, is one of my issues.

I believe I have many.

For example, on my way to becoming that independent adult I vowed at age nine to become, I have bypassed the joy of being my age. Here I am approaching thirty—my absolute goal for success and happiness—and I have let the demographic of my eight to five crowd start to crowd out my youth.

Exaggeration?

I receive the AARP newsletter instead of *Vogue*.

I call out bingo numbers instead of giving out my number to eligible men.

While people my age are investigating safe tanning methods, I have a file filled with the latest research on hip replacement surgery.

Lord, help me.

I have started to wonder if that overused prayer has become a useless, mute plea to God. Because he certainly doesn't seem to listen, and his response time doesn't take into account the "window for success" that a career demands. For the past five years I have prayed for a way out of this job, but student loans, the economy, and two crashed hard drives possessing my recent résumé derail good intentions. I cannot see my way out of this current life. The thought gives me goose bumps. The fear kind, not the inspired kind.

Then again, could be the flu. Even my health cycles are that of the over-seventy-five crowd.

Spending too much time with these folks is a bit like being trapped at a baby shower. You inevitably hear terror stories of physical anguish and are offered advice against your persistent yet polite wishes that they really not go there. *Oh, I never thought I would have problems with* [insert any private body function] *either. Learn from me, deary. Eat your* [insert remedy…soy, yogurt, iron supplements, etc.] *now.* To which you cringe and inevitably turn to the person on the other side of you, who initially looks normal, until her mouth opens and she says, *Learn from me, deary. Don't ever eat soy or yogurt or take iron supplements, etc.* It is a wash every time.

After a while these crazy personal horror stories start to sink in. I imagine chills, sniffles, and aches where there is nothing more than typical working girl fatigue. But just in case I am ever on the verge of faulty [insert private body function], I had my friend Sadie come over and help me install a lazy Susan in my kitchen cupboard so I would have easy access to the latest multi-herbal-combo-infused-coated supplements. To alphabetize said medicines was completely Sadie's doing. I am not obsessive.

But I am regular.

"Mari, you have a visitor. Front lounge area." The loudspeaker bellows this just above reading group leader Kay William's purple-and-yellow striped hat—a carryover from her days as an elementary school librarian. She starts with a bolt of nerves, her large hands losing their place in the book. She licks her fingers and smears coral lipstick onto the white pages to regain her spot, and the other residents give me dirty looks.

"Sorry," I whisper under my breath and sneak out to the hallway. I am thankful to leave. Why can't Mad Hatter choose something peppier? There are so many happy books.

I trundle down the hall listing off optimistic stories. "*Wind in the Willows. Anne of Green Gables. All Creatures Great and Small. Huckleberry Finn*—"

"I shot Kennedy." Fran, a woman who laps the facility in Mickey Mouse slippers and fabricates a new history of her life daily, whispers into my ear. The smell of the peppermints she steals from my supervisor's office wafts toward my nose.

"Just as I suspected." I nod at her and keep walking. I turn back and see her talking into a pretend phone. She's probably discussing her legal strategy now that her secret is known by the woman who leaves these corridors and surely tells the FBI or at least NPR about such confessions.

My smock stretches tight across my back when I reach for colorful streamers and balloons as I walk the corridor. This action allows me to cross the masquerade ball off my long list of annual activities. "I am Julie, your cruise activities director," I say, mimicing reruns of the *Love Boat* to nobody. As freeing as it is to speak nonsensical, fantastical thoughts out loud, I'm still stuck on a boat that never docks in exotic ports promising parasailing, genuine handcrafted baskets, and that most requested excursion of all…love.

My sights are set on a horizon more golden than this one, indeed. I am determined to have the life I want by the time I am thirty. However, I just turned twenty-nine a month ago, and I have no plan in motion to exchange this charity job for a glamorous resort recreation director position or for attaining an enviable love life…and all the other imagined trappings of a perfect existence.

"Hey there." I say before the person in the waiting room stands up and turns around to greet me. Answering the phone or greeting a guest does not allow for surprise. My life consists of three people with a few minor characters thrown in here and there.

"Thank goodness they found you. It takes them forever. Forever."

A deep and full-bodied voice that should belong to a jazz singer belongs to my friend, who is five foot two and tiny and cannot carry a tune. I expected her to squeak like a mouse the first time I met her.

"You'd think they could locate an employee—" She stomps her foot without effect because she is wearing fuzzy slippers.

"Hey. Caitlin. What brings you here?" I say, encouraging her along. She goes through this spiel every time.

"I was just over at the resale shop on Seventh and, of course, thought of you. Can you believe it has been three years since we met that day you went in to look for those pants? Corduroy, were they?"

"Yes. Good memory. A resident had left his only photos of his wife in the pocket. We looked for nearly two hours that night. I still cannot believe you helped me."

She smiles, remembering our beginnings. "Well, when I overheard your reason and the manager's lack of compassion, I just had to. And we found them! And each other."

"Ahhhh." We croon this simultaneously.

I check the clock on the wall over Caitlin's shoulder. "I'm off pretty soon; I just need to lock all the outside doors. Want to come with me?"

Always agreeable, Caitlin salutes me and then says, "I brought you a vanilla latte."

"Mmm. You, Caitlin Ramirez, are my best friend." My mood is altered just in the anticipation of something warm and sweet.

"I spoke to your other best friends. We have decided on Freddie's for breakfast tomorrow. Are you on?" She drains her latte, tosses it, and pulls a file from her leopard-print purse to work on her long, bright pink nails.

"Sure, I'm on. But you mean Bible study."

"Yeah, Bible study." She looks up from a hangnail. "You seem down. Are you down?"

"No, not really."

"Not really?" She hiccups as she often does when doing two things at once.

"No, just tired." I notice Caitlin's short, black hair is sprinkled with pink glitter.

"Just tired?"

"Could be a cold." Why am I extending this dialogue?

"A cold?"

A conversation with Caitlin is like a monologue in the Grand Canyon.

"No. I'm fine. Glad the weekend is here." I don't lament out loud that my only planned activity is our breakfast gathering. Surely if I am tired of my state of being, so is my wide circle of three. Once a month we meet for what started as a Bible study. Lately we have done less delving into spiritual matters and more dissecting of life moments. I figure life moments are what lead us back to spiritual matters, so in our self-absorbed way, we are right on track.

"Yes…the weekend. I think Sadie has big news," Caitlin offers.

"Really? What?"

"You know Sadie. Lock-lipped. Lip-locked? No, that would be kissing. Well, you know…she won't talk. But she did allude to some guy. Which could be lip-locked, I guess." She laughs at her joke and then sighs. "Sadie is so deserving." Jealousy taints how much she means this. "At least we will have something to discuss this week."

"In addition to…"

"In addition to…?"

"We will have something to discuss in *addition to* the book of Matthew."

"Matthew?" She pauses, and I assume she is recalling a boyfriend from college. I can almost hear her flipping pages of her diary. She sighs ever so audibly between hiccups.

The grandfather clock next to me begins to announce quittin' time. I was not about to stay a moment later. It is dangerous to get stuck in these hallways at night; one is likely to get talked into a round of dinnertime dominos. I made that mistake once. Okay, five times.

"Do you want to come over and heat up a pizza?"

"I have to head on to Fab to hang up some inventory, but thanks. I just wanted to honor the day we met while I was thinking about it." She reaches around my paper cup to give me a quick hug.

"Thanks, Caitlin. This made my day. See you tomorrow?"

"Tomorrow."

As I lock the door behind her, I think about Sadie. No, I think about levelheaded, act-together Sadie and a guy. Has she found someone?

I am probably the only one of us who could say "congratulations, it's a boy" without a hint of envy. Four years ago I decided I would wait until just before my thirties to date seriously. I wanted all the other things *by* thirty, so it would follow that a serious somebody would appear immediately after. So far, nobody has attempted to interfere with that declaration. Perhaps if I approach the "new job, new life before I am thirty" conviction with similar resolve, it will also come true.

I don't dwell on the fact that the first commitment has been easy to fulfill because nobody asked.

Bible Study

Thanks for the ride." I fold into my friend Angelica Ross' baby blue BMW, catching the edge of my linen pants on the door handle.

"Did you check the bottom of your shoes? I just had the car detailed. I have to pick up a client on Monday. Some new doctor from San Francisco. First impressions are very important."

I stifle the urge to tell her that "pick up a client" makes it sound as though she is a lady of the evening, not a pharmaceutical rep.

I open the door and tap my heels like Dorothy in *The Wizard of Oz*. "There's no place like breakfast. There's no place like breakfast." I swing the soles of my feet in her direction and wait for permission to be her passenger.

"Good enough." Angelica adjusts her rearview mirror to check her lipstick and adjust the blond swatch of bangs across her forehead. "You hear about Sadie?"

"How is it that everyone knows about Sadie except me? What do you know?"

"Just that she has been seen with a guy in all the best restaurants lately. You know Sadie. She doesn't share juicy details about her personal life."

"Unlike someone I know," I say, laughing. Only Angelica has a love life to speak of. Actually, Angelica has a dating life. Love is not part of her current plan.

"People with broken-down heaps of scrap metal should not make fun of those with nicely maintained cars who drive said people to breakfast."

"Guilt taken." I see Caitlin getting off the bus just as we pull into the parking lot. So does Angelica.

"See. That could be you. Does she still not own a car?"

"She refuses. She says she doesn't want her personal reliance on cars to add to our nation's reliance on imported oil. Besides, she used to get parking tickets all the time because she forgot to feed the meters."

I am not into palm readings, horoscopes, or tarot cards; they all go against my basic understanding of how God works. But I do firmly believe in the power of reading breakfast-food preferences. This, I am sure, is of God.

"I'll have the huevos rancheros with extra salsa and sour cream, and could I also have guacamole? And breakfast potatoes with bacon…and iced tea." Caitlin places her order first, though the waitress is looking at me. Last week Caitlin ordered blueberry pancakes with whipped cream and chocolate pudding on the side. Ever since I introduced her to Angelica and Sadie a couple years ago, her eclectic taste in clothes and food has been a source of endless entertainment for us all.

"I will have…hmmm…maybe the fruit platter? What is the soup today…it is too early for that, huh? Oh, dang…give me the Super Cheese omelet." Ironically, Angelica was voted "most decisive" in our college marketing class and is now a pharmaceutical rep for a company that makes medication for Adult Attention-Deficit Disorder. These days she rarely sticks with anything or anyone.

She once told me that she fell into a rut. And it apparently was the worst experience of her life. I imagined her lying twisted and helpless in a large chasm…but, of course, she was really talking about the kind of rut that is my life. Predictable, boring, and not in need of a PDA or other self-organizing device because every day pretty much looks the same. Sometimes Angelica sidles up and looks at me as though I am the edge of that rut—intriguing and a bit fascinating, but if she gets too close, she might fall in.

"Granola with dry wheat toast, a sliver of skim cream cheese, and coffee with skim milk and sugar." Sensible Sadie Verity hands her menu to our server dressed reluctantly in '50s attire. Sadie is a classic. We are all the same age, but Sadie is the only real adult among us. Angelica and I were sure she was older than us when we met her in college at a Bible study through the campus ministry. We started going to the study because we thought we might meet decent guys. It turned out to be comprised of all women. We stayed because Sadie was an excellent leader.

We all watch her when she isn't looking. She has the body of Alicia Keys with long legs; the affective speech of someone much older, like Maya Angelou; and the calm demeanor of a counselor. It is funny how you imagine yourself a certain way with certain people. When I stand next to Sadie, I want to tug on the sleeve of her impeccable suit and ask her to lean down so I can whisper questions into her perfect ear.

What choice should I make?

Which way should I go?

Why are you friends with me?

The waitress has made her way back to me. She tucks her blond hair with black lowlights behind her triple-pierced ear and sighs. "One egg sunny side up, a cup of oatmeal, whole grain toast, and black coffee." I hand her the menu but she doesn't take it.

"The Senior Sunrise Delight." She slurs this, extreme boredom freezing the function of her tongue.

"I really wouldn't know." I nonchalantly examine the salt-and-pepper shakers. They are mini-replicas of Chevys and Fords from the 1950s. I'm willing her to go away.

Nope.

"Right panel. Big green letters…exactly what you ordered." Malicious pause. "S-e-n-i-or S-u-n-r-i-s-e D-e-l-i-g-h-t." Her fuchsia mouth outlines the words as though she were on Sesame Street.

She returns to the kitchen, where she probably makes the cooks cry.

I smile as I imagine how I'll spend her two-dollar tip.

"Tell us. Tell us. Tell us about your boyfriend!" Caitlin bounces up and down like a child.

A child with a large basket on her head.

Caitlin is third in command at a trendy boutique, Fab, in an eclectic part of downtown where galleries and tattoo parlors share city blocks. Determined to get to the post of second in command at the store, she is always trying to initiate the next big trend. Her goal is to get one big claim to fame so her boss will have to promote her. Today's stab at fab is a huge rimmed hat…the kind found atop bicycling women on soy sauce labels.

"But what about our spiritual dilemma of the week?" I interject, a strict traditionalist.

"This is more important. Besides, what Sadie thinks of this guy is a spiritual situation. Please, Sadie. Details?" Caitlin nods to emphasize her point and causes her basket to slip to an awkward angle.

Sadie wants to appease her friend but cannot quite get past the hat.

Nobody can.

The busboy has to push the next table over three feet to wedge by her head extension. "*What* is that, Caitlin?"

"It's a non. From Vietnam. They are made of bamboo and are quite durable and exotic, don't you think?" She touches the pinnacle of her new find.

"Anon, Anon," I say, and only Sadie laughs at my literary joke.

"Yes. A non. The owner of Yi Li's Tea House had one on the other day, and as I stared at it over my rice crackers and green tea, I knew it would be a hit. Not only is it a great conversation piece, it protects you from the sun in the summer and light rain in the winter." She is a home shopping network of one.

I can barely make out Caitlin's expression under the bamboo cone, but we all know she is serious. Sadly.

Sadie, seated next to her, can only see the large sloping side of the hat-mountain. "Well, it would certainly give one a lot of...distance in crowded situations like on the subway or...at a party..." Sadie is trying to be optimistic.

Caitlin nods under her non and adjusts the blue fabric tie beneath her chin. "The only problem is that sounds are muffled. It's like going through a tunnel."

The only problem?

Despite her quirky taste in fashion, Caitlin is a glass-half-full gal, God bless her. I shrug at Sadie as Angelica flips up the tip of Caitlin's hat and gives her a thumbs-down. Angelica does not sugarcoat anything for anyone.

"I have a spiritual dilemma that will be a nice segue into our exploration of Sadie's love life." Angelica stirs her coffee rapidly. Half her morning caffeine is now pooled in the saucer. She pauses to weigh her statement and makes a correction. "Actually, it is more of a moral dilemma."

"Go for it," I say, though I am frightened about what she might bring up. You never know with Angelica. Shock is her primary goal in any setting.

"Is it okay to dump a guy after a pretty decent first date just because he sells insurance?" She looks up and scans all of our faces for a first response, not the filtered politically correct answer we tend to present in case anyone is listening.

However, on this topic she need not worry. We all reveal our dark sides gladly.

"Yes." Caitlin chirps innocently. "And no fair. That isn't a dilemma; that's a rule."

"I hate to say it, but yes," Sadie follows on the heels of Caitlin's definitive approval. She looks embarrassed.

"Ouch. Way to make us start out the day shallow." I disappoint myself, but we all have had stalker experiences with insurance salesmen in this town. At first they look dashing in their suits and manly with their briefcases and business cards, but the next thing you know they are downloading your personal address book and crashing your friends' barbecues looking for new clients. The last straw is usually the "only because I care about you" conversation in which generic man—we call them all Brad—shares with you, over a candlelit dinner, how likely it is that you will lose a limb while feeding a parking meter or poke an eye out when baking quiche, should you ever take up baking.

I shake my head at our lack of compassion. "Okay...but that is the only reason to dump a guy after a good first date." How do we get to a place of setting up such ridiculous standards for men? Sadly, this one rule rules out about eighty percent of the male population in Tucson. The other twenty percent are physical trainers who rent converted garage apartments from their parents. "On this note reflecting our moral descent, please save us with your news, Sadie. Tell us about a great man who breaks the mold and who, I take it, is not in the field of insurance."

Sadie doesn't look as if she is sure she is ready to tell us. Can we handle an adult conversation? "Well...I can say that lately a gentleman has been calling on me."

"Calling on you?" Angelica says. "Like a telemarketer?"

"I'm dating, okay? I'm dating a guy."

"Oh, you are so lucky, Sadie. Of course you found a guy. What guy wouldn't want to date you? You are so...perfect. We are all confused, but you have your act together." Caitlin has a tendency to turn a compliment into a platform for self-deprecation.

"Hey, speak for yourself," Angelica says as the waitress arrives with food. But we all know it is true. How is it that women of the same age and basic beliefs can be on such different ends of the "act together" spectrum?

The waitress hands me a black-and-pink deco plate and a coupon good for a senior's discount at a local movie theater. "Special promotion for a special order," she says with a side of sarcasm.

I smile again. I guess she will get a tip after all. I tuck the coupon under the plastic map of Route 66 that serves as my place mat.

"The one dating gets to pray," says Angelica. She does this to avoid our usual system of taking turns. It's her turn. Angelica doesn't like public displays of faith.

Caitlin takes her hat off and reveals her matted-down, short, supposed-to-be-spiky hair. Sadie offers a blessing.

Between bites of her sensible meal, she shares a few details. The gentleman, Carson, is a new donor to the Tucson Botanical Society, for which Sadie is the development director. He is sponsoring the creation of a new fountain and night garden designed to showcase a community telescope.

"He is so romantic," Caitlin whispers to her caloric breakfast.

"He also is…well, a bit…"

"Portly?" Angelica says randomly.

"No," Sadie sighs. "He is a bit older."

"What is a bit?" I bring my index finger and thumb close together measuring a small portion along the continuum line of time and age.

Sadie's downward glance isn't shame. It is a "they won't understand" glance.

"Wait. I love *The Price Is Right*. That game where you have to guess which of the two prices is the right one." Caitlin claps her hands with glee.

We don't know what to do with this stroll down latchkey child entertainment lane.

"We can each guess how old he is," she continues with a big smile.

"Leave me out of this home version," I say and look at Sadie pleadingly.

"Okay. Sixteen years. For pete's sake, sixteen years." Sadie sits up straight with no apologies. "He knows what he wants out of life and he is…a real man. Not a boy pretending." She peers across the table to squelch anything Angelica might want to add about "real men."

Not that there's anything wrong with that. But I wasn't expecting that much of a difference. However, Sadie is beyond men our age.

"Wow—" Angelica starts to share her opinion, but I cut her off at the pass.

"A toast to real men." I motion with my coffee cup and the others follow my lead. Sadie's relieved look tells me the discussion is over. Possibly forever.

Snide waitress refills my cup while I am toasting the only stable man of America. "Free refills with the senior breakfast," she says, so pleased with herself.

I may be the butt of her joke, but I just got me a free cup o' joe. I smile sweetly at her. Toothy and one moment away from a "har har har" sound.

We all make plans to meet up separately and together in the near future. The sun shines on us as our designer shades slide down our foreheads to settle on our noses at the same time. Well, mine clunk. I lost my Ralph Lauren's and resorted to borrowing a pair of the large black optometrist glasses on hand at Golden Horizons for folks with dilated pupils or light sensitivity.

"Next month we will really discuss Matthew." I offer this up as if I don't say it every month.

They nod seriously as if they don't nod seriously every month.

As we are about to part, each to her own weekend errands, the busboy with red cheeks and an apron that wraps him like a burrito comes running out after Caitlin. His steps are short from the tightness of the fabric, so his walk is a little bit Geisha—an even funnier visual comparison considering he is waving her non in the air.

"Lady! You forgot your cornucopia."

Strange Girl

My neighbor from the basement is standing in front of the apartment complex. It looks as though she is waiting for a bus. I wave rather than point out we are not on a bus route.

She absently turns her wrist to check her watch. She seems to notice *not* that it is almost 10:00 P.M. and long past bus route hours (if that mattered), but that the face is dirty. She wipes it across her monogrammed terry cloth shirt that has elbow patches. A bright yellow Y against the lavender background tells the world as much as she is willing to share of herself.

I understand her without knowing more than the Y. I personally wear a straight, noncommittal smile as my bit of sharable self. And though I don't wait for buses that do not come, I am not above waiting for new versions of my life.

My landlord, Monty, had mentioned Y when she moved in last year. I was jealous when I discovered that she works from home…until I found out her home was the nasty basement space. Not really an apartment. And not really a basement. More like a lower-level supply closet.

Monty had tried to unload it on me several years ago, but I had Sadie with me. As he opened the door and years of must and dust invaded our breath, Sadie just laughed and laughed. Soon it was way too uncomfortable for Monty to do anything other than pretend he had been kidding about renting a broom closet for seven hundred a month. Sadie's perfect response saved me from the dungeon. But now Y has to live there.

We had one exchange when she first moved in. An elderly man in a plaid shirt and black slacks carried boxes bearing the Tom's Ketchup logo and containing mysterious contents. By the stagger of the man, those boxes were heavy. I remember watching Y's face closely as she watched the man. There was not any appreciation or gratitude in her expression, only worry. Somehow I guessed he was her father, though he was considerably older than one would figure her father to be. As she watched his progression to and fro across the concrete courtyard, her straight lips and stitched brows said it all. She seemed anxious for him to be gone.

I had introduced myself on my way to my car. She seemed uncomfortable. She spread her arms wide and said in a mournful monotone, "Home sweet home."

"I hope you like it here. The location is great." I stopped before opening my car door. "I'm Mari…15C."

And right then, before she could speak her name in return, her father yelled it from the lifeless dwelling. She grimaced and shrugged. "That's me…and that's mine." I knew she was claiming the dungeon and not the man who was breathing hard in the doorway. I heard her name, I saw the Y on her chest, and yet it did not sink in. Maybe because I was focused on a way to save her from living in that room.

Tonight, a year later, we still do not exchange more than glances. And I have yet to recall her name. A habit I hate about myself.

As I continue on my way to the store, my mind stays fixed on the Y, and all I can think of as my feet move forward is the rest of the Mickey Mouse song, "because we like you."

Hindsight

I stroll toward the Grocery Bag just four blocks from my place. It's a perfect winter Tucson evening with the haze of desert sage. Nothing bad could happen on a night like this. After my nightmares of being eaten by coyotes or javelinas subsided, I have always felt an incredible sense of security here where the saguaro cacti, tall and strong against the night sky, seem to stand guard while I go about my business.

I enter the "Bag" and casually nod at the guys on duty. My many food obsessions over the years (salt-and-vinegar chips, taffy, cookie dough, and cheese-in-a-can, etc.) have enabled me to make friends with the young men assigned the late-night post.

The cliché about men looking good in uniforms holds true even for minimum wage occupations. These boys, even the awkward ones, are handsome. White shirts with wrinkles circling the underarms and at the elbows show signs of admirable labor and repetitive tasks. Drooping ties that are probably pulled from couches, car seats, and overflowing sock drawers just minutes before clocking in give the guys the appearance of bedraggled stockbrokers.

They smile as I enter their world, and a few nod a greeting before continuing their conversations about college life…football games, girls, and cars. Once again, a feeling of security comes over me. My limited life has its benefits, I think.

Lost in the variety of choices on the shelves, I take comfort in knowing that I have nowhere else to go tonight; this is my outing before I face limited television options and resort to another viewing of a Cary or Hugh Grant DVD. The aisle with towers of stacked tuna cans is my final destination. Anything else I find between here and there is a bonus.

"Hey, Mari." A male voice I should recognize catches up with me in my fog.

I look down to see if I'm presentable. The boys of the Bag don't count; they accept my late-night self. My quick downward glance reveals a stain-free T-shirt, loose-fit jeans, and bright green velvet Chanel loafers. Presentable enough.

I turn around to find Chad Warner, the physical therapist who works at Golden Horizons three days a week. We call him Nomad Chad and are jealous of his flexible schedule and his white teeth.

"Oh, hey." My hand goes up to my hair for a nervous run through. My turquoise ring gets caught in a tangle, and for a moment I panic. Luckily he looks down to fix a twisted wheel on his cart, and I have a chance to free myself from a humiliating pose.

My hand is detangled but still poised in the air as he approaches me… so I wave. Big.

Given the three feet of distance between us, this looks a little close to crazy. He turns to see if there is someone an appropriate distance away to receive such an exuberant gesture.

No. I'm just weird.

"So, is this your turf?" He seems only slightly thrown by my behavior.

"Yep. I live just down the street. How about you?"

"For a while. Rooming with a buddy right now. They hiked my rent, and now I need to find something that accommodates a nomad's income." He winks but it doesn't seem slimy, only friendly.

"I figured in this town you made a good living. Lots of hips need adjusting."

"Speaking of which…" he pauses to crack his knuckles and his look becomes serious.

I start to run my fingers through my hair again but catch myself. Oh, please don't be asking me out. Please don't say something that will make me blush. I just want to grocery shop in peace.

He continues, his manner professional. "Well, when I first noticed you, I didn't realize it was you exactly. And I kinda have a habit of assessing people's walks. I know, a bit weird, right? But it keeps me on my toes professionally."

Oh, great. The man watched me walk my tour of aisles. There is nothing worse than having someone watch you walk except having them do it without you knowing. And then reporting on it.

I'm what? A specimen? A case study?

"Oh." My eyes don't want to connect with his, so I look beyond. I notice Chef Jace's canned spaghetti sauce is on sale…two for a dollar. French bread pizza sounds really good about now.

"And I noticed that you…well, you shuffle."

I could add toppings like cheese and pineapple. My mind catches up to what he just said. "I shuffle?" I raise my voice because I am appalled, not because I want further explanation.

"Your left hip drags, and so the right side seems to follow. I call it an old man's shuffle. This case would be an old—"

"I get it." My tone reflects my state of perturbedness. I realize the guy is just being professional. It isn't his fault. He wouldn't know that I am on a personal roll of humiliation. That every corner I turn leads to someone happy to point out that I have an elderly person's tendencies.

"Your sacrum might be tight."

"Oh, you know what?" I laugh with a wild lilt to make up for my tight sacrum and uptight tone. "It's my shoes. These things are a size too big, but I love them because they are…" I am about to say "old," but I catch myself. "Uh, because they were a gift. I think my sacrum is fine. It is so nice of you to notice, though." I say this as if he mentioned the delightful way my hair flipped up in the back. I want to end this encounter and go hate my television options.

He nods. "Okay. Well, if you do ever need an adjustment, I can schedule you on one of my Golden Horizon stops."

One of my men in uniform comes up to rescue me and breaks up this awkward moment.

"Ms. Hamilton?"

"Yes?" I raise my eyebrows out of curiosity, but I am thankful for the interruption. Chad starts to move his cart forward and waves a little "catch ya later" wave. But not before he hears the innocent words of the grocer boy.

"Carl wanted me to tell you we got that extra large tube of scent-free Muscle Heat in yesterday. Do you want me to get it for you?"

I shout, "Oh, great! Millie has been asking for this every day at Golden Horizons. Thank you. Millie thanks you." The grocer boy responds exactly as Chad had just moments before. He turns around to see who I must be calling to at this decibel.

Dang. This all happens because I broke a very important rule…never, ever buy personal hygiene or health care products at the place where they know you by name.

I spend forty-five minutes roaming a store with five aisles because I don't want to run into Chad at the checkout. If the twenty-year-old manager is not talking to his girlfriend but is actually watching the store monitors, he would see me turning corners again and again, craning my neck forward to be sure Chad is not in sight.

In the monitor of my mind's eye, I resemble the scary lady who wears a tutu over her denim jumper and shouts at children, cats, rocks, and meter maids down by the University of Arizona.

How did this happen?

I walk home not noticing the brilliant sky. Evidently something bad can happen to a girl on a night like this. Even the thought of a large tuna fish sandwich on toasted sourdough does not help.

I can only focus on how my left hip seems to drag my leg along the sidewalk.

Alien Messages

Wednesday:

Beep.

"Um, yeah. I couldn't find long-stemmed lilies, but I hope you like the flowers. Oh, this is Ken. Screen name the Whiz. I love the movie *Citizen Kane*. Anyway, I hope you aren't allergic to rosebuds. Ha, ha. I will be in touch. Um…bye."

Beep.

Thursday:

Beep.

"Sal here. I've got bundles of lavender with your name on 'em. Thought it would remind you of France. Hopefully it reminds you of me too. Sal. Screen name SensationSal. You won't forget that one, I'll bet."

Loud laughter followed by the sound of dropping the phone.

"Sorry. Sorry. You there? [more loud, nervous laughter] Well, that is stupid…this is a machine. Of course you aren't there. Hey, think of me."

Beep.

I have a rash of strange phone messages from men who seem to think they know me. Sal's message conjures up images of an open madras shirt, dark chest hair, and long silver rope chains that tangle up in that chest hair.

I try to recall if I signed up for any vacation giveaways or enter-to-win contests that would have placed my name and number on any unfortunate sales lists. Only one comes to mind. In a hurry last month I did sign up to win a brand-new hybrid convertible.

I just know that these disturbing calls from overzealous males are warding off good, life-changing calls…like the one that offers me a brilliantly fancy new job in a lush resort or that shiny, environment-friendly car.

To Be Made Worthy

A frantic Golden Horizons volunteer wearing a wedding-mint-green frock comes rushing up to our main station. "I have a report! An attempted suicide…I don't know…" Her frizzy hair is Medusa-like and her blue eyes are tiny in the white of shock.

My coworkers spring into action. Lysa picks up the phone to dial 911 and has a thin leg up, ready to jump over the counter. Chad stands between the volunteer and us. First response man. "Who? Who?" He wildly reaches for her lapel like a detective asking for a rookie cop's badge number. It takes him a moment to read the tag. I watch him sound it out in his head before speaking the odd name. "Petulia. Who? Where?"

"Miss Tess…she is threatening suicide."

I laugh. I played the lead in this scene five years ago. My coworkers pause to look at me as though I am the wicked witch of the west.

"Let me guess…she threatened to take herself to the pearly gates if you refused to slip her a Gibson drink and sneak her out at midnight."

"Yes!" Petulia is incredulous.

My peers are in awe.

"Pearly Gates." I pause to savor the power of the moment. "It's a retirement home on Fifth and Martin." It takes a moment for this to sink in. When it does, Petulia's face melts with relief. Her pale skin reddens with embarrassment.

"She does this to all the new staff people." I turn to Lysa and motion for her to put the phone down. "Although Petulia here might need that ambulance."

They laugh heartily and I stand front and center willing to take any affirmation I can get these days.

While Petulia goes to take a much-needed Sprite break, I offer to address Miss Tess and her behavior.

I take a long route to Tess' room, allowing me time to work up an attitude of disappointment. I further stall by reaching my hand into the south wing suggestion box—an idea I implemented last year to help ease the direct verbal complaints from residents and funnel them in a more orderly, constructive system. So far, the boxes have served as waste baskets, ash trays, and collection receptacles for humorous and often feisty observations of the facility, its people, and this culture.

The one I found yesterday was written by Myrna Frederickson. It was not signed, but I knew her chicken scratch from too many games of hangman. "We should all gather our money and see if there is any way to buy back the fine services of Beau. He never threw people out of games and was a most delightful young fellow. And cute. Our staff now is mostly ugly. Ugly and decidedly mean." For once she used the collective "staff" instead of my name directly.

Today I'm afraid to reach into the pine square with a grinning slit at the top. Only one crumpled piece of paper lies in wait for my retrieval. At first I assume it is someone's fast-food burger wrapper, but I see my full name written in big, loopy letters and smooth it out to read the mysterious note. "Mari Hamilton walks on by and doesn't even notice that the scenery has changed. She had better pay attention."

I reread it at least three times. Did the insightful writer have something specific in mind, or is he or she intuitive enough to know I also have just stumbled upon this truth for myself? My thoughts sift through my phobias until my feet bring me to stand before room 312. I'll assess my own problems later. For now, I anticipate the smile of my favorite resident as I slowly push the door open with the toe of my sturdy shoes.

Tess sits in an already muggy room wrapped in a luxurious mink stole that forty years ago fit strong, perfectly toned shoulders. Now it dwarfs the eighty-year-old into a little girl wearing her mother's clothes. She looks down with false guilt and readies herself for my equally false reprimand.

"Tess Childers, you cannot scare off the new volunteers like this. One day we will all stop believing anything you say. You know that, don't you?"

"Sorry, Mari." Her favorite line of all time. "We would both be better off at Pearly Gates. I hear they have great benefits for their employees."

"Benefits? What are benefits?" I tease her. Neither of us would go there. She, because Pearly Gates is where her second husband lived for years. Their divorce settlement actually stated they could not reside in the same retirement home. Me, because I would never work somewhere called Pearly Gates. Out of principle.

"You do know what this means," I say, trying to sound stern.

"You'll be the one to read to me." From beneath her wrap she pulls a delicate pink envelope heavily scented with Chanel No. 5 perfume and filled with sweet details of her friend Gisele's life in New York. These two were inseparable from debutante years to their lives as young, affluent, married women. They shared a charmed existence until Tess lost her first and only great love to cancer.

In the irrational state of grief, Tess married a man who did not deserve or truly have her love. His awareness of this made him all the more eager to remove her from the things she did love.

This wrong man—she never uses his name—moved Tess from the opera houses, society columns, and Broadway premieres of New York to the rodeos, dusty bars, and jean-clad denizens of Arizona.

I take the note from its envelope and settle into the velvet-covered chaise. Tess' single room has the grace and charm of a suite at the Plaza. I know because she tells me this. And despite our rough beginnings, I believe every word she tells me.

She closes her eyes and prepares to connect with her friend through my voice and her tender memories of a better time. I clear my throat, but the lump remains. Gisele describes snow-covered Central Park, which she can see from her parlor room. She laments how nobody knows how to make a Gibson cocktail anymore, and she states the tragic glut of pathetic and apathetic hired help in Manhattan. She has requested her fourth in-home nurse this month.

"You two sound like two onions in a martini glass." I fold the letter and place it in Tess' jewelry box with all the others.

Her large collection of precious stones and diamond jewelry is secured at a nearby bank; only a few sentimental pieces from her first love are kept beside her at all times: a gold watch, a pair of modest emerald earrings, and a wedding band. I check to make sure they are there every day.

"Not so fast." Tess wants to continue with our routine. Her lids are heavy with sleep, but her hands are still nimble enough to remove her charm bracelet and hold it up by its small, brass key. "Choose something divine."

I gave up protesting three years ago when we started this part of the ritual. I open the armoire and take in the gorgeous fabrics, styles, and colors that are mine for the choosing. My fingers return to the silk, the chintz, the satin. It is not difficult to imagine Tess dressed in these garments—young, vibrant, and the envy of every stranger at the jazz club, theater, or reserved tables at the Rainbow Room.

I pause over a light gray Christian Dior. It is my favorite. Tess knows it. I know it.

Too many childhood years of sharing…giving up…any item of importance or perceived significance prevent me from believing I deserve something so beautiful—and so meaningful to a person I adore. As my fingers glide forward, I know there is something else behind my unwillingness to remove the piece. I need not explain it to Tess. This item from a part of her life that she misses, that she loved…I want to save it for last.

I put off such a gift from my friend because I want her to be here forever.

"Skipping the finale?" She chuckles with understanding.

My sight lands on a color I have not noticed before. A faded apricot scarf? My hand disappears into the folds of the Burberry coat it hides behind. I can barely feel the silk; it is as smooth as polished glass and as light as air. I reach up for the satin-covered hanger and remove the most breathtaking dress I have ever seen. It is art. It is dance. With one look at Tess' smile, I know, too, that it is mine.

"That, my friend, is a fine selection. Rudy Mangione, one of Broadway's finest musical dancers, brought that back from Paris for me." She looks off toward the hallway, but I know she is in her Fifth Avenue apartment, folding back silver tissue paper and taking in the first sight of this creation.

One glance takes in the deep curves, soft folds, and subtle peplum. "I couldn't wear such a thing. Your life was made for splendor, Tess. But mine…" I look down at my sad uniform and can barely hold back the tears.

"Mari, you have not yet learned to recognize greatness, beauty, and purpose in your life. Please believe me. You might not prance around in all these pieces or attend a high tea at the Plaza, but there is still a reason you are the one who holds the brass key right now." Her delight and belief lessen my self-consciousness.

"Oh, Tess…your gypsy talk is going to me head."

Tess howls with one strong laugh. "Gypsy! Oh, Mari." For a moment her smile turns to teacher-serious contemplation. "We don't talk about it much, but I know we have the same faith leading us." She pauses when she sees the apricot draping my shoulders. "Amazing. It is as if Rudy picked it out with you in mind…even if he didn't know you."

I hadn't identified, or wanted to explore, the sense of loss in my life in recent months, but the hope and purpose behind her words reveal themselves as the missing ingredients.

I start an Ella Fitzgerald record and leave Tess to her afternoon nap. Out in the hallway I pause for a moment, lifting lush layers of silk to my face. And in front of the bulletin board listing "101 Things You Can Make with Jello," I make the one thing I have been afraid of…a prayer request directly related to my own future.

I pray to be made worthy—not of the fine clothes—but of the kindness and the belief in my future. Because right now, I don't feel it.

Taxation with Representation

Strange girl stands by the mailboxes. Today she is wearing a leopard-print T-shirt with a cursive Y and red pants with green stripes. She reminds me of a leftover Christmas decoration gone very wrong. Her shiny black hair splays against her shoulders in chunks that are not chic, just indifferent. Odd neighbor pretends to read her mail. Behind old-fashioned wire-rimmed glasses her eyes are moving too fast to really be taking in words. She is practically in the REM stage. The lingerie catalog she is looking at belongs to the woman in 12C. I know this because I got it by mistake yesterday and placed it in the mail-swap box this morning…along with a note asking 12C to please notify all her favorite exotic clothing distributors to correct her address on file.

I sense I am supposed to speak to basement-dwelling neighbor, but I am dragging; I just want to walk on by. My vow, as of late, has been to *not* ignore these tugs at my heart. I'm hoping they will eventually lead to something life changing rather than just polite mailbox encounters.

"Hi…" I say this with the pause where her name should go. How does one forget a name that begins with Y?

"Oh. Hey. Do you have cable?" She looks up from a display of garter belts to ask me this most important question.

"Yes. And you?" I regret the conversation already.

"No. But I'm thinking about it. Have you traveled to Asia?"

"Not yet." But it sounds good about now.

"What do you do for fun?" She surprises me with a normal get-acquainted question. My mouth opens to introduce the long list, but my mind spins trying to pick up on anything that I do outside of work, let alone "do for fun." Little does she know she has brought up a touchy subject for me. I must wear my lack of frivolity on my sensible sleeve.

She offers some assistance. "I'll bet you do fascinating things like rock climb and go to art exhibits." Her activity pairing is as compatible as her top and pants.

"Well, not lately." Now I am disgusted with myself that I have no plans to scale the wall of the Tucson gallery.

"Do you spend a lot of time online?"

This exercise in chitchat is not making me feel better about my life. "No, hardly ever. Though I did just get email at work."

"I had you pegged for a real active type. Like dating a lot and going out. Having friends…" her voice trails off as she starts to walk away, leaving me dazed and confused.

"Good to see you," I say to her small backside with a bit of sarcasm. How do I go from following a tug of the heart to being sarcastic?

I gather my mail and quickly survey the bills vs. correspondence ratio. All bills except for one Golden Horizons envelope, which must be my W-2 forms. For some people, this is a momentous occasion, even a welcomed event in the cycle of their year. I have never found it to be such.

Elmo, my cat, is waiting for me in the entryway. I rush past him to the bathroom. "Sorry, guy," I offer as he follows me and waits for me to appreciate him. On my way to the kitchen, I scoop up this blob of gray-and-white fur and kiss his tummy. He hates this and regrets greeting me at all.

I feed him his usual half can of nondescript mush and deprive myself of any people morsels until I have made a call to my new accountant.

A brusque, nasal voice answers the phone. "No One Lewis' Accounting, can I assist you?" He says this with great reluctance and without a hint of the humor (albeit terrible humor) the business name suggests.

"Yes, you sure can, Lewis. This is Mari…Mari Hamilton…Sadie's friend?" I wait for recognition and get zilch. "You said to call when I got my W-2s."

More silence. I can hear the tap-tap-tapping of a laptop computer on his end. He is busy helping people who have assets worth assessing.

"Well, I got 'em. The forms. Those forms you mentioned. Got 'em." I say this over and over until he interrupts.

"Can you meet after hours?"

"Sure."

"How about eight. And bring that other paperwork I told you to round up."

"Tonight?" I feel rushed. I am one who likes to gently enter the arena of financial details.

The fingernail to chalkboard sound of an inkjet printer reminds me that Lewis awaits my response. "Tonight is great. So your office will be open?"

"I don't meet here. Too many banker boxes. I like to do business at LuLu's. There is a booth I practically rent there." He snickers at this. I knew his sad sense of humor had to surface eventually. Great. My accountant works his numbers like a bookie from a back booth at the most archaic restaurant chain in America. I believe this location is one of its last links.

"Do you know the place?" He asks this seriously. As if anyone can miss the bright green roof and the purple-coated brick front. Should I inform him that there are days I deliberately drive a different route to work so that I do not have to face this building before 9:00 A.M.?

"Should I ask for you at the counter?" I jab.

"Margo will be expecting you," he reveals, once again, his brilliant lack of humor and hangs up the phone without ending the conversation. Apparently, when numbers are your friends, social niceties are not required. I run through my multiplication tables in case there is a long-buried passion and the excuse for indifference I have been seeking all of my life.

Nothing. Just bad memories of lining up in fourth grade on Fridays for math flash card competitions.

Numbers Breakdown

Right this way." Margo pulls a worn, laminated menu from the bin at the hostess pulpit. She has several buttons pinned to her striped mock apron. While staring at her uniform's graffiti, I am informed that LuLu is crazy for the new Hawaiian salad that has coconut, pineapple, and crisp lettuce greens. Another reminds people to not smoke in this establishment. A personal picture shows Margo and her pet Chihuahua playing the piano.

The maze of turquoise-and-pink booths makes me dizzy as I walk behind her. She nods to each of her favorite customers. It is like being the runner-up and mistakenly following Miss America down the aisle. A child in a high chair tosses pudding at me.

Margo reaches the very back booth of her service area and motions me toward the man who would be Lewis. He wears braces, which actually add an element of appeal to the boy. He doesn't look old enough to have established a business with a reputation that Sadie, of all people, could and would vouch for.

He makes a false effort to stand up as I approach and motions his hand toward the entire other half of the pastel C-shaped booth. A stack of manila folders is on the table by Lewis, who is seated directly in front of a potted palm; his face is framed by strands of green. He resembles a cartoon lion…one that would be the star character in a kid's show promoting how great it is to wear braces and add numbers for a living.

"My order is coming, so feel free…" he says, pointing toward Margo, who is still standing at attention. He seems unaware of her affection.

"I'll have a malted. Oh, and French fries." This comes from nowhere and somewhere. There is something that screams "get a malted" in the vinyl-and-chrome chairs placed at smoky-hued glass tables.

I choose the steak fries over the regular, skinny ones and turn my attention to Lewis, whose head is already buried in a folder with my name on it.

My folder is recycled. Through the white label I can read a name scribed in thick black permanent marker—"Frankie Valducci." I imagine his name being crossed out when the feds busted him for running yogurt stores as a front for laundering mob money.

"What happened to my predecessor?" I ask, pointing to the evidence bleeding through the sticker.

Lewis shrugs. He won't talk. Accountant-client privilege.

By the time Margo makes her way to us with our food choices, he is almost finished inputting my information into his miniature laptop. He scarcely looks at Margo as she places extra ketchup packets next to his grilled cheese.

It turns out that my big ol' steak fries and malted are fantastic. I'm inhaling my dinner selection and licking my fingers. Lewis bites into his large sourdough sandwich. Strings of American cheese graze his chin and form a large shiny blob on his front teeth. Margo has thought this through; a tiny ceramic basket with toothpicks is at his elbow.

Disappearing momentarily beneath the table, Lewis fumbles in the box by my feet and emerges with a tabletop printer. As its annoying printing sound overrides the instrumental version of "You Don't Bring

Me Flowers Anymore" on the speakers above our heads, he becomes more animated.

"How long have you been working with the elderly?" he asks, suddenly aware he is with another person.

I cringe at this phrasing. It removes me from my area of expertise, which is recreation instruction and therapy. Working with the elderly sounds like a candy striper. I don't want to discuss my job.

"Five years. It's just a detour." I am compelled to remind myself and everyone I meet that I do have a timeline. That this life is not as limited as it first appears.

"From what? According to your records this has been your primary career...caregiving." This pencil pusher is a darn good button pusher.

"Let's just say I am trained for more...fashionable settings. And more lucrative," I add this part to counter my measly income that by now is quite apparent to Lewis.

"What you do is noble." He is serious, and this makes me even more depressed. Noble is another phrase for "nobody else'll do it." I have a plan for something better.

"Are we about done?" I ask, brushing off his grand sentiments. Pushing my glass and the red plastic wicker basket to the edge of the table, I make my desire to leave clear.

Lewis asks me to read through a small stack of forms, mark the appropriate personal information on the page, and sign. I'm cruising through the personal information. Same residence as last year. Yes. Had someone else prepare my taxes. Yes. Want to contribute to political campaigns. No. Want to contribute to any charities. Yes. I indicate several that are connected to some of my favorite residents at Golden Horizons.

Married or single?

I'm tired of questions.

"Under 65 and not blind." I mark the "yes" box and my spirit is temporarily buoyed as I replace the idea of single with the idea of being young and sighted. But as my overanalytical mind tends to do, it takes the devil's advocate position with fervor. While my peers are dating, getting married, or climbing corporate ladders in expensive heels, the two best things I have going for me are 1) I am not on Social Security and 2) I do not order my issues of *Aging Grace* in brail.

On a scale of one to ten, my version of twentysomething living has to rate a negative three. Hot tears escape from the corner of my squinting eyes. Lewis looks up from gathering his belongings and seems frightened by my pale and sweaty visage.

"But you get money back." He is perplexed. Nobody has ever responded to a refund in this manner. "Did I do something wrong?" He slides around the booth and pats my back as though I am choking. The Boy Scouts never taught him the proper procedure for nervous breakdowns. My rigid muscles try to contain my sobs.

Lewis calls for Margo, who turns out to be the safety advisor for this shift. She also pats me on the back. "I have an aunt who is allergic to potatoes. Could it be that?" Her concern is kind, but I question the quality of her safety training.

"Call Sadie." It is all I can think to do. "Sadie, please."

Lewis grabs one of his file folders and locates Sadie's number. Margo points to the swinging kitchen door as the closest phone available and starts to count aloud as she measures my pulse. The next time I see her, she is wearing a "I'm quite a LuLu, just ask me" pin given only to successful managers, honored cooks, and on that rare occasion, hostesses who prevent hyperventilating customers from choking.

A Life Examined

Psychologists, psychoanalysts, and monks consider life examination a worthy investment of time and energy. To be thrown into it, however, like the deep end of the pool when you are still clinging to an inflatable dolphin, is not something I would recommend. But here I sit, on my secondhand couch, surrounded by a jury of my peers, who are all now doing their job…peering at me with looks of concern and staring into my life with the same fascination one has when watching open heart surgery on the medical channel.

Sadie called them all here. She says for emotional support, but I know what an intervention looks like. When I am not engrossed in the medical channel, I skip over to the latest twentysomething angst in the city or affluent suburbs show where interventions can begin with a social hour, hors d'oeuvres, and polite talk of rising stocks. But in this eastside Tucson version, chips and salsa served on paper plates are followed with talk of why we are gathered in my small living room at 9:30 P.M. on a weeknight if it is not to watch a chick flick or to discuss a relationship breakup.

"The idea of being under 65 and not blind was depressing…was that it?" Caitlin is trying to understand my complexities.

With my head in my hands I try to explain for the umpteenth time. "No. It actually made me feel good, and then *that* depressed me. For someone so close to their absolute goal date, my proximity to the life I envisioned is so far away. I'm pathetic by anyone's standards." I force myself to look up. Angelica is nodding in agreement with this last statement and is reaching for more Doritos.

"You know what I love?" She kicks off her Marc Jacobs ankle boots and sits cross-legged on the black wicker chair I painted last year. "Those baked chips, the really crispy ones with the scalloped edges. They are so much better than these. Oh, or baby quiche. I could eat a dozen of those." She lifts up the snack that does not pass her standards and shoves it into her undeserving mouth.

Caitlin, scattered but well-meaning, is turned directly toward me. She is wearing glasses with a diamond-studded ladybug on the right lens. As hard as she tries, her one eye is not able to see beyond the dazzling insect.

"I have always wondered what it would be like to be interrogated by a Latina version of Colombo," I say to break the tension.

"Very funny," Caitlin says, waving away the joke she doesn't get.

Sadie taps her mason jar, the only glassware I own, to start the official intervention. "We need to share words of support for Mari. We all know she has been struggling for quite some time…"

Sadie has just given an invitation to my friends to come forward and dissect my life. I should be more insulted than I am. But I'm a bit curious. It isn't as though I haven't been aware of my problems; I just didn't know my friends were dying to point them out.

The vulnerability makes me feel cold. I reach for a fleece blanket that since moving to Tucson has been more for decor than function. Bundled up, I await the onslaught of personal advice. Am I strong enough to weed through the petty and get to wisdom that might actually help?

Unfortunately, Angelica is eager to go first. I don't trust her with my feelings. "Mari, let's face it. You live the life of my grandmother. Look!"

She rummages in the wrought-iron magazine rack and pulls out a stack of magazines.

Dang it.

She holds them up, fanning the pages and rotating them so that each person in the room can clearly view the cover images of white-haired models biking, playing cards, and enjoying their patio sets. "*Aging Grace, Movement and Health, Aging Monthly, Retirement Weekly…*" One by one she slaps them down with a thud on the glass coffee table, each an added exclamation mark tagged to the point she is making.

"Those are for my profession. Sadie, don't you have scads of periodicals about plant life? It's normal…" My shoulders gravitate toward my ears and my body tightens. I'm ready to defend myself if nobody else will.

"What's this?" Angelica holds up a lively photo of twentysomethings laughing and mingling by a pool. "I don't believe it…a brochure for Canyon Crest condos. This gives me hope for you."

"Is that a different retirement home?" asks Caitlin.

"No," clarifies Angelica. "It's the hottest place to live in downtown Tucson."

"I do have dreams," I whisper.

"But do you have a chance of this," she points to the brochure, "if you keep your current lifestyle?" Angelica goes over to my stereo unit and grabs a basket of CDs. "There isn't one recent CD here. Sinatra, Dino… Rosemary Clooney, for pete's sake."

"There is nothing wrong with the classics. I have all of Sinatra's work." Finally, Sadie steps up for me.

"And how about this one? Do you have this in your collection?" Angelica tosses a case to Sadie's open hand. Sadie turns the disk so she can read the bright red lettering. I try to remember what it is, but all I can think is how thankful I am that I have not received my online order of…

"Muzak. *Best of the '70s?*" Sadie blatantly questions my taste.

Drat. Secret pathetic life fully revealed.

"Why is this getting so personal?" I direct my question to Sadie, my supposed caring friend. Why hasn't she put a stop to this attack?

"Mari, this isn't easy for any of us. Just hear us out." She looks at the other two and speaks as though I am gone, locked up and trying out straightjackets. "If you had seen her at LuLu's…" her voice breaks off and her head shakes side to side at the horror she had witnessed. "As difficult as this is, we must be very honest with Mari. And she knows it."

Angelica needs no prodding and continues her list of my problems as though Sadie has not interrupted her. "You spend money on large-print books for your Golden buddies and then are too broke to join me in Cabo. When's the last time you took a vacation?" She takes a deep breath before adding, "Or had a date, for that matter?"

We don't have enough time for me to try and remember. Besides, I'm hazy from the muscle relaxant the urgent care doctor gave me. Sadie had whisked me away to Holy Cross as soon as she observed my mental state at LuLu's.

Caitlin raises her hand to speak. I reach across the table and remove the ridiculous glasses. Her eyes flutter and try to refocus. "Mari, of course you are sad. You moved to Tucson from D.C. with dreams of working in a resort…a place of luxury, opportunity, and affluence." As she describes the life I had envisioned, I feel my conscience pull back a little. The practical Christian in me has not yet made friends with my personal ambitions. She tries to soften her assessment. "I am that way too. Maybe in a way we are dreamers who struggle with the doing part." She toys with her glasses.

"Good point," Sadie interjects. "So how do we help get you from the dreaming to the doing? What do you want most?"

"The job. Definitely."

Sadie removes the ocean blue scarf from around her hair and lets her thick, black curls fall. Letting loose. She wants to settle into this moment. "How many résumés do you have out right now?"

"I have to update it. I want to include some recently acquired skills and talents…" I stop. Nobody is buying this excuse. Not even me.

"I'll take this one." Sadie raises her hand to sign on as my résumé mentor. While Angelica makes a good living, it is Sadie who knows the ins and outs of the job market.

"I want to dress her," says Angelica.

"That should be me," Caitlin counters as she eats guacamole by the spoonful.

They stare at me with territorial eyes. I cannot afford Angelica's taste. And I don't know that I have the courage to take on Caitlin's sense of style. Sadie sees the dilemma. "Actually, Mari has great clothes. She just forgets to make the effort."

She is referring to my closet full of Tess' contributions.

"I have a bunion. Anyone want to claim that as their area of specialty?" I ask.

Is "mass ignoring" a phrase? Because it just happened here, in my living room, among my snacks, by *my* friends.

"Well, I have dating then. I'm the only one out there meeting people." Angelica needs to win one of these points.

"No. You are out there dumping people. Sadie actually has a boyfriend." I feel I need to clarify this because Angelica's dating world scares me.

"We'll take turns setting her up. How's that?" They follow Sadie's lead as I watch my life go up for bid in pieces. "Now, when is the last time you visited your family?"

"No." I say in a voice that startles Elmo from his comfy perch on the back of the sofa. "This is not about home. Let's not spin this one weak moment in my life into an opportunity to scrutinize my childhood." I cross my arms in front of my chest like the child I say I do not want to discuss. Everyone notices.

"Fine. Then let's talk about your adulthood, Mari. You say you are unhappy, yet you do very little to change your attitude or circumstances. I mean...it is as if..."

Even I, who does not really want to hear this, wait with bated breath.

"It's as if you don't even have faith. Maybe you don't want to examine your feelings about home and your parents, yet it is the very thing you are still trying to get away from. When did you last visit?"

"Four years ago. And I told myself I wouldn't go back until…" Dang. I am such a sucker.

"Until?" Sadie knows the answer.

I give her the "you know" look but she won't settle. So I begrudgingly continue, "I suppose I don't want to go back until I can prove to them that I can be successful in the world and still be a good person."

If this were live in front of a studio audience on the *Dr. Phil Show*, an applause sign would be held up and we could go to commercial.

Angelica checks her watch. "Hey, now. Isn't this supposed to be a time of prayer? How about I start?"

"Thank you, Angelica." I am relieved and shocked, frankly, that she wants to turn this to prayer.

"But this is the point we should be discussing." Sadie tries to dissuade Angelica who, we find out later, had a date waiting for her at El Charros the entire time.

"Mari clearly doesn't want to discuss it. She is half-drugged anyway. Let us pray." Angelica bows her head to lead us.

Sadie seems reluctant to bring this session to an end, but she, like the rest of us, is too surprised by Angelica's suggestion to stop her.

As we bow our heads and get quiet, a voice that is loud, blunt, and unmistakably Angelica's belts out, "Lord, would you just get Mari to start acting her age? Amen." And as if just remembering the setting for the prayer she adds, "Oh, and let us be a help in her time of trouble. Amen again."

Before they leave everyone clarifies their assignments. It takes a village of type A women to change my life, apparently. Angelica has to make sure her patronizing prayer didn't cancel out any plans we have made. "You know what is so unbelievably perfect? You promised to join me for my company's golf tournament next week."

"Oh, I almost forgot. And how is that perfect?" Two disasters make a right?

"Consider it our first outing after this..." she draws a circle in the air with my last Doritos chip. "What could be better than a fancy golf tournament loaded with eligible, successful men?"

"A hangnail that morphs into a tumor?"

"That is what we need to change." She points at my heart but means my attitude. Satisfied that she has fully assessed my problem and apparently her problem with me, Angelica turns to face the mirror by my bright red door. A quick slip of lip gloss and a tweak of her cheeks for a fabricated glow of youthful enthusiasm and she is ready for her date.

"Don't you care that I cannot play? I hate to hold others up." I try a new angle.

"We will just tell them to play through. Besides, the people I work with...they start toasting one another's accomplishments a little early in the day. By the time they are hitting the fairway, you will look like Annika Sorenstam."

"Who?" I scrunch my forehead. "Hey, nice BlueBerry, by the way." I point to her fancy PDA. "One of the residents has one just like it." For once I am with-it enough to know what Angelica is up to.

She types "Project Mari" on several dates to create a spreadsheet of opportunities to fix her pathetic friend and then rolls her eyes at my comment. "Wrong fruit." She doesn't offer any more information. It is enough to know that I am absurdly out of touch with real life.

"What? What'd I say?"

Angelica holds up her BlackBerry to keep it between her life and my ever-deepening rut.

Saving Vase

Delete.

Delete.

Delete.

Three more weird calls from even weirder men. If this were not the night of my favorite show, I would start investigating this phenomenon. But I have only five minutes to make popcorn and settle in for an evening of *Castaways*, the reality show about ten people who are forced to compete with one another to stay on a neglected Caribbean island. It's a cheap rip-off of a more popular reality show; the characters even have less personality.

I blame my captivation with this low-rent version of human drama on my teen years' obsession with *Gilligan's Island*. Shown on the late-night classics station, my opportunity to watch it depended a lot on how soundly my parents were sleeping. Imagining the castaway experience to be the most adventurous thing ever, I used to pretend my top bunk was the island. If my foster-siblings approached me to tie their shoe, make them a sandwich, read aloud another issue of *Ranger Rick*, or perform some other mundane activity, I would point to the blue rug and call it my deep ocean.

Being shipwrecked would be a tragedy for most folks, but it was certainly a salvation fantasy for me at the time. Like a message machine response I would say, "I'm sorry, I cannot be reached. You are in the ocean. I am far off in the distance, beyond the vision of your telescope and far past the range of your communication efforts." They would walk away rolling their eyes or calling me names…and I would sit up tall, glad to be alone on my island of pressboard, a hand-me-down mattress, and a *Kate and Allie* comforter, contemplating not how to get rescued, but how to remain, survive, and build a life apart from others.

My doorbell rings. This shakes me for a moment because Paul, the rodeo clown from Colorado, is just about to say who he is voting off the island, and because nobody has ever used my doorbell before.

A peek through the peephole reveals a funhouse rendition of Y's torso. I just walked by the uncovered living room window, so it is too late to pretend I'm gone.

As I open the door I am quick to look over my shoulder to indicate that something…someone…important is waiting for me in my living room. So important I really shouldn't take my eyes off of them to get the door. But I will…just for a sec. I say the last part out loud, "Just for a sec." She falters on the step and pushes up her sleeves nervously while deciding whether to run away.

Afraid to sound rude, I backpedal and say I meant that for someone else. She waits a moment for me to explain who my guest is, but I don't.

For obvious reasons.

I pull the door in closer to my body so she cannot see beyond me to the vacant chairs or to the wobbly island shots. I have always been ashamed to admit to friends that I watch this drivel, but after this past week's confrontation I am hyperaware of any and all behavior that is socially derailed. This show is one of my few private comforts.

"Hi. Mari, right?" Y stands with her legs wide apart and her hands on her hips.

This is the perfect time to ask her what the Y stands for, but I want her off my step so I can get back to the voting. I nod and look over my shoulder again, indicating my guest is rather needy and demanding of my time and attention.

"Do you have a vase I could borrow?" She asks while glancing at the gutters above my door. She doesn't see such things from her grave-level apartment.

"Oh, sure. I believe I do." I think of a cupboard where I have numerous vases I have gathered from flower orders sent to me for holidays and birthdays from my family since I never go home. I don't have *a* vase; I have a vase outlet.

"What size or color would you like?" I soften a bit and step up to a customer service role.

Hands leave slender hips and hesitatingly motion the general size requirements for a bouquet. "Any color," she mumbles, and then she adds, "but purple is nice."

"Coming right up." I smile and push the door shut, realize this doesn't look right, and open it again, ever so slightly. "I have to close this…my cat…had a terrible accident before. Outside. Be back…" I leave her to imagine the horrors my cat has endured beyond the parking lot after dusk.

My assortment of vases is dusty but large and varied. I select a clear one with thin marbleized strands of blue and purple streaming throughout it. It reminds me of my plastic lab partner in freshman anatomy class.

"Thanks," she says, looking at it as if I have handed her a treasure. Treasure. My mind returns to the climactic ending taking place just a few feet away from me.

I look over my shoulder again and say loudly, "Be right there." My smile concludes our encounter and Y looks at me with a bit of concern. I try not to blink a lot because that would be a clear indication that I know that she knows that I am certifiably insane. I watch, with dry eyes, as she leaves my stoop. I want to make sure she doesn't glance into my front window. As soon as she disappears around the corner by the laundry room, I rush back to my sofa just in time to see the final vote. Sandy is not voted off. Nor is Paul. But the former Miss Tulsa with sizable talents is forced to pack her bags and return home to her duplex and pet poodle.

I sit there rubbing Elmo's belly, wishing I had someone to share this extreme television moment with. Regret covers me as I wave a high five to nobody. I should have asked Y her name. I should have swallowed my pride and told my imaginary company to leave and invited Y to stay.

Sunday Morning

I try to wiggle my feet fully into my brown leather loafers just outside of the large wooden doors of Eastside Christian Church. Before stepping into the foyer, I pop a breath mint into my mouth. Love thy neighbor.

Clive, the Elton John look-alike organist, is well into a song. His patchwork coat displays the gold-and-purple tones of a painter's color wheel. As the words of a favorite hymn calm my nerves, I am thankful I resisted the urge to sleep in today.

Congregants file into the same seats every Sunday. When Caitlin was first exploring Christianity, she attended with me for a few months before settling on the Episcopalian church. After an upbringing geared toward psychology rather than theology, she immediately spotted the church-perch syndrome. She interpreted this as too complacent and too inflexible, traits already assigned to churchgoers, fair or not.

I agreed at first, eager to have her opinion validated in a new setting. But soon I noticed the behavior in other settings. People gravitate toward a placement that is familiar to them. In the boardroom, on the transit bus, and even in public bathrooms—three stalls in to the left for me, personally. When I pointed this out to Caitlin, she agreed. "It is kinda like when I put on my rings. I start with my belly button ring and only then can I put on my finger rings. Maybe there is an order to most of what we do." I think I had spun this into yet another reason to believe in God. It was a time in my life when witnessing took on the feel of cattle roping.

Running late means you run the risk of losing your preferred seat to a newcomer or someone shaking up their personal perspective. Such is the case today. A young couple sits, holding hands, in my favorite spot in my favorite pew. It's the only survivor from the original sanctuary that burned down in the early '40s. The wood is worn smooth from worshipers placing their hands on the side rest for support to stand, to sing, to pray. But it is the view which sold me on my piece of pew property. As I look toward the front of the sanctuary from this angle, the pulpit is placed squarely between a stained-glass image of the Garden of Gethsemane and one of a bright light shining from an empty tomb. Even before I recognized the symbolism of this spot, I must have intuitively realized that my life is stalled in the middle of these biblical moments. I'm waiting and wanting to move closer to a life resurrection but feel caught up in my time of doubt and fear. Even with faith, it can be difficult to fully, wholeheartedly believe divine hands transform human lives.

Stumbling along with my shoe still caught on my heel and no time to pray for a different seat, I slide into my backup. The spot is always available. It took some time, but I figured out why nobody fills this space.

Her name is Rose Waverly.

Her white hair is held in perfect formation with delicate, gem-lined bobby pins; she is refined and royal in appearance. Her suits are impeccable and expensive. Always there is a nice piece of jewelry that looks made to match her designer suit. Her bracelet is loaded with silver icons from enviable, foreign travels, yet her subtle power is so strong that her jewelry does not clink and jingle during the service. It merely speaks in whispers of her charmed life.

I am her antithesis with my plain light denim skirt—one Angelica actually has begged me to burn—and a short-sleeve blouse. Minimalist. The small turquoise-and-silver earrings that should float on air as I walk sound a bit more like wind chimes in between the hymns and prayer silences. Now, if I had any remnants of confidence and emotional security, clothing would not matter; however, I have been prodded, chided, and tagged by my peers as a twentysomething washout. The last thing I need is to disappoint a woman I barely know.

I paste on a smile when the pastor introduces the time to greet one another. I'm waiting. Watching the coiffed hair. The shiny nails. I see her finish chatting with another fine woman to her right. Then her shoulder drops a bit and she is about to pivot and greet her fellow worshiper to the left.

Turn. Her smile is broad and filled with beautiful teeth that would be the envy of all the residents at Golden Horizons.

"Hello, Mari." She flaunts those teeth and a bit of the emerald brooch at her neck. She fingers it lightly to showcase it.

"Hello, Mrs. Waverly." I start to scan the crowd for someone else to greet.

She doesn't read the cue. "And where is your husband today?"

Not again.

"I'm single." This is as rote as the AA introduction. My name is Mari, I am single. Under my breath I add, "Just like last week."

"That's a shame. A girl your age…not married." She scans my clothing and finds several reasons for the sad state of singledom that I am in.

I notice it is never a shame because I am so sweet or a good woman of faith or because I am pretty in certain low-light situations. My status is clearly a shame because of my age and apparently because of Mrs. Waverly's limited expectations for the single girl standing in front of her with a pasted-on smile.

And it is a shame *every* Sunday.

At first I chalked it up to bad memory. But I know the flow of conversation when talking to a person with dementia, early Alzheimer's, or selective memory. To be honest, I think Rose is a bit mean. It sounds ghastly to consider that an older woman could be intentionally not nice, yet we are surrounded by personalities every day that relish situations that make others squirm.

Angelica comes to mind.

Do we really think that young taunters become delightful once they are subjected to Medicare, Social Security, and a culture geared toward youth and beauty?

Rose's chagrin leads to a tsk-tsk movement of her head and a slight clucking of her tongue. Meanwhile, my eyes dart about nervously, my cheeks redden with frustration, and my tongue confesses that I am, this Sunday and every Sunday, single.

Finding Excuses

The workstation I share with several other employees takes me back to dorm life. I have the equivalent of the narrow twin bed and the courtside patio—an old metal typewriter desk with a limited view of the paling stucco maintenance building.

To break out of this adult version of a limited life, I look at the stack of calendars given to me from industry reps. Tropical locations, pristine waterfalls, and private beaches beckon me beyond my private prison. My favorite calendar is the one featuring women and men in wheelchairs living out their days in exuberant, fulfilling ways. They are lucky people who travel the globe by the seat of their pants.

I play "Which one is me?" a game which evolved from my belief that within any group of people or selection of possibilities, there is always one person who is like me or at least like a part of me. I always seek this person out at social gatherings, grocery stores, matinee crowds, or in photos of strangers that hang in museums or rest on the nightstands of the residents. It can take a while, recognizing oneself when out of context, but eventually I always see me.

In this instance I have my identity narrowed down to two choices. Am I the politically minded sightseer twirling in front of the Washington Monument sporting a stylish haircut and Donna Karan from head to toe? Or am I the carefree, "I've never been more daring" woman who spins her chair perilously close to the edge of a designer pool in Scottsdale while sipping raspberry lemonade?

I am about to ask my supervisor, Rae Vandersleski, which she would cast as me, but I catch myself when I see her mood. The woman has mighty moods. She storms by me and *is* not in the mood for such stupid talk. In other words, I decide to keep this job one more stinkin' day.

"Good morning, Rae," I say to Rae o' Sunshine.

"Yes, isn't it." She looks over to be sure I am doing something productive, and by now I am feigning such. Rae has not figured out that "Good morning" is not actually an assessment of the day thus far...it is a greeting. One to be reciprocated.

If it were an assessment of the day thus far, I would have to alter it slightly and say, "A bit like eating soap, Rae." Yes...yes, it is.

The end of January means you can loosen the cinched belt of unreal resolutions and go back to breathing properly. This freedom allows me to return to my gluttonous ways. I am hungry for old favorites...like imagining I am a person in a calendar. Or avoiding the reworking of my résumé, which is pulled up on the screen.

"What's a highly marketable way to say I am depressed and moody...oh, and sick of work that requires effort?" I ask Lysa, our latest in a succession of file clerks. Rae's assumption that everyone is either incompetent or aspiring to be incompetent usually has new employees job hunting by lunch. But Lysa, who is in her last year of nursing school, seems to be quite intelligent and patient.

She looks up from a file and gives this some thought. After just a few months of employment she is completely used to my out-of-the-blue questions. "Type this..." She gives me advance warning and I poise my fingers over the keys as she continues. "As a passionate and reflective

person, I am in pursuit of a career that matches my desire to work effi-
ciently, creatively, and within a team environment."

"Oh, I like it. Team means others can pick up my slack when I am too
tired." I type madly, suddenly inspired to turn all my faults into exceptional qualities. After I run out of ideas, I turn to Frank, our custodian.
"You know, I told myself I would get out of here last year."

"That is dangerous thinking. You might want to turn that idea into
something positive as well. Something like…if this is my last year here,
what would I want to accomplish?" He is filling out a report as to why the
Sunset Canyon wing is closed off.

"Too positive. Baby steps." I look at his form upside down and read
aloud as he writes. "Reason for limiting access to portion of building: wet
floors from leaky pipe." That is his way of covering for resident Perry, who
insists on taking his fish in their bowls for morning walks.

"You're a good man, Frank." I smile at one of the most caring people
here at Golden Horizons. Frank is my adopted grandpa. I haven't told
him in case he would decline the honor.

I save my résumé for another day and face the empty calendar
awaiting notations that represent a life lived. I consider borrowing some
appointments from Angelica's crowded social planner.

This reminds me…

I write down "Dreaded golf tournament" in next week's expanse of
unused life. I put a smiley face next to this entry, just to bug myself. I have
been around Angelica's coworkers. This will not be fun by any stretch of
the handicap.

"What can I break to get out of golf?"

"Your clubs," deadpans Lysa.

I am very impressed to find that she can keep her sense of humor
while handling the projects she is assigned. The state just issued a new
series of codes related to residents' follow-up care and treatment. Her fingers are covered with an assortment of neon stickers representing physical therapy (red), psychiatric counseling (blue), speech therapy (yellow),

and a kaleidoscope of other services. Right now she looks ready to self-prescribe a blue sticker.

"Wouldn't the rotator cuff do it?" I'm desperate. I keep tracing over the word "golf" on my calendar square.

Forward…Golf.

Backward…Flog.

How appropriate.

Chad walks by, and though I am still horrified by our grocery store encounter, I have to work through the awkwardness. "Hey…you." I toss a bean bag paperweight at his back.

I find that juvenile tactics learned on playgrounds still work amazingly well in the adult world.

"Mari. You're losing your beans. Ha." He return volleys the plaid fabric bag along with annoying third-grade humor. I'd mock him, but I started it.

"What can I break that will let me get out of playing golf with a friend." I rotate my arm to give him a clue to the answer so obvious that even I, a non-golfing, non-physical therapist, know it.

"Your word, apparently." He chuckles and starts to high-five Lysa until he sees that she is Edward Stickerhands. "Actually, the problem we discussed a while back could affect your swing," says Mr. Back to Business.

Yes, I will be sure to call Angelica and tell her I have the shuffle of an old man.

I hold up my hand. "That will be all."

Fore Eyes

Top of the morning to ya," I say with my best Irish accent to the small-stature man in the kilt before me. He stands boldly, the breeze whipping about his tartan (and quite spartan) plaid skirt. He was offering me a metal basket of golf balls, but now the offer is revoked. He turns and walks toward the clubhouse and, my guess, another highball before high noon.

"Why would you say something like that?" Angelica, who will say anything to anyone at anytime, is appalled by my behavior here at the Oasis Golf Course.

"I know…I spoke Irish to the little Scottie-man. It was the first thing that came to my mind."

And I thought it would get rid of him.

"That little Scottie-man happens to be my regional supervisor. I was going to try to get us on his team, but I can kiss that goodbye."

I am even more thankful for my haphazard remark.

She doesn't want to let go of the argument. "He is wearing a kilt for a reason…" She does a top to bottom survey of my wrinkled pink polo shirt and too-big khakis held up by an old man's belt. Subconsciously she assures herself that she is not me. Her hands smooth the fabric of her pristine Anne Klein taupe slacks and her dainty knit sweater tank. I sense she wants to ask what my excuse is for my clothing choices.

But I really am perfectly dressed for the part. When Angelica invites one of us to her events, it is not usually to introduce us around or to have a good time in our presence. It is to make herself feel good by comparison.

Her eyes meet mine and she knows I know. I almost detect a nod above her strand of pearls.

I put on my dilated-pupils glasses—I really meant to get some normal ones for this—and prepare to have my rut pointed out in many different ways over the next few hours.

"Why are we in teams? Is this like a sponsored fund-raiser or a... what? Why are all these people here?" I always like to have a reason for enduring pain and humiliation. I am hoping for a children's charity or Save the Wild Canyon Horses. Something redeeming.

Angelica shrugs her defined shoulders. "It is a morale booster for employees. You know how hard I work...we all work. It is a thank-you." She settles on this last version as a nice compromise between something that benefits needy people or animals and something that is an extravagant pat on the back.

As we get our own baskets of golf balls she notices my face guard. "No. No. Not those glasses." Her cheeks turn red and the muscles beneath her rose-tinted Gucci lenses are twitching. She must be rethinking her strategy of bringing me here. The flip side of hanging out with an undesirable is that one is seen hanging out with an undesirable. "I brought you here to help you to get you within normal distance range to your own peers. You are so..." She is speechless. There are no words in her social, contemporary, and very with-it vocabulary to label exactly what I am.

I remove the glasses and drape them on the neckline of my shirt. She winces at this barely better offer on my part.

I shut up at this point and practice my swing. I do more chucking in the general vicinity of the ball. My metal basket is still full when Angelica has depleted hers. Without a word she sets off to find us a beneficial duo to latch on to for the tournament so this whole day is not a wash for her.

After sending a few more errant balls toward the clubhouse, I take a break from the heat and head under the covered observation area. I hear Angelica's voice off in the distance. "You're kidding. You are such a kidder. Don't even say that." I don't have to look to know she is surrounded by good-looking men and flipping her hair frequently in place of authentic dialogue.

"What am I doing here?" I ask my friend Empty Chair and slide an ashtray to the other side of the wobbly wrought-iron table.

"If you are like everyone else, you are here to network, schmooze, drink, and get a promotion, if you are lucky enough to get your supervisor to drink even more than you." I turn to face the face of the voice. It is oval, beautiful, and comes with a set of the most amazing green eyes.

I do a Vanna White motion of my outfit and say, "Obviously I am not like everyone else," in my usual self-effacing way with an extra touch of nervousness.

"Obviously." He says this in a nice "and that is a good thing" way. "I'm Peyton Foster."

"You don't seem to be drinking. So what is your strategy for these games?"

"I prefer to work the old-fashioned way. Beat 'em at their hobby and then hold it over them in the boardroom the next week. Besides, these tournaments feel too much like fraternity years as it is." He pushes his blond hair out of his eyes.

I decide that if I can remove Peyton Place from my memory, his is a rather nice name. "Hi." As I reach my hand toward him I catch the edge of my mondo-glasses. They end up beneath the table. Now that the glasses are not making Angelica feel silly but me feel stupid, I have my own regrets.

He tries to decide whether to shake my hand first or retrieve my glasses. This is a gentleman's dilemma. I want to say, "Your mother raised you well," but I know that will sound...old.

He grabs my hand and bends over to snatch up my sorry eyewear. There is no way to look at these and not mention them. He holds them up to the light and acts really impressed. "Aren't these the kind Jeff Gordon wears for the Indy 500?" He is mock-serious but in the spirit of friendliness, not facetiousness.

"That they are. Well, that and a bit more advanced, I might add. I test drive endurance glasses and other products for sports celebrities. I have another pair here somewhere." I fumble in my pockets. "Tiger Woods is interested in trying them out. So I'm here today really just to test these for Tiger. Testing for Tiger."

He laughs and doesn't seem at all put off.

"And you?" I see he is beautiful enough to be "one of them," but his personality seems a bit too…present.

"I don't have a tester." He shakes his head, disappointed by his bad luck.

"What are you doing here? Are you here with the other socially acceptable drug dealers?"

He laughs again. "You caught me. Though I have a very good lawyer if you should choose to prove it."

"And ruin my chance to get a free neon Just Focus pen? Never."

We go back and forth like this for several moments. I almost feel social. If I were looking at me…well, and if I ignored the outfit and the special needs glasses, I would think I was someone like Angelica. Sure, confident, and hip.

While we are chatting away, I notice that he keeps rubbing his hands together and looking at them. "Are you planning a sinister plot for a B movie?" He looks puzzled. "All that hand rubbing." I realize I am being as bold as Angelica, and probably as rude.

He gets it and laughs a very nice laugh. "In this heat the golf glove really irritates my hand. See…" He removes his Michael Jackson paraphernalia and reveals a bumpy heat rash.

Though I act disgusted, I am secretly delighted because I can offer my beautiful new friend a cure. "Well, I know just the thing for you." I reach into my bag and pull out Garden Glove hand mask. "This stuff is wonderful. You smooth it on, and it creates a layer of protection on the surface of your skin. Put the glove on, and I guarantee at the end of a day like today, everyone will think you skipped a few holes and hit the Elizabeth Arden spa for a manicure."

"You are amazing. So you really are a tester of some kind?"

"No." Here it comes. Do I admit what I do for a living or make something up? No time to be clever. "I...I work at Golden Horizons Retirement Center." His face still says "interested," so I continue. "Our maintenance and landscape guy told me about this because a lot of residents with casts or bandage wraps end up with ghastly rashes...though not nearly as scary as yours." I turn the attention back to his shortcoming in case my job status was too much information.

"I just wish I had met you sooner." He says this while flapping his hands to get cool air on the sores.

From the corner of my eye, I see Angelica rushing over. I am not sure who she is set to save, but it turns out she likes Peyton and misinterprets his motions as a wave.

"Peyton. So good to see you. Remember the Miami tournament? Crazy. Crazy." She makes the universal motion for crazy...finger twirling outside her ear. Her right-hand diamond ring blinds us both.

"Yes. It was crazy...uh..." He wants my name. I realize I have not yet introduced myself.

Angelica interrupts me. "She is with me. Peyton, I wish we had spoken sooner. I just set up a foursome with Dr. Ravin and Winchester. I'd try to get out of it, but you know Winchester. The guy can make or break your career with a call. Right?"

Who is she? Why am I with her?

"Well, it was nice to see you again Angelica. And to meet you...?" He tries to get my name.

"Mari. Mari!" I yell this as Angelica hurries me toward the two fake-tan, old Ken dolls poised by their cart just yards away.

"Thanks for the great tip!" He waves the tube of lotion in the air.

Angelica gives me a dirty look. "What kind of tip could you possibly give Peyton?" Her pearls pull tight against her enlarged neck veins. "He is one of the top golfers. I hope you didn't just embarrass me."

"I wouldn't dream of taking that away from you." She doesn't get the slight because she is marching me along the green to meet Howie and Stu, the secret names I use in my head to separate these clones with clubs who seem to have matching divots on their heads.

Our foursome turns out to be so bad I actually am searching the course for Scottie-man in case I can make amends. Our teammates are just Angelica's type, playboys who forget that innuendos are supposed to be subtle. She is flirting back at them while I watch indifferent and uninvited in the background. I am the nerd serving punch at Angelica's prom.

By hole eight I am dragging. Sweating. Tired. Sick of their stupid, intoxicated jokes and Angelica's willingness to laugh. I keep checking her water bottle to be sure it really is from Artesian springs and not the flask Stu keeps in tow.

As Angelica is about to swing she sniffs the air. I assume this is a way to see which way the wind blows, so I lick a finger and stick it in the air beside her.

"Pretty mild," I say with authority.

"What is that smell?" She says this in my ear but quite loudly.

"I'm not sure what you mean." Though as I hold my arm up, I get a whiff of my shoulder...the Muscle Heat, which is supposed to be odorless, seems to turn quite rancid in ninety-degree weather. I quickly put my arm down.

"It is *you!*" She leans away from me and actually pinches her nose. Pinches her nose! And waves the air about her. The LA guys are taking this in as though they are hopeful it will turn into a chick fight. Howie, the doctor, removes another clandestine beer from his golf bag. The caddy looks the other way. Either that or he is trying not to smell my shoulder.

Denying this seems useless. "Okay. So I used Muscle Heat on my shoulder. I pulled it helping Walt to the bathroom yesterday. All week I was hoping to destroy my rotator cuff because I wanted to get out of this spectacle and then this shoulder thing happens, but it is too short notice for you to find another pawn…so I caked on the ointment and showed up. For you." I point at her and her pearl necklace and her sleek tank sweater with a vengeance.

Angelica drops her club and stands with her hands on her hips, looking to Howie and Stu for moral support. They are talking about leather vs. fabric upholstery in the Tucson heat. So she takes a deep breath away from me and comes in for the kill. "Why do you insist on all of this?" She motions up and down as though I am a life-sized model of disease. A disease which leads to social death, no less.

By now I have my sorry sunglasses on and am perspiring more than usual. My odor is the last straw.

"I only signed on for nine holes anyway. So me and my stink will be gone in no time at all."

"You only signed up for half? I could have joined the three Rogers from Chicago. They are all in the top five for sales this quarter. And they totally love me."

"So go join the Rogers." I am tumbling toward another breakdown. "This stupid event isn't even for charity. It is like a traveling cocktail party—pretentious players, lousy appetizers, and not a chance of good conversation."

I toss my club at Charley, our caddy, and start speedwalking toward the Halfway House Café, which is a mock-dilapidated shack that charges twenty dollars for a burger and fries are extra. I know how bizarre speed-walkers look…like they are animated with their hips popping out. With my baggy khakis and wrinkly shirt, I'm sure my movements resemble that of the Pillsbury Dough Boy on his way to a kitchen fire.

It doesn't occur to me until I am halfway to the Halfway House that Angelica is my only way home.

Second Opinions

"When I pray for my life to be changed, that is one thing." I reach for my Americano from a harried barista and keep talking to Denton, who stands behind me. He is the minor character I have chosen to help me process my ambush intervention.

I stop speaking while we wander around the coffee shop looking for a table not occupied by the unemployed clutching classifieds or pairs of Brads going over their monthly figures. A corner booth opens up, and I clear it of breakfast debris.

"But when others pray for someone to change in front of said person, then it is hard for one to not feel like their life is a complete mess." I have switched to third person. It is safer from a distance.

Denton sips his green tea. I am counting on his nature as a peacekeeper to not add insult to injury by agreeing with my confronters. An administrator at a nursing home, he was my table partner several years ago at a conference entitled "Staying Healthy in Health Care." We exchanged phone numbers, compelled by a force larger than us. In a room of mostly over-fifty-year-olds, our twentysomething souls felt obligated to consider pairing up, mating for life, procreating, and perpetuating the species in the face of extinction. One date later, we realized we would have to leave the populating of the earth to another couple…a couple that perhaps found more than safety issues and state codes to discuss.

Still, though Denton and I are a boring combination, he is like a thick cotton sweatshirt that resurfaces in the bottom drawer just when the weather changes—a never-failing source of comfort that is forgiving and fits perfectly every time.

"I believe they assessed you properly, Mari." The pressing of his tea bag occupies his field of vision while I sit and stew across from him.

Did I say comfy sweatshirt? I meant unforgiving, lace-up, full-body corset.

"Geez, now I'm sorry you didn't get an invitation to the big event." Bitterness coats my tongue, and it isn't the freshly brewed French roast. "You could have joined the club or signed up for the newsletter that must be circulating. I haven't seen it, but it has to exist because suddenly everyone is inspired to comment on my life." My frustration pours out and sets like concrete. Something else for me to carry around.

The shoulders of my counterpart shrug slightly. Then he sits back and puts his mug down with a ceramic thud. A judge passing a sentence. "Mari, my evaluation is made only because you brought the subject to my attention, not because you are so pitiful I feel compelled to fix you." He motions his flat hand up and down, like a crossing guard requesting a driver to slow down.

"True."

"Maybe you take your work home with you too much." He doesn't look down this time, knowing he hit a kernel of truth.

"Look who's talking." Yet even as I say it I know that he speaks as one who has crossed over to the other side of workaholism. And not just because he is drinking tea.

"I've taken up with a book club at the Reading Room bookstore over by campus."

I nod to honor his big step, but I roll my eyes on the inside.

"I started training for a 10K run and have just signed on with the Trail Tweeters, a hiking and bird-watching group that has the lofty, admirable goal of walking a different trail and identifying a different bird each week." Denton pauses to literally put his finger on the right word. He points to his phone resting by the napkin dispenser. "Connected. Mari, I feel connected to my peer group for the first time in my life."

I want to comment on the way his ridiculous suspenders would be evidence to the contrary. But as I consider my list of reasons for not connecting, I notice that Denton has a chic edge to him. The difference from old Denton is subtle, but nonetheless, he is slightly more attractive. What is it about him? A bit of stubble darkens his narrow features. Once-beady eyes seem brighter and more observant, ready to identify an Ash-Throated Flycatcher or, if one is lucky, a Yellow-Billed Cuckoo.

"Want to go with me this weekend? We are hiking a trail on Mount Lemmon and hoping to catch a glimpse of the mating Ruby-Throated Hummingbird." At the mention of mating, his cheeks flush the shade of this rare bird's throat. Could there be more than birds and lack of connection causing Denton to take to the hills? I imagine a college girl clad in REI attire embarking on the Catalina Trail. Her tousled hair and drooping safari hat blends with her bookish nature to camouflage what is model beauty. She lifts her binoculars to her bright blue eyes…no, hazel…but she doesn't direct them toward the bird as the leader has suggested but toward her fellow fowl-tracker, Denton. She scans him from bottom to top and becomes flustered when her close-up view reveals that his eyes are not focused on the wing span of fowl but are peering right through the convex glass of her standard equipment to her soul. She loses her balance. Denton is so sensitive he instinctively knows she is about to tumble. His surprisingly strong arms reach out, pulling her back from the abyss.

Isn't this what all of us want? To be pulled back from a fatal misstep by the very person who will eventually agree to keep us from falling into the bottomless void forever after?

The force of his modest changes and my overindulgent imagination pushes me back in my chair. All I can think of at the moment is that everyone is doing it. If Denton is merging with society, I don't want to be left behind. I mean sure, we weren't meant to populate the earth as a couple, but we still comforted one another in our shared, uncouth universe.

"The world of birds is really quite fascinating. Before, I used to shoo away anything with wings, and now, after looking them up in the *Little Big Book of Little and Big Birds,* I am compelled to spend moments contemplating their vibrant colors." He is peering out the window, willing a bird to land on the shrub outside so he can introduce me to the nirvana of air vermin.

"No, thank you, Denton." I mean the no and the thank you. I am not sold on his version of transformation, but I am inspired. Here I wanted Denton to be on my side. To say, "Mari, you're perfect as you are." But instead he offered a glimpse of what life can be like if we give ourselves over to risk. I consider what new things could be a part of my future: respectable job, recognition, exotic travel, a broader circle of friends, clout at the best restaurants, a new apartment in the trendy part of town, a date.

We leave our breakfast chat without making plans to meet up again. Between his day job and his extracurricular activities there isn't time to laze about with someone who isn't yet crazy for cuckoos. He strides over to his dazzling silver SUV with a "Tucson is for the birds" bumper sticker; the morning sun glints off of his compass watch, waterproof up to fifty meters, and I sit on the torn vinyl driver's seat of my lackluster car and know that dreams do come true for others.

Maybe…for me too.

Lost and Found

"Did you feign cardiac arrest? Angina? Or did you stick with the clichéd broken rotator cuff excuse?" Lysa asks from her file cabinet corner. She is compiling a demographic study of the residents. Sadly, this institution often knows more about these people's lives than their families do.

"I did not fake anything, including my hostile departure from the green. I ended up taking a cab home."

"Uh-oh," she says knowingly. Lysa had witnessed Angelica at her finest one day when the queen of blunt stopped in before a lunch date. The female cyclone kept ranting about the Golden Horizons' color scheme "that would make the seventies gag itself with a spoon" and the "whole *One Flew Over the Cuckoo's Nest* creepy vibe." Later, when Lysa politely asked what Angelica and I possibly had in common, the answer "God" didn't seem like a great witness. I had said I was obliged by court order to spend time with her.

"It was not pretty. Probably rather humorous for our caddy, though. The good news…the court order might be canceled after my out of order behavior on the course."

"That is good news." She clasps her hands together in mock rejoicing.

Her fake, over-the-top smile reminds me of Wendy Skies, a former weather girl who is now a popular anchor on the local news station. "It is time for the news," Frank says as he walks by with his push broom. He nods and he salutes with two fingers to his gray baseball cap, signaling that he will take care of it.

"What was that about?" Lysa asks raising her eyebrows. "Your club have a special handshake too?"

"Walter Simmons…the guy who carries the backpack and his checkers wherever he goes…"

"Yes. And smells like sandalwood. He's sweet."

"Very. But sadly he is the father of KTSN's Miss Popularity—Wendy Skies. You know, the one who presses her palm to her heart and says 'God bless ya' as her sign-off."

"So very fake. Does she come in all the time and act superior?"

"I wish she did for Walter's sake. She doesn't visit at all, but the poor man still religiously watches her show. He says her God bless you sign-off is their little way of communicating. It just breaks my heart."

Lysa considers this. "Well, maybe it is something they used to say when she was growing up."

"I understand wanting to give her some credit. Nobody wants to assume a gentle man like Walter is ignored by his only daughter. But I've looked into it. The woman lives about five miles that way." I point in the direction of Paradise Properties, an elite development where each mini-mansion has its own pool, courtyard, tennis court, and the sure sign of money—an irrigated, lush lawn. "She has to go by here to get to the station, so she has no excuses."

"I'd give anything to be able to visit my dad." Lysa's voice softens, and I remember that her dad passed away two years ago. Her catalyst moment to start nursing school.

Guilt conviction sets in. I quickly step off my soapbox and my mind replays Sadie's inquiry about my avoidance of home. I may not drive by my parents' house every day on the way to work, but am I really so different from Wendy? "Maybe she is busy and plans to visit, but…" I don't let myself finish the pathetic remark meant to assuage my guilt rather than grant Wendy grace.

"Don't forget that you have a meeting with Rae at 11:00. She asked me to block out quite a chunk of time for you to be with her in her royal chambers."

This annual planning meeting is my life assessment marker. I preface it each year with a short prayer, "Lord, let this be my last planning session. Move me on to greener pastures. Amen." This year I will add, "May I never have to pray this prayer again."

I roll my creaky chair out into the hallway so that Lysa can see from her corner corral that my tongue is stuck out. Unfortunately my chair's momentum forces a collision with Mr. Emil Shannon, who is storming toward the desk with the self-appointed authority his short and corpulent body betrays.

Just as Wendy was to be crowned worst spawn of the year, we are reminded of this poor excuse for a child. Cursing, Emil bends down to rub his shin while his other hand is waving madly in the air, pointing, accusing, searching for a target.

"I'm so sorry, Mr. Shannon, but you will have to hail a cab outside." I roll back behind the counter so there will be a sound-and-fury barrier between us.

He rises and glares over the faux-granite surface at me. "Once again I have had something of great value stolen in this unchecked crime ward." He waits with nostrils flaring, his breath as shallow as his spirit.

I offer him the look of shock and outrage that he expects followed by an insincere frown of disappointment. "Unfortunately, we don't have a place for stolen items. They don't remain in the building, what with all the pawnshops in the area. But if you think you might have lost something that someone else found, then we do have a *lost* and *found* bin—"

"I haven't got all day to spend in this—" He stops talking when he sees that I have stopped searching through the bin so I can listen for his insult. In a lower version of his angry voice he seethes, "Just look, please. It's a gold watch."

This runt of a man is the son of Pamela Shannon, a woman with only slight dementia who has picked up a bad habit in her old age. She picks pockets. At first the stack of hundred-dollar bills, Emil's driver's license, and a silver pen in her nightstand after visiting hours were a mystery. We finally caught on and confronted her. She laughed at our slow detective work. When she was told that stealing from a son sweet enough to visit regularly was abominable, she laughed even louder.

Pamela's devilish, in-the-know grin later made sense. Frank heard the bridge room gossip that Emil was robbing Pamela blind and was probably responsible for placing the high-functioning woman here well before there were any signs of physical or emotional need. A quick search through a local real estate website confirmed that Emil was selling pieces of his mother's property at top market prices.

Now when the metal doors are closed to visitors, we congratulate Pamela on whatever fine object she has acquired and then place the item directly in the lost-and-found bin. It doesn't bother us at all when Emil shouts, spit building in the corners of his mouth, and reprimands whoever is on duty about the loose security. Important lawyer-man still doesn't realize that his mother is only doing to him what he is doing to her.

I asked Pamela why she even allows him to return. It turns out he brings pints of butter pecan ice cream each trip as a guilt offering. She just loves butter pecan ice cream and watching him squirm when she refers to him as her "special tubby boy."

Tubby's small, bloated face is now hovering just inches from mine. "You do not run a resident community but a home for thieves and vagrants. I should take my mother out of here because of all the criminal activity that goes on."

I hold out the orange container that has an assortment of books, eyeglasses, and as of last week, Mr. Shannon's gold Rolex.

"When I get done with the high-profile case I am working on, this place will be my next investigation. You can be sure." His stubby hands grab for the watch, reaching and retracting like a turtle's head returns to its shell after an offense.

"How old are you, Mr. Shannon?" I give him a pensive, evaluative look.

"What on earth does that have to do with it?"

"Well, you are right about the lost items scenario happening too often."

He looks as pleased as a gargoyle can look. Uncoordinated, nervous fingers replace the watch on his thick wrist.

"You know, dementia can set in early in a person's life. And it can be hereditary…" I leave the deduction to this great lawyer working on a high-profile case.

With a shrug of his shoulders he straightens his suit on the top half. The middle of the jacket is wedged onto his extended belly. Nice suit, evil fit. He spins on his heel and storms toward the glass doors, which he tries to slam, until he realizes they are hinged to close slowly for thieving people with walkers. This really gets to him; he kicks the steel frame of the door and limps off.

Bullied in a China Shop

Rae is a tall, big-boned woman who comes from a long line of linemen. She bellows my name and beckons me to her office. I enter the only room in the building with functioning air-conditioning and breathe in the strong fake scent of gardenia air freshener.

She stands with some difficulty and motions for me to sit in front of her. Mother-of-pearl glasses rest on her nose as she takes in everything about me. I do the same to her. She towers over a glass desk. The light from the backdrop display case of Hummel figurines glows through her thinning hair, giving her a ghost-from-Christmas-past look.

One late night after Lysa and I had written up Medicare qualification reports on residents, we became giddy on Mountain Dew and Goobers from the snack machine. Neither of us wanted to go home because going home meant going to bed and eventually waking up and having to return here. So we restarted the antiquated computer and researched on eBay what we could get if we kidnapped the Hummel porcelain cherubic children and animals. It turns out they are worth more than enough to cross the border and live comfortably for a few years.

The problem with fantasies like that for a somewhat logical person…
you always ask the "what then?" question and the dream balloon deflates
faster than you can purchase a one-way bus ticket to Mexico. Over-
analysis is my own worst enemy.

Our stare down ends with Rae extending a candy dish to me. A cheap
peace offering before the battle begins. To be polite I select a red hot, but
it is stuck to a wrapped peppermint, and she has to hold the dish while I
wrangle the tiny dot of sugar loose. Unfortunately, her patience allowance
for me was spent the moment I walked in the door and sucked in some
of her private cold air. She makes it clear that she is at wit's end. Since she
was born with a shortage, this comes rather quickly.

Her thin silver pen taps on the glass repeatedly. I chose the wrong
candy, so she is going to make me wait and consider how much better life
would be had I chosen a golden butterscotch or a root beer barrel. My
mind immediately conjures a neon sign that flashes: "Bull in a china
shop." There is no way to avoid such a thought when you are in Rae's
office. This woman, who is one plaid flannel shirt away from a Paul
Bunyan portrait, surrounds herself with fragile items that teeter on the
edge of possible doom. Delicate crystal figurines in indistinguishable
shapes, origami birds midflight, shell saucers holding glass marbles,
antique lace doilies draped over the arms of her leather wing-back chair.
I want to ask her if she does this to feel powerful. And whether she places
herself among fragile bones and tender spirits for the same reason.

Instead I focus on a smear of mascara that is below her right eye. She
looks like a heavyweight boxer, and somehow this identity is more user-
friendly to me than that of wicked supervisor. So I keep it to myself and
refer to her as Sugar Rae in my head.

"Let's get right to it, shall we?" She adjusts her blouse so that I see
mostly the tropical red tank beneath. She is a large stop sign planted in
my path. I'm tempted to run it…grab the Hummels and dash for the
border after all.

"Well, plans for the Golden Golden party are well underway. We'll be ready after a few minor details are ironed out, but I'll have those secured by next week. Blanche, the head of the resident committee, and I are on top of all details." The big fiftieth anniversary party for Golden Horizons is a bit of a scam, really. The facility is only twenty years old, but apparently an original Golden Horizons started up in Yuma fifty years ago. I guess services to the aging are prime franchises these days.

"What's left?" Rae twirls the small gold chain around her thick neck. Each time she twists it to one side it disappears into her flesh on the other.

"I just have to confirm the play time and rate for a fantastic fifties band. The Doo-Wops. I thought it would be nice to commemorate the music of the original era. I was only able to get them through a personal connection; they are in high demand throughout the Southwest." My mouth is rambling along. I don't know why I need to build up these details to Rae. I'm doing a good job and she knows it. Why do I become so defensive in her presence?

I tell myself to shut up, but I keep on talking to avoid the silence. "This music will go well with the decorations and those invitations you approved last month. The pretty ones with the balloons rising up the side of the page." They are horrific juvenile invitations instead of the very classy version I picked out. Rae had refused my choice, saying this wasn't an inauguration or a funeral but a real party. "Parrteee" she had said, like a seventeen-year-old.

"Forget the music. I have that covered." She stops twisting her chain in favor of pulling my leg.

"You're kidding, right?" As soon as I say it I try to suck back in the breath that carried those bad, bad words into her space. She never kids. She punishes, insults, tortures. Never kids.

Her Mona Lisa-esque smile quivers. "I have arranged for the band. All that fifties music can still be the theme." She opens a folder in front of her. I know by the colored label that it is an employee file. I'm several months from a review, so my heart skips a beat. Is she taking over the party plans for a reason? Could this be my firing? Could this be my free pass to another life?

"Beau was spectacular and quite a planner." She praises the employee who quit.

As sick as I am of this guy, at least he had the sense to quit. "Oh, the one who quit and left you on short notice?" Ha. Take that. I was the savior when Beau the wonder boy left her high and dry.

"Did you ever meet him?" She skips over my comment with the greatest of ease. And her voice even catches with emotion.

Here we go. "Uh, no. Haven't had the pleasure." I start to roll my eyes but she is watching me, so I keep them still at the top and pretend to focus in on a mosquito. I grab the air to snare it midflight. My aim is excellent. I ask her for a tissue, a burial for the imaginary bug.

Her usually smooth forehead now has several layers of creases. She looks at me as though I have eaten the bug and scrounged around for more. "Well, he was a good planner." She pauses to note the obvious contrast between former and current employees. "He left us with some anniversary party ideas before he left five years ago. They're quite good. I want you to use as many of these as possible."

She shoves the folder at me. It falls onto my lap and the papers inside start to slip out.

"But I have the party under control." The last thing I want is to work my behind off creating this big event and have all the credit go to Beau. I'm so sick of him.

"And I don't need to remind you that personnel files are *personal* and confidential. I want this back next week. I shouldn't even be doing this, but his ideas are so great…" She stops talking. A small laugh escapes her throat. "There are even some excellent recipes in there. The residents used to love his lemon chiffon cake, and his black bean, chipotle chili is award winning." Her fingers go back to the necklace, and she seems to forget I am here. It crosses my mind that possessing Beau's personnel file is a gift. Maybe in between casserole secrets and event-planning tips there is one write-up. An early bad review. A string of unexplainable tardies. I organize the folder and get up to leave before she wakes up from her daydream.

"Sit," she barks. I obey

"Our pilates instructor is leaving. I'll need you to cover for her until you find a replacement."

"But I'm not trained in pilates. And don't *you* hire?"

"Do I need to remind you again that *you* are the recreational director? First you leave the party details to me, and now you want to get out of leading some harmless calisthenics. These people just want to try and touch their knees, for pete's sake."

I'm elated to hear my professional role reduced to inciting knee touching. Renewed conviction to distribute more résumés this week is fueled.

"Is that all?" I'm pouting now. My job description keeps mutating. Even perfect Beau couldn't keep up the act forever. Maybe he had a breakdown and now lives in the psychiatric ward of Holy Cross Hospital. I grip his file even tighter.

"You should be thrilled that we can hire an instructor at all. I shouldn't tell you this, but since it relates to you..." She shrugs and opens her drawer. She pulls out a piece of black licorice and starts gnawing. "Our budget is getting slashed at the end of the year. Big time. Whatever you are planning for the fund-raiser had better be huge. Don't try to push through era bands and plain invitations or the first cut will be your job. Got it?" With each chaw her mouth is getting darker from the licorice. Black is beginning to fill the creases her red lipstick had carved out earlier. "Do we understand each other?"

I stand and look at her...black eye, black lips...and think maybe she is morphing into the devil right before my eyes. "Perfectly." I spread my healthy pink lips into a broad smile and think bigger. Maybe Beau's file will include favorite recipes and instructions for a good ol' fashioned exorcism.

Confessions

I need some breakup advice." Angelica accepts her plate from our favorite Freddy's waitress—whom I now refer to as Cruella the Gruel Slogger—and removes her pink tweed Prada jacket, draping it casually but deliberately label-side out on the back of the chair. There is nothing more pretentious than the blatant subtlety of a socialite.

Caitlin points a fluffy-mittened hand toward Sadie. "Don't ask Sadie to help. All you have to do is look at her and you know she is smack happy in love."

Sadie smiles shyly. Happiness is indeed written all over her face.

"Slaphappy." I correct Caitlin with the edge I have adopted since my conference with Rae. Not even my large bowl of coffee softens the stark truth revealed that day. I so need to step out of this version of my life.

"Meeeowwww." Angelica motions cat claws, indicating my feisty mood is now not only in my head but out on the breakfast table for all to judge.

Caitlin's eyes are half-covered by yet another hat. A rainbow-colored knit afro has replaced the long-gone non. "Oooohh. Guess who should offer breakup advice? I'd say Mari is in just the right mood."

"Fine." I don't even try to argue. Bring on the ridiculous dating situation Angelica wants to present so I can wallow over her active love life rather than dwell on my nonexistent one. And why does Angelica always get to present our dilemma topic?

Angelica nods, glad that my bad mood will serve her well. "Perfect." She pushes up her white poplin sleeves and then slides her silver charm bracelet to rest near her elbow, saving it from dipping in her granola with banana chips.

"It's my regional corporate partner, Josie." She hisses so the sound of her partner's disliked name can sink in. "She is driving me crazy and I must get away from her. She is ruining my reputation."

"Goodness! Not your reputation. Do tell." I place my hand to my forehead in Scarlett O'Hara fashion to mock her openly. If she wants to exploit my mood, so be it.

"It's true. I was all set to start dating this fantastic doctor from the clinic on Centennial. He travels a lot for Doctors Without Borders, and I'm pretty sure he is interested in me."

"Are you sure that isn't Doctors Without Boundaries?" I make my judgment known. "Shouldn't you keep 'client' and 'boyfriend' as two separate entities?" I use the double finger quote/unquote gesture for added emphasis.

"Well, you don't have to worry. Josie-Nosey mentioned my faith to the doctor." Angelica's fear of public faith has turned into a phobia.

"So what terrible thing happened? You know, it isn't the end of the world if people realize you actually believe in God. Maybe she saved you from going out with someone who is completely void of faith…or anti-faith…" I pause to take a poll. "Which is worse, do you think?"

"Anti-faith."

"Both no good."

Angelica interrupts my runaway commentary. "As it turns out, he's a Christian. A deacon at his church even. So that's that." She wipes away granola crumbs and the chance at romance in one motion.

"So while the rest of us would give anything to connect with a Christian guy, let alone a *doctor,* you find this combination to be repulsive?" Even though I first challenged the ethics of the situation, my devil's advocate persona has jumped to the other side. I cannot help but pick apart her line of reasoning.

"He'd expect too much. You know, serious dating, marriage, kids. The whole package. That is so far from what I want. So, Josie has to go."

What's written on Angelica's face is easy for me to read because she and I have had a few soul-searching discussions about this very thing. Angelica's darkest fear isn't that a guy will want the whole package. Her fear is that a good Christian guy, doctor or not, will not want *her* whole package, including emotional scars she is slow to release after early years of rebellion.

"Wait a minute." Sadie holds up a strong, manicured hand. "Didn't we just have a series of conversations about Josie? When we discussed how to make friends with other women in this day of female envy and cutthroat competition?"

"Yes! Good call, Sadie. I knew her name sounded familiar." I continue this conversation to save Angelica from discussing the real problem.

"And that advice was great," interjects Angelica. "I met Josie for lunches to get a feel for the friendship, just like you suggested. And then we went out after work a few times, just as you suggested. And my boss eventually noted my efforts at camaraderie. So it was perfect. But what you all forgot to mention was that courting a woman friend has the same natural curve of interest as dating men." She shrugs and opens her hands out in the pose of helplessness.

"So we helped you make friends with this Josie and now you want to break up with her? Can you break up with friends?" Caitlin looks worried and turns her pitiful question in my direction.

"Apparently, if we no longer serve a purpose, we begin to slide down that natural curve."

Caitlin rotates her rainbow head-puff around the circle to see if we are

playing with her. The anxiety is rising to her flushed cheeks and her
middle-child appeaser is kicking in. "You know what I do when I get mad
at Mary Margaret?"

"Who?"

"You know, my coworker."

"The scary one?" I am shocked that a woman who wears dog collars
and growls at her customers is named something as innocent as Mary
Margaret.

"Exactly. And that is why it is hard to like her. Not because I am competing with her for a promotion, but because she is just so very mean.
Anyway, I pray a lot about it."

"Sure, prayer. I can do that. But can I pray for Josie to quit?" Angelica's
statement makes us all hope that our names are never mentioned in her
evening prayers.

"There's another thing I do that helps. You might like it, Angelica.
Sometimes I daydream about going ice-skating. In my fantasy the store's
owner, Linda, has invited all of the employees to the ice-skating rink. As
an exercise in bonding or something. Well, nobody can skate, right?
Because we all live in the desert. And while everybody else is falling
down," Caitlin smiles and starts to giggle at what is about to happen in
her dream, "I am stalling, pretending I cannot lace my skates. Then all of
a sudden the song 'Friends Are Friends Forever' by Michael W. Smith
comes over the loudspeaker. You all remember that one, right?"

"Yes." We all admit. And though a few Christian camp talent night
solos of this song clutter my mind, soon the Muzak version floods my
brain. This I don't admit.

Caitlin continues, breathless and lost in the moment. "And as the first
chorus begins, I rise, step over the crumpled bodies, and begin to skate
like Michelle Kwan. Everyone is moved spiritually by the words and
moved emotionally by the power of my moves. My last figure eight before
the triple axle finale is done around Mary Margaret and Linda. I see the
tears streaming down their faces, and Mary Margaret begs Linda to give

me the promotion because I am beautiful, talented, and the most inspiring thing ever." As Caitlin's arms reach out to accept imagined applause we notice the flaw of her latest fashion choice. The funky hat is connected to the fuzzy mittens by a crocheted scarf. It is an all-in-one unit. As her arms stretch wide and the scarf starts to tighten around her thin neck, the need for a choking hazard warning is apparent.

But we don't say this. We are all too stunned to speak. Not because we think her daydream to be demented, but because she admitted to the warped fantasies we all have.

"If you think I am going to waste a daydream on Josie, you are nuts. I'll break up the old-fashioned way."

"Flowers?"

"A phone call?"

"No call?"

We all offer leftovers from past breakups.

"No. The 'It's not you, it's me' speech, only I will wear my new Gucci dress with my new Kate Spade bag, and it will be so obvious it *is* her and *not* me."

This, of course, is the perfect way for Angelica to end it. We agree in silence, stirring our coffees and rearranging the last bits of breakfast on our plates.

"Oh, I almost forgot." As Sadie reaches into her Louis Vuitton briefcase, she is gleeful. I didn't even know glee still existed in our culture of personal angst and drama. But here it is, right in front of me, all rosy and optimistic. She distributes silver metallic envelopes tied with deep blue ribbons.

"No, you didn't." I challenge my friend, wondering if she is about to request the honor of our presence for her nuptials.

She blushes ever so slightly and shakes her head. "Don't you think I would introduce you all to him if we were headed into that level of relationship?"

I shrug. "I don't know. I have never seen you in loooove before, so it's hard to say what you would do."

"A fancy night out." Caitlin has opened her invitation and is reading it out loud. "Stare into the mystery. A night of exploration and discovery awaits you as the Tucson Botanical Society unveils the Carson Curtis Midnight Garden for Gazers featuring the Galaxy Telescope, nature's most romantic show of light and wonder, a rare nighttime garden, and the chance to dine and dance among the stars." She holds the linen paper to her heart as she imagines a night of opulence and catered eats.

"So this is the unveiling of Carson as well?" I inquire, draining the last bit of caffeine from my mega cup.

Angelica turns to me and points to Sadie with her fork. "I seem to recall Ms. Verity stating that if a wedding was in her future, we would meet the man. Did you catch that?" She teases warmly, daring Sadie to admit to love.

"I did indeed hear that, Angelica. Good point." We look to our friend in unison and she laughs.

But she doesn't deny it.

The rare occurrence of cold weather chills us as we step out of the restaurant. It isn't the best time for true blue Southwesterners, but I personally love the chance to pull on favorite sweaters from my D.C. days. I tug on a J. Crew cable-knit to cover the increasing expanse of skin between my jeans and my tops.

"Hey, Caitlin." Angelica is smiling, but we all know she is about to give her friend a hard time. "This new creation…the scarf thing…it is for urban women, right?"

"Urban and trendy," she clarifies.

"Pretend you have to hail a cab."

I should close my eyes, but my morbid curiosity keeps them open to watch as the obvious happens. Caitlin's overzealous arm shoots straight up in the air and the scarf strangles her midsentence. "What's this got to do with hai….eecchhhhh." She doubles over coughing.

"You know, Caitlin, I would never break up with you. You provide way too much humor in my life."

"Maybe I'll just have the hat and scarf attached."

"Good call." With that Angelica pats the top of Caitlin's head and links her arm through the arm of her unintentional comedian friend.

"So Matthew next time?" Try, try again.

"Matthew." Three nods of agreement return my effort.

As Caitlin and Angelica head off to a movie, I check my home messages. Some guy named Lazarus wants to know if I received his flat of daffodils.

I am perplexed. "Sadie, is there like some big fund-raiser going on with the Botanical Society? I keep getting calls from men about flowers."

When she hears about some of the messages, she grows concerned and promises to find out if any other organizations have phone campaigns going on. "If not, Mari, you need to change your number. That makes me really uncomfortable."

I stare at my friend's face and take note of every fine feature. How can someone be so delicate and strong? I wonder if it is her strength that makes her reluctant to confess her obvious feelings about Carson.

"Sadie, just between us…"

She knows what I am asking. "Just between us…if I can just let myself believe a man as good as Carson not only exists but actually loves me, I know this is it. I've never thought in terms of marrying. My work has been so fulfilling, and it seems every year I have had more responsibility and success…"

"You might keep that part to yourself."

"What I mean is, somewhere along the way I started to believe it would have to be one or the other. Happiness at work or happiness in relationships."

I want to dispute this theory by stating that I am unhappy in both, so logic would follow that one could feasibly be happy in both. But that would be making her happiness all about my unhappiness, yet another habit I am trying to quit.

"You will be able to come to the event, won't you? I'll deal with the comments from the peanut gallery, but it is most important to me that you really like him, Mari. You are my sanest, wisest friend. I trust you."

This confession tells me that Sadie doesn't know me very well, but I accept her compliment graciously so she won't suspect her trust is misplaced.

As we each walk to our cars, I think how sharing these crazy fantasies and distorted theories is exactly why we have friends we can be totally honest with…and why the best of friends also keep your secrets.

A Case for Grace

One pew has a gap as obvious as that of the *MAD* magazine cover boy. It is, of course, the gap by Rose.

We nod to each other as Clive leads us in the first hymn. If I went to the singles class I would have a friend here. But that leads to commitment, obligation, calls during the week, plans for after the service...I sound like Angelica assessing the little known pitfalls to actually having a relationship. I need help.

"Let us greet one another with the blessing and peace of the Lord. New folks, be sure to hold up your visitor's card for our deacons." The minister has a bright red card in each hand and waves them like a spiritual traffic controller.

Rose starts with me this time. She grabs my elbow with a firm grip and jostles it a bit. "How are you, darling?"

"I'm good. May the peace of the Lord be yours. I hope...that for you. And blessings...lots of blessings..." I've never been a good conversation closer.

"Where is your husband?" Her eyes peer past my shoulder only to find my very large purse, which was actually a small travel suitcase from Tess' first trip to Europe.

I consider my options and somehow, someway…a lie forms in my mind. Then on my tongue.

"He's on safari, actually. You know how tough it is to be a photographer for *National Geographic*. If he isn't shooting lions, he's shooting politicians. With a camera, of course."

And she rejoices.

Somewhere in the dark swamp of insecurity that is my mind, I decide that professing a sin is better than confessing to "single."

I create excuses to walk by the suggestion box frequently, hoping to catch the prophetic seer or the prankster. Since the first message appeared a few months ago, a significant pile has accumulated. I'm fascinated. Like a Broadway actor who cannot quit reading a bad review, I want to know what they know that I should know.

When I hear the bingo crowd applaud the first winner, I sneak into the nearest bathroom to read my new life clues. The first is written on the back of a church bulletin. "Mari should visit the computer club. She might just find out how popular she really is." I should alert my intervention group that I'm popular; I wouldn't have to mention who with. I reach into my pocket and pull out part two…a long, thin strip of newspaper.

"Kenny pees in the whirlpool."

I guess everything isn't about me.

Hire Power

Is this the best you got?" Haley calls out like a Wrestling Mania contestant from her reclined, tangled position on her pilates mat.

"I didn't sign up for the pansy calisthenics class." Typically mild and kind Walter is raising a fuss and his fist as I call out the next routine.

"Elbow across the chest stretch series...right arm across the body, press it in with the palm of your left hand." I try not to grimace as pain shoots through my right shoulder blade. "See. Like this."

Rae's theory that these folks just want to touch their knees is pure hogwash. I'm being heckled by seventy-year-old group-exercise participants because my couch potato workout (their words) is not difficult enough. My innovative routine (my words) is mostly stretching moves combined with a few aerobics steps learned from classes I had taken a few years ago between January resolutions and the season of Lent, for which I gave up my gym membership again when Angelica promised to give up low-carb diets, again.

"You sure don't live up to your namesake." They are all in the know about a professional pilates guru name Mari who sells videos and DVDs.

Their collective belly laugh at this clever dig lasts for fifteen minutes. It is the first time they break a sweat.

I'd like to make Rae touch her toes from a backbend position about now.

"You'll be happy to know that I am interviewing an instructor right after class today. Save your kind hospitality to bestow upon her this Friday, God willing." There is a thunderous round of clapping which echoes terribly in the low-ceilinged sunporch that serves as the exercise studio.

I don't even receive the Golden Horizon's traditional mid-five slap of open palms as the participants exit. This is the ultimate "face" in their world. Even Rae got one after trying to take away Lloyd's telescope after it was discovered angled questionably in line with the vast, open windows of suburbia across the main street. The residents adamantly opposed the use of force, yet deemed it to be quite a fair match when the two large figures ended up exhausted and breathless and the telescope firmly in Rae's grip.

This official rejection by my own people inspires me to check, for the fourth time today, my home phone messages from the hallway pay phone. No job offers. No vehicle grand prizes. But, of course, I do have yet another disturbing caller.

"Warren here. You probably will remember me from the email series about saving the baby seals. I head back out with Greenpeace in a month and hope that we can get together before then. I hope my package of tree saplings was welcome in lieu of flowers…I prefer proactive expressions of joy. Email me with some possible dates. My mom would like to meet you first, if that is okay. Save the earth. What's it worth? It gave you birth."

Beep.

I'm all for saving baby seals, but who are these men? Who is *this* man who rhymes his way into a woman's phone line? This time my imagination conjures up an image of a squinty male whose knit cap slides back on his head, revealing a lack of hair and the very edge of a globe-shaped tattoo. He scratches the tip of Africa while he poetically praises the earth.

With my résumés out circulating, I cannot risk changing my number. Not yet. Though Sadie questions whether I am living as though I have faith, I have deep faith that good things are in the works.

For example, I have great faith that no matter what I think of Sonya Freidman during this interview, I will hire her. It is either that or I will have to invest in instructional DVDs before Friday.

Sonya cannot be missed. Not in this setting. Her long blond hair gracefully flows down the length of her back. Thin yet strong arms and legs move with assurance. Her posture as she stands by the office area is erect and the epitome of yoga health. Lysa chats with her and they are laughing like long-lost friends.

You're hired.

"I'm sorry to be late, Sonya. I'm Mari. " When she shakes my out-stretched sweaty hand, the upper part of my wimpy arm shakes as well. "Thank goodness you missed seeing my class just now. It was not a pretty sight."

"I did peek in. I felt your connection with participants. That was lovely."

She's being gracious.

You're hired.

"Well, you are kind. Shall we head to Rae's office? She's at an all-day conference." I point toward the only door with a nameplate. "R-a-e" is spaced out but then the creator of the plate realized his planning error, so "Vandersleski" is crammed together.

I follow Sonya into the museum of fragility. She takes in the shelves of glass miniatures and hugs her body with her longs arms—the chilly air-conditioning and delicate decor causing the same effect.

"Have a seat." I motion to one of the two chairs in front of the main desk. When Rae gave in to my request to meet here, she insisted that I not use her power chair or eat her stash of pistachios. I am tempted to offer

Sonya some of Rae's candy, though she probably feeds on grass and leaves.

Sonya was referred to us by her godmother and one of our newest residents, Camille St. John, who transferred from a retirement home in Phoenix. Considering she is one of the wealthier residents, Rae was more than glad to oblige. I was more than happy to not place an ad in the paper and field all the subsequent inquiry calls.

Her résumé is printed on aqua paper with an "80 percent postconsumer recycled" watermark. I realize I should skim her credentials or take great notice of her objective, which is "to connect individuals with their physical strength while empowering them with emotional tools to live a richer, more active life." But my eyes immediately rest upon three very impressive words following the current place of employment inquiry… Majestic Vista Resort. Which happens to be the number one location on my career move wish list.

You're hired.

"You are at Majestic Vista…and you want to work here?" A part of me is hoping she will say that her work there is so unfulfilling that she prefers to join the ranks of the poor and noble.

So I can take her job.

She laughs and showcases brilliantly white teeth. "I do love Majestic, but unfortunately they are only able to offer me a few classes. I was fortunate to join their team teaching pilates, yoga, and yogalates sessions when their primary instructor went on maternity leave. Now that she has returned, they are unable to provide me with enough work…so I am expanding my horizons…at Golden Horizons, I hope."

Now I see her in the pristine setting of Majestic Vista, with its marble walkways and jade fountains, where people sip espresso from tiny cups and nod to each other on their way to the sauna, the salon, one of the six pools, or the vast system of naturally lit corridors that weave their way to expensive guest suites with private balconies and Jacuzzis and where fresh papaya juice and organic bran muffins are delivered with the morning paper, which is delicately rolled and tied with a black silk ribbon. She greets her coworkers…no, her teammates…with a genuine smile and a healthy glow from the free sugar-rub massages she gets weekly as a perk for being a part of the team.

The only time Rae has used the word team was to describe what it would take to drag her to participate in a round of Scrabble. A team of rabid oxen, I believe was the complete phrase. Though I have never heard of or seen rabid oxen, I figured the disturbing news stories of mad cow disease were an accurate reference. I liked the idea of them running down the hall, drooling as they knock over precious collectables on their way to collect Rae from her leather chair and drag her to the Scrabble table, where her little wooden letter shelf would contain only vowels.

"Mari?" Sonya looks concerned for my well-being and mental state.

My train of thought has derailed more than a little. This is what coveting does to you. First you have a physical sensation and then your mind starts to wander and wish bad things on the people who keep you down. I snap out of it and focus my eyes on her very well-proportioned facial features. Everything is in the ideal place.

"Wonderful. I do hope you will make this your home…or second home."

"I'd love the chance to work with you. I like your style and manner. I find it refreshing." I am liked by this goddess. I find that a little hard to believe, yet…

You are hired.

"At first I was afraid that my slight connection with Beau would not open this door, since he has not been here for…" she pauses.

Beau? Beau? Sorry…b-bye. Thanks for coming in to flaunt your résumé and shiny hair, but we are already overflowing with Beau worshipers.

"Beau?" I cannot help but repeat his name out loud. My luck is so consistent.

"Oh, yes, I thought that was why you were interviewing me. You see, I knew Beau from my undergrad years at Arizona State and Camille… Mrs. St. John…knows Beau from her former retirement home in Phoenix. He's the director there now. I'm very flattered that my name even came up between them. Did you know that he also finished his PhD and is heading some studies for the Aging and Movement organization?"

"Of course he is."

"So you know him?"

"No. Just of him. He's quite…" I want to say successful and accomplished in a way that has a negative connotation.

"Amazing," she says, smiling at me, and I am thankful she cannot read my dark thoughts.

I really don't want to keep discussing Beau. My stomach feels sour…as if I just overdosed on French fries with malt vinegar. But I have to ask out of sick curiosity, "So, were you two close?"

She blushes, which on an average person reveals skin flaws. She radiates an immaculate, blemish-free complexion. A thin, strong hand brushes her bangs out of her eyes. "No. Just friends. But I have always been fond of him."

I don't know if it is courage gained from the mention of my opponent or my overall desperation, but I turn the direction of the interview drastically in my favor. "Sonya, I probably shouldn't bring this up, seeing as how I am interviewing you and trying to sell you on the wonders of Golden Horizons, but I wasn't expecting you to work where you do and…well, I have recently applied to Majestic Vista." I cover my open mouth showing my "oh, my gosh" mind-set while Sonya opens hers with mutual surprise. I finish my explanation quickly before my courage subsides. "They posted their guest recreational coordinator position, and I sent my résumé." Just like that I cross a professional and probably ethical line.

And it feels tremendous.

She doesn't look appalled, afraid, or around for an exit. She poses her arms up in the air as if she is about to yell "goal!" "I would love to put in a good word for you. After all, you've honored an out-of-nowhere referral just to visit with me. And like I said, I felt a connection to you right away. You'd fit in perfectly."

I would?

Her enthusiasm almost makes me believe her.

"I've got an idea. If I am not mistaken, you are interested in what I can offer the residents here. So how about we serve two careers in one day? You come to the Majestic to watch me lead a class, and I will just happen to introduce you to the director. It can't hurt to meet the man in person. Lionel Richardson is everything you'd imagine a successful entrepreneur to be, and he is also very personable. I happen to know that he reviews all hiring candidates for every position. It's his way to keep the team working smoothly. I'm sure he'd take to you right away."

I *should* tell her that she would have to pretty much light one of her students on fire for me to not give her this position, but I decide that it feels incredibly good to have her think that she needs to prove herself to me.

We look at our respective calendars. I cover mine with the length of my arm so she cannot see how available I am. As she jots down the day I plan to visit her class, I notice that her bracelet has a single charm and it is a cross. I resist inquiring about her faith, considering I have already broken half a dozen interview etiquette rules.

We are just about to leave the office when Sonya doubles back. "Is it just me or is there something strange about this room?"

"You, me, and anyone normal considers this to be a freaky room."

"Would you mind if I had a pistachio?" She eyes them as her hand goes to her flat stomach to indicate hunger.

"Take them all." I extend the silver bowl to my new friend gladly.

You are so hired.

Lady Luck

I'm telling you, my breakdown has led to a breakthrough. It is as if my efforts to put myself out there have placed a universal welcome mat for Lady Luck." I stir my diet soda with a thin red straw while Angelica examines the menu from Nonconformity, a newer club downtown intended to help revive the commuter city by bringing patrons back into its fold after the usual five o'clock hour of exodus.

I look around at the stucco walls and take in the framed black-and-white photographs of different mob scenes from the pages of history. They all represent bad collective gatherings so the trendy restaurant can state its case for individuality. Waiters and waitresses are each dressed differently except for hats that have working, flashing lightbulbs on the very top.

"Angelica, isn't this more of a Caitlin kind of place?"

She looks at me with a wounded expression; I have stripped her of her individuality.

"This happens to be the newest, hippest spot in the downtown revival movement, which means it is completely an Angelica place to be. Thank you so little." She unfolds the menu toward me and points to the coconut prawns as her appetizer of choice. Then the calamari. Then the nachos.

"Don't you want to wait for your friends?"

"Nobody gets out of the office on time. They could be a while." She motions for the waiter, who is wearing a toga. "We are unfashionably early for a Friday night. To be anywhere before seven, even at your starter club, is socially useless."

"If you desire to be here *because* it is trendy, wouldn't that be a sign of dangerous conformity?" I point to a nearby portrait of Hitler.

"Mari, get over it. You aren't going to generate this level of conversation the entire evening, are you? I have invited some very fun people. Please don't ruin this by sucking everyone into your philosophical, over-analyzed world."

Nothing like a compliment to help one feel good about oneself. I'm already self-conscious about this get-together. Angelica pulled one of her sly moves by telling me she was taking me to her reading group. It turns out this is her usual Friday night group from work, a case study of my generation that I have always managed to avoid...until tonight.

"Prawns then. And you are buying since I thought I was going to discuss *Silas Marner.*"

"I lied a bit. You needed this, Mari. This is all part of that Lady Luck mind-set anyway, so just sit back and have a good time with people who know how to live."

By "live" she means "live it up." I'm already judging how badly this evening could turn out. But maybe she is right. This could be a part of my new Lady Luck lifestyle. I check my watch and set a timer. Tonight is the start of the countdown challenge on *Castaways.* I plan to make up a story about meeting up with another group of friends at nine-thirty. Lady Luck wouldn't insist that I give up all my socially uncouth behavior, would she?

"What are you doing?" Angelica looks at me struggling to push the small buttons on my functional watch.

"Hey, Angel!" A guy at least six foot five struts across the restaurant floor and arrives at our table in three steps.

"That's a first." I whisper his take on her name with a measure of sarcastic shock.

Dirty look from Angel.

"Angus! I didn't know you were going to join us." This, of course, meant that he wasn't really invited.

"Peyton mentioned the group was meeting up here and I've been dying to try it. My brother-in-law is the sous-chef and says it is the place to eat." Angus looks at me and smiles, but I don't reciprocate because my mind is replaying the name Peyton. He didn't seem to get sucked into the Angelica charm vortex at the golf course. Why would he be a part of her group? Now my throw-caution-to-the-wind attitude is interrupted by the nervous jitters that signal a mild case of infatuation.

"Angus, this is Mari." Angelica looks at me a bit worried about my lack of response and nudges me. I notice she does not say "my friend Mari."

I stand up like a polite guy and shake his hand. "Mari Hamilton… Angelica's dearest friend." Take that.

"Fantastic. May I?" He motions to the seat right next to me. I am relieved. My theory is that if a guy liked me, he would want to sit directly across from me, not beside me. He probably wants to fawn over Angelica "Angel" all night.

The prawns come and Angus mentions once again that he is related to the sous-chef. Our waiter acts thrilled but could really care less. "I'll tell him you are here," he offers limply. We watch him head back to the kitchen with his lightbulb flickering.

"Mari Hamilton, eh? That sounds so familiar. Do I know you from somewhere?" This sounds like a line, but he actually looks perplexed trying to figure out when our paths might have crossed.

"Not likely," Angelica and I respond simultaneously, and I give her a dirty look this time. She rolls her eyes and offers Angus a clarification. "It's just that even though we are dear friends, Mari doesn't get out much. She's sort of a shut-in…a social shut-in."

"Well, too bad for us. You probably have some guy who doesn't want to share you, right?" His flattery is flat from overuse and insincerity.

"You got it." I point at him like a game show host.

Now that I am sitting in this lie of a boyfriend, I immediately feel more confident. How warped is that?

"I'm going to go say hi to Rob. You two want another round of…" he looks at our empty glasses.

"Diet Coke," I say.

"She means scotch on the rocks. Make that two." Angelica does a parade princess wave as tall boy makes his way to the bar, which is covered in Christmas lights.

When he is out of earshot, Angelica looks at me. "Look, we don't have to drink it, but please…Diet Coke? At least order an expensive seltzer or something."

"Don't you ever get tired of pretending, Angelica?" My fatigue and anxiety over Peyton's possible appearance combine into a truth serum.

"I'm not pretending."

"I think you are. It's as if you are always challenging yourself, tempting yourself to return to your old life. When are you going to give yourself a break by stepping away from all of this? How do you know who you are apart from this scene?" By now there actually is a scene as twentysomethings come in herds to the watering hole. For most, this is their first stop of the evening, so they head for the bar. A few groups order appetizers and pitchers of beverages and settle into booths around us.

"Overanalyzing again," she singsongs. I see her checking out the male and female populations. In her world, they are all competition for attention. It must be exhausting. She sees something she likes and stands up partway to wave toward the door.

My fear and my hope rolled into one person approaches the table. Peyton maneuvers through the crowd with ease. I see women turn to check him out. Some don't wait until he passes to be so obvious with their admiring stares. He seems oblivious, but there is no way he could be.

"Well, what a great surprise. Hi, Mari." Peyton doesn't see Angelica point toward the seat immediately across from her just for him, so he moves around beside her and sits squarely and amazingly across from me. He is genuinely pleased to see me. And he remembers my name.

"Peyton, right?" I say trying to act coy, but my lower jaw is shaking.

Angus returns to the table with our drinks. The one I won't be drinking is placed right in front of me. "Peyton, bud. Can I grab you something while I'm up? I'm kinda making a move on the female bartender, so it wouldn't be a bother." His dimples cut into his baby smooth skin. The guy probably only has to shave once a week.

"I'll take a seltzer with lime, man."

"You know, that sounds so much more refreshing," I eagerly push my drink and my opinion toward Angelica. She looks as though she wants to join me on this choice but holds up her hand in an "I'm fine" gesture.

She isn't, though. I forget about Peyton for a moment to consider the state of my friend's life. I don't know if she is falling, tempting fate, or carving her way through this time in her life the best way she knows how.

Maybe Angelica invited me here not only as a way to force me into our generation, but also as a way to hang on to the faith she commited to back in college. Our paths crossed just when she was diving into religion with a vengeance. There was a time when she was going to Bible study four nights a week and leading a sorority-run chapel service on campus. Her weekly rounds of the dorms to witness put my faith to shame. She challenged me to grow during a time when I was falling toward mediocrity. And now maybe I am here to do the same for her.

Angelica scoots her chair up next to Peyton and rests her chin on his shoulder. He has no choice but to acknowledge this.

"Long day, Angelica? You had to go through those training reviews, didn't you? Those are so harsh." He starts to explain what these are for my benefit, but Angelica interrupts.

"Could you hand me a prawn?" She bats her baby blues, and when

Peyton places the prawn on her plate, she awkwardly opens her mouth wide like a baby bird starving for affection and coconut shrimp.

Peyton looks at me and smiles as if we share a sense of reality and pops the tip of the prawn between Angelica's Bobbi Brown-lacquered lips. He lets go as soon as it barely touches her tongue and only her fast reflexes catch the appetizer before it can mar her Dolce & Gabbana shirt with a grease stain. She looks insulted when she should look embarrassed.

Angus breaks the awkward silence by bounding up to the table along with several other folks. I assume they are people he met in the bar, but it turns out they are the new arrivals of Angelica's group.

Two scantily clad women, Lorna and Wanda, and a guy who looks a lot like Danny DeVito in hiking boots take up the remaining chairs. Thank goodness it is Peyton that I get to look at.

As Angelica introduces me around the circle, Danny Devito, whose name is Roger, reads from the same boring script that Angus did. "I know your name from somewhere..." a smirk is evident beneath his confusion.

"That is what I thought!" Angus, who now has a few drinks in him, overreacts to this coincidence.

Peyton speaks up this time. "She is the one who introduced me to that Garden Glove stuff. I'm telling you, Mari, that is amazing. Look." He holds out his hands for me to check like a kid proving he has washed before mealtime. Sure enough, every bit of the rash is gone.

"She's the one?" Angus asks.

"No, I've heard her name somewhere else. But that garden stuff is pretty cool."

"Whatever are you talking about? You don't garden...any of you?" Angelica struggles to find her way back into the conversation.

Peyton explains so I do not have to defend myself. "That day at the golf tournament, Mari told me about this great ointment that basically cured the rash I get from wearing the golf glove. I told everyone about it."

Angelica looks at me with a mix of newfound respect and reluctant belief. "That was your idea?" This news seems to be as hard to swallow as the prawn tail she just inhaled by accident.

"To Mari!" Even the women who only seem to be there for decoration raise their glasses to toast me. Angelica raises hers and promptly drains it with one gulp. By being accepted into her circle, rather than ostracized as she had expected, I have driven my friend to break the only commitment she has kept for three years…to abstain from alcohol.

At that very moment, five cell phones ring in unison. Wouldn't you know that all of the folks at this table have set their phones to ring to the tune of the song of "Call Me" by the eighties band Blondie.

Angus looks at his text message and announces, "It's a flash." He reads it for those of us who know restaurant etiquette and turn off our phones during dinner. "Meet at the courthouse at 8:05 wearing a hat and carrying a Pez dispenser to leave on the edge of the fountain. Pass along to five people."

"I don't get it," I say as the buzz at our table and at others nearby rises to mania levels.

Only Peyton hears me. "A flash is when an anonymous someone sends an email or text message to hundreds of people to gather. The point is to bring together a crowd to do something pointless…usually in a public place. Sometimes they have a real purpose, but usually they are sent just to see how many lemmings will follow." He looks around and is as surprised as I am how many lemmings are in our midst.

"We had better go if we want to find Pez dispensers in time. Good thing we are close to the courthouse." Angus drops a fifty on the table to cover his tab and rallies the others to follow his lead.

As badly as Angelica is feeling about taking a drink, she seems thrilled that something has detracted from me in this moment. She stands to join them. Peyton and I remain seated.

Angelica doesn't even ask if I am game to come along. She knows the answer and is not-so-secretly pleased, even if it means I will be left alone with the guy she likes. "So you can cab it home?" Her question is asked on her way into the throng heading for the door. I don't bother to answer.

At this very moment my watch alarm goes off. Though it isn't to the tune of an unclassy dance song, Peyton assumes it is my cell phone. "Oh, no. Not you too?" He says this while watching after Angelica. I see the disappointment in his eyes.

I turn off the alarm and let him think I am "in" enough to have received a flash TM. "I'm pretty sure that is what the delete key was meant for." I watch him still watching the exit. The obvious yet surprising question blurts out. "Do you like Angelica?"

Peyton's eyes return their gaze to our table. He is sweetly shy about this confession. "I do. When she isn't putting on her show, I sometimes think we could…get along. I know she can be hard on people and unaware of how she comes across, but I've seen her laugh. I've seen her talk with kids at the children's hospital, you know?"

Okay, I didn't see this coming. Yet, I am inspired by this guy's ability to see the real Angelica. "You don't have to sell me, Peyton. I know that side of her too. She's sort of going through a rough patch, but she'll come out on the other side."

He nods reflectively, considering this possibility.

"Do you think she is remotely interested in me? I hope this isn't awkward…"

I wave my hand. No big deal. "Not at all. I mean, not at all awkward. And absolutely I think she is interested. Even if she doesn't know it yet."

Peyton laughs at this and clinks his glass against the edge of mine.

Since my "sit across from the one you like" theory has gone up in smoke, I am tempted to find an excuse to leave and make it home in time for my show. Then it occurs to me that while the rest of my generation jumps on the group mentality bandwagon, staying in Nonconformity with Peyton and our seltzers with lime is a very mature, hip thing to do.

Besides, my VCR is recording *Castaways*.

Baby steps.

From Outdated to
Out Dating

Torrents of raindrops do cannonball splashes on my *Tucson Daily News* umbrella as I maneuver around people too confused by precipitation to move forward quickly. Up ahead I see the lime neon Fab sign. It takes the pressure of my body weight to push open the grand, Gothic door. Standing barely five foot four, I have to duck to avoid cranial collision with the brilliant red paper lanterns hanging like stalactites from a black ceiling.

When Mary Margaret, a small woman with graying temples, sees that I am just a friend of Caitlin's and not a commission possibility, she returns to the slim leather-bound volume of vampire poetry in her hands.

"Is Caitlin here?" I rest my hands on the counter by the old-fashioned cash register and force the woman who looks more librarian than retail aficionado to address me. She turns her face to avoid looking at me, and I notice something that changes my librarian assessment…a tattoo of a copperhead snake winds along her jawline and slithers behind her ear. I shiver.

The red tip of her clove cigarette directs me to the back curtain. "Inventory," she explains.

I make my way around the circular clothing racks that are packed with delicate and mysterious and occasionally furry items. I touch each piece, enjoying various tactile sensations until I reach the back room. Stepping into the tented area, I almost step on Caitlin, who is gathering bangle bracelets from the cement floor.

She looks up at me. Her face is innocent and open…angelic. As hard a time as we give her, she is one of the most endearing people I know. Caitlin embraces that quality which I avoid at all costs…vulnerability.

"I've been such a klutz lately." She grabs my arm and stretches it out and begins to load it with bracelets. Once I look like the tin man, she motions for me to download my booty into a wicker basket. She seems nervous.

"Mari, I feel bad about how we ganged up on you that night. It seemed okay in the moment, but not later after I thought about it." She touches my arm and looks directly at me. "The heart of it was right, but I realize now that you felt attacked. And I said something that probably made you feel even worse…"

While I have tried to block out a lot of that night, I am most certain that Caitlin had not said anything too ruthless. I shake my head.

"No. I did. I said…I said we are the same. The whole dreamer thing—"

"There is nothing offensive about being called a dreamer, Caitlin. I didn't—"

"I really look up to you, Mari, and your job and the way you help people. And you would do that in any setting. My life pursuits right now are so material by comparison. I think I put you down without meaning to."

"That wasn't a put-down." I grab a halter top covered with rows of plastic streamers, the kind that flair off tricycle handlebars, and hold it up to my chest. "What do you think?" Like I said, vulnerability ain't my thing. Caitlin smiles and accepts my plea to change topics.

"Help me put these out? And then we'll get started on the makeover for your date." She emphasizes the word "date" by following it with a wide-open-mouth look of awe. "You did bring a few of your things from home, right?" She starts to roll a rack of camisoles out into the cave. I follow her and try not to focus on the fake braids she has poking out of her head. They are Pippi Longstocking tentacles angling from her jet black hair. I worry that Caitlin's fashion inclinations might be better suited for circus tryouts than for a first date. But after her show of kindness and empathy, I shove aside my plan to beg off this experiment. If it doesn't involve permanent dyes or surgical procedures, I should be able to work with whatever she creates. Is that what Frankenstein thought before he looked in the mirror?

"I grabbed just a few odds and ends. I really don't know what look to go for." I hand her the grocery sack and my wimpy contributions. Since I had planned to back out of this, my selection effort was halfhearted.

"How did it go last night? Angelica's outing of you as a socialite?"

"So everyone except me knew I was not headed to a reading group."

"Um, you went with Angelica."

"Touché." I smile at the friend who some write off as ditzy and clueless. Yet even she understood that Angelica and reading group are not a likely match.

"It turned out nice, actually." I tell her of my time with Peyton and how he is one of the few guys of faith I have ever met within Angelica's circles. She never mentioned it, but then again, she is always pretending to be something she is not, so she probably doesn't inquire into other people's level of belief.

"That sounds promising," Caitlin mumbles as she unhooks one of her pigtails from a display of Velcro shirts.

"For Angelica. He secretly likes her but is somewhat scared of her. You know how she is." We both say "yep, yep, yep" at the same time.

She stops going through my bag of items and looks at my face to read my emotion. "You really don't mind that you spent the evening hanging with a guy who likes someone else? Could you lend me some of that self-esteem?"

"Is that self-esteem or just me knowing my role so well? Always the friend of the love interest and never the love interest. Actually, when I first met Peyton, I was flattered by his friendly attention. Now that I have a sense of him…I like him all the more, yet I also know he is not my type."

"Yeah. Christian, handsome, and nice. I can see how that would get old." She mocks me while our observer releases a big sigh. Caitlin has described a complete dolt in Mary Margaret's opinion.

"A guy can have all the right ingredients and still not be your favorite dish. You know what I mean?"

"Please don't use food metaphors. I haven't had lunch. And yes, I know what you mean. It's why I broke up with Micki. He was perfect in so many ways, but there was no…"

"Wait. Isn't that the guy who was trying to grow his fingernails to beat the Guinness record? I thought that was why you broke up with him."

"You're exaggerating. He had nails so he could play his ukulele. And you know me. If it is for the sake of a person's art, I'm all for it. But Micki's fatal flaw was less obvious." Her slight shoulders rise and fall with the burden of love lost. "He didn't get me. He liked me. Enjoyed my company. Laughed at my jokes, but he never got me."

We both sigh at this. I figure the "he doesn't get me" factor creates what most single women call chemistry. No matter what name you want to give it…it matters. The reverse is true as well. I experienced a few catch and release dating cycles because I was attracted to guys I didn't understand or connect with. And when that's the case, no matter how cute or how attentive a guy is, a self-respecting single girl who's holding out for the real thing will always move on.

Caitlin holds up a see-through sarong from the rack in front of my body, draping the ends over my shoulder and waist as though I am a giant paper doll. I keep my head still so that it does not shake "no, no, no" violently. I breathe a sigh of relief when she wobbles her braids side to side and moves on to another style.

I have breathed too soon. The new concoction she has me try on is a chartreuse peasant blouse, houndstooth vest, and black miniskirt that teases the eye with a lining of purple.

"My neighbor would love this." I offer a positive notion and pray for her braids to signal that this selection too shall pass.

The sound of chimes turns both our heads to face the door. A Keanu Reeves look-alike trips down the one step and falls into the warmth of Fab's womb. Each time he gets halfway up his army boots catch on the chains that drape from the belt loops of his long shorts, and he contorts in a backbend and falls again. His fourth try is successful because Caitlin props up the human muppet until he is detangled.

"Zane, are you okay?" She shifts his backpack to a centered position.

"Whoa. Whoa. Thanks." When Zane stands upright he is a good foot taller than Caitlin. He pats her on the head, an endearing gesture.

I turn all the way around so I can take a good look at this creature. I realize he did not stumble in, but rolled in. A beat-up, sticker-covered skateboard is gripped in his gloved left hand.

The two chat together for a while, and the register chick watches them closely. I catch her primping the gelled curls at the nape of her neck. I can tell she is willing Zane to look her way.

But instead Caitlin turns his shoulders to square with my side of the room. First there is shock in his eyes.

Caitlin laughs and covers her mouth with her hand. The little spots of black nail polish look like a parade of bugs across her cheek. I look down ready to say I had nothing to do with this outfit when I realize I have stepped directly behind a disrobed mannequin. I am an X-rated version of those tourist gimmicks where you poke your head through a cardboard cutout that places your face on the image of Nixon's or Donald Duck's body.

Zane looks relieved that he did not just catch me in the buff.

"That was freaky," he says, eyes downcast.

"Not as freaky as the real thing would have been. Believe me." Oh, no. Did I just refer to myself in the naked person? Change the subject.

"So…you are a skateboarder? Either that or you carry a very large key chain."

"He calls it Earth Surfin'. Isn't that clever?" Caitlin points to one of the stickers on the board that confirms the catchphrase.

"That is clever." I try to figure out how old Zane is. He pulls his hair back with a rubber band, and I notice a few crow's-feet around his eyes.

"Sorry about my crash landing. As soon as the rain comes my wheels freeze up, and I go from thirty miles per hour to zero in two seconds flat." He laughs a quiet chuckle that is soothing in its gentleness.

"Did you bring the invoice?" Caitlin steps behind the counter, completely ignoring the other girl, and opens up a three-ring binder.

"Yeah. Got it here somewhere." Zane pats himself all over and then retrieves a thin piece of yellow paper with a dozen creases from the lowest pocket of his shorts, which graze his ankle. Does an entire segment of my generation really dress like Oompa-Loompas? Or is Zane one of a kind?

Apparently it is the former. Caitlin explains that Earth Surfin' is the name of Zane's clothing line, which is starting to sell like crazy in the Southwest and California.

"Well, what I really need to do is get online action. I spent too much time lost in literature in college. I don't know anything about computers. But I know if I want a piece of that multibillion dollar retail pie, I need to step it up."

"I have just what you need," I offer.

Zane winks. "Do you now?"

I tear off a corner of the invoice and use a pen with a plastic sunflower on the end to write out my suggestion. "Grease and Go. When the rain mixes with the dry dirt on the bearings, it creates clumps. This stuff dissolves it on the wheelchairs at work."

"Excellent. I'll be indebted to you for life if this helps." He waves the piece of paper at me and starts to back up. Caitlin gets the door for him while he tucks his ponytail beneath the waterproof safari hat, an item he stole from a mannequin dressed in a military uniform and a boa. "Wildly interesting outfit, by the way."

I look down at my clothes and wonder how to take that comment.

"I'll be indebted to you for life…" Caitlin repeats Zane's words and flutters her eyes in mock flirtation once he has zoomed by the display window.

"Oh, please. I was just educating the boy."

"He went to Yale." She responds to my look of surprise. "See, appearances can be deceiving. He dropped out his senior year to start his company."

"Really? Hmm." It occurs to me that if Zane judged me by my attire, he thinks I am wildly interesting. I can live with that. I give my outfit a second look.

Mary Margaret sighs a big sigh and lights some incense in the ceramic hand that is meant to hold gum. I used to put my retainer on one just like it.

"Now…back to it. You've got a date to get ready for." Caitlin adjusts my skirt.

Date. The word sets my nerves reeling again. My stomach flutters as though it is on its own fair ride. Back up on the little platform in front of the mirror, I spin for Caitlin.

"Something is missing…" Placing a finger to her lips, Caitlin contemplates my urban version of *Death of a Salesman*.

Praise the Lord she noticed. About five inches of fabric on the hem is missing. Style is missing. Potential to not be mocked in a nice restaurant is missing. But I keep my mouth shut and hope for the best.

"So what is this guy like, anyway?" Caitlin's eyes light up as she considers her many possibilities and my one.

"I honestly don't know much." I think of the few emails Sadie sent me encouraging me to take the first step toward change. "Sadie says he is really into community service. Handsome. Makes a very good living as a chef. Does not reside with his mother but treats her to clever Mother's Day dates. That is how Sadie met him." I pause to twirl again like a good model should. Caitlin is evaluating which bangles and bobbles might go with her creation. I close my eyes and continue to think about my first date in years. "He actually rented out the botanical gardens for his mother last year so he could take her on a walking tour that ended up in front of a special species of a rose he had named after her."

"Lift your feet one at a time." Caitlin forces me to lean forward so she can apply proper footwear. To maintain balance, I grab a leopard-print lamp shade that hangs from the encompassing blackness.

"I hope this isn't a mistake," I say about all of it. The date. The clothes. My attempt to reenter my generation.

Caitlin does not take this in reference to the clothes, which to her eye could not possibly be questioned. "If Sadie says he is nice, then he is nice." She pulls on the fabric of my skirt to see if it should be tighter. "Sadie would never set me up with one of her associates. She wouldn't say it...but she doesn't think I am good enough..." Caitlin pauses to rummage through my bag of items in search of something compatible...or in this case...something in total contrast to the other pieces.

"No, that isn't true." I say this as halfheartedly as I mean it, so I repeat it for emphasis. "It isn't true at all."

The rustling stops for a moment. "Who could blame her? The way I live and dress is considered strange by those in her circle...in my parents' circle."

As she speaks, two thoughts go through my mind. First, as sad as it is that she feels this way, it is even sadder that she is probably right. Sadie does separate people into categories without meaning to. She has always considered Caitlin to be scattered and living below her own potential. By Sadie's standards, this is unacceptable. Second, Caitlin is transforming me into the very type she says will not fit into Sadie's circle. Am I mad? Am I determined to sabotage my first date in years?

But the most daunting realization stabs me in the pit of my soul. If I don't pull this off, it will not be because of what I wear. It will be because of me. Why *did* Sadie think I could handle going out with a guy who owns two restaurants? I make up an answer. "I'm sure she just thought that Jace and I would get along because of the community service thing. Nothing else."

"Jace?"

"I know. Weird name, right?" I laugh really loud so we can share in the silliness of this truncated, uppity version of Jason.

"It might be if it weren't featured on a very successful line of chicken sauces and luxury desserts."

"That's him? I just bought his marinara. How strange." Now I am more nervous.

"Open your eyes." Caitlin spins me toward the mirror. I avoid looking at my reflection and catch the look of happiness in her eyes. I cannot begrudge her this moment. It isn't as though someone will be taking pictures. I become hopeful. She is clever and trendy by peripheral-society standards. I look.

"I love it!" I decide that honesty should be the missing piece of my response.

"You aren't just saying that, right?" She digs through a drawer and pulls out an instamatic camera. "I want this for my portfolio."

Caitlin's coworker takes another big breath; I see her slightly smile. She loves the outfit because it is unmistakably, undeniably absurd, even by a snake lady's standards.

This is when every part of me, including my conservative taste, decides to jump on board with Caitlin. She is trying to prove herself in front of a tattooed naysayer. She is helping me take extreme measures to pull my life out of the mire of the mundane. Maybe I can pull this off for her sake.

Without letting myself look at the outfit again or consider a fabrication of elation, I find a truth to tell. "You are the most creative person I know, Caitlin. I mean, who else would have thought to combine this outfit with my nineteen-fifties orange tulle apron?"

I glare in the direction of the mean lady and repeat myself. "You are so *very* creative, Caitlin."

The door of castle proportions shuts behind me and separates me from my old way of living and dressing. With my head down, skirt flying up, and apron strings streaming, I rush out into the rain and forge my way from the land of the dismally outdated into the world of the out dating.

Attempts at Social Behavior

I slump like a child in the back of a limo with my feet dangling ever so slightly above the floor. Jace Burch sits next to me with an air of normalcy. I want to ask if he picks up all his first dates in a limo, but it would lead to a no-win answer. A yes response would intimidate me. And a no would add an element of expectation and pressure to like the guy...or at least the date.

He checks his watch.

"Uh-oh. So soon?" I tease but mean it.

"What?" He looks up and realizes my point. "No. Of course not. I'm sorry. I just think in terms of timing. It's very important for an evening to come off perfectly. Wouldn't you agree?"

I start to say yes, but Jace uses a small intercom by his head to shout to the driver, "Jonathan, please take Eighth and circle around. I don't want to arrive before seven."

I don't ask why because I know this one. He must live by the same social timing rules as Angelica. Never make a formal date before seven because the waitstaff will not take you seriously.

"I hear you work with the elderly. That is very refreshing…and noble." There is that cliché again.

I notice that he is smiling but his eyes reflect a mind that is elsewhere. I respond because the man has picked me up in a limo, which will make for a good story later. "Not so noble. There are days I want to run for the hills." Literally.

The silence reprimands my negativity. Think positive, light thoughts. God, give me positive, happy thoughts. Silly Putty. Ice cream. Home early *and* eating ice cream.

"When Sadie told me about what you did for your mom…I was really touched by that. She is so fortunate to have a son who showers her with respect and love." Good. Good. "Believe me, I see how neglected some parents are by their children. It's a tragedy." Bad. Bad.

"Forgive me if I seem a bit distant right now. I'm thinking through the menu in my head. Like an actor rehearsing lines for an evening performance, I'm afraid going through the details of a meal is part of my preparation."

"At least tonight you aren't in charge of the meal." I say this to ease his tension, but he looks at me curiously. I look at my watch and continue when I realize we have another fifteen minutes to kill. "I mean, if I hate the filet mignon at Lily's, we can make fun of their chef, right?" I laugh a little fake, nervous blip.

"If you dislike anything, it will be my fault." Beat. "Lily's is my restaurant."

Oh. Nevermind.

Jace tries to lighten this slip of conversation. "This is why I am nervous. I really want tonight to be perfect." Another beat. "For such a lovely lady."

I don't like the term "lady." It makes me think of Jerry Lewis' squawking version that is drawn out, high and hard, on the eardrums. Jace seems nice enough, but I have the strangest feeling that he is on a date with someone else.

We settle back into the temperature-controlled seats, and while Jace thinks through the upcoming menu, I rethink tonight's outfit. I ended up talking to Tess just before the date and had no time to alter my attire. To Jace's credit, my warped schoolgirl's uniform did not cause him to visibly cringe when he picked me up. Of course, he was probably mentally chopping ingredients for today's special.

At last the stretch limo pulls up in front of Lily's burgundy awning. The valet opens the door for us and by surprise greets us both by name.

"Thank you." I stall and read his name tag. "Pierce." My fingers hold the hem of my skirt down as I exit the car. I'm against flashing on a first date.

Jace and the valet chat for a bit. His manner is controlled yet gracious. The rapport between him and his employees is evident as we step into the candlelit restaurant and are greeted by large smiles and approving glances. I have always wanted to come here but know it to be quite expensive and romantic. This rules me out on two counts.

Women are dressed in either long gowns or perfect black dresses, both choices elegant in their simplicity. I am graffiti against a backdrop of pristine silk.

Handsome faces turn toward us. Everybody wants to see the chef and his date. Their eyes fall to my tulle apron, and I can just hear their thoughts of admiration for the respected restaurant owner, who is secure enough to date a waitress from fast-food row.

I step toward the chair that would place the table between me and the jury, but Jace reaches to pull out the chair which situates me front and center. I look at him and then down at my clothes, hoping he will take this as an acknowledgement of the situation.

"Allow me," he gestures to the seat and I sit. If the guy wants to commit social suicide on my watch, go for it.

Jace has selected everything in advance—from the entrée choices to the music played by the violinist to the waiter who is serving us. Even my phobias are not strong enough to keep me from enjoying this perfect night. I warm up to him.

Our conversation is light and friendly. We do have a lot in common. He grew up in a modest home filled with foster children. Only later, when his mom remarried, did they have the luxury of a bigger house with a kitchen large enough to allow more than one person in it at a time. It was here, in a new setting and a home filled with new love, that he began to experiment with recipes.

For a brief moment he excuses himself to check on the progress of the dessert. Alone at the table the discomfort of being on display returns.

Jace returns with a genuine smile, apparently satisfied with the dessert's status. He continues where he left off. "You can imagine how much flak I got. Here I am, a big kid in Jersey who should be studying football plays instead of soufflé recipes," he reflects tenderly. "But Mom— Lily—was my biggest cheerleader. I thought it was an interest, a hobby. She recognized it as a gift from the beginning. You know, I have considered Golden Horizons as a place for my mom. It's a very nice facility. I want her near me, and she wants a nicer climate than Jersey can offer her."

I sense there is a bit of buzz about the room, but we are deep in conversation, and I am deep into the exquisite chocolate dessert. The tingling sensation I get when someone is standing right behind me kicks in. I turn around as Jace looks up to greet a man with a camera. One of those romantic extras a place like this has…an on-site photographer to capture the mood of a good date.

I shake my head but Jace has already nodded approval. The photographer steps over to get both of us in the shot. It is not an instant camera that spits out the image in seconds. This moment is recorded on real film.

We are having a good time, but I really doubt Jace wanted a memento of this evening. He probably sends the photo, autographed, to the women he brings here. "I'm just curious. How does the restaurant then get the photos to the guests?"

Jace motions for our dessert plates to be taken away. My torte is replaced by a cup of after-dinner tea. It takes him a few thoughts to get what I have asked. "That wasn't a staff photographer. That was Kevin Milano."

Kevin Milano. Kevin…Milano. I can hear Sadie and Angelica discussing that name. He came to one of Sadie's events. He's…oh, no. "From the Style section?"

"That's the one," he confirms. "I hope that is okay. You aren't hiding from the mob, are you?" Chuckle, chuckle.

Oh, man of food. Don't you know the fashion police are more brutal and less forgiving than the mafia?

Apparently not. Jace couldn't be happier about what just transpired.

Our return trip in the limo is relaxing. I realize that this man of influence and cooking savvy, who is successful enough to be able to name a restaurant after his own mother, has managed to put me at ease over the course of several courses. The conversation is familiar and not at all forced. I feel what I assess to be "normal" in this moment…even in this slightly moronic outfit.

At my front door, he kisses my cheek with friendly affection.

"Thank you, Jace. It was such a nice time."

"It couldn't have been more perfect," he says, and I see his mind begin to shift elsewhere as he makes his way down the stairs.

I have a sneaking suspicion that it is the idea of getting on the society page he deems as "perfect."

As I remove my military boots, I cannot decide if the angst I try to express to God is associated with my important visit to the resort tomorrow or the fact that I may have single-outfittedly destroyed a man's reputation.

It's a toss-up.

Scenes from the Other Half

The coffee shop is packed with people preferring refills over timely arrivals to work. Angelica edges an indecisive, borderline bickering couple over to the side so she can place our order. Her Fendi bag is between us, so I try to peek inside. She says she has brought something for me. I am hoping it is an Angora sweater of hers I was coveting the other day.

"Thanks for the coffee," I say as we take an open table by the electric fireplace.

"Welcome," she mumbles between the two bites it takes for her to finish a scone. "That is so annoying. I think people with kids should wait until working adults have left the coffee shop. It's only right. Equal time." She points behind her.

My glance falls past the woman and child at the next table to a stylish woman dressed all in pink reading the morning newspaper. My eyes stay on the upside-down image on the folded half of the paper. It looks vaguely familiar. The "crash position" angle of my head causes Angelica to turn in her seat. At first she doesn't see what has caught my attention, but when she faces me and reaches into her Fendi, she looks disappointed.

"I wanted to be the one to show you," she whines. "Better prepare yourself." With the manner of a lawyer introducing case-winning evidence against her client, she slaps the paper down in front of me. Just a few inches down from the Style Scene masthead I see the familiar image right-side up. Even positioned as it is supposed to be, it is still so very wrong. There I am with Jace. I look ruddy, as though I work on a potato farm and am going to break out into a whistle any moment. Jace gazes adoringly at the obvious star of the table, the chocolate torte. Here I am grinning away, thinking this image will be seen by nobody, while Jace is obviously showcasing one of his finer creations.

"This is a tad humiliating. I look like some attention-starved bystander who forced my way into the photo."

"Try fashion-starved. Who dressed you…Caitlin?" Angelica is shrill and quite disappointed that I am focusing on the wrong humiliation factor.

"It's not a non or anything. Easy." I take a moment to read the lengthy photo caption first to myself and then aloud because I discover, with great pleasure, that it is the cause of her frustration. I clear my throat and do my best newscaster impersonation.

"It looks like love. Restaurateur Jace Burch puts a stylish spin on an old favorite with his double-layer chocolate torte drizzled with caramel and sautéed Oregon hazelnuts. And while Jace only has eyes for his own creation, it was the melding of retro corporate with vintage homemaker worn by his date Mari Hamilton that captured the attention and hearts of our fashion editors. A note to Ms. Hamilton…maybe we are just old-fashioned, but the next time you dress to delight the senses of the hip and happening, go on a date with someone who recognizes an original when he sees it."

"They like me. They really, really like me." I give her a Sally Field acceptance speech. "Didn't you read this part?"

"I did, and I'm beyond shocked. I cannot believe you were going out with Jace and never told me."

"Where's my 'Congratulations on being a fashion icon for a day, Mari'?"

"That will pass. Everyone knows the fashion editors from the Style section are ruled by paid advertisers and not a true sense of taste or culture."

"I didn't pay them. And I wasn't wearing any known labels. You just cannot accept the fact that I was…what was it…" I read with a loud voice, "hip and happenin'." I know Angelica worships this section and is always hoping to be caught in one of those montage shots taken at parties where people look distant, unaffected, and completely noteworthy.

"I cannot wait to show Caitlin. It could be her ticket to the buyer position." And I had doubted her taste. I'm so happy that in the end I was running late and had little choice but to forge ahead with my mismatched clothing.

"I'd be ticked if one of the most eligible bachelors in town used my Kevin Milano moment to promote his dessert."

"It worked out for everyone. He got the mention and I wasn't tagged as being the 'ignored for a reason' and overly beaming date. Besides, it was an amazing torte. I'd go out with it again."

"What about him?"

"Not so much." I try to pick the remnants of polish off my nails. As there is no time to repaint them before I visit Majestic Vista, this is the next best option.

She slaps my hands down. "Stop that. If you do have a run as a fashion icon, you should at least pretend to care about such a responsibility."

"Does your agitation have anything at all to do with the other night when I stayed behind with Peyton?" I pegged her.

I keep picking.

She rolls her eyes. "Oh, please. Like I want anything to do with someone so—"

I cut her off. "Totally infatuated with you? Yeah, I agree. Obviously he has little common sense."

"Really?" Her joy sneaks out before she can control it. "A lot of the guys at the office like me…" her voice trails off, and I let her wander for a moment. If she wants to turn this into nothing, I'm not going to stop her.

"It turns out that the guy is intimidated by you. Next time you come here for coffee, maybe you should invite him and not me. That's my last mention of it. Cross my heart." I make a crisscross motion over my zippered sweatsuit top. Which brings it to her attention.

"Are you trying out to be a fly girl?"

"Today is my day. You know, project Lady Luck. I'm going to Majestic Vista and hopefully networking with the owner."

"Right!" She turns chipper and supportive. The coffee drip has taken hold of her personality just in time. "I hear Lionel is fabulously gorgeous. And rich. I guess sweats are a safer choice than your June Cleaver gone wrong look." She points back at the paper and I almost lose the coffee in my mouth.

By going just a bit later than the usual morning drive time, I am able to move through town with ease. Hauling along Tanque Verde, I feel ecstatic. I don't know if it is the possibility of what might happen or the fact that I have not played hooky *ever* in my adult life, but I'm breathing bigger, fuller breaths and my head feels clear and ready to discern opportunity's knock.

Two miles before the resort, I see advance signs promoting the most luxurious spa in the Southwest. When the huge copper sculpture of mountains at sunrise appears, I know to turn right. How many times on my way to the grocery store or to Sadie's house have I taken this detour so I could look at that sign and imagine the life beyond?

The curve of the long, private driveway causes the litter in my car to sail about the interior. A Big Slurp cup comes dangerously close to the brake pedal. I give it a Mia Hamm kick and it rebounds over the middle hump and onto the passenger's seat.

I check my clothes for obvious Elmo fur balls and find only random strands that are next to impossible to remove. I'll walk quickly, with purpose, and nobody will notice.

As if in a 1940s musical, my entrance triggers a practiced and graceful response from all the attendants. They rush up from the left and the right and form two greeting lines. I am tempted to dance down the center of their human tunnel like a square dancer. My imagination blends genres, but one thing I am singularly focused on is my goal to end up here among the chandeliers and the golden-hued wood walls. If I could walk on marble tiles handpicked in a small town outside of Rome every day of my life, I could get rid of my functional shoes that place a minimattress between me and the cement slabs at Golden Horizons. If I could look at a mural of rushing water and mountain peaks against a sunny, opalescent pink-and-yellow background, the dark thoughts that plague me throughout the day would vanish into the ceiling skyline.

The male closest to me has a clipboard, and a pretty girl next to him has a decorative coffee mug on a tray. "Welcome to Majestic Vista. May I have your name, please?"

"Mari Hamilton."

"Mari, welcome. Would you care for a morning espresso, latte, or soothing tea?" He skims his list, and once he is sure I am one of the chosen ones who belong in these hallowed halls, he is all about service.

"I am here for Sonya's intermediate pilates class. She is expecting me."

His brows come together but only for a quick instant. The woman next to him whispers in his ear and a light goes on. "Ah, yes. That class is just about to start. Right this way. Halo will escort you to the sanctuary room."

My personal tour guide heads over to a long wooden bench that faces short lockers and cubicles, where designer shoes rest until their owners return to claim them. Halo invites me to remove my shoes and replace them with fuzzy blue slippers that give the bottom of my feet a gentle massage with each step.

"Weren't you at Lily's last night?" she asks in a friendly manner.

"Yes, I was. Do you go there?" She must have seen the photo. Maybe Jace is a member and I just scored big points.

"I would if I ever got asked," she offers in the humble manner of someone who is born beautiful and feels obligated to downplay it.

The sanctuary room lives up to its name. Along textured vanilla walls are rows of sconces holding candles of all sizes. A vast alcove cradles a kidney-shaped stage where Sonya is rolling out her mat alongside large stone vases holding stems of lavender. I try not to think about the screened-in porch my exercisers are forced to endure. They should have this kind of setting.

Sonya promised to place me in the back so that when Lionel shows up to observe her class, I will be near him to introduce myself. I stand against the wall taking in the ambience and watching as attractive person after attractive person files in.

Sonya gives me a familiar smile. She greets a few of the others rolling out their deep blue mats on her way over to see me. She twirls around to showcase the room. "What do you think?"

"I'm in love," I say while pretending to pinch myself.

"It is incredible. Did you see much of the foyer and social area?" She gives an okay sign with her fingers and opens her eyes wide. "Oo la la. I really thought I had died and gone to heaven when I started here. This feels too meant to be, you know?" She motions her finger back and forth between us.

"I couldn't agree more."

Turning on her toes to face the group, Sonya checks her watch, and amazingly morphs into an even more elegant creature…part swan, part cat. "All right, everyone, let's step into our breathing. Lie down on the mat and feel the length of your body pressing deeply into the floor with each breath."

I quickly set up the mat Halo had given me. What parents name their child Halo? Probably hippies. I feel every part of me sink into the floor. The first few series of moves relax me; there is no sweating or torture. If not for the sharp sound of quick breaths from the woman next to me, who must be a Lamaze graduate, I would fall into a deep slumber.

The instrumental music in the background rises in energy level. Some native drums are incorporated into the piano and harp harmonies. From here on out, Sonya kicks up the workout. The sweat begins and the word "stretch" takes on deeper meaning. Stretch the limits. Stretch too far. Hopefully, stretched thin as well. I'm keeping up but only because there is a second person on stage providing examples of the modified version of each exercise. Forty minutes into it, I am modifying the modifications and checking the clock every few seconds, praying for it to be over.

Breather woman next to me asks if I need a glass of water, perhaps with lemon? She hands me her perfectly folded hand towel with the MV monogram. I mop my brow and, while everyone is facing the front, I mop my armpits and beneath my chest. So this is what my militant-exercise residents want? They're crazy.

My short rest during an abdominal exercise series that is difficult to watch, let alone mimic, helps me regain my energy and composure. It is during this time that a sharply dressed man with perfect hair and manicured nails enters the room. I see him nod to Sonya and offer the smile of a liked politician. You know he is older because he has an air of wisdom and maturity, but his skin is flawless and very few wrinkles remain to support anyone who might question his youthful vigor. He takes a seat in an antique chair.

This is it, I tell myself. Kick it in, Mari. Show him and yourself what you are made of.

The last thing I remember is the sound of my heart pounding (or was it the drums?) and the outline of the breather woman's contacts as she leans in to examine what a living version of rigor mortis looks like.

Humiliation Squared

"Mari, how many fingers am I holding up?" a booming voice engages me in a scene from hospital dramas featured on the major networks. Have I fallen asleep while watching television in Golden Horizons' lounge?

"Can you tell me your last name?"

"Ham...Hamilton." I squint and can begin to make out the figures above me. There is no candle glow, only a sharp, piercing light directed at my pupil.

Now that I am blinded by the spots that linger after light exposure, I use my hands to feel about me. I'm on some kind of cot or table and dark walls are close-in.

"Mari, it's me." Finally the sound of a familiar voice. My vision clears, and I can see Sonya's chin and then her full face tilt toward me.

"This has never happened to me before." I strain forward for a moment to measure the look of concern in Sonya's eyes, but I succumb to the weight of my own head.

"This is Dr. White. He's our on-call physician. It seems that you passed out from...?" She is baffled.

The man next to her is not in a white lab coat but in golf attire graced with logos promoting a life I know nothing about. They have called him in off the green to check on me. He speaks with stern kindness and authority. "Actually, the way you were holding your right glute, I believe you were in the middle of a muscle cramp. Though it is very uncommon, the pain of a muscle seizure can cause a blackout. Are you still in pain?"

No matter how I feel, I am determined to say no. I start to shift my position. He must be right because I am favoring my right cheek. Which is funny, my mind interjects, since I have never been particularly fond of either. I release my back and press down on my right side. A shriek escapes my lips. The scream is so loud the doctor steps back instinctively to preserve and protect his ear drums and his love of the symphony.

"Mari, I feel so bad. This has never happened before. I should have been watching you more closely." Sonya doesn't blame me for ruining her class.

"You are so hired," I whisper as the doctor makes a quick call on his cell phone.

"Are you sure? Look what I did to you." Sonya is horrified.

"Believe me, this represents the way my life works. It has nothing to do with your teaching methods. Our exercise group will love you."

She hugs me gently. I cannot believe she is this excited to join Golden Horizons. I hope I'm not around when she realizes what she is signing on to.

Now the doctor is speaking to someone just outside the door. Sonya is helping me try to slide off the table to see if I can put my full weight down on my legs. While the pain is not as excruciating in this position, it becomes clear that I cannot hold my body upright for long without triggering the spasms.

"We are bringing in our best masseur to rub out the cramp, Mari." Sonya has given me some aspirin and a little purple paper cup with daisies on it. She is removing what looks like a designer hospital gown from the cupboard near the rock fountain in the corner. The doctor has left us alone to give me privacy to change.

"It had better be a woman." I laugh, but her expression makes me nervous. "It's a woman, right? I mean, this is my never-before-seen right buttock we're talking about."

"Charles is the best, Mari. And I will stay in here with you if that makes you feel more comfortable."

Tough choice…alone with a guy while wearing an open gown or alone with a guy *and* the woman who is my only link to a new life and who, up until now, thought I was somewhat professional. I will never be able to hold my head up if I ask her to hold my hand through a stinkin' massage.

"No. No. I'll be fine. I'm just feeling groggy. Of course I am fine with Charles. He's a professional. He is a professional, right?" I'm a dithering dupe. "It is so nice of you to take care of me like this. I cannot believe I missed my chance to meet Lionel. You kindly set it up and here I go and ruin it. After all of your effort, the guy still doesn't know my name."

Sonya wrings her hands and looks away from my rambling mouth toward the peaceful bliss of the fountain.

"He does, actually." She visibly cringes at the scene she witnessed.

"What? What, Sonya? Don't tell me he was still there when I… cramped?"

"Mari." She is reluctant to speak. She motions for me to sit down and remembers that is not my best position of comfort right now. "Mari, he is the one who carried you in here."

The scene in which Lionel was my heroic leading man to my passed-out damsel in distress flashes through my mind like lightning. My future goes up in flames. One by one the symbols of beauty and success melt away…the mural, the complementary cup of tea, the marble polished to a sheen, and the heavenly slippers that forgave my calloused feet. These are erased from my recent past. But, of course, the biggest tragedy of all is that they have been torn from my future.

"Nooooooo," I wail. My humiliation is complete.

Sonya pats my back and comforts me as well as a stranger is able, but it is no use. "I had better let you change. Do you need any help?"

"Not unless you are a licensed psychologist too." I try to lighten the moment for her sake, but I am too deep in irrationality to find humor in any of this.

After the door closes behind her, I wish I had accepted her help. Wiggling out of my sweats is proving difficult. I cannot lean over the way I normally would, and squatting isn't a pain-free option either. I figure out that if I lie down on the massage table and bend my knees, I can get my sweatpants as far as my lower thighs. My logic is that if I then stand for just a few seconds, my sweatpants should fall the rest of the way to my feet.

I am thankful there are no mirrors in this place. If I had a glimpse of what Charles will soon be exposed to, I'd never go through with this. I copy the Lamaze lady's breathing pattern and prepare to stand. One breath. Two breath. Three breath…Go.

My feet hit the floor and the pain nearly cancels out any further breathing. These form-fitting sweats do not quite fall to the floor as I had hoped. I brace my hands on the table and walk in place to loosen the grip of Lycra. "Onward Christian soldiers…breathe…marching as to war, with the cross of Jesus, going on before." I hum a vacation Bible school favorite to mask the pain.

"Hey, I know that one."

A voice startles me into action. I try to turn and squat and pull my pants back up—an impossible motion that triggers searing pain. And that thing that never happens to me…that passing-out thing…happens for the second time in one day. In the most compromising position imaginable, I fall to the marbled tile that will never be mine to glide over in self-massaging slippers the color of sapphires.

Charles the beautiful masseur is in the room.

And Lady Luck has so left the building.

Helpful Accessories

Higher," I say in between groans of pain.

Caitlin adjusts the ice pack on my lower back. I cannot feel my buttocks, but I can feel the undertow of muscle cramps.

"I cannot believe the guy who could offer me a life makeover had to carry me twice. And he saw my junkie car."

"He left you passed out in your car? That doesn't sound like a good man to me."

"No. He placed me on the backseat. Sonya drove me and then took Majestic's car service back." I cannot bear the humiliation of this.

"It's a good thing I made this." Caitlin digs through her colorful Mexican artisan bag.

I glance down at the woven bracelet she hands me. Among amber beads and threads of blue and brown are the initials WWOMD. My friend's revised take on the What Would Jesus Do concept.

"You are supposed to ask yourself What Would Old Mari Do? and then do the opposite."

I recall a *Seinfeld* episode with a similar theory. Is it possible that my instincts are so messed up that I should run in the opposite direction when they surface?

So WWOMD? I'd hope to never run into Lionel again. I'd be so ashamed that I wouldn't follow up. Why give him the chance to say, "I'm so sorry, but you are one clumsy, inept, odd woman. We don't serve or employ your kind."

"Hand me a pen and some paper," I say, pointing to my desk, and Caitlin retrieves my monogrammed thank-you notes. "Lower," I add, indicating my pack needs adjusting for the hundredth time.

I decide to take the new theory out for a spin. New Mari won't let anything—not even possible rejection—get in the way of her dreams.

Music Man

My volume raises another octave as I describe once again my vision for the decor theme to be implemented for tonight's Golden Golden Gala to Blanche Adams.

While I do appreciate her last-minute idea to transform the event into a Jane Austen tribute, it is giving me a mental seizure. I find myself doing Rae's "you give me a migraine" hand to temple motion before sending Blanche on an important mission to retrieve electrical tape. This will occupy her for hours, but it also means I am left to complete the last-minute details by myself. Rae conveniently trundled out of here at two for a hair appointment and will not reappear until everyone is in attendance so she can make a regal entrance in a radiant gown that supposedly once belonged to Oprah. She bought it online and made a big to-do about its level of luminance. We all have our doubts but will praise her nonetheless. And I have my special glasses just in case it is indeed a ten on the scale of brightness.

In my arms I hold reams of gold lamé. It is the volume and style of fabric that would incite fear in any woman who has ever been a bridesmaid. But as a table covering and a display draping, it turns out to be perfect material. Only two more of the dining tables need to be covered, and then I plan to affix some to the exhibit table, where I have arranged large photos of Golden Horizons and its residents during each of its decades of existence. Beside each main black-and-white image, I have placed a photo album containing more images, menus, activity programs, and other paraphernalia from that time period.

The large black-and-white photos had been Angelica's idea. She had just returned from a conference where they had displayed large images of people before and after taking the newest medication. Though I found this disturbing, I was able to envision how it could work perfectly for this event.

I have not yet called Angelica, though she left a couple of messages. Just the thought of replaying the incident at Majestic, to Angelica no less, was too much to bear. I needed to throw my thoughts and energy into this event. Prior to my on-site spasm, I secretly dreamed that the Golden Anniversary party would be my send-off...I could go out with a bang before transitioning into my new life. Now the success of this event is necessary because it is all I have. The perspective shift leaves me flat.

I look around at my surroundings and can plainly hear a line from a favorite movie...Jack Nicholson leaves his peers in the psychiatrist's waiting room with poisoned food for thought. "What if this is as good as it gets?"

"Mari dear, I'm ready for a hand here." Tess is at the far end of the grand room, where she has agreed to display some of her finest garments from the 1950s. As I approach her and her work, I am utterly in awe. It is breathtaking. The entire expanse of the wall is decorated with dresses pinned to look captured mid-dance, shoes dainty and intricate dangle from nylon thread anchored to the ceiling, and several mannequins I borrowed on a whim from Caitlin have been transformed either into tiara-adorned princesses or sophisticated figures clutching sequined clutches, umbrellas, and dog leashes with stuffed toy poodles attached.

"Oh, Tess...I do believe you have saved me from certain mediocrity tonight." I praise the lovely woman still hemming a Bob Mackie gown the color of raspberry sherbet. "I had no idea you could do such things."

"Darling, haven't I ever told you that I was a window dresser for Saks?" She bats her made-up eyes and grins the smile that only cherished secrets can inspire.

"You left that out of our many conversations. I don't know why I just assumed—"

"I was a spoiled debutante turned spoiled housewife?"

"That would be it. Well, except you forgot the 'turned spoiled resident' part."

"I'm ashamed of you, Mari. You know me so well and yet you really thought I was among the idle rich? Me?" Tess bites off the bit of string remaining after the knot has been secured. "I was rich, but never idle."

One of the biggest joys in this job is discovering who these people have been and what they have accomplished in a lifetime. Against popular opinion, this place is not a place of lamented regrets. Except perhaps that there is not more time to live good lives. Just when I thought Tess couldn't surprise me anymore, she silences me with her still-agile hands and creative flair.

"Has anyone ever told you that you are one classy dame?" I help her hang the last gown and adjust it to look as though the wind has caught the hemline. A fan on the far left side of the display oscillates and catches the edges of various garments from the poodle skirt to the evening ball gown. It is as if they are dancing to a song not yet written. I tell her this.

"Actually, I've been told that I'm *the* classy dame." Her frail hand rises to cover her mouth as she laughs. "I love that idea…about the song not yet written. Every display I have ever created always had an element of whimsy. An unknown that was meant to invite the viewer into the scene with their ideas and interpretations. In a way, I have always invited people to offer a bit of their personal, evolving song to accompany the visual. I do love how you think, Mari."

We both stand and face her creation, mesmerized and transported to a time when elegance was incorporated into a lady's lifestyle, no matter how rich or poor. I know the event is going to be enjoyed by all the residents, and I cannot wait to tell Rae that I did not use one idea from Beau's file. In fact, after tonight, I do believe that talk of Beau's great feats will be no mo'. There is room for only one of our songs…and this chorus is mine.

Tess' eyes still sparkle as she turns to face me directly for the first time this evening. "Mari, you look beautiful. Didn't I tell you that dress was made for you? If Rudy Mangione were alive, I'd be sending him a picture of his dress finally on the right person. Gisele insisted that we get a photo together before the night is through."

"I'd love to." I twirl once so the dress mimics those on display. "It is an honor to be wearing this, Tess. Thank you."

"No, thank you. Just think how I would feel if one of my evil step-daughters discovered that I have this collection." Trouble passes over her face as quickly as a cloud in the breeze. The sun shines brightly on the other side of her unhappy memory. "You have given me happiness by accepting a few items this past year."

We both tear up some. Then she says, "Are you trying to ruin my freshly applied mascara? Now stop that. I have to go get my dress on so I can show you up." Gathering her sewing kit items, Tess heads toward her corridor. Before she is too far away, she turns with a look of hope on her face. "Please tell me that a gentleman friend will be here to accompany you tonight. I see you dancing with a special boy in that dress."

I blush, more from personal disappointment than embarrassment. "No. You know me, Tess…I'm waiting for just the right one to deserve me and this dress." I say this as a flip fill-in comment, but as I finish the sentence, I know it is exactly how I feel.

"Good girl. When it comes to love, it really is hip to be square. Waiting for the real thing will never go out of fashion."

Her words give me comfort and hope. It is the real thing I am after. The kind my parents have. I think of them for the first time since my social intervention. I check my watch; there isn't time to call them. It

seems I only think to communicate with my family when it is not convenient to do so. It is convenient for excuses, however.

A loud cymbal clangs and sends thunderous echoes down the hallway.
I'm pulled from my guilty thoughts gladly. Running as quickly as my
floor-length dress allows, I have a near collision with a man and his runaway cymbal.

"You rang?" I try to lighten the mood as I can see he is feeling foolish.

"Hi. I'm Rick...with the band. We're here to set up, if that's okay.
Actually, we are not really a band, just guys who love playing jazz. It's our
buddy who has the contact here." He straightens his jacket, which looks
three sizes too big.

Great. They aren't even a real band. "That would be Rae."

"No, his name is—"

"Rae is my supervisor and the one who apparently thought a love for
jazz was a good enough résumé." I interrupt him with my attitude.
Thankfully he is still flustered from his trip down the hallway, so I have a
chance to snap out of my mood. "Over there you'll see a small stage
behind the area marked off as the dance floor. If you need any additional
cords or outlets, let me know. I'll be finishing up some last details here
before I go check on the catering staff. I'm Mari."

Rick nods, shakes my hand, and gives me a thumbs-up. I sense he is
about as comfortable with social gatherings as I am. With a cymbal under
each arm he makes his way over to the stage. As I finish my work I notice
the arrival of the three other members of the band—a pianist, saxo-
phonist, and base guitarist.

In between warm-up songs I am about to request "Moon River," but as
I look their way, Rick is very blatantly pointing me out to the pianist. The
pianist happens to be quite cute. His dark curls, brown eyes, and olive skin
are just my type. No wonder I was fine with surfer-blond Peyton's friendly
rejection of me.

My face grows warm, this time from embarrassment, and I hurry off
to check with the caterers. One more glance at my watch reminds me that

it is almost showtime and there is still no Rae to be seen. On my way to the kitchen I spot several eager beaver residents who are dressed and migrating toward the grand room.

"Sorry, folks. I need you all to remain in the commons area or your rooms for another half hour. But I must say, you make for quite a dazzling crowd. If I didn't know better, I would think this was your prom." They smile and begin to reminisce about past occasions and events as they reluctantly about-face.

Pretty piano boy crosses my path on his way from the drinking fountain. I want to ask him if he would like a pitcher of water for his band, but when I see his face, I forget the word for water…and pitcher…and that leaves little to work with.

He stands and dabs his tie, which has a few raised droplets on the silk. The watermark is soon obvious. He keeps smearing the water, so now large streaks are evident.

I reach into my matching clutch and remove a handkerchief. "May I?" This sentence requires two words I am able to recall in the presence of cuteness. Now, if my hands will stop shaking, I can help the man.

"Thank you. Good thing they hide me behind the piano, wouldn't you say?"

"Yes, I would." I laugh and keep dabbing at his chest. "Whose the leader of this non-band anyway? I'd like to thank him for this. I mean, for hiding you behind the piano."

"That was a self-imposed sentence. I'm the sort-of leader of the sort-of band. I got the guys together as a favor to Rae."

I'm shocked by this, though I shouldn't be. Rae is good at networking with handsome men. Often they are pretty boys (case in point) but are usually much more petite. I stop dabbing at him, and he takes the cloth from me to give it a try.

"Rae?" I squeak out. I quickly try to recall if I have said anything derogatory about her in his presence.

"When she told me about this great night, I was more than happy to make the trip. I'm rather fond of it here."

"Oh, are you a Phoenix band?" I consider asking him if he knows the Doo-Wops, but I think better of it.

"I'm a Tucson boy who has relocated to Phoenix. For now, anyway."

"What is it that you do? I mean, when you aren't a sort-of band leader."

"Mari!" I hear Lysa calling from the kitchen. She has begged me not to leave her alone with catering-related decisions, and I have clearly abandoned her.

"I'm sorry. I must go. You're nice. Your band...I mean, it's nice. Thanks for being here."

Piano man watches me as I back up down the hall and then finally duck into the kitchen to save Lysa from difficult dilemmas, such as arugala vs. iceberg or spiced red potatoes vs. mashed. After much convincing, I persuade the chef that when you are serving people over the age of seventy, bland is haute cuisine. He looks insulted but instructs his staff to follow this advice.

By the time Lysa and I have finalized all last details, the musician is gone. But Rae is wobbling down the hallway toward me. Her brisk steps on stiletto heels is comical. As she steps out of the hall shadows and into the brightness of fluorescent lights, we are able to take in the dress in its full, glittery glory.

"Uh-oh. She ordered Oprah's comforter by mistake." Lysa giggles this into my ear before the unfortunately dressed woman is within earshot.

Rae glances into the grand room on her way toward us. "Are you going to finish decorating?"

This is a perfect Rae kind of comment. She makes her dislike known without blatantly putting a person down. I'm sure this has saved her from many former-employee lawsuits over the years. There is never enough solid evidence of abuse, only the lingering sock-in-the-gut feeling of disappointing a person over and over.

"Wow. Some dress, Rae. Some dress." I am as polite as possible. "Your musician is here...what's his name? Your friend?"

Rae bares her teeth at me. She is braying like a mute mule. Lysa looks at me and then we both smile at her. "Pretty smile…for a pretty dress," I offer in a tone like Cruella the Gruel Slogger.

Her lips close like a steel trap. "No. I want you to check for lipstick on my teeth."

She stretches her lips once again; this time Lysa looks away. I nod in the affirmative and Rae smiles pleased as punch. She walks fitfully away from us.

"So just to be clear…a nod can mean 'yes, your smile is clean.' Or it can mean 'yes, in fact you do have maroon smeared across your jagged front teeth.' Right?"

I bray at her and largely mouth, "Thawt wooold be cawrect."

My feisty good mood could be inspired by "the boy" or the fact that I sent Rae out into the limelight with purple teeth. But I believe it is a bubbling sense of faith that tonight is going to turn out just as it should.

It's My Party...

The non-band is a hit in more ways than one. Everybody is dancing, loving the music, and it seems the gathering of young men in ill-fitting tuxes is enough to inspire swooning. Within forty minutes of the program there is actually a gathering of groupies that sways like a cluster of reeds in front of the musicians. I see Haley toss her handkerchief on the stage. Tess later tells me that Haley's email address is written on it in lipstick.

Family members of current and former residents also join in the fun, taking in the displays and sharing their memories. As a nod to the system, I have placed my suggestion box on the exhibit table with a note encouraging folks to write down a favorite story or incident at Golden Horizons. For once maybe I will receive happy reading material.

Much of my time is spent tending to details and troubleshooting. We run out of seating, so Lysa and I headed to the storage room to round up old folding chairs and benches. Twice, the sparkling cider fountain clogs from the pennies thrown in by people mistaking it for a wishing well. The caterers almost serve Perry the fish platter, which surely would have killed him. The man collects live fish because he cannot dine on them.

The evening is almost over before I have a chance to see Tess in her incredible Versace dress. Spectacular. She is the belle of the ball. The color of her cheeks gives her an adolescent glow. The men keep asking her to dance, and the classy dame keeps accepting. She snaps her fingers to favorite tunes as her partners lead her across the entire length of the room. And though this evening is a mere shadow of her glory days in New York, it is more than enough to give her joy.

Breathless, she saunters over to where Lysa and I stand. "Picture time, my dear, before this old woman faints."

"Yes. I almost forgot. Shall we?"

My date and I walk over to the backdrop adorned with cutouts of shooting stars. The photographer positions us a bit closer to one another. I usually stand a couple inches taller than Tess, but this wisp of a woman has finished off her look with a pair of knockout heels. "Mother and daughter shots are my favorite," smiles the photographer's assistant, a tall, thin woman wearing a black shift with pearls.

Tess peals with delight at this mistake. "She does have my style, doesn't she?"

"If you don't mind, I've been wanting to dance with Tess all evening." Walter bows to me first and then to Tess. "Shall we?"

"It's hard to see my mom dating again," I say to Lysa.

"Watch out. Crazy quilt cometh. I repeat, crazy quilt cometh," Lysa whispers out the side of her mouth. I nonchalantly look to the left and am tempted to run to the right. But my pride stops me. I have nothing to run from. I dare her to criticize this evening.

"There's a shrimp shortage, platter number three." This is her greeting.

I just smile. I dare you, Rae. I dare you to not like this party.

"We will get right on that." I keep my composure because if that is the only thing she can find to complain about, I have won.

"It's incredible, don't you think?" Lysa leads Rae toward unknown territory...a compliment. I tried this when I was wet behind the ears and naive. It always backfires.

Rae puffs up her chest and looks about the room as if she hadn't noticed that a smoothly run party was going on around her. But now that we have brought it to her attention, she must take it in to make her judgment. She leaves rash decision making for online purchases only.

"I do think it is going well…"

Nothing she can say will change the fact that she just acknowledged that I, Mari Hamilton, have pulled off the event of the year. I, Mari Hamilton, have…

"Beau saved the day."

Except that. Sock-to-the-gut feeling returns and pushes out my optimism with a force that throws me against the wall. "What!" I am tempted to grab this larger-than-life-sized Cabbage Patch Doll and shake her. This woman assumes that I used Beau's notes. I work night and day on this so that people can give her praise, and she turns the appreciation back to my predecessor. No more. I can take this no more.

"Rae, for your information, I did not use one idea from Beau's file. Not one. All this…" I circle my arms like a child playing whirlybird so she is sure to get my point. "All of this is my doing. Tess did the fantastic display, but all else…mine." I thump my chest like an alpha male gorilla.

I hear a faint "Go, girl" comment from Lysa, but Rae shifts her weight with displeasure and discomfort. After all of this she still does not take me seriously. She looks at me with disdain and pity. Nothing I do will erase the bright memory of Beau.

"Mari, one thing you have yet to learn about serving people is that it isn't all about you. Nobody does this work alone." She shakes her head and walks out onto the dance floor. She grabs the frailest man within reach and forces him to dance with her.

"Don't go, Mari. This is your night…don't let her win…" Lysa shouts down the hallway, but I have gathered my skirt and am running before the tears can start. I know it isn't just this scene. I am used to Rae's harsh style by now. It is everything. And it is nothing going as planned in my life.

I don't stop until I am outside in the large courtyard with our own man-made Golden Pond. My favorite spot awaits me, and I plunk down on a bench centered on the foot bridge. I sit for a while as silent sobs rise up and escape into the warm night.

"Give me something, God. I'll even settle for Sadie's former theory… one part of my life can stink…but not all. Not all at once. Give me something." I'm not usually a talk-out-loud kind of drama queen, but I am dressed for the part and nobody is out here…

"Will punch do?" Piano man is out here. He must have come out just in time to hear me. We are both embarrassed.

He hands me one of two crystal glasses. "I'm sorry that I barged in on your personal—"

"Breakdown?" I wave my hand in the air casually. "Don't worry about that. You'd be hard-pressed to find me when I'm not in the middle of one these days." My breath shudders as my lungs try to catch up poststorm.

"I was going to say prayer. It sounded like a prayer."

"Maybe if I did more of that, I would be doing less of this." I can only imagine how pathetic and puny I look right about now.

"I hear you. I'm sure he did too." He points up at the sky with his glass.

"You guys are a hit. Rae was smart to request your group. The residents love you." I inconspicuously wipe my nose with the back of my hand.

"Thanks. It feels good to be here. I love seeing them smile as they recognize each song." He sits down next to me hesitantly. I nod, giving him permission, and he turns toward me with eyes that melt my tension, "Can I ask what you really want? That sounded less like a request and more like a plea for mercy."

I start to speak but remember that he knows Rae. "I can't say. It's about a lot of things lately, but a part of it relates to a friend of yours and I wouldn't feel right."

"Let me guess…our Queen Rae? If it makes you feel better, we are more acquaintances. I don't think she exactly cultivates friendships, do you?" We both laugh at this ordinary yet absurd idea. He doesn't seem to be looking at the door longingly or searching his mind for an excuse to leave. "I've got a few more minutes before our break is over. I'm all yours."

"There might be a riot if they can't dance. You don't know how tough this crowd is."

"Ahh. You see, we thought of that. We have Sinatra spinning on the turntable right now. I figure I have…" he looks at his watch, "at least ten minutes before they join forces and revolt. I personally prefer Sinatra." He strains his neck toward the faint sounds from inside. We can just make out the song "Fly Me to the Moon."

"So…would you want to…" He moves his torso in a slow dance rhythm. A grimace follows his smile. He's changed his mind already.

Don't change your mind.

I say yes just as he says, "That wasn't a very smooth invitation for a girl who is having a difficult night. Sorry."

My acceptance of his bad invitation surprises him. He leaps up and places his glass on the bench. His hand extends to greet mine, and he pulls me toward him with practiced flair.

For the two remaining minutes of the song, we are circling the small space of the bridge together. I'm thankful for all those dance lessons we have had at Golden Horizons over the years. I do not stumble, nor stub my toe on his.

"Do you think tonight is successful? You have probably played at lots of fancy shindigs, but for an anniversary party at a retirement home… how would you rate tonight?" I'm obviously leading the guy into a one-answer corner. He did, after all, witness my personal waterworks display beside a man-made waterway.

"The best night ever. And not just for a retirement home version of a party. I've never seen people respond so well to each aspect of a gathering. The exhibit, the photos, the clothing display…"

The song ends, and we return to the bench like teens at a school mixer. We don't have much time left before he must return to the piano.

For some reason I am determined to focus on the negative of this night rather than the possible romance of this moment.

"Me too. I mean, I think that too. It has gone so well, and yet Rae cannot acknowledge that. In fact, she not only won't compliment me, but she gives all the credit to some guy who has not worked here in years. She thinks the details are ideas from his file, and…and…I can't take it anymore. I can't compete with the golden boy of Golden Horizons." My hands fold into fists and I hate how out of control I feel in front of this really lovely guy, who probably just came out for some air.

He looks surprised by my emotional rant and then smiles ever so slightly.

"That's crazy. You should set her straight. Clearly this memorable gala is not the work of Beau, who, between you and me, knows diddly about pulling off these things."

My mind is scanning my words. Did I mention Beau by name? I certainly hadn't meant to. "Please don't tell Rae about this. Sadly, I will not be leaving my position here as soon as I had hoped. I'm stuck until…wait a minute…" I finally get what his comment means. "You don't know him too, do you?"

"If this were a movie, I'd string this out for another ten scenes so we could have zany run-ins with very Shakespearean moments of mistaken identity, but I'd rather not waste time that could be used getting to know you."

The fact that I am still confused at this point only serves to point out how distraught I am.

He reaches for my hand, lifts it to his lips, kisses it, and says, "I'm Beau. And your friend Lysa told me who you are because I asked to see two people…the person who planned this incredible evening enjoyed by everyone, including Rae, and the beautiful girl in the amazing dress who helped me with my tie."

I pull my hand back and stand up. My stance is shaky, and I realize I have not eaten anything yet. My head throbs from crying martyr tears. I have to brace myself against the wooden rail of the bridge.

"And though this won't surprise you, I was amazed to discover that those two fantastic people are one and the same. Her name is Mari Hamilton. And here she is, doubting herself when she has pulled off," he searches above to pluck the right word from the same sky I was cursing minutes ago, "a miracle."

I position myself toward the door that leads back to the center and quickly assess that it will take many awkward steps to exit. It will be better if he leaves first. "I'm feeling pretty stupid about now…" I cannot speak his name. "Could you leave me alone? I do…I do appreciate your effort, and the punch." In the gut. "But I'm afraid nothing can rescue this evening."

Not even your beautiful eyes and a perfect dance.

He stands near me for a few moments. As I look at the ground, Beau gazes at the water. I'm feeling dumber and more childish by the second. I want to start the entire evening over and retrace my actions so that I could be standing here, with him, sipping punch and laughing about the coincidence. But I can't. It's too late to be a grown-up.

He then walks away, not with a stride of defeat but rather a stalled "what just happened" gait. Rae's point was valid. The band did make the event. Beau and his band are responsible for elevating the evening I planned to a more magical experience.

For now, my pride does not allow me to accept the other more upsetting truth: I really like this guy. And that just cannot be. You don't get a crush on the enemy.

The automatic door opens to allow Beau to disappear into the building. Sinatra's voice wafts over to where I sit. For a brief moment I am surrounded by upbeat, catchy music and lyrics…"Luck be a lady tonight…"

If I could just make nice with irony, maybe it would stop ruling my life.

Blogged

Gusts of wind blow into my face and adhere my contact lenses to my eyeballs as each car in the opposing lane speeds by. I am replaying last night's incident, amazed at my bad luck. I consider small bits of dust pelting into my skin as just punishment for such Old Mari behavior.

"Please, Mari. Put the window up. Sadie, don't you have those parental controls up there?" Angelica seems agitated. Could be because we are trading breakfast for a walk.

Since we all signed up for the Tucson Trot, a breast cancer research fund-raiser a few months away, Sadie suggested a practice walk might be in order. A smart idea because not one of us has been doing anything resembling exercise. Even Angelica, who is a spin class addict, seems to be in slug mode.

And slug she does…my shin until I push the button to raise the window.

"Everyone out." Sadie takes on the voice and visage of a soccer mom more than happy to unload her car full of bickering children. It is the first time I see her clearly as a mom. A someday mom. My eyes drop to her hand just in case there is something she has not told us. You never know with sneaky, to-herself Sadie. While Angelica is always talking about how to get out of faux relationships, Sadie is quietly going about nurturing a real one.

My mind goes to Beau. I haven't told anyone about last night. I want to process it first. Maybe the walk will help.

The morning is warming up, and we all take time to stretch our legs in the sun and step away from the topic en route. I lift my leg and place it on the back of a bench; my hip and lower back scream, reminding me of the other incident I have not yet shared.

"I almost forgot!" Caitlin rushes back to the van and removes a large bag from beneath her seat. We are afraid to ask.

With great excitement and care, she removes four small, strapped pouches that look like fanny packs—something I have not seen much of in the past decade, except during my vision of Denton surveying the hills and shrubbery for birds with long hair and even longer legs.

I was wondering when Caitlin would introduce her next big idea.

"Great. A fanny pack is perfect for my keys and pack of gum. Thanks, Caitlin." Sadie is delighted to find that this offering is actually functional.

Caitlin gleams. "Close…but think lower."

Now we are very afraid. None of us really wants to drape straps around anything lower than our hips.

We get a "duh" look as she unhooks one and wraps it around her thigh, which happens to be the size of my bicep, which happens to be large by female arm standards but quite small in terms of legs.

"Ta-da. It's a thigh purse."

We consider this without a direct response.

"See? It doesn't bounce up and down like a fanny pack. It is still easy to reach down for a cell phone…or for keys and gum."

"Honey, for those of us with real thighs, this might not work out to be a good idea," Sadie says, examining her bright yellow nylon bag.

"The straps are adjustable. I know that women come in all shapes and sizes. In fact, I like to base my ideas on that very premise." I'm sure this has just occurred to her, but she speaks it with conviction.

I extend my strap; its full length unfurls to a yard's length. "You did consider a large mama leg. However, those of us *with* meat on our bones still might—"

"Rub our skin off. Hello?" Angelica does not tippy-toe around the possible pain we could endure.

"I was going to say chafe…but yes…rub our skin off."

Caitlin thinks for a moment and seems to decide I am the best model of meaty. Cinching the black strap, she places the neon blue purse at the first place left leg does not touch right leg. This, sadly, is barely above my knee region. "There. I could call it a leg purse so women could place it anywhere without feeling left out of the product's original purpose." She seems satisfied with her solution and we all nod to the logic.

We are off. Soon we are lost in conversation and don't even notice the small zipper tab making a "chink, chink" sound with each step.

I try to avoid bringing up my recent disappointments, but the job hunt and the anniversary party have been my primary topics for the past three months. Eventually the conversation cycle returns to these.

Well, almost.

"I completely forgot my big news for you, Mari." Angelica is delighted to recall something of great importance.

"What?"

"It will explain a lot of recent events."

We offer blank stares as we wait for her to stop gloating and start informing.

"All this time, Mari wanted a new life and she has one. Only it isn't really hers. And she doesn't even know it exists."

I'd like to know why God has apparently put Angelica in charge of being the first to know anything about my life.

"Is there a beginning part to this conversation? Because I didn't get any of that." Sadie extends her stride, and Caitlin and I hurry to keep up with both of them.

"Ditto." I say. I'm perspiring but not from walking bowlegged to avoid the knee chafe. The sweat is from anticipation.

"Well, you know how some of the guys you have met lately seem to know your name? And those phone calls, the ones you dither on and on about? I have found the secret."

My mind cannot get past Angelica's usage of dither. Who says that?

"It's beyond crazy, but it answers my biggest question. When I went to the flash with Angus and Roger, it occurred to them again how weird it was that they both knew your name, and somehow they connected it to emails." She is about to burst with the news but leans over to catch her breath. We have been speed walking inadvertently. "Well, yesterday Roger comes by my office and says he figured it out and wants to show me this big news." She stalls again and bends down to tie her shoe.

"Spit it out!"

Angelica steps out of our walking order and comes over to me. She places a hand on each of my shoulders and looks me squarely in the eyes. "You, my friend, are somewhat of an online novelty. I don't know how it happened, but a very, very loose version of your life is being shared in a popular blog. So popular, in fact, that it is the number two blog listed on the Personally Speaking website, which closely monitors the number of hits each diary gets. Your site receives more than 40,000 a month."

"Please speak English to me." Sometimes I think I have dyslexia of the ear. Only a few words are coming back to me in any logical order, but none of them make sense.

"These are online diaries, Mari. People share their thoughts, their hobbies, how they take their coffee or prefer their toast, and in your case…what they like in a good date."

It is still sinking in. Ever so slowly.

Angelica feels compelled to lead me. "Like flowers sent in advance of a first date…ring any bells?"

"You're wrong. I don't even read my work email regularly, let alone send people notes about my life on some blong." But a bell has been rung. All those calls and the talk of flowers from strange men. They had taken their cues from someone or something. Apparently it was my cyber self.

"The word is blog. And believe me, I know you didn't create this. You are not savvy enough. But someone is telling whopping tales about you and your amazing life." She uses those annoying finger motions when she says the word "life" to bug me because I do that to her for the same effect.

"This makes no sense." This is all I can say over and over until we are circling back and the car is in sight.

"I know. It didn't make sense to me either. Forty thousand hits is a lot. A very impressive number for blogs, which are usually read by relatives, bored friends, and boring Web surfers. But I figured out one of the reasons…they posted a picture of you. Only it isn't you; it's the lead actress on that show about the agents who pose as nurses. It was canceled about three weeks into the season."

"You mean Cecilia Jade!" Caitlin says, all excited about my glamorous life double.

"Yes. Her. She. Whatever."

Sadie, who has been silent throughout this entire dialogue, reminds us of Angelica's first comment. "So what big question do you get answered by all of this?"

"How in the world Mari could possibly become more popular and known than me, of course."

We all look at her expectantly.

"The answer had to be fiction. Absolute, pure fiction."

On the way back to town we strip off the thigh purses and the group votes to go look at the blog together at the local library. Though I would rather see it alone, I think it best if I have people who understand the world of such things.

As we are about to pull into the parking lot, Sadie asks yet another clarifying question. "No offense, Mari, but who would waste their time fabricating a blog on your behalf? What could they possibly gain?"

All of a sudden, I know where we will find the real answers.

Back in *Charlie's Angels* mode I lean forward, my troubled face poking between Sadie and Caitlin and my outstretched hand pointing straight down the road.

"Change of plans. Golden Horizons, and step on it."

Though I am disgusted by what I have deducted, the rush of adrenaline is delightfully more invigorating than the rush of desert wind just an hour and a half earlier.

Caught

I raise my weekend employee pass up to the scanner and the door swings open with a creak. It occurs to me that if this pursuit leads to what I think it will, this might be my last tromp through these halls. One's pride can only fall so far.

My first stop is to check in on Tess. I ask to be alone with her for a few minutes.

"We'll go get coffee in the cafeteria," Angelica offers.

"It tastes like tar," I warn.

"Better suggestion?"

Nope. "I'll call you, Sadie, when I'm ready. See that room with the orange door and the 'keep out' stickers? That is where we will meet."

"This is all so exciting. And I don't even know what is going on." Caitlin's eyes are bigger than usual and her feet are tapping to use up her mounting energy.

I can see Tess rocking in her chair through the window in the door.

"Morning, Tess," I say, greeting my friend and ally warmly.

"I'm still humming from last night. Splendid, my dear." She claps her hands and then stalls midclap. "Shouldn't you be resting after the big night?"

"Tess, what do you know about the bets going on regarding my social life?"

"Well," she purses her lips and thinks a moment. "I know only that my twenty dollars is on you finding love. When I saw how Beau was looking at you, I was most certain I would cash in big. Big enough to retire from retirement." She chuckles.

"You knew that was Beau?" Of course she did. She moved here a year before I started.

"A few of the gang who are betting on your love life encouraged Rae to ask Beau back for an encore, so to speak. They meant well, honey. Didn't you like him? I had forgotten how handsome he was. Did you notice that?"

I did. That's the problem. "I'm afraid I have bigger concerns right now, Tess. I think that this group has been using our computers to talk about me. Or a version of me."

"You mean advertise your availability?"

"That's certainly a nice way to put it. But do you see how invasive this is? Strange men have my phone number, Tess. And apparently they think I do things like rock climb and attend art gallery openings..." As I say these things, a bell is ringing from a past conversation. "And they posted the picture of that actress..."

"Cecilia Jade." She laughs at being in the know on this part. "I do recall a dinnertime vote on who they think you most resemble who is currently on television. I had no idea it was to be used in such a way. How can I help?" Her little shoulders hunch forward and her small eyes peer into mine. She's all business.

"Who would have the most to gain from this?" I repeat Sadie's question.

"Of the residents? Well, I suppose Maggie, Sally, and, of course, Chet."

"Why 'of course' Chet?"

"He was a politician, you know. The man is not worried about taking big risks."

I ignore the fact that she just called betting on my finding love a big risk. "Thanks, Tess. I'll keep you out of this."

"So back to Beau. I saw you two, dancing on the bridge. It's exactly as I envisioned it…in that dress."

Since the evening crumbled so soon after that brief dance, I had wiped her prediction from my memory.

"Beau and I…did not click. I have been hearing about him for years. I certainly know enough to know that he is…"

"Perfect?" she says in a flighty, romantic way.

"Not for me." I focus on my cell phone to avoid looking directly at her. "You know, Tess, this whole promoting my love life thing might be it for me. The catalyst I needed to head for the Pearly Gates."

She nods, affirming how I feel. "Could be. Though I think the biggest catalyst for change will be that dance on the bridge. Mark my words."

I ignore her optimism and make the call to Sadie. At this moment, getting a grip on my "now" seems far more important than wagering bets on my future.

I decide first to gather evidence before confronting the guilty residents. I call Lysa, a much more active computer user, to come in and help me check a few of the residents' online accounts.

Once she arrives, I barricade the door with an orange plastic chair and we start our investigation. First we go to the site. Angelica shows us some of the major collective blog libraries. My site's link is accessible through several of these sites.

"Wow! There's Cecilia Jade. Get a load of the list of positive attributes that preface the blog." Caitlin looks as though she has won the lottery, jumping up and down and grabbing my shirt. I don't see the list because my hand is over my eyes.

"If you are going to bust these people, you had best be strong enough to at least look at this."

Angelica is right. First glance reveals a very nicely done site. I'm impressed with myself. That is, until I start reading the headings and subtitles cruisers can click on:

My favorite foods

My favorite dates ever

What I want in a man

What I hate about wimps

My daily deep thoughts about life and love

Photos of Mari on Mount Everest

Photos of Mari in the Caribbean shark hunting

Photos of Mari skydiving

My top ten books

My daily activity log created by my fan club president

Write me

Wear my promotional T-shirt

Favorite prints for sale

Top ten romantic places in Tucson

Why I inherit a million if I'm married before 30

"Well, they are clever. Look at that last one. I might even marry you for a million." Lysa skims these and randomly pulls up the categories. When she gets to the photos, the evidence of digital editing is obvious only because I know I have not scaled mountains and danced in Zimbabwe. Pages from art and outdoorsman magazines have been scanned. A cutout of Cecilia's face is pasted atop whatever body is in motion.

"Okay, can we trace who is updating this account?" Angelica sits on the desk the way they do in the movies and takes charge of the investigation.

"Well, someone with more expertise should be able to trace a few of these entries. Like this daily log of Mari's activities. This person wrote in almost every week, so the link should be traceable. We should contact Rae."

"Rae!" I shout in her ear. The one she is now holding as she rocks back and forth in pain.

"Mari, you can't do a private bust. To close down this operation, you need Rae's authority. What did you think you were going to do?"

She got me. I have no idea. "I just found out that I am living this double life, so I had no plan." I pace in the small room and wish I had asked for a cup of tar with sugar and cream earlier. "She will find a way to turn this against me. I know she will."

"Does it matter, Mari? I mean, at this point?" Sadie comes over to give me a sideways hug.

"No. Thank you for the perspective. You are right…it doesn't matter."

"Maybe you should put up your own picture and keep this site. Maybe the right guy is already on this list." Caitlin wears her heart on her naive sleeve.

"Negatory." Reminiscent of those war movie scenes where the president orders that final red button to be pushed, I tell Lysa, "Do it. Call Rae."

"Yes, ma'am."

As we wait for Rae to show up, Lysa verifies that Chet, Maggie, and Sally are all part of this plot to expose me to the dating world. We figure out that the primary contributor who submits my activity log is referenced by others as the fan club president. But that is as far as we can get.

"While we are waiting, could we pull up the Botanical Society's page? I posted a promotion for the Stargazer Gala." Sadie types in the name.

We read all about the telescope and the rare plants that have been placed in the center of a star-shaped garden until we see what Sadie was likely focused on. There is a small image of Carson followed by a brief bio. He is very distinguished looking with a kind smile.

"Wow. He's a looker." Angelica compliments as she knows how, but it has an edge that makes Sadie only half smile.

"He looks compassionate…and strong. Nice combination," I say.

"I can see you and him together forever," Caitlin offers, sounding a lot like Tess and her visions of me and Beau.

Beau.

We hear Rae breathing before her large knuckles hit the door. She is in sweats, and it surprises Lysa and me enough to make us giggle. We hope she has been exercising because her face is beet red and frightfully puffy.

We show her the evidence, and to her credit she seems mortified by its existence. That makes me feel a bit better and safer.

"I really don't know how you bring a stop to this kind of slander. Should we contact the company that runs the server? Maybe they could be sure we block any and all access to my personal information."

"No!" Puffy face does not want that kind of attention brought to this place under her watch.

"I love these residents as much as you do, Rae…" I assign human sentiment to this typically unfeeling supervisor so she will like me, "but they are giving out my address and phone number. It's amazing that I haven't had men come by my apartment."

She won't budge. "No. I said no. What if that triggered police involvement? We'll handle this situation ourselves. Chet will cancel the site immediately and give me the names of all those involved." She sends Lysa to round up the main culprits and continues to peruse the site. "They certainly have imagination, don't they? Cecilia Jade!" She cackles at this comparison.

That safe feeling I was getting….gone. Very gone.

As the guilty parties file into the hallway space outside of the office, an impromptu perp lineup takes place. I glare at each person as if on the other side of a one-way mirror. Only Chet is making eye contact with me. His tufts of gray hair on either side of his large, shiny head give him the appearance of an owl.

"We just thought we'd help, Mari. We think the world of you and want you to find love and…"

"Stop right there." I wave away this line of reasoning. "This is a violation of my privacy and my life. You have no right to do this just so you can win the bet."

"Did you bring this to an end?" He asks Rae bitterly. Their eyes meet, and I sense there are more words exchanged within that look.

"Yes, I did. This is completely out of line, Chet, and out of character for you two, Maggie and Sally. I cannot believe you would take it this far. Mari was ready to press charges and close Golden Horizons down for good. I had to talk her out of it."

"Wait a minute! That isn't true." I counter her, but the rumor is already out there. I'll never get back into the good graces of the residents if they think I tried to take their home away. Nice twist, Rae. Now, no matter what, she is the one who has tried to save the day.

Maggie and Sally start to cry. What a mess.

Chet is seated at the computer and reluctantly pulling up the site specs. When I ask him about the outside contributor, he shrugs.

"Spill the beans, Chet, or you will lose your courtyard and matinee privileges." I am stepping up because Rae has taken a backseat all of a sudden. Chet has something on her, I can tell.

"Give us that daily log keeper's info, and then, while you are there, pull up the list of everyone who has placed bets." I know I am right when I see Rae's crimson cheeks turn pale and pasty.

"Gladly." He sits upright and types in a few key words for a search. Within seconds a long list of names is called up onto the screen.

"We don't even have that many residents."

Chet laughs a master-of-the-universe, guttural laugh. "We went global. See." He points to the small pink letters by each person's name, indicating which country they live in. Some names are accompanied by an icon of a camera. We click on one and it shows two young Japanese men holding up a sign that reads "Mari rocks our world. Beautiful American woman we hope to marry you." They are wearing the "Will you Mari me?" T-shirt from the site with their torn jeans. Each holds a flower in their teeth.

"No!" This goes beyond surreal. I thank God my real picture was not used. I can always change my name, but plastic surgery is definitely beyond my budget.

"I have to say, I'm impressed with how well done this site is." Angelica nods her approval until I cock my head sideways and give her my "that's enough" scowl.

"Thank you. You're quite a smart and pretty young lady." Chet is still a mover and a shaker. He recognizes a kindred spirit in Angelica.

"Chet, stay with me. Who is this fan club president?"

"Here it is. All that we know, anyway. This is not someone who was in on the creation of the site. They just started adding great info. We all thought it helped the site, so we never questioned whom it might be."

I am shaking my head in amazement as a screen name appears against a black background. Bright cursive letters display "Yvette101."

"Well, that isn't much help," Sadie surmises.

But it is something about the curve of that Y that brings to mind a fabric version of the letter. My strange neighbor's sweater-clad chest flashes before my eyes.

That's it.

Another piece of the puzzle has just settled into place. I motion for the girls to follow me out. "Rae, I am going to check on this site, and if it still exists in one hour, I'm calling the police."

"Where are we going?" Caitlin asks but doesn't care. She's loving the action.

"*We* aren't going anywhere. I have some personal research to do."

Everyone except Caitlin, who grew up reading Nancy Drew mysteries, is glad to conclude this chapter of today's adventure. Sadie has a date soon and Angelica really wasn't as interested in resolving the situation as she was in springing it on me and watching my reaction; which, it turns out, has not only been emotional but physical. I'm breaking out in hives all over my face, neck, and chest.

"Is this stress or something from the walk?" I ask the others as I scratch my chin.

"We went where you went and we look normal. Enough said?" Angelica offers.

"What do you think, Caitlin?" I ask my nice friend directly.

"I think it's a good thing they used Cecilia." And only because it was Caitlin and not Angelical who made this joke, I laugh. I laugh until my hives sting and my sides ache. What else can a girl do when she realizes that her lack of a social life has been made globally public?

What else can I do when Russian men are using money they earned by selling a milk cow to bet that I will not find love for three to five years?

Laugh and pray it all goes away.

The Why Behind Y

Casually I wave to the landlord as he rakes invisible leaves. I have always suspected that he watches for renters with cable to leave so he can watch ESPN or the cooking channel. He picks up his shears and moves to the side yard to trim the shrubs, and I make my move over to Yvette's unit. I realize I have stumbled over her name because the initial sound is that of "E" not "Y." How trick-e.

Her sole window is level with the sidewalk. From my crouched position I can see worn, ugly linoleum the color of sludge running beneath a thirdhand table. There are books beneath two of its legs to keep it level for the computer and the short stack of dishes that burden it. Yvette passes just below the window and I pull back. Flattened against the stucco exterior wall, I realize that my body is casting shadows into her one room. I step over the length of the window to the other side. Dozens and dozens of flowers fill vases, many of which are mine, and cups, buckets, and the rust-stained sink. Lots of them are past their prime, and Yvette is gathering the dead leaves and petals into a paper bag. These endless bouquets are proof of her involvement with my site, though I hadn't expected the direct link to the bizarre phone calls.

Why would someone concoct such a scheme to get flowers from strange men?

I rap on the window and a startled Y looks up into the shaft of sunlight. I wave but she does not know who it is. I hear her release the chain lock and wait a moment for her to peek her head around the corner.

"Mari!" She swallows big and makes a Donald Duck sort of quack.

Watching her squirm is not as satisfactory as I had imagined.

"Yvette. Yvette. It's so good to see you. I was just passing by and thought I would ask if I could get a couple vases back. Out of the blue I received a ton of flowers. And a big platter of sushi from some guys in Japan. It's the weirdest thing." I pause to see if she will understand that I am on to her.

She closes the front door behind her and spends a moment figuring out a plan, an excuse, a distraction. "I could bring you some later today. I…they're kind of full right now. Would this afternoon be okay?"

Though it goes completely against my initial mood, I'm feeling nothing but compassion toward her. Here's a girl who spends hours on end in a one-room closet with a chair, a lopsided table that holds her computer and a few plates, and a rickety cot. Her only decor and view are posters that promote skateboard parks and software.

"Do you work with computers for a living?"

I think back to when her father carried those large, heavy boxes that must have been filled with cables, monitors, hard drives, and other tools used to pry into another person's life.

The rise and fall of her adam's apple gives away her self-conviction. "Yes. I design purchase sites for retailers."

Of course.

I typically avoid confrontation, but I don't want to spend the rest of my time living in these apartments avoiding her. "Yvette, I know about the postings on my site. That you have been discussing my life with total strangers."

Her eyes grow big and her hand goes to the doorknob. "Oh," she says meekly.

I wait for an explanation that doesn't come.

"How did you even find out about the site? This is all so strange."

"After we met, I did an online search of your name. It's a habit of mine. I search anyone I meet. I figured I would see mostly the usual…any appearances in the daily paper, any arrests…"

"Arrests!"

"Well, anything that is public record. But then I see several sites with your blog listed and wham! It didn't take long to see that most of this site was falsified, but the posted snail-mail address was yours." She shrugs and giggles. "Cecilia Jade. That made me laugh."

"And the flowers?"

She shrugs again. "After a few conversations with you, I figured that the site was not your doing. And I don't know anyone around here, so I went online and started chatting with folks at your blog-turned-site."

"And the flowers?" My patience is thinning.

"Look at this place. I barely get any light. It's a gopher hole. Where I used to live, with my mom, we had a huge garden. I missed the colors, so I started to mention your floral preferences."

"But how'd you manage to…?"

"I said you could only receive deliveries on Tuesdays."

"The day I stay late at work. Smart. Then you would just sign for them." I feel as though I am reciting the closing scene of a *Scooby-Doo* episode. "I have been plagued by weird men calling me!"

Yvette's small hand rises to cover her mouth. She is shaking. "I am so sorry. They must have looked up your number. I never gave it out… promise. Oh, Mari. I hope you didn't get frightened by anyone."

I decide to leave out my many fearful visions of Sal, Warren, Ken, and the others. "No, but I was starting to wonder who was out to get me."

"You know that first day I came by to borrow a vase…I almost told you everything. But you were acting sort of strange, and I thought maybe you already knew and were mad at me. I stopped interfering with the site after that."

Her confession evokes my compassion once again. How could anyone stay mad at the girl with Y on her chest?

A big idea sprints into my mind. Maybe I could interfere in her life. "I want you to come to my place tomorrow night. Say, around seven? I'm having a couple friends over, and I'd love to have you join us."

Her mouth opens but nothing comes out. The back of her hand pushes her wire-rimmed glasses up her nose so they can slide back down. It's the first time that I notice more than the Y or the distant look of preoccupation on her face. She has beautiful eyes with rich, thick lashes. Like Caitlin, she is a fortunate soul born with the look of eye liner and mascara.

"Yeah. That'd be okay. You aren't mad?"

"I won't have the SWAT team waiting or anything. I've wanted to invite you over several times before. Why not start off on a new foot?"

"Okay, see ya. Thanks." She opens the door with her hand behind her back and promptly ducks into her cubbyhole.

The girl doesn't have to pretend to be me to find happiness. God only knows I am struggling with that objective. But she does need something I do have—friends.

I spend the afternoon tidying my apartment as a way to control some kind of mess in my life. I keep the television on for company, though this isn't necessary because every half hour I get calls from my concerned friends. Incuding one from Angelica, who says she printed the entire website in case I need to go to the police.

Then the call from Rae, who sounds puffy and full of whatever it is she uses to keep her meanness afloat. "The deed is done per your request, Mari. I'm so appalled that you threatened this place. You talk so much of service, but when push comes to shove, you only care about yourself. Don't think I don't know about the résumés you have circulating." She pauses to breathe her heavy breath pattern.

I take in her toxic words because she reinforces the question I ask of myself: Are my efforts all about me?

Even during this unpleasant stay in the state of guilt, I recognize that Rae's next line is undoubtedly all about her.

"You don't know the meaning of service."

She huffs and she puffs.

And she blows my little job away.

Phone Home

I spend the next morning in a haze of uncertainty. I don't know if I really lost my job or if Rae was just letting off steam. Either way, I stay home. If she didn't mean it, let her sweat it out. If she did, I have little desire to step onto the premises and give her a chance to reinforce her decision in front of God and everyone. Yes, I have fantasized about such a confrontation, but when such an opportunity is real enough to taste, only the bitter is guaranteed, never the sweet.

I consider calling Sadie to ask her about my rights and whatever else someone who manages people would know, but I'm afraid she will coordinate another intervention. I'm not up for too much honesty right now. Besides, my cupboards aren't stocked.

My stomach aches because this is what it knows to do on command to warrant a day off. In grade school I missed a couple days a month due to mysterious stomach pains. Excuses to stay home were necessary because it was the only time I could have my mom to myself. I wonder if she ever knew.

There is that urge to call home. This round I cannot claim there is not

enough time. In fact, I cannot think of any of the usual excuses that surface to prevent me from a gesture of need.

I arrange the couch and surrounding area with all that I require for
this effort. My blanket, a cup of coffee, my slippers, a glass of water, a
toaster pastry, and Elmo.

I position my finger to autodial 1. I programmed that as my "in case
of emergency" number, which is funny, because if something did happen,
my folks could not do much from several thousand miles away. But here
I am, in what I consider a crisis if not an emergency, and it feels good to
know they are only one digit away from me, here on my couch, in this
place of sagebrush and bull snakes and magnificent sunrises. One of
which fills my living room window. I watch for a few minutes and then
press down.

I imagine Mom with her loose ponytail and Land's End long-sleeved
shirt, and Dad with his big feet encased in Timberlands, rushing around
as they clean up after breakfast and organize last details for the volunteers
coming in the afternoon. They each have a list of people to call taped to
their phone. Not a day goes by that they are not expressing their passion
and conviction to someone at the city, county, state, and federal levels.
Mom's theory was that as soon as a decision maker asks his or her secretary to not put their calls through, they are on that person's radar. Just
where they want to be.

"Schmidt?" My mom's voice is stronger than I remember. We have
spoken only a few times in recent months. Once I started submitting my
résumé, I was reluctant to talk with her. She, like Rae, would know something was up.

"It's me, Mom. Mari."

"Hey, you! Ted, it's Mari!" She calls out to my dad excitedly, even
though she clearly was anxiously awaiting a call from Carl Schmidt,
county commissioner.

I can hear her place the cell phone in the cradle and the familiar echo
of shelter sounds as she switches me to speaker phone mode.

"Hey, if it isn't our princess of the South. How are you, dear?" Dad's voice, in contrast to Mom's, sounds pale and tired. His exuberance is heartfelt but only surface level in energy. My own heart beats quickly as my spirit remembers how often stress was a part of our daily experience. Money was tight. There was always a battle to be fought. Conflict between several of the children was imminent. And always there was no time for rest.

I tap together the heels of my slippers and am glad to be home. Right here.

"We're so glad you called. You know we are well into preparations for Resurrection Week. Wish you were here."

Sure. Getting free labor is always good.

"Knowing you two, you have it all under control. It's only disguised as chaos."

"How long since you last visited?" My dad laughs, implying only that I must have forgotten that the underlying current at the shelter was always chaos. But the answer to that question replaces my fake stomach-ache with a full-fledged ulcer.

"How are the plans going?" This upcoming week is second only to the Thanksgiving Festival in the shelter's annual cycle of fund-raising. Resurrection Week follows Easter and is a full seven days of celebrations and efforts to involve the community with the shelter and vice versa. Several open houses and tours kick off the week. Then the kids sign up to do chores and errands for area residents or for businesses. The event has grown so big that there is not one politician associated with children's services, foster care, or social services who does not make an appearance. Usually they wait for the street fair on the last day so they get the most publicity for their small effort. But there are a few who personally care about the work and help lead tours and arrange interviews from the site to raise awareness and hopefully money. For them and the shelter.

As they share, in tandem, the plans for next month's party, I do feel excited about their ideas. Only a bit of me acknowledges that I did get this part of their genes. They ask about the Golden Golden Gala, and I play up the success without mentioning Beau...Rae...

Me.

Fah so la ti do.

"I visited one of the resorts this week. Majestic Vista. You should check out their website. It's incredible. And they host several charity functions each year." I introduce the topic with a service slant, hoping this will soften what I am telling them. They knew when I moved thousands of miles away that I was determined to end up in a world other than the one I grew up in. But when I landed a "temporary" spot with Golden Horizons, they had been so proud.

"That sounds really nice, dear. Sure does." They give me their reassurances. "But I'll bet after that big successful anniversary party, they won't want to let you leave the retirement home."

The very blatant segue to the obvious point of my call comes and goes. It's one thing to disappoint them with a well-paid position that has benefits and perks. It's quite another to tell them I got booted out of a low-paying, no perks, "doing it for the ministry" kind of career.

"Oh, hey. You'll never guess who our latest boomerang is." Mom peals with absolute Christmas-morning delight.

While suburban parents use this term to refer to their grown children who return home for a rent-free existence, "boomerang" is my parents' term of endearment for those kids who go through the shelter and later return to help in some way. Many times it is for Resurrection Week, but occasionally it is someone who returns to assist on a regular basis. Even though my inability to return lowers their percentage of these boomerangs, they unofficially have the best record among shelters in town.

"Thalia?" I say this name after ten years of not. She was my nemesis in the house, but I liked that she played a motherly role with the other kids. It meant that I did not have to.

"Oh, wouldn't you love that!" Dad, at least, remembers the rivalry.

"Marcus is here."

My heart stops. Another name I have not spoken in years. Not since I left Washington, D.C., with a vehement commitment to break all ties to anyone and anything relevant to my childhood. The biggest break was not with my parents or the tree-lined street I knew as my only home. It was with Marcus.

I can hear on the phone that Dad is calling upstairs for him. By "he's here," they mean right there.

"Please no, please no," I whisper.

"What dear?"

I forgot about the magnification of speaker phone. "Oh…I said Elmo. He's getting fussy."

"I miss that crazy kitten. Actually, he's gettin' to be an old man by now."

Yet another indication of how much time has passed confronts me. I hear Dad say he cannot find Marcus and how disappointed he'll be to miss my call.

"Mom, I have to go. Um…good luck with the plans, and I'll let you know if I make any big career moves."

Liar.

"Dad thinks Marcus might be down in the kitchen prepping lunch. Can you hold on? It's so good to hear your voice."

"I really need to go."

Mom doesn't know all that upsets me, but she senses I'm not up for talking to Marcus. She makes an excuse for me. "Honey, Mari is a busy woman, like her mother, and she needs to get back to work. She'll catch him next time."

"Thanks, Mom. Love you."

She chuckles with understanding. "I love you too. Don't be any stranger."

Our usual sign-off feels good. But when I hang up the phone, I feel very alone. I go where I rarely go…to my old photo album. It was a project for high school and one I bemoaned endlessly. But this cheap, three-ring binder was one of the few possessions I brought with me to college in Arizona.

My fingers know which page to turn to by feel. The edge of this photo page has a slight indentation from so many visits.

I close my eyes and open them. Close again…flip to the page…then open. My eyes go straight for Marcus' face. He was one of the only guys at the shelter who had to shave. In this shot he has a five o'clock shadow that serves to contrast with his bright smile. At age thirteen, Marcus had come to the shelter very hardened, yet he was one of the first to embrace everything about his new home. By the time he reached high school, the social worker's reports reflected that he was a serious student and a very well-adjusted individual. A real success story.

In this photo, his Cubs baseball cap is angled to the side; the tip is hitting my big hair as I lean my head toward his shoulder. Our arms are linked, and we have on matching Cubs sweatshirts. I didn't give a dang for baseball, but Marcus was from Chicago, and he was passionate about this tie to home. When your mother forgets your name because she is high, and your father forgets your birthday because he wasn't around for your birth, a baseball team can serve as a substitute for family. This version comes with posters, emblem-covered attire, and statistics that are good to pour over and memorize. That way, if anyone asks about your childhood, you can distract them with fascinating facts about your home team. It's the oldest trick in the book of denial.

Elmo resituates himself, placing a paw onto the page. With my finger, I retrace the face of the only boy to ever capture the attention of my heart.

Until recently, that is.

Matchmaker

The residents are up in arms over your firing, Mari. The rumors were growing with each hour. They had to shut down the game session because people were chanting 'Mari' instead of 'bingo.'" Lysa enters my apartment with a box that used to hold copier paper. Now it holds the very limited proof of my past five years of work. She catches her breath and then hugs me.

"Thanks for doing this. Once I realized it was true," I point to the box, "I couldn't face going in to retrieve my things." I'm shocked at how choked up I am.

She shakes her head. I can tell she has been crying.

"I'll have to find a way to say goodbye to the residents." My mind wanders for a moment, and then it occurs to me who I will miss the most. "Tess!" I put my hand over my mouth to stifle a sound that does not emerge. To not be able to talk with Tess again would break my heart.

"These should help." Lysa hands me the stack of notes in her right hand. They are tied with a yellow ribbon I recognize from Tess' stationery supply. I skim through the signatures on the various sheets of paper;

these goodbyes and condolences are from my favorite residents. Lysa's kindness has touched me. I get teary against my personal vow not to. It's a good thing, I tell myself. How many times have I almost quit on my own accord?

I excuse myself to the kitchen as Lysa trades one of her health care industry white shirts for one of my slouchy sweaters. I quickly reemerge from my galley kitchen with all that I can offer the person who has saved me from humiliation with Rae—a box of crackers and some canned cheese. Like two thirteen-year-olds at a sleepover, we kick our shoes off and get comfy on the couch. Feeling the need to expand for comfort, we take up lots of room, digging our toes into the nubby fabric to press our backs into the arms at each end. We face one another and at first just grimace our disbelief back and forth as we reach for crackers. But halfway through the can of cheese we are laughing and trying to make sense of the past two days.

"It's brilliant, really," Lysa says with her arms stretched out. "Rae figures out that you are planning to leave anyway, so she takes advantage of this computer caper as a diversion. She fabricates a story that you were ready to press charges against your own residents. She comes off like she, of all people, is defending these folks." Lysa slaps her forehead with incredulity.

"You think it worked?" Sadness covers me. I can't bear that people believe such lies about me.

"Maybe one small faction believes that garbage, but only her pets. Even Chet is telling the truth about the situation. I saw him confronting Rae once the news was out. I think there is something between those two."

"I thought that too!" I shout and then backpedal. "You mean, something like a conflict or a secret…not like they're dating, right?"

Lysa can barely breathe, she is laughing so hard. A silk embroidered pillow comes straight toward my head.

"Hey! No beating up on the unemployed. The downtrodden. The misplaced worker. The unjustly booted."

"The free. Don't forget that part. In some ways I am jealous of your…" she pulls a positive angle on my situation from the air, "your life without commitments."

"No commitments except rent, food, car payment…but those are silly things." The gravity of my situation sinks into my skin, my spirit. Not even the last squirt of cheese will save me.

As the conversation hits a wall, there is a knock. I have completely forgotten the matchmaking I had planned for this evening. I slog over to the door in my baggy jeans and the T-shirt I use when painting furniture. On my stoop I find the first half of this blind date standing with several vases in her arms.

"Yvette!" I welcome her by speaking her name, and it feels good. "Come on in. I'd like you to meet my friend and former coworker, Lysa."

"F-former coworker?" This news gives her good cause to worry. But what she doesn't know is that I have forgiven her.

"Oh, that's a really boring story. Short and recent, but no twists of interest. Lysa and I were just discussing the benefits of being unemployed."

Another knock returns me to the door. I open to find Caitlin in a tulle shirt with black jeans and Zane on her arm. After taking in all the details of Yvette's life, I made a call to Caitlin to see if she had any possible interest in Zane. When she answered no, I asked if she would help me hook him up with my neighbor and cyber spy.

I introduce everyone, and while Caitlin compliments Yvette's monogrammed peasant blouse and Yvette openly admires Caitlin's boots covered in old-fashioned travel stickers, I make plans to get the right couple out the door.

"I feel really bad, everybody. Here I had these tickets to a viewing of Extreme Skateboarding, but after today's events, I'm just not up for it." I look at the floor for a while, letting the silence become awkward.

Zane and Yvette's eyes light up simultaneously at the mention of the original plan. I'm this close to closing this deal. Zane graciously inquires about my day.

"She lost her job." Caitlin announces, and when she sees the appropriate look of shock on his face, she plans the handoff cleverly. "I was really excited to go to this film, but now I feel I should stay with Mari. To comfort her. You understand, don't you Zane?"

"Yes. Absolutely." His disappointment is only slightly apparent. "Mari, this is probably a silly consolation, but I just wanted you to know that your tip about the Grease and Go was brilliant. I've been telling all my friends about it. I think I'll sell it at my store."

Perfect topic Zane-man. "Zane, I remember you talking about wanting to get Earth Surfin's website going…and it turns out that online retailing is Yvette's expertise."

"I should get in touch with you sometime, if you wouldn't mind." Zane gives Yvette a glance, and she shyly nods.

"Hey, why not now?" I play up the brilliance of this coincidental arrangement. "Why don't you two take these tickets and have a good time? Please. I'd feel terrible if everybody's night was ruined because of my unfortunate circumstances."

The two future soul mates look at each other to get a feel for what the other is thinking. They reach for the tickets at the same time, bumping hands.

We all bid them farewell, waving from the top of the stairs until they climb into Zane's jeep.

"Did I just witness an ambush date?" Lysa inquires as she rummages through my kitchen in search of the largest spoons. We both noticed the vat of ice cream Caitlin has brought with her.

"I prefer to call it a double blind date."

"Maybe you could earn a living doing this matchmaking thing. Tonight was very clever; I'd hire you." Caitlin considers one of the many possibilities before me. "But why'd you do it? After all Yvette has done to you?"

"What'd she do?" Lysa asks with a mouth full of butter brickle. Her utensil of choice, a soup ladle, comes in for another humongous scoop.

"She's the outside hacker…the fan club president," explains Caitlin.

"No way!" Lysa swallows the calories and the news. "So why *did* you do such a nice thing for her?"

"The way I see it, if a person is desperate enough to pretend to be me, she deserves a new gig."

Nobody disagrees, and my official pity party commences with a round of brain freezing bites of butter brickle.

Passing Notes

My back feels the pressure of a gaze. I turn expecting to see Elmo perched on top of the bookshelf, but it is the suggestion box that wants to be noticed. Lysa smuggled it out for me so I could read the fruit of my labor from the party.

A childhood memory flashes in my mind. I hold a red construction paper heart folder close to my own and rush home after our Valentine's Day party at school. Unlike my friends who tore into theirs between suckers and chocolate kisses, I wait until I am alone to open each small envelope and read notes of friendship, hoping to find hidden references to a crush.

Now, I reach into my box with similar anticipation. Small, crisp pieces of linen paper with gold embossing that I had placed by the display are now filled with short, sweet thoughts and memories. Many family members recall the difficulty of bringing their loved one to live in a facility, but their sentiments express gratitude for those who made that difficult transition easier. A mental checklist reminds me that I was the one to initially welcome many of the people who enjoyed the dance floor the other night.

One by one, their childlike expressions of fear, worry, and even abandonment fill the space of my mind. It felt good to ease their concerns each time.

Sinking down into the sofa cushions, I unfold the last note. At first glance, I don't match the slanted cursive with writing that I should know. "Mari, In case I do not tell you this more than a dozen times, tonight is spectacular and you, my dear, are divine in that dress. All my love and admiration, Tess."

It's sweet. But it's not…

I realize that I was hoping to have word from him. Mine enemy.

Just as I am about to revisit the disappointment from days in that overstuffed lobby chair twenty years ago, I see my handkerchief through the slit in the box.

The handkerchief that I forgot to get back from Beau.

Though I am sad he did not feel comfortable returning it to me in person, it does provide me with a chance to thank him for his thoughtfulness. I reach in and grab the embroidered, wrinkled fabric. I take care of people every day. But when I stood on tiptoe and blotted his tie, I realized, for the first time, how great it could be to take care of one special person.

Lifting the handkerchief to my nose, I inhale the scent of his cologne. I smooth out the wrinkles and know this square piece of fabric won't be washed for a while. This is a bit pathetic, but I am learning to be honest with myself. As I press down and eliminate the creases, I see a bit of blue. Slowly, I unfold the white cotton and discover a message scrawled in crayon just for me.

"When you are ready for our second dance, call me. 602-555-4325—Beau. P.S. I got this idea from Haley. Watch out for her!"

I outline his phone number over and over until my fingertips store it in memory. Could this new life I have been forced into include the courage to call a guy like Beau? Angelica wouldn't hesitate for a second…unless she liked the guy. Is that what will keep me from dialing this number? I hold a blatant invitation in my hands and still assume he is merely being courteous.

Before the night is over and exhaustion consumes me, I have written Beau's number down in five different places, just in case I lose the handkerchief, or toss the address book, or crash my hard drive (known to happen), or forget where the yellow piece of legal pad paper is tucked in my Bible. But it is while I am engraving the ten digits into my toaster that it hits me…I don't want to risk losing this number because, for the first time, I might be willing to risk my pride for a boy.

Correction, this boy.

For five years I have built up such a defense to the name Beau that I shudder when the name comes to mind. Anything I have done, from organizing bingo tournaments to teaching residents how to knit, has been compared to his abilities. And I never measure up. How could I ever feel anything except small and useless in his presence?

Yet I did feel something else. I felt safe and strong and able to express myself around him. This perfect person who set the bar so ridiculously high for my glamourless job did not come across as judgmental even when I stood pouting.

While getting ready for bed, I notice my briefcase has fallen over during one of Elmo's pursuits of imaginary bugs. I'm restuffing the leather with random notes, a crossword puzzle, issues of *Lucky, Self,* and *Contemporary Woman* from my recent effort to understand my age group, and then I see what I have forgotten all about.

Beau's file.

His face comes to mind instantly. And because of our encounter, my possession of this personnel file is even more invasive and wrong and—let's face it—incredibly lucky. Without calling him, without swallowing my pride, I can get to know Beau. I clap to turn on my bedside lamp, and for the next hour my thoughts are all of him. I read every review (all excellent), every recipe (Rae wasn't kidding; the guy did win local cookoffs), every comment submitted by residents and coworkers (he's a god).

By the time I have read it all, I am more relieved than disappointed. I didn't really want to find dirt on him.

Not now.

But just so I can make peace with this picture-perfect file, I add one small blemish. On his last review I add the notation, "Seems too good to be true. Someone should look into this further."

Before I drift off, a question enters my mind. If I have faced the enemy, and he has kind eyes and a squeaky-clean record and doesn't seem to be an enemy at all…who have I really been battling all these years at Golden Horizons?

Taking Chances

Do you believe in plagues?" I ask at a volume loud enough to be heard over the yells and shouts of pre-Easter shoppers. (I have yet to hear a hosanna among them.)

"Like locusts?" Caitlin runs her fingers over the latest fabric combinations. "This is sad." She looks with disappointment at the department store's version of a display.

"More like…lousy luck, date drought, faith famine…contemporary plagues."

"Oh, what's this one?" Caitlin points to the speakers overhead.

"I dunno," I say, an unwilling participant.

"Sure you do. Name it," Caitlin chirps.

I listen to a few beats of the song. "Muskrat Love."

She listens for a bit and nods overzealously. "Incredible. And no, I don't think you are experiencing personal, contemporary plagues, if that is what you are getting at."

"Maybe not full-fledged biblical plagues, but perhaps these days God serves up plaguettes. Mini-disasters to remind us of his power."

She rolls her eyes at my twisted thinking. "I can explain your date drought plaguette, as you call it."

"Oh, yeah? Do I want to know?"

"You are picky. Holding out for something great. You, Mari, have had dates lately and you just aren't interested." She says this while trying on a hat of purple fake fur. "Whereas I have not had a date in nearly two years. If anyone has been infested by plagues, it is me."

"Correction. One date. What is your plaguette?" I don't tell her about Beau. Not yet. Besides, I probably ruined a perfectly good chance at a real date. I wish I knew if he put the handkerchief in the box before or after my childish outburst.

"Mary Margaret is trying to take credit for the outfit I created for you. Can you believe it?" She adjusts her revised apron look self-consciously. Two aprons tied together create a skirt and a third apron tied in the back over a turtleneck. It reminds me of a baby's bib, but I know she is hoping the apron look made locally famous by the Kevin Milano photo will be noticed out in public.

"I'll vouch for you. Just tell me how. I'd love to take on Mary Margaret." I pantomime rolling up my sleeves for a fight.

"I don't suppose you will have any more photo ops? As great as that caption was, I'm afraid I'll need a second chance."

I examine the combination she has just pulled from nearby shelves and racks: a striped blouse, pencil skirt, and a pair of Doc Martens. She is discreetly draping them over the display figure closest to her while watching for the salesclerk. "You'll get your chance; I just know it."

"Miss! Miss, can I help you?" a salesgirl comes from behind the counter and approaches us as fast as her white boots can carry her. Blond, sleek hair is rolled in giant, old-fashioned rollers. I think she and Caitlin should get along, but they eye each other with distrust and disapproval. However, there is a moment just before the woman's lip curls like Lisa Presley's that I see something that resembles respect for Caitlin's impromptu display.

"No, just looking. Thank you." Caitlin waves and we rush out the door.

"Let's just go home. If we put together a noteworthy outfit for my date with Jace, it should be easier to plan clothing for Sadie's event." I desperately want to cut this afternoon short so I can look at those ten digits and consider the possibility of making a call.

"Practical, but shortsighted. What if this weekend presents you with an opportunity and you are not dressed for it? I've seen your closet, and you definitely at least need a stellar pair of shoes. Ah," she shoots at my forthcoming argument. "I'm right. We need to go two blocks and take a left."

I play the reluctant child who insists on immediate gratification while shopping. We stop at an ice cream stand and a corner coffee kiosk before arriving at the store, Best Foot Forward. "That's so Angelica," I say when I see the stiletto-logo adorned door.

"Well, they do carry her overly promoted brands, but they also include a lot of unknown, fabulous labels."

"No, that's Angelica. Look." I nod my fudge-dipped cone toward the woman just passing through the doors.

"Stick with me. She'll lead you toward a shoe purely for the name. Just watch. Down the cone or toss it."

"No fair," I whine. My nap time is approaching quickly. As we enter the very chic narrow store filled with well-lit glass shelves, I mimic Angus' greeting. "Angel!"

This must be Angelica's code name within her inner circle because she turns around with an air of popularity and known-ness. But when her eyes take in two old friends, she puts on a more casual countenance. The one she uses for everyday intimidation purposes.

"Looks like we all need shoes for the stargazer party." Caitlin decides to start us all off on the same foot, so to speak.

"Need, want…all the same when it comes to shoes." Angelica's eyes brighten with purpose as she looks down at my raggedy pair of Converse sneakers. "I'd say it's a blessing I am here." With authority she turns to the saleswoman and beckons her by name. "Lucinda, let's start with these, and these, and where is the April release from Manolo?" She grabs various styles by their skinny straps and dangles them in front of Lucinda's permanent smile.

I shouldn't be surprised to find that Angelica knows the store date for shoe arrivals the way I know the dates for new Muzak compilations and books on aging.

Caitlin stabs me in the side with her sunglasses to be sure I am noticing Angelica's gorilla label tactics. I hold my hands up, submitting to whatever unfolds and not taking any responsibility.

"Lucinda, is it? Nice to meet you. I'm Caitlin and this is Mari. Could you bring out Revel Yell's new four-inch heel?" She positions herself between Angelica and the woman in charge. "And if you have any of last year's divine black leather boots from GaGa, bring those with you too. The ones with the tassel wrap, not the buckle. Thank you."

Two can play this game, apparently.

I sit down on a large scoop of a chair that resembles a guitar pick more than a piece of furniture. Such comfort. They can fight over my feet, but my rear belongs to this goofy chair. Lucinda snaps her fingers and I start to rise, thinking I am not worthy to sit here. Her command brings out two assistants. One to take our size and style requests, and one to serve sparkling cider and petits fours while we wait.

Nobody told me snacks were involved. "We should have my next intervention here." I lick pink frosting from my finger and am ignored. Caitlin and Angelica are facing off, peering into tissue paper and sleek boxes to accept or reject offerings from the back room. My unsolicited comments and shoe opinions are clearly irrelevant to today's outcome.

Half a dozen petits fours later, Lucinda is looking haggard, whereas Angelica and Caitlin seem energized as they near a consensus. Torn between two cults of fashion, I'm the disheveled recruit they would all love to shape, dress, and use to bring others into the fold.

Assistant one clears a path from the back room to my feet. And as she bows down and removes my sneakers, Angelica and Caitlin stand on either side of her like the little shoulder-perching devil and angel that appear in dream sequences about temptation. They both are grinning widely. Could it be that the shoe will fit and I will be transformed into some version of myself that pleases both?

Breath is held all about me as I watch a pair of lavender shoes emerge from the rubble. The heel is considerable, but the trim is a very delicate, an iridescent weave of fabric so fine that at first I think it is merely a shaft of light from Lucinda's diamond ring reflecting off of the satin. This thread winds the length of the shoe, from the heel to the very tip of a slim band of satin where the most intricate, understated fabric flower adorns my big toe.

I am captivated but don't want to give in too easily. "I'm afraid of heights." I take a few steps and then tell my group of observers about a speech I gave in seventh grade against the Chinese practice of binding women's feet. Seems my generation has introduced its own version of social status through podiatry pain.

"You get used to it, believe me. And the downward slant makes you look like you have somewhere to go," Caitlin responds while Angelica likely wonders how on earth we all remain friends.

"Oh, hey…that could work for me."

"Shall I wrap these up for you?" Lucinda moves so quickly I almost don't notice the price tag. It is the extra zero that catches my eye.

Now I hold my breath. "This is not practical. Maybe if I had not blown my only chance at Majestic Vista…and lost my job…"

My two friends are delighted with their selection. They have crossed the great divide for the sake of shoes and friendship and will not accept no for an answer.

Caitlin repeats her view of dressing for opportunity and Angelica could not be more agreeable. "Yes, you must. I just wish you had a date to see these shoes."

The smile sneaks up on me.

Angelica notices. "Really? Do tell." She strings this out with great amusement.

I tell them about Beau, the party, and the handkerchief...but nothing of engraving the number on my toaster. Still, they understand the seriousness of my interest.

Angelica hands the shoe box to Lucinda and places her hand on top as if taking an oath. "That's it then. You absolutely must. She'll take these."

Caitlin is equally thrilled. "Wear them for confidence when you call Beau and ask him to Sadie's event. The timing is too perfect."

I protest while downing the last of the cider straight from the bottle. "But will these really be in season ever again?"

Caitlin has the answer to this. "Taking chances, Mari, is always in season."

I look at their faces, which are so often scrunched in opposition to the other's viewpoint. But today their best foot forward is in a common direction.

As I hand Lucinda my zero-balance credit card I am telling myself, "I must take this chance." I'm not a shopper at heart, but today I am buying wholeheartedly into this ideology about life and fashion...and other important things.

Suddenly, I have a fantastic desire to make toast.

Stars and Stripes Forever

I wait as though Beau is not going to show up. I have told myself to not put on my new shoes until he knocks at the door so that I don't appear overly ready. I pace, my stomach aches, and I check the television schedule again to see if there is something worth canceling date number two for, or that will be a consolation prize if I am stood up. All I have to do is look at Beau's personnel file to know he is a stand-up guy rather than a standing-up guy.

Elmo senses my anxiety and hides beneath my couch where he is howling a personal sonnet of fret. I try to coax him out with canned cat food, but he is determined to stay put until I leave, taking my nervous energy with me.

The bell rings. I do a Rae mule impersonation in front of my mirror before opening the door. A big bouquet of flowers is extended at eye level. Lily petals tickle my nose and I sneeze.

"Sorry about that, Mari." Beau removes the flowers from my breathing path and points the blooms toward the floor. "I didn't know you were…"

"No, I'm not! At all. I love flowers," I shout and grab the colorful bundle from his clutches so he'll feel good about his gentlemanly efforts. "Look, no sneezing." I wave the flowers in front of my nose at a respectable distance as he steps into my three by five entryway.

By now I have most of my vases back from Yvette. All except for two because Zane, it turns out, is quite an old-fashioned romantic.

My former enemy now sits on the edge of my couch and takes in the limited space of my dwelling. "Nice. I really love your style, Mari." I like that he likes using my name. It sounds nice gliding toward me on his deep voice. "You seem really calm. I'm more nervous than I thought I would be."

I glance over at the toaster and laugh at my obsessive nature. If he only knew. "I avoided caffeine for two days so I would come across this way." I confess the most acceptable part of my strange behavior and slip on my divine new shoes. At the door, I reach for my coat and Beau moves toward me to help me angle the sleeves to my arms. I had seriously considered wearing one of Tess' mink stoles, but I figured a gathering of plant and nature lovers was not the place to strut my animal exploitation attire.

"Are your friends meeting us there?" He asks with nothing better to ask.

"Yes. I'm so glad you will have a chance to meet them in one setting. I hope it won't feel like overload for a first…" I don't want to say the word in case he would choose different terminology to describe this encounter.

"Second date." Beau raises two piano playing fingers to correct me.

I smile inside and out.

I step out the door first, which is awkward because I have to double back and lock the door with my key. Standing face-to-face on the narrow step, I squeeze past him as he steps back as best he can. This motion actually juts his knee into my thigh and propels me forward with pain.

I have been humiliated in the fanciest resort in town. This is nothing.

The lapel of his jacket is now sticky from my lip gloss, and I am beginning to suspect that we will be the couple the normal or just-shy-of-normal couples look at for comfort. We each turn to face opposite directions, he toward the descending stairs and freedom, me toward the door, the solitude of my apartment, and Old Mari behavior.

Click. I turn the lock, refusing to let my past ways interfere with tonight's potential for a good second date.

Sadie looks like a model. The perfect hostess, she greets us graciously as we walk through a small covered courtyard and into the outdoor fairyland. She raises her eyebrows at me when Beau steps forward to take a small lantern from a large bamboo basket. I nod and scan the vicinity for her significant other.

Her slender hand points to the basket so I will follow Beau's lead, and then it discreetly directs my attention toward a sharply dressed man over by the telescope. He is even more handsome than the photo Sadie showed us on the website.

Angelica and Peyton and Caitlin make their way up the front walkway. I wave to them and motion for them to follow Beau and me as we choose a table near the band. As casual introductions are made around the circle, we set our individual lanterns down to mark our places and head for the dance floor.

I have only danced four times in my adult life. Publicly. And two of the times have been with Beau. We step onto the floor without the awkwardness I have planned on. My chin rests comfortably below his shoulder when we slow dance. This gives me time to try and rub out the still-mucky look of pink lip gloss on his nice suit.

When I finally called Beau, he confessed to just calling Tess to get my phone number. I thought that was exceptionally nice of him. He could have played it cool like other guys would. Let's face it…like I would. Who acts interested anymore? Expressing one's simplest desire to get to know someone further seems the kiss of death if you listen to anyone out there dating. I count on one hand the number of friends and perimeter people I know who are seeing other people. It becomes clear I have put way too much stock in what comes out of Angelica's mouth as being the voice of our generation.

The downside to his chat with Tess—he also got the latest news about my job status. Honestly, I am glad my holey laundry is out in the open. And it just keeps flapping. Throughout several dances and the start of our dinner, I ramble on and on about Rae's ridiculous accusations and the pressures of working at Golden Horizons. When I confess my recent goals and lifelong aspirations, he doesn't make me feel guilty. "A change right now might help you choose the next course of your path," he says while we nibble on endive salads before the formal program begins.

"That's what I was thinking." And how great it would be to survive the date drought and end up with Beau.

"Sometimes it's good to change lots of things in your life at once. To get it all over with." Beau laughingly presents a theory for disaster, but also one quite in favor of a new relationship.

I don't respond but keep my eyes fixed on the flickering luminarias that cast small halos around the gilded rose petals scattered about the table. I think of pretty Halo and how we will never be shoe locker buddies at the resort.

"Mari, Caitlin, Angelica, and friends, I'd like to introduce you all to the guest of honor, Carson Curtis. Carson...my dear friends."

As Sadie savors the moment, I turn to face my friend and the man who has captured her heart. "Hello, Carson. This garden is lovely. Such a wonderful idea for a contribution to the community."

He nods and accepts other congratulations and greetings from around the table.

"It's such a pleasure. I feel as if I know you all by now. I've told Sadie how lucky she is to have such a close group of friends. And how lucky I am to have met her. Why, I really think this entire garden came about because I wanted excuses to keep calling her." Carson speaks his heart, much to Sadie's surprise. She has remained professional around him for much of the evening, I noticed. This comment causes her to step closer to him and gently place her hand on his arm.

"We must make the rounds before the entrée is served. We'll see all of you afterward over by the telescope. Oh, look, Carson...the Ramirezes have arrived. I really must thank them for their generous contributions." Sadie looks beyond us to a table near the champagne fountain.

"As in Kay and Ricardo?" Caitlin, who has a complexion the tone of a latte, actually blanches. Her red lipstick is a stark smear of color across the canvas of her face.

"Why, yes. How do you…" Sadie's eyes are wide, and a look she rarely offers to others—pure surprise—crosses her features. "Are they relatives?"

"Parents," Caitlin says from behind the napkin into which she is spitting out a bite of garlic roll. She chokes slightly and reaches for her water glass.

"Parents!" All of a sudden Sadie doesn't know how to think of eclectic, strange-but-true Caitlin anymore. This friend who barely pays her bills, lives in a questionable neighborhood, and complains against corporate structure has affluent, socially revered Kay and Ricardo Ramirez for parents. By Sadie's look, their contributions are noteworthy. And so is this bit of information. "Well, let's walk over together." She motions like a kindergarten teacher rounding up kids from recess.

Narrowing her eyes a bit at Sadie's shock, Caitlin puts down her napkin with a tight fist. She stands slightly hunching over so her parents won't see her. A bizarre topiary is a gracious blocker for her small frame. "Don't tell them I'm here. That is the last thing I need. Promise."

"I…I won't. I mean, I promise. But wouldn't they know we are…"

Caitlin's look says it all. No. They know nothing about her or her life, and she plans to keep it this way.

Unable to contain myself, I try to peer over the tree shaped like a star to see the unknown parents. All I ever got out of Caitlin was the fact that the one is a psychologist and one is a scientist. I forget which is which. But I always knew or understood that they were wealthy. Obviously, this point had never crossed Sadie's mind. After all, she hadn't thought to ask Caitlin if she was related to these major donors.

When I turn back to Caitlin's chair, she is gone. I see the edge of a shrub still moving and hear her hiccups just beyond. I start to go after her. It takes Angelica, of all people, giving me the "how rude can you be" look to remind me that I have a date.

"Beau, I'm just going to go check on her. I'm sorry. Will you be okay here?"

"Definitely. Peyton and I have some common interests to discuss."

I'd like to think he means me. But I know he doesn't.

Caitlin sits on a stone bench and rubs her arms quickly, as though the warm night cannot penetrate her chills.

"Didn't you think they might be here?" I ask. The thought had occurred to me, but I figured maybe she and her folks were in one of their civil cycles.

"No. I don't know. I was excited about dressing up. Meeting Carson. And Beau…" She leans toward me and bumps my elbow affectionately. "I didn't think through the *they* factor. Did you see the look in her eyes?"

"That fancy shrub with a crew cut was in my way."

"Not my mom. Sadie. Her look was of acceptance or worth. It made me sick."

I don't ask why. I understand. Caitlin longs for Sadie's approval almost as if Sadie is a surrogate parental figure. And it is only when Sadie knows Caitlin comes from money that she seems to recognize her friend's worth. I don't want to get in the middle of this. And it is Sadie's night. I stay silent but show my support with a return nudge.

Tears roll down Caitlin's cheeks. After a few moments of silence her hiccups are replaced by several sighs to catch her breath. "It isn't Sadie's response. Or *just* her response, I should say. I'm sad because my dad's birthday is this weekend and we haven't spoken in quite a while. I'm mad at myself."

"Every story has two sides…" I present the appropriate cliché.

"Yeah, but if I express my opposition to their materialistic, status-oriented life with such conviction, I should also express my faith to them. They should see how I have changed because I am a Christian. Instead, I act like the petulant child who couldn't wait to leave home. I'm doing this all wrong, and I hate it."

I don't know whether to say it or not. When is encouragement a lecture? "Maybe tonight could change that. Maybe this entire night is not about Carson, Sadie, Beau, or the stars." I made a grandiose gesture to the brilliant night sky. "Maybe tonight is about you."

She pushes her cheeks back and forth to the side as though she is gargling with mouthwash and ponders this possibility. Just on the other side of a flowering cactus we hear a woman's startled cry that ends abruptly. I stand up and rush around the prickly arms of the plant and find an elegant woman in a lavender gown crumpled on the ground. The heel of her shoe is caught on a loose piece of flagstone.

"Oh, ma'am. Let me help you." I practice the art of picking up fragile bodies with expertise that comes from experience. I use my legs and am careful with her frame as I bring her to an upright position in two moves.

"Goodness gracious," she says, a bit faint from the quick motion. With only one shoe on, she falters and grabs my arm. When her eyes focus she sees her shoe…in three pieces on the stone walkway. "Wouldn't you know I bought those just for this event. That will teach me to impulse buy. Won't I look like the silly, old lady for the rest of the evening." She says this with a slight laugh, but I sense she is quite upset by the situation. "I only wanted to see the rest of the grounds."

"You know what? My friend Caitlin and I…" I point toward Caitlin but she is no longer by my side. "Well, my friends over at that table…we were talking about going without our shoes the rest of the night. There is something so romantic about dancing barefoot, don't you think?"

She responds as I expected her to. "It is a romantic thought for the young, I would agree."

"It also means I won't be needing these. What do you say?" I slip my feet out of *my* impulse purchase shoes. They have already worked their magic. They gave me the courage to call Beau, and that was worth half-a-month's rent.

She shakes her head to resist the offer, but the graceful flower on the toe catches her eye. "They are lovely..." she looks down at her dress and laughs. "And can you believe how well they match? Honey, do you really want to give up your shoes to a perfect stranger?"

"You aren't perfect yet..." I tease her with the shoes and she reaches for them.

We exchange names and information, and then Grace and I return to the party.

"Did I miss much?" I ask to point out the fact I am back. Beau and Peyton are talking up a storm while Angelica chats it up with some wealthy patrons who turn out to know the owner of her company.

"Hey there." Cute eyes are glad to see me. "You missed the unveiling of the telescope and Sadie's great speech. But I think her scope was set on Carson, so she'll never know."

"I cannot believe I wasn't here for that. Does that mean the evening is almost over?" I feel as though I could stay forever. Because we are outdoors, I don't have my usual gala jitters and subsequent desire to bolt for the nearest exit.

"It cannot end till the pretty lady dances. Come on." Beau grabs my hand.

"Angelica, let's get another twirl out there, shall we?" Peyton interrupts Angelica's schmooze session, and she doesn't seem to mind at all.

"I should look for Caitlin. I'm worried about her," I say privately to Beau.

He turns my body to face the dance floor. "Looks like you have nothing to worry about."

Caitlin, dressed in a creation of her own inspiration, is dancing with a man I presume to be her father. He exudes pride, and her petulant child expression has been replaced by a grin of contentment.

I'm a bit teary, actually. I feel blessed by tonight's events.

"Mari." Sadie and Carson are coming toward me quickly. I wonder if she is trying to get away from the dignified gentleman who follows her as she winds her way around the group of dancers.

"Mari. Before you take in your last dance, this gentleman wanted to say hello." She steps aside and reveals a man I know well, but not so well. I blink a few times and it comes back to me. Lionel Richardson.

"Such a small world," I say, offering my hand in greeting.

"It is indeed. I saw you earlier and had wanted to chat with you. And then you disappeared from sight." He motions toward the shrub.

"Sorry about that. It is so good to see you again. I hope you have enjoyed the event."

"It is a lovely event. Sadie always does an exceptional job." He pauses to refocus on his original intention. "I couldn't find you or my mother, and then she told me why you disappeared!" He points over to Grace, who waves in return like an excited child at a parade.

I have to laugh. What are the odds? Lionel reaches to shake my hand again.

"I'd like to welcome you to my team, Mari. That is, if you are still interested?"

Is this a pity hire? He never even interviewed me.

Does it matter?

No.

"Yes! Mr. Richardson, yes!" I shake his hand a bit violently, but he seems pleased nonetheless.

"I'll plan to see you Monday morning. My crew will be expecting you. Welcome aboard."

I look at Beau, who is beaming at my good fortune. My cruise ship, which never lands in any promising ports, has just maneuvered its way into the most fabulous location imaginable: my dream life. And there are still seven months until my thirtieth birthday. That is not only on track, but ahead of schedule.

And as if to mark the occasion, a camera flash goes off in our faces. I drop Lionel's hand and place mine over my eyes to shield them from momentary echo flashes. When vision returns, I see Kevin Milano, who gives me a quick nod before disappearing into the crowd for another photo op.

"Well, I think there will be a record of our agreement. See you soon." Lionel bows and walks past me toward another wealthy gentleman.

"Tonight couldn't have been more perfect," I say as I take in the scene about me…Caitlin's moment of truth, Sadie's look of love, Angelica's real laugh with no flipping of the hair, and Grace, who looks regal over by the champagne fountain. It occurs to me that I have repeated Jace's end-of-date line.

"Mari…" Beau pulls me toward him as the music begins.

"Yes?" I cannot handle mush. I want it, but I cannot handle it. Don't…

"It's our song." I realize that the last melody of the evening is indeed our song "Fly Me to the Moon."

I laugh in a bizarre tone. One-part joy and three-parts disbelief that I have met someone…a guy…who would even say "our song" on a second date. He must be the last guy on earth who would be so wonderfully old-fashioned and, let's face it, a bit cheesy. Angelica would be appalled.

I think of Tess' advice that it is hip to be square when it comes to love. Instead of focusing on the fact that Beau returns to Phoenix in three days, without wagering my own bet about my chances of finding love, and without thinking through the ways I might mess up my new job, I surrender to a night of miracles that turns my gratitude toward the keeper of those glorious stars above.

Saturday's Style Section

The photo features Sadie, Carson, Lionel, me, Beau, and a portion of Angelica's face as she looks on with shock. The short article occupies my attention all morning.

"The unveiling of Carson Curtis' night garden hosted by the Botanical Society was a festive affair that beckoned the likes of Majestic Vista's Lionel Richardson. Once again, Milano's camera has captured the fabulous look and style of Ms. Mari Hamilton, pictured here with bare feet, adding a surprising touch of whimsy to her fairy princess vintage Valentino. *Tucson Style* has found its fashion muse for the year. While always-elegant Sadie Verity directs attention to the stars, we'll keep our eye on Ms. Hamilton. It looks like Angelica Ross of Rex and Hunter pharmaceutical is already doing just that."

As I put the paper down on the kitchen table, I notice the real estate section. There, framed by a drawing of an intricate garden gate, is an ad for Canyon Crest. "The last wing of luxury condos will be available in six months. Reserve today!" I carefully tear it out and put it in my purse. Monday I will use my first lunch break as a fabulous Majestic Vista employee to call and reserve my future home.

The phone rings; on the couch Elmo resituates his large body away from the annoying sound. "Hello?" I am expecting Sadie but am pleasantly surprised to hear someone else.

"Did you see the paper? Is Angelica going to flip or what?"

I laugh with delight. Beau not only does the proper thing by calling me the next day, but he already knows my friends well enough to peg their response to the photo.

"Absolutely!" We laugh as though we do this every Saturday. I toy with my woven bracelet—Old Mari cannot believe this is real. The new Mari considers how incredibly real and normal this feels.

Third Date

The dark paneled walls of Divine, a posh restaurant in a resort even more exclusive than Majestic Vista, provide a rich, peaceful backdrop for Date Number Three. Angelica says it is the absolute best ambience for Date Three. Curiously, she hosts her top clients, doctors and psychiatrists, in this place of hushed conversations and violin music. And she wonders aloud why her clients become infatuated with her.

I don't think she really wonders.

Beau steps forward to check on our reservation. I use the opportune vantage point to admire the width of his shoulders, the tailoring of his suit, and his kind manner toward the hostess. He looks back to be sure I am okay. I wave from the damask-upholstered mahogany bench. All I need is a pillbox hat and I am royalty.

He does a little wave.

I am resting on a cloud—a silky, damask-covered cloud—watching this bit of heaven ask about "our table."

Our reservation.

Our future.

Our life.

"Our" is not a word I have used very honestly. I toss it out when I need to imply power. "I have a team of people backing me. I am not alone." This is what a false "our" is meant to connote.

Just last week I called the cable company to report my missing Classics Network. Said repeatedly to the customer service rep, "our" was intended to conjure up visions of a bulky husband—surely standing next to me, breathing just inches from the receiver—who would be very, very upset if he missed the Gene Kelly film festival.

But "our" in the amiable, amorous, collective "we" meaning has not been a part of my vocabulary. Hearing Beau say it several times in the span of minutes makes me want to try it out.

"It's *our* third date," I say to the gentleman next to me, who is reading the *Wall Street Journal* with great interest to show his great disinterest in my presence. My ears recognize that I have said the "our" part a bit like Tony the Tiger. He shifts to cross his left leg over his right, careful to match the original pant leg crease. He would rather face the wall than a girl who is using annunciation too big for her slight Midwestern accent.

"Just a few more minutes." Beau assures me with his words and his arm around my shoulders. He rubs his thumb sweetly over the thin straps of my pink vintage dress (thank you, Tess).

I like this action because it is done without thinking. It is a casual and familiar motion. His fingers say, "This is our way of touching our girl-friend. This is our routine."

I am certain that there is nothing that could make this date more incredible.

I am certain that nothing—not slow service, cold food, or an incompetent violinist—could put a damper on this…*our* incredible third date.

Destructive Third-Date Behavior

There are many theories about what constitutes destructive date behavior. If backers of all these theories were seated at the next table, ordering seven-course meals at the expense of the Third-Date Research Institute, they would agree my conduct throughout the rest of the meal constitutes honorable mention in their house of records.

Leon serves our freshly baked cheddar rolls. He introduces himself as though he is our butler or our favorite respected uncle. I sit up straighter because of Leon's pleasant and proper manner. He makes me want to be a better dining woman.

Beau serves me the basket and watches my selection process with interest. I am no dummy. I know this devoted gift of observation will fade by date four, but I like it. "Basking in someone's attention" now makes sense. My heart is actually warmed by this connection.

I add butter to the porous surface of my roll. A random light shaft from the crystal chandelier above catches my knife. The prism lasers my eye. All dangerous date behavior is triggered by some shift in the single woman's brain. I still blame the prism-in-the-eye moment.

I start talking about my life. La, la, la, la, la.

It is normal to tell your date about your life. And if it is the third date with a guy you really, truly, admit-it-out loud *like*, it is practically a requirement.

It is not normal, however, to flood the conversation with references and detailed accounts of negative traits, behavior, and quirks. It can be confused with cute and humble...the first five stories. The Institute examiners would probably cut one off at three stories. Anything after that turns into destructive behavior.

I have passed story thirteen.

"Remember Randy? The guy who always wants to play four square or race down the hall in his wheelchair?"

"Yes..." Beau is still giving me all his attention, but a quick look of concern crosses his face as our meal arrives.

"I got so tired of him challenging me to those stupid corridor races that I started putting glue in his wheels. I said it was WD-40 so it could be a fair race and all, but it was glue. His arms fatigued by the first inter-section, so I was in the clear to run ahead and, frankly, disappear..."

"More salad dressing?" Beau asks because apparently Leon tried a few minutes ago and I was lost in conversation...with myself.

"Oh, sure. Thanks." I watch him carefully pour the Italian dressing from the silver server and I continue with the story. "So here I am hurrying down the hall to get out of his sight, and then I hear a huge crash. Collision. Like steel hitting steel."

Beau raises his eyebrows with an appropriate look of shock. He is practicing Polite Third-Date Behavior.

"Yes. You got it. That huge, triple-tiered drinking fountain with the hand rails...he hit it hard." But before Beau can think too badly of me, I temper the horror. "Oh, at an angle, not head-on...because I had accidentally used more glue in the right wheel. He veered. Thank goodness."

"Yes, thank goodness." Beau motions to Leon.

I reach for my glass of lemon water because suddenly I am exhausted and dehydrated. When did the meal get here? As I gulp my beverage, fielding lemon seeds with my tongue, the shine from my lapis bracelet reminds me that I removed my WWOMD since it didn't exactly match my outfit. If I ever needed that, it is now.

Feeling the prechills of self-loathing, I realize I have been going through my "reasons you could reject me and get out now" repertoire for nearly forty-five minutes. Beau's meal is almost finished.

Now I recall him praying before starting in on the risotto and eggplant. I didn't pay attention to *our* prayer. I should have been memorizing it, but I was planning a witty way to share the story of tying my pastor's shoes together while he was praying at my baptism when I was eight.

I recall Beau feeding me some risotto a few times. It was very good, with a slight nutty taste and the tang of capers.

I feel sweaty, clammy. I have lost track of time and my senses.

Completely.

It is so obvious that Beau is not motioning for Leon to request the dessert menu. He is trying to get the check before I can start one more looney-bin story.

How can I salvage this? One "just kidding" does not override twenty-four tales of disturbed living.

Leon shows up and looks at my face carefully. Has he been listening? Or is it the beads of sweat resting on the crease between my eyebrows that causes the look of concern?

"Yes, sir?" He turns his deep brown eyes toward Beau's hazel ones. They need few words.

Beau gestures for Leon to lean in toward him. Beau whispers. Leon whispers back. Beau says, "Perfect. I cannot thank you enough." And Leon disappears quickly.

Well, it is obvious to me that Leon has left to gather reinforcements. Beau has asked that I be removed from the premises. They may not have a cover charge at Divine's, but I bet they have bouncers for this and other occasions: An older, rich man is seen with an underage woman. Two business partners break up over tiramisu. A married couple exceeds the espresso limit and starts a fight about the tube of toothpaste. There are many unfortunate reasons for bouncer services even at upscale restaurants.

It does not escape me that Beau has fed me carb-loaded food during my diatribes to slow me down before I can beat Leon and his Leons to the stained-glass doors. I push back my chair, just waiting for Beau to bring this disaster to a close or for Leon and gang to gag me and tie my hands behind my back with linen napkins.

Before I can stand, Leon is back.

The only reinforcement he has brought with him is a silver bucket holding a bottle of chilled champagne. A very expensive bottle of champagne.

"What?" Are we not experiencing the same date here?

"I know you don't drink a lot, but I thought we should toast this special moment."

"A toast to what?" Toasting a breakup is not polite dating behavior, I'll have you know.

"You have told me of your every wrongdoing, indiscretion, bad decision, inclination toward evil, and moment of weakness..."

"Well, not all." Like, I altered your personnel file, for instance.

Beau holds his hand up, his first protest all evening. "And I am more infatuated, interested, intrigued, and captivated by you than before."

"Charles Manson had quite a following," I say quietly as I sheepishly raise my flute to meet his at the epicenter of this self-made disaster.

"To Mari. The woman who is not capable of ruining this third date. No matter how hard she tries." He smiles and I turn the color of the merlot the imaginary Institute committee is drinking.

Then Beau raises his glass even higher, motions for me to do the same, and leans forward to kiss me. Right there...in the eye of the storm. And just like meteorologists are always telling us, there is a surprising peace.

After our short but memorable first kiss, he takes a sip of champagne and clears his throat.

"So...those things...they don't bother you?" I want to know how he could figure me out so easily. "Didn't any of those stories—"

"Scare me? Just the one about encouraging your cousin to jump from the top of the barn to test the shocks on his new tennis shoes."

"He never grew as tall as his brothers. Did I mention that?"

"Yes." He waves it away as though my violent tendencies are a fly at a picnic. To be expected. "Now a proposal..."

That I delete his phone number from my cell directory?

"We leave."

Here it comes.

"To quickly put an end to date three...choose a new restaurant for dessert...and officially start our fourth date."

I love that word "our."

Fitting In

Mari, it is so good to see you again." Halo greets me with a half hug. I make a note of the style so I can duplicate it tomorrow. She nods as she peers at me over maroon-rimmed glasses that look fresh off the designer's table. "You look great. So colorful. But of course you do…you are a fashion muse, right?" I realize she has a slight foreign accent. The first time we met, I had been so focused on her long legs that I had not noticed her long vowels.

All weekend I was tormented about what to wear to Majestic Vista. A corporate-appropriate outfit would seem ridiculous here. I settled on a pair of slacks, a multicolored microfiber shirt, and a short scarf tied close to the neck. Later, when I catch my reflection in the glass wall fountain, I realize I look like a sailor on leave from the Good Ship Lollypop.

"Lionel will meet with you later this week. He wanted me to introduce you around and show you the layout. As the member and guest experience designer, you will have full access to the facility. Here is your pass. Lucas will enter your fingerprints into the security scanner eventually." Halo is walking briskly up a slight incline in the hallway. Colors of the desert are woven into the plush carpet that feels a bit like shifting sand beneath my heels.

A few swipes of her security card lead us to yet another hallway. At the end of the last one there is a receptionist desk where a young woman stands awaiting guests. "This is Amy. She is the guest hostess for all the individual therapy rooms."

I scan the girl's name tag. Her "Amy" is spelled like the French word for friend, *Amie*. She shows me a series of well-appointed small rooms for massage, aromatherapy, facials, hot stone treatments, mud baths, and every other imaginable physical and beauty treatment. Soft instrumental music plays overhead in the hallway, but each spa space plays its own version of relaxation.

"You are in for a real treat. Your first month here you are allowed to try every type of therapy we offer. Lionel insists on this so that you can become familiar with our services. It's the best time, isn't it, Halo?" Amie's calm manner matches Halo's. I will have to work on that effect.

"Divine. And then every month you are entitled to two hours of services. It's quite a perk. Most treatments cost between sixty and two hundred dollars an hour for guests," Halo mentions.

Maybe that is how they stay so calm.

Amie furrows her defined brow slightly. "Too bad they don't compensate all the professionals for that expensive rate." She is speaking in a low voice and looking all around her.

I look around too before responding, not sure who to look for but most certain I could recognize an evil listener should I see one. "The pay is really bad?"

"Let's just say that it varies. We have several incredible Latino masseuses who don't get the same rate. I don't think that is a coincidence." Amie is all about secrets and inside information. I can tell right away she likes to be the revealer of dark news. I notice Halo becoming a bit bothered by the conspiracy theory.

"I'm very sensitive about such things, and I don't know this to be true,

Amie. Let's not unload too much on Mari her first week here, okay?" Halo organizes a stack of brochures about the spa treatments.

I try out a soothing voice. It just sounds patronizing. "Halo, you mentioned my title as being an experience designer? Would this be a new term?"

"Lionel's invention. He doesn't like the sound of director or coordinator for this setting. His belief is that Majestic Vista is a personal experience with health and serenity. Your job is to cater the spa encounter to every guest's needs. Some people are here for fitness, some for rest, some for energy, some for illness recovery or remedy, and others are here for a sense of pampering and pleasure." Halo checks each of these off in the air.

"Don't forget to mention other deciding factors. Some are here for discretion and some for exposure. There is another wing just like this one across the interior river, but guests enter the spa rooms through a populated central area that has an eatery, a small theater, bridge games, and a cocktail hour. People who want to be seen paying obscene prices for a massage go there," Amie says.

When I am done saying the word "eatery" to myself over and over until it twists into "eat a tree, eat a tree," I decide that Caitlin and I would head for Amie's secluded territory. Angelica and Sadie would probably rush across to the other side. Wait until I tell them I am working at a place that has its own river.

The other two sense my awe.

"It really is an amazing place to be. Work used to be so stressful for me—I was a legal secretary—and now I look forward to Mondays. That sounds over the top, but I mean it," Halo says with sincere eyes.

I believe her. I believe her.

"Believe me, I understand. The job I left was very stressful." I say this as if I left my post as head surgeon of a major hospital. "I got to a place where I didn't even believe in my future anymore. Or if I did, I was afraid of it. I questioned faith."

Amie leans forward over her receptionist desk. "My Buddhist monk friend says that the future is behind us. Our past is in front of us. That is why we can see our past, but we cannot see our future."

"That's interesting," I say, not certain what it means, but I do find it interesting. What we can see is all that has come to pass. What is out of our range of sight, the scariest part of life, is the unknown…the future.

"That concept changed my life. That and daily meditation. Do you meditate? You mentioned faith." Amie is very enthusiastic about her faith regime, but when she turns the focus to my beliefs, I feel a bit awkward.

Why is it that I can appreciate someone of another faith speaking so openly, yet I cannot appreciate myself enough to volunteer details about Christianity? I'm a wimp surrounded by authentic people. God must get so very tired of my pathetic efforts. But I must say, I enjoy this setting and these new friends who share their deepest selves so soon.

"I pray a lot as part of my faith," I say in a noncommittal fashion. "Amie, you know your name means 'friend' in French…were your parents Buddhists from France?" I face them both. "And Halo…your parents must have been flower children. My name is so drab by comparison." I smile a wide, honest smile in celebration of my new friends, who are vulnerable, caring, true, honest…

As I stare at my new coworkers, I imagine us shopping downtown, eating big bowls of pasta at Ricardos, playing volleyball with guests in matching tank tops, talking on the phone after work to discuss the meaning of life and faith…Just me and my new amazingly authentic friends.

"These aren't our real names," they look at each other and then toward me.

Hold everything. "What?"

"Most of the girls and a few of the guys make up names here. Security reasons. I'm Laura," Amie whispers her given name. "And I'm a Lutheran from Montana. I just happen to have a Buddhist monk friend."

"I'm Carol." Halo reaches out her manicured hand to grip mine. "My parents are federal judges. Not a tie-dyed shirt between them."

"And your accent?"

"Fake," admits Carol.

With a shake of hands I am let into the inner circle. But as I head home that night trying to think up a good fake name for myself, I am unable to shake the fact that things are not as they appear.

Domino Effect

Not the usual?" Cruella challenges my shift in breakfast preferences.

"Blueberry crepes, like I said," I repeat to her crumpled face. I figure a new life warrants a new order. She leaves, defeated, shoulders as limp as her apron. "With real whipped cream, please," I call after her.

"Oo la la," says Caitlin, picking at her faux-rabbit fur, thigh-high boots.

"We need a new place to meet," I say with conviction.

"The Santa Fe is popular," Angelica offers, brushing her hair behind her ears.

She looks pretty today. Clean, I think…but I don't say this.

"But then we'd have to wait longer," says Sadie. She is the one who has plans immediately following our study group.

Possessing a long-distance boyfriend who has survived date three… correction, date four…and still calls is the best of both worlds in my opinion. Lots of girlfriend time and then every other weekend I have great, focused, one-on-one time with Beau. I am glad to be back with the girls, and yet I am inspired to make changes here and there. This must be what a new life allows you to do. Scrutinize the old from a safe distance and offer suggestions whether they are welcomed or not.

"It'd be good to shake things up. Carson would wait for you." I think how nice it would be to trade in these car-shaped salt-and-pepper shakers for those in the shape of saguaros and prickly pears that grace the tables at the Sante Fe.

"Possibly," Sadie concedes with a sigh of fatigue.

We are all tired. So much has happened recently. Angelica is still "seeing" but not officially dating Peyton. Caitlin has been getting calls and emails about her sophisticated mod look ever since Kevin Milano snapped me in the two shots. I gave the paper Caitlin's info so I would not be the recipient of such inquiries. She is thrilled with the notoriety and I with the anonymity.

"Okay, I have a dilemma," Angelica begins as she adds sugar to her coffee. She doesn't even look around to measure our interest. She just starts in. "I'm wondering if it is okay to break up…"

"I do too," I say, determined to not let Angelica always rule this portion of our breakfast. "I have a dilemma. I'd like to start with mine this time." I do take the time to measure the interest of others, and there is very little, but I forge ahead anyway. "I need a new apartment that suits my new life." I watch them nod "no big deal" nods. "And…a new name."

"What?" Angelica is now adequately surprised.

"Are you still getting calls and emails from the blog?" Caitlin asks while scratching her legs again.

"No, that seems resolved for now. This is for work. It turns out that those people with cool names—Halo, Amie, Siena, Petal, and Earl Gray—" I run down the list of fellow coworkers I have met over the past few days, "have *fake* names."

"You are surprised by this?" Sadie deadpans in typical Old Mari fashion.

"Well, yeah. Sort of. I mean, I wouldn't figure the clientele at Majestic

Vista would require workers to remain anonymous. Don't you think it is a bit…odd?"

"You cannot be disillusioned with your new life so soon, Mari. That would be Old Mari behavior. I'm still waiting for you to start picking apart Beau, who is, I believe, a great match for you." Angelica reveals my demons.

She is right, but I don't like the idea of Angelica speaking truth into my life. "I need a name, please." I make designs in my whipped topping and long for the old breakfast choice. Maybe I am an eternal "grass is greener" gal.

"Chi-Chi," Angelica volunteers after a sigh of resignation. "Or Goddess. Kate Moss?"

"You just are mad about the event photo and that it referenced that you were looking to me for fashion ideas."

"That's where you're wrong. I was thrilled just to be in a Kevin Milano shot, Miss Too Big for Her Britches."

I shut up. I *am* too big for my Majestic Vista Lycra britches. How'd she know?

Time to create a diversion. I'll focus on other people's problems. "I need to use the restroom. Sadie, come with?"

I can tell she doesn't want to join anyone who says "come with" to the bathroom, but she is too nice to leave me hanging there alone with my debutante wording.

"Don't tell me you do want to pick Beau apart," she challenges me as soon as we are in the black-and-white checkered ladies' facilities.

Now that I am face-to-face with her, I am not sure I want to tell her that she is not perfect. "It's about your event, which was lovely." I start off friendly.

"Thanks. It turned out great. I think that even though I was hoping for more people, the number was just right. And Carson and I did a lot to advance the awareness of the gardens…"

"It's not about the event, actually," I interrupt. She stares at me baffled and a bit impatient. I continue while staring at the soap dispenser. "It's how you responded to Caitlin when you found out who her parents were. You hurt her, Sadie. She looks up to you so much. We all do, but it was obvious that you were suddenly impressed with Caitlin when you found out she comes from money." I want to add, "Which you would have known if you ever spent time one-on-one with her," but I leave this for another time.

A manicured hand waves in front of my face. Sadie's eyes are closed and she is shaking her head back and forth. Mad? Confused? In denial? "You are mistaken." She looks away, but other than the framed print of ketchup and mustard bottles dancing together, there is nothing to focus on. She continues. "I…at first I was impressed, I'll admit. But not as you think. It was respect for Caitlin because she is who she is in spite of coming from money. I understand now that all her craziness and eccentricity is about courage…not…"

"Laziness? Lack of direction?"

Sadie looks up convicted. "Yes."

I'm so glad she isn't mad at me for bringing this up. "You need to let her know this, Sadie. It would mean so much."

"I do. I do. You are right." She stomps her foot and the sound echoes. "I can be so hard on people. I have such high standards for myself, and then I try to force everyone else into this ridiculous shape of perfection. I push people away. I'll end up with regrets if I don't…"

I realize she is not talking about "people" in general but Carson in particular.

"What's up, Sadie?" I try the soft tone I learned from Amie and Halo.

Without her usual reluctance to reveal details, she opens up. "Well, you know Carson is older, but what you don't know is that he is divorced. He has a kid, Mari. A ten-year-old…Harry…who lives with his mother in New York."

She has been carrying this around all this time. "Sadie, people go on to create good, whole lives after divorce. Are you afraid it means he isn't marrying material?"

"It's a lot to contend with, you know? I mean, relationships are hard enough without the idea or the reality of your significant other having had this other life. I don't know if I can get past it. Maybe I'm scared he won't be able to get past it. It's the ultimate 'been there, done that' situation." She sits down on the very short bench. Her knees are almost up to her chest and she looks defeated.

"Oh, honey." An endearment I usually despise seems to be a comforting choice. I sit next to her in silence in the midst of a room resembling NASCAR purgatory. "Is this what he is telling you?"

"No. He seems to want to move forward. These are just the thoughts that consume me. I woke up last night at three o'clock in a cold sweat, certain that I have to break things off before he does. I have never been out of control this way, Mari."

I pretend to crack my knuckles. "Well, welcome to my world, little lady. I am always out of control. Let me guide you through this time of emotional upheaval. It's not so bad once you get used to it. There are lots of unknown benefits." I see her smile out of the corner of my eye and keep up the routine. "You get to have a massage while passed out. You can go on dates with men who just want their picture in the paper. Umm…Oh, you might even be lucky enough to have a website created in your honor. Or…or you could have your friends gather round and reveal your pathetic lifestyle…or…"

"Thanks. You sold me." She laughs, and I realize how tired she looks. We all think nothing can get to Sadie, and yet she has been quietly suffering.

"Let's get back out there. He adores you, Sadie. Pray about it…and let all of us pray about it too. Who says you have to have the answer right now?"

"True." She dabs her eyes with a tissue and then grabs onto my shirt and pulls me back before I can exit. Apparently, when you get Sadie talking, the girl won't quit. "You know my philosophy about only having one great thing in your life at a time?"

"Yeah, but I'm personally hoping that isn't true. There is too much potential in my life right now."

"It's as if there was a domino effect of backlash when I decided to believe otherwise. I found out more about Carson's background, I started doubting everything, and now I think I'm sabotaging what could be a really good thing."

"Maybe the dominos are going in the right direction. Maybe all of this is leading you toward good things. Did you think of that?"

As soon as we are back to the table, Caitlin and Angelica try to read our faces.

"How about Chanel? It's classic, sophisticated, and associated with fashion and style," Caitlin suggests while recrossing her legs. A few tufts of fake fur that look an awful lot like ceiling insulation swirl about her.

I like it. Although rich, old women throughout Manhattan probably have poodles named Coco or Chanel, I still like it. "Thanks, Caitlin. Good thought."

"Now, my turn. Please?" Angelica raises her hand in submission. "Is it okay to break up with your manicurist if you have heard of someone far superior…"

"Yes," we say. Such an easy one.

"I didn't finish. What if it is a manicurist I have been witnessing to?" She lowers her voice at the end of the confession, but we all understand exactly what it means.

Angelica is back among the professing Christians.

We take in her admission but give her the grace she requires.

"Is she bad? Like, does she choose cherry red nail color instead of crimson red or tear off your skin when she redoes your nails?" Caitlin offers a way to a decision.

"No. She's good. I just heard about Fidel Gray, who is supposed to be incredible. Maybe I will give it more time. Usually the initial buzz is all publicity hype."

"Yeah," I agree. "Give it more time."

"Yes. More time," Caitlin repeats and raises her eyebrows at me with a hint of pleasant surprise at our friend's new leaf.

That is what looks different about Angelica. With her tough outer shell gone, she is softer, warmer. We take a moment to observe her changes. This one push toward a kinder direction changes the course of the rest of our morning together. Our individual conflicts fall down, one right after the other. Sadie says a few words to Caitlin privately and they embrace. Angelica seems relieved to have outed herself. And I don't try to convince everyone and myself that I don't belong in this new life.

After listening to Sadie's struggle with Carson's past and witnessing Angelica's change of direction toward faith, I am tempted to bring up Amie's Buddhist monk friend's idea about the past and future for discussion among Christians.

But I'm afraid Angelica would want to get her own Buddhist monk friend.

And then break up with him.

Phone Dating

"Guggle. Guggle. Urch."

"Guggle. Guggle. Urch?"

"That's the one."

"It might be your carburetor," Beau offers, though I suspect it is his version of my rotator cuff answer. Something you have heard that sounds worth repeating.

"Do you know anything about cars?" I laugh.

"Not a bit." He laughs.

"And I was going to ask you to look at a car with me this weekend. I might really buy it. Guess I will need to get a date with a car guy."

We laugh.

This is me talking to a boyfriend. The boyfriend. He qualifies as a boyfriend because he asks me about the most boring details of my life with interest. He is the only person to know about my *Castaways* viewing pleasure and the word "pathetic" did not leave his lips.

"How do you feel about the job? It's been a couple months now. Have you adjusted?"

"It's good. A bit strange. All that money and attitude…it is so different from Golden Horizon days."

"That's what you were hoping, right?"

"Yes." I guess.

"I understand. I had such big expectations when I moved to Phoenix and took this management position," he says. "Eventually the realities of the fantasy emerge."

"Exactly." He gets me. This makes me feel better. Unless…what if the fantasy he is talking about is our dating relationship?

"Do you think I should go blond?"

"Not if that means you will have to date your own kind."

"It's really more of a honey blond…the signature color developed for Majestic Vista employees only. Don't you think that is a bit strange? And how sad that I didn't even catch on that they had dyed their hair to match. I don't know what I thought. Inbreeding, I guess."

"Or pod people?"

"Yes. Pretty On Demand people. That would be appropriate."

"Give it time, Mari. You are an anthropologist in a new culture. Or a missionary. Think of it that way."

"I'm not offering much in the way of spiritual wisdom to these folks. I am, however, teaching ten people how to knit. Can you believe that is a coveted hobby?"

"See? You are popular on your own terms. That's not so bad. Have you survived the probation period?"

"The first one. At six months they make an even bigger decision. If Lionel likes me…correction, loves me…enough to invest in my future with Majestic, he sends me to his spa in Mexico so I can observe the best of the best in action."

"You'll make it to Mexico. How could anyone not love you?"

Pause.

How could anyone not love you. Beau is a someone, which means he is part of "anyone" status. I rephrase the sentence: How could Beau not love you…me.

"Oh, my gosh! I forgot I have to meet up with Angelica downtown. I'm so sorry." I stammer a bit and write "meet Angelica" on my Mexico wall calendar so it isn't an unprovable lie. A few days over I see a note about Tess' bypass surgery. "I will call you as soon as I hear how Tess did in surgery this week. I'll be seeing her tomorrow just to check on her."

"I will be up for your walk-a-thon this weekend; maybe we can go see her at the hospital afterward. Tell her I am praying for her full recovery. I expect her to dance with me at the sixtieth anniversary dance."

"Who says I will share you?" Uh-oh, that was a reference to future ownership. "Gotta run. Talk with you soon."

We hang up. Leaving me alone with my hang-ups.

Did Beau really intend to link me to the word "love"? Could someone make this leap in affection after only a few months? Am I the guy in this relationship, so afraid of the next step that I won't be honest about my feelings?

My hands are clammy. I've got a bad case of Sadie's fight-or-flight syndrome.

Covert Operation

Go! Go!" Lysa motions me into the back hallway of Golden Horizons. I am dressed in the volunteer uniform down to the white nurse's shoes that stick to the linoleum as if it were freshly laid pavement.

Tess insisted that I visit her prior to the surgery rather than come with her to the hospital. She said she wanted me with her before the drugs changed her "charming personality."

Once we are standing near the faint light of an exit sign, Lysa's eyes take in the new me. "What did you do to your hair?"

"Do you like it? It's Sunrise Blond. All the rage at Majestic." I pat the back of it in Britney Spears fashion, but I am not convincing my friend. Nor myself.

"How do you say 'I like the old you better' in fancy spa lingo?" Lysa gives me a "get a load of her" sideways look. "Though I like the new look of your car."

I blush and make excuses for the things I want. "My car broke down, and repairing it was going to cost the equivalent of four times its actual blue book value. So I…went shopping. I know it's a bit much. I've never had a new car."

Lysa raises her hands. "No explanation needed. I love it. I've been wanting a friend with a decent rig."

Her genuine acceptance of my choice almost relieves me of my self-judgment.

"Here put this on. I got it in case Rae saw you, but now it serves an even greater purpose," she says as she hands me a hairnet.

"Oh, great." I shove random strands of Sunrise Blond into the cap and start to giggle out of control. So does Lysa.

We laugh silently and with convulsions as we walk through the hallway.

There is a crack of light coming from beneath Rae's door. People from the state are doing a location inspection tomorrow; otherwise the woman would not be here at eight o'clock at night. I know I am risking a confrontation with her, but for Tess, I'm willing to take the chance.

"If Rae catches us, just look down at the floor and say you are Frieda, a substitute night nurse. Use an accent," Lysa instructs as we make our way through the maze that I know like the back of my hand.

I avoid looking at my old desk for reasons I don't want to admit. I had thought that a return visit would be my chance to compare my two worlds. The ridiculously pathetic "before" contrasted with the spectacularly fabulous "after." But now I won't let my eyes take hold of the rickety chair and metal desk in case they will recognize them and miss them.

"Come in! Hurry, before you-know-who awakes," Tess whispers with little girl joy beneath a serious look.

Lysa and I are still both laughing hysterically.

"Lysa, you stay too. You girls are my best young friends here." Tess pats the side of her bed. She is looking pale and fatigued, and for a moment it is hard for me to see the Tess I know and love. But she is there. After a few familiar mannerisms…a wink, a smirk, a shrug…and I see her.

"Tess, we are glad to be here to celebrate your upcoming surgery and your renewed strength." I pretend to toast the health of this good woman.

"That reminds me!" She raises her finger and points to her minifridge. Lysa obeys the direction and returns with two bottles of sparkling cider.

"Hey, aren't those from the…" I recognize the brand from my Golden Golden party order.

"You didn't want the leftovers to end up in Rae's personal kitchen, did you?"

"Here's to health and the future!" We each sip just a little of the honey-colored liquid.

"This cider almost matches Mari's new hair. Did you see it, Tess?" Lysa wipes her hand over my head and removes the netting.

"Well, I'll be!" Tess says. She begins to laugh and we start up again. I am amazed and blessed to have a friendship with this woman who is more than two and a half times my age.

"I miss you. This…" I motion around me, surprising even myself with the words I don't let myself finish.

"Did you hear that they aren't going to replace you?" Tess asks me.

"That's impossible," I respond with shock. I didn't think I held the place together, but I certainly thought my role was significant to the quality of life of the residents. This news is devastating to me.

"Is it because of the fund-raiser? Will it not happen?" I ask, not really wanting to know if my leaving has caused serious loss for the residents.

Lysa says, "Rae wants to use that as the excuse, but you know as well as I do that it is because she is a lousy business manager. I'd be all for her bizarre system of accounting if it were advantageous to the residents, but it isn't. This is my third center to work in, Mari, and it is suffering the most. It isn't your fault."

"No. It's not, dear. Don't think for a minute that you are not supposed to go on with your life. I do wish there was something I could do right now to help this place, though. I would in a heartbeat. I've been racking my brain trying to think of a solution." Poor Tess, just days before her surgery, and she is worrying about trying to save her home. Her expression changes with a new thought. "How is Beau? Or how are you and Beau, is the real question?"

"They're great," Lysa says.

I blush and I doubt. The struggle with shifting my status from single to dating still causes me some strife.

"Give it the time you need, Mari. We know that in all things God works for the good of those who love him…"

"Who have been called according to his purpose." I finish the Scripture from Romans and hope it is true.

"I'd like to pray before I fade here. Mari, will you?"

"Sure." I look at Lysa, who has told me that her faith suffered greatly during her father's illness and death. She nods for me to go for it.

My prayer is simple…and a bit wandering. I pray for Tess and her surgery, for this place and its survival, even for Rae and the leadership here at Golden Horizons. I throw in a bit about God's will for all of us…that we cling to it even when we face uncertainty. Beneath my prayer is another prayer, a silent, personal supplication…God, use me in this situation. Let me be a part of the life you have for me.

"That was so nice, dear. I feel better already. Lysa, would you get my stole? I left it in the recreation room."

"Certainly," she says, her voice a bit shaky.

As soon as Lysa exits and Tess faces me, I see she is all business and heart. Her little hands reach for mine. She gives me a knowing nod and I feel what she is referring to. The charm bracelet with the single key is in my hand. The weight of it represents the weight I feel in my spirit. This isn't just our usual routine, I sense. I ask her if I am right.

"No, it isn't. It's time for you to have the gray Christian Dior, my dear." She wags her finger at me, ready to counter my protests with her deeper wisdom.

"Tess, this is a procedure they do several times every day at the hospital. Your doctors believe you are strong enough for this, or they would not choose to operate. Please don't act like this is…"

"Mari, if there is anything I have learned in this life, it is that my joy, my pain, my journey is never about or between me and another person or a situation. Doctors, surgery, or otherwise. My life is between me and God." Tess reads my face, which is twitching and turning away.

She continues. "Are you hearing that? It is a great blessing to finally understand this. Take it…along with these material items," she motions to the key, "and may they unlock the life between you and God."

I look up startled. She is the only person to really understand my struggle lately. I clutch the key tightly and then embrace the sweetest gift of all, my friend, Tess.

We hear Lysa's shoes squeaking down the hallway. "Do you want me to take the dress now? Or can I wait till after the surgery?" I still do not believe this is goodbye. My friend is a sentimental gal, that is all.

"You can wait. But just so you know…some keys open more than just one old bureau. You will read this when the time comes," Tess presses a ribbon-tied note into my hand as Lysa enters wearing the stole.

"Sorry to disturb you two, but Rae is on the loose. I think she is in the other wing, so we had best hightail it out of here. Come on, Blondie. Tess needs her rest for tomorrow."

Leaving Tess is not easy, but she assures me everything will turn out as it should. I exchange my WWOMD accessory for this single-key charm bracelet, and as I step out into the night, I am hopeful that I am also stepping into the life that is between me and God.

Y Knot

"Chanel, you have a call holding on line *cinq*," my coworker and newest friend Sophie calls out to me from the glass desk in the mirage wing.

"*Merci*, Sophie!" To pass time, we pretend we speak French fluently. Together, we know twenty words and two phrases.

Clad in her bathing suit, Sophie is ready to lead her synchronized swimming class. Well, almost.

"Are you wearing your Timberlands into the pool? Very graceful flippers."

"You like? Earl Gray told me someone broke a glass over by the pool. I'm not risking these *pieds*. They are ensured, baby." Sophie does a little tap dance.

I press five on my headset. "Hello? Who are you and what business do you have with me?"

"Mari? It's Yvette. Your neighbor. Former neighbor, actually."

"I'm so sorry for my greeting. I thought it was someone here at work." Yvette's sentence sinks in. "You moved out?" I have been so caught up in my life that I haven't even noticed strange neighbor moved out?

"I did more than that. Zane and I eloped!" She squeals. The former no-personality girl squeals into my ear. I do a dance of pain.

"Eloped?" Are you nuts? I want to shout out the limited number of months she has known Zane. Uh...one, two, three, four, five months. Who could possibly know they want to marry someone after...the same amount of time I have known Beau? Could I make such a rash decision? No.

I adjust my judgment and turn it into happiness for the girl formerly known as basement dweller.

"I know. It is crazy. Maybe I should have made a website of my own and taken bets. I would have won big, for sure. It is too soon...but I just knew. We just knew. And we owe it all to you, Mari. You hardly knew either one of us, yet you made this happen. We want to take you out to lunch today as a thank-you."

"Today?"

"We leave for a month-long trek through Europe tomorrow. Please?"

They are not only sure enough about their love to get hitched but secure enough to pitch a tent in the Alps together. I feel uptight. Reaching into my pocket, I find the email from Beau that I printed last night. Allowing my eyes to glance at the first line is enough. "Mari, how about we live together...in the same city?"

Returning to the situation at hand, I get my bearings as quickly as possible. "I only have an hour...and Majestic is so far from any places to eat..." I'm making excuses rather than celebrating my friend's big moment. Their relationship is between them and God...and surely it was God who tugged at my heart that day to set them up. "Wait!" I act as though I just stumbled across a great idea rather than tripped over my list of excuses. "Eat here. I can leave passes at the door for you. And..." I'm on a roll now, "dress in sweats or comfortable clothing."

"I thought that place was fancy." Yvette seems to doubt whether she is Majestic material. This puts me in high gear to make her feel comfortable.

"Fancy in a casual way. You will feel right at home. Besides, I will be your personal experience designer. Can you spend a couple hours here?"

Yvette's muffled voice talks to her significant other. "Yes. We'll see you soon."

I hang up just as Lionel rounds the corner. His nice suit flows in slow motion and his smile appears undaunted by the stresses that plague this business mogul. "Mari, just the gal I wanted to see."

Gal? Golly gee, Lionel.

"I have good news for you." He reaches over and grabs a clipboard from the desk. "This is your schedule for next week. You are a month away from your six month approval, yet I feel confident you can handle this privilege."

"Privilege?"

"Take a look at who is on your schedule. I wouldn't usually hand over a top client to a beginning designer, but somehow I just knew this was the right thing to do."

I skim the list of client names, hoping I will recognize the one he deems as important. My eyes catch on one that takes my breath away. Not...

"You saw it...Wendy Skies. On your shift. She expects the full treatment and always requests extra bottled water and fresh, peeled kiwi after her massage. There are a few other important specifics about her preferences and a few allergies as well in her file. Become familiar with it before next week." Lionel sees the frozen look on my face. "You do know Wendy Skies?"

"Not personally, of course. But we know someone in common."

"Excellent. Then I was right to do this. Don't let me down, Mari... Chanel. I know you won't."

He walks away satisfied with my silence. Though Mari has visions of torture massages dancing in her head, Chanel won't let Lionel down.

Before I can forget, I schedule Yvette and Zane for a deluxe couple's massage with Charles, the best masseur in town. Even if I don't know how I feel about my love life after just five months, I can offer up a wedding gift to two people who are willing to ignore the what-ifs and embrace the why not to tie the knot.

Moving Toward Something

Are we there yet?" Caitlin moans as she clip-clops next to us along the Tucson Trot route. We hold our tongues rather than mention that she is the one who chose to try her lace-up clogs today of all days.

Only Sadie let out a brief "What were you thinking!" under her breath, but the sound of wood dragging on pavement muffled the rhetorical question.

"How are you doing, Rachel?" I ask Angelica's new little sister. As in Big Brother, Big Sister program. We are all scared for this impressionable fourteen-year-old, who already seems in awe of Angelica's life force. Yes, we want to yell "Run, Rachel, run as fast as you can," but we are afraid she will think we just mean to the finish line. Just as I'm wondering if I have time to adopt Rachel should Angelica decide to break up with her, Caitlin says she will sister-share with me.

"Being outside feels pretty good. I thought it would suck because I prefer to shop." Rachel looks about her at the mountainous skyline and the surrounding flora with mild appreciation that, while it is not the grandeur of the mall, it does not "suck."

We all nod at the family resemblance.

"We are getting close. I see some folks walking the finishing circle," Sadie says optimistically. We are all dragging, though it is only five miles.

"Next year, let's run it," I say for shock value. Caitlin pegs me with one of her heavy feet.

"Hey, Pinocchio. If I have splinters, I'm lighting a match and tossing it in your general direction."

"Oh, my gosh. I don't believe it. Look who is here!" Caitlin is excited about a celebrity sighting. A small golf cart is careening around the corner and edging just a short distance from the paved walkway and toward the end of the trail. I see only a glimpse of blond hair and a long stretch of tan legs. Whoever this is, she is cheating her way to the finish line.

"It's Wendy Skies." Caitlin claps her hands. Even Angelica does not buy into this version of celebrity.

"Oh, please. Big deal. She'll be a hostess at LuLu's within two years. The woman has no sense of fashion—"

"Or kindness," I add.

"Or fairness, apparently," Sadie commentates as we watch Wendy rush over to the trail in front of us just in time for a photo op in the finishers' circle. It turns out this woman who is too good to visit her elderly father is just good enough to serve as this year's breast cancer awareness event emcee.

"You've got to be kidding me. Way to taint this fund-raiser," I say, pouting.

Sadie nudges me. At first I think it is her cue to be nicer, but then I see what she sees. Standing at the finish line are Carson and Beau. I cannot help but smile.

Instead of looking at Wendy smiling for the cameras, wiping her brow, and stretching out, I focus on how good it feels to be walking toward something. Someone.

Beau looks at me with pride, but there is something else in his eyes. And though I consider he could be overheating from this extremely warm

October day, his red face causes my stomach to go funny. I kick up my pace.

"Congratulations," the two handsome men say in unison. They are holding pink roses for each of us, including Rachel.

"Ahhh. That's so sweet," I say and give Beau a hug—an act I never thought would feel normal. But today it does. I look into his red-rimmed eyes. "Did you eat Thai food again?"

He clears his throat. "No. I need to speak with you, Mari." Suddenly he realizes a big change in my appearance. "Your hair. It's…fun."

"I don't do serious all that well, so just spit it out," I say while my mind comes up with lots of possibilities for his behavior. He has to move to the East Coast. He is tired of the long-distance relationship. He found out we are brother and sister…

"Tess passed away this morning. I decided to go check on her before I came here. The doctor said the surgery went really well, but her heart gave out." He is crying because he adored Tess, and because he knows what this will mean to me. Beau watches my face for a response and grabs my hand in support.

I don't cry. Thoughts of Tess' goodbye replay in my mind, and I hold a very unexpected peace within.

"Mari, are you okay?" Sadie is standing beside me. By now they have all caught on to the news.

"We did it, everybody! We walked, we ran, we strolled, we rolled for breast cancer! Let's give ourselves a pat on the back. We can be proud of this fine effort. Today we are not just people of the Tucson community, we are friends…no! We are family. And that's what makes all the differ-ence," Wendy Skies' voice spews from speakers resting on a bench right beside us.

Now I cry.

And I don't stop until I get home.

The Fork in the Road

Your order is leaking. Not my fault." Our Chinese take-out guy shoves several plastic bags at Beau and exits as soon as he gets his money and tip. Leaking indeed...kung pow sauce drips a trail from the door to the kitchen.

"I'll clean that after we eat. Deal?" Beau asks as he pours our numbered dinner choices onto paper plates.

"Deal." I'm ravenous after hours of crying and blowing my nose. I keep looking at the key on my bracelet. Now it and what it opens are all I will have to remember my friend by.

In silence we chow on Chow Fun and speak not of the loss of Tess. This silence also surrounds the email I still keep in my pocket. The email that asks me if I want this relationship to be real, serious, and possibly long-term.

I don't know if the email is disconcerting because I have had enough change to last me a while or because the long-distance relationship has protected me from having to think about what the next step might be. I'm not someone who grew up with grand visions of the white fluffy dress and the white picket fence. Fantasies about lifestyle and career crowded out the whole "I do" plotline.

Apparently Beau has been thinking about this. A lot.

"So, Mari…that last email I sent you. Was it too much?" He is looking right at me because he is the kind of guy who can look you in the eye when talking about real things. Even a shared zip code.

I am tempted to use the news of Tess' death as an excuse to avoid this conversation, but I know our in-person sessions are few and far between. It matters, I tell myself. Speak. "No. Not too much. Just…so soon. I don't know." My favorite line in life is "I don't know," as if this becomes a universal pass to avoid any confrontation. I can see it doesn't exactly meet Beau's need for information.

"Do you not know about us? Or is it about moving? Because I gave that a lot of thought. You have just found the ideal job…so you should stay. I should be the one to move. If anyone moves." His nervousness is palpable. My heart wants to send him a lifeline.

"It isn't the move. It's…" What is it? "It's the expectation that comes with such a move." Don't guys feel this kind of relational pressure? "I thought asking you your opinion about my new car choice was a huge step of commitment. What if you move back here and it doesn't work out? Then what?"

"That 'what if' doesn't matter. The 'what if' that matters is 'what if we don't give this a real shot?' " He speaks seriously and unintentionally waves a wonton at my face until he realizes he is waving a wonton at my face. "I'm sorry. I've never been…I've never felt this way about someone before."

"Neither have I," I offer. I don't know much about most things, but I do know I have to admit to the feelings that I have. I am almost thirty; if I cannot learn from past mistakes by now, I never will.

"We're back to the age-old question: Where do we go from here?"

I'm silent. My mind is scanning all the recent events of my life: meeting Beau, my posh position at Majestic Vista, my hair color alteration, my name change, the loss of Tess, having real conversations with a significant other. Talk about systems overload.

"If I ended up here…in Tucson…you would be okay with it?" He rephrases the question.

Wouldn't it be nice to spend more time with him? To have him ask me over for a game night with friends? We could go for walks in the morning or meet up for coffee or lunch or dinner. This is a life I could envision…right?

I sound confused as I pour out my thoughts. "I admit that the long-distance relationship has been convenient, but if you had been living here when we met, I still would have been excited about getting to know you better."

Noodles hang from Beau's mouth as he considers this somewhat compliment. "So this is a yes to us living in the same town?"

"I'm still worried about expectations. What if—"

"You bought a wonderful new car. That is a commitment. You didn't seem to dwell on what-ifs over that. No more using the what-if defense. Mari…you are what…almost thirty?" Beau seems energized by this and takes a bite of hot mustard.

I sit back in the couch and give him the evil eye. I can barely get past the car comparison to our love life, but if he uses my age in a line of reasoning about life being short or the ol' biological clock argument, he will have to reckon with my diabolical side.

He glances at my look but doesn't waver. "I'm a few years older. Don't we both know by now that what-if's make life harder, not better? I just want to move forward…with you."

This is the first thing that makes sense to me. Hasn't my entire past year been about moving forward and into the life I am supposed to have? And today, walking toward the finish line and seeing Beau waiting for me was a moment I will treasure forever. But in this moment of intimate conversation with plastic utensils, all I can offer is a smile and a quick nod.

Elmo curls up in my lap and purrs as if there is not a life-changing choice on the table. I pet him in order to avoid looking into Beau's eyes.

"I want to be someone who can move forward too." I do. So I say it to the first person to really get me in a long time.

I gaze into Beau's brown eyes.

"Mari, this is new for me too." He looks away just for a moment, as if to gather courage. "But I want to give it a real try. This distance thing…it is too easy to make it all about convenience or a future possibility rather than a now reality. You know?"

"I know. I just need time to think about all this." I have to be honest. My emotions are very raw from the news of Tess' passing. The force of my sadness causes me to stab my plastic fork into my mound of noodles. A loud snap follows.

A quick look of disappointment passes over Beau's face, but soon it is replaced by a look of understanding. "It's been a hard week. Take your time. We'll find our way, Mari. We will." He hands me his fork.

This is exactly what I need. An offering. A gesture. And some time to ponder this question: When one faces the fork in the road too early in a relationship, is there any hope that a single girl will reach her intended destination?

Rubbed the Wrong Way

She's late," I complain to Sophie and Halo, whom I have chosen to assist me with Wendy Skies' intricately planned spa day.

"It is always this way. Watch. She'll arrive harried and blame the weather, traffic, or her horoscope for the delay." Sophie nibbles on a pear and does a quick imitation of a harried look much to our amusement.

"Do that again," I say.

"You know this is a test, don't you?" Sophie inquires.

"Lionel said he wouldn't usually give someone an established client prior to the end of the probation period. I must have already passed his test." I shrug and check my watch again. Wendy is like those irritating girls in high school who got out of gym class by feigning cramps when it was really vanity's allergic reaction to the dismal gray gym shorts.

Sophie reaches into a cloth backpack and pulls out her latest attempt at knitting. "No, this *is* Lionel's test. He does this to everyone. But don't worry. We are here to make sure it all goes smoothly. Meanwhile, can you fix my scarf, Chanel?"

The knot in my stomach is as twisted as Sophie's random rows of stitches. Of all people, why Wendy Skies? I sense this is not just a test of my professional skills but of my spiritual disciplines.

"I choke on tests," I say quietly. My hands repair Sophie's project while my nerves unravel.

"Showtime." Halo nudges me and we all stand upright like soldiers. In unison, we flutter forward to form the welcome "v" like the one that greeted me more than half a year ago. Now I am the one who stands at the vortex and makes the initial greeting with a warm smile and the offer of all-out luxury.

Wendy does not acknowledge my greeting, nor does she make eye contact with me. She is speaking to an imagined crowd of people beyond us. "Can you believe that today of all days my driver decides to fall and break his leg? Unbelievable. The service took half an hour to replace him."

"I hope he recovers quickly," I say in response.

"Well, it'd be too late to be helpful." She tosses her gloves at me and accepts a water spritzer with lime and a thin, red straw. Who wears gloves in Tucson? I envision her in the LuLu's uniform of Angelica's prophetic vision and cannot help but laugh.

"You think his injury is funny?" Now she looks into my eyes and pretends to have a heart. But I know that if she had a heart, she would recognize me as someone who had helped care for her father. But there is no look of recognition in her fake blue eyes, only superiority and entitlement.

"Not at all. I just hope he has family to care for him during his recovery." I am not off to a good start. Sophie steps in between us and presents Wendy with the schedule I created to make her day perfect.

Like a queen before her charges, she claps her hand to initiate the start of her service for the day. Halo and Sophie both respond appropriately, reaching for Wendy's jacket and lifting her feet one at a time to replace her Manolos with blue slippers. I stand a bit in awe of Wendy's manner. She is an anchor in a secondary market, for pete's sake. Where does such undeserved self-importance come from?

"Shall we?" I motion for Wendy and her new entourage to follow me across the bubbling brook and to the "primping for exposure" side of the facilities. As if on cue an older woman with a green facial mask approaches us and makes a beeline for Wendy. I quickly check the notes on file to see if Wendy prefers us to deter or welcome fans and cannot help but roll my eyes when I read, "Wendy appreciates recognition but will not shake hands with other patrons unless she first approves. Air kisses and nods are okay if Wendy makes the gesture first. Autographs are up to the celebrity's discretion. Our guest requests a distance of three feet be maintained between her and her fans."

My timing is perfect as I step up to the raccoon woman and wrap an arm around her shoulders to guide her to a spot on the carpet approximately three feet away from our star guest. Wendy cleverly places her hands behind her back away from shake range and compliments the woman on her choice of facials. The exchange is brief and kind, and the woman seems pleased.

"Chanel, is it?" Wendy flips her hair in my direction.

"Yes."

"Nice maneuver there." I receive her nod of approval with relief. At least maybe now my job won't be in jeopardy. From this point on the day goes smoothly. She continues to keep her hands to herself, and I keep my opinionated, internal commentary to myself.

After lunch Lionel comes by to see how I'm treating his guest of honor. "I've seen your catered experience for Wendy. Very nice. Scheduling her pedicure in the pergola was a very creative touch. How did you come up with that?"

"I read the notes in her file, and they said she likes the scent of roses. So I had the gardener relocate a potted vine from the meditation garden to the pergola."

"Excellent. That is what I mean by 'experience designer.' You are really understanding the vision I have, Chanel."

Getting a compliment under an assumed name doesn't feel very genuine, but I smile with gratitude and suppress the urge to say my real name out loud ten times.

Once again Lionel is off and moving down the main wing, straightening furniture and artwork as he makes his way to his office.

"Chanel...do you read?" Sophie's voice crackles through my headset.

"Yes." I scan the schedule and see that we are down to the final element for the day, a mud bath followed by a full-body massage. In the margin I have written that Wendy only likes a gentle surface massage because of her exceptionally tender skin. "I'll take her to the massage with Michael." A former piano player, Michael's our lightest touch masseur.

"Well, we have a bit of a problem in the mud spa. Could you come and take over? She refuses to listen to any of us."

"What is the problem?"

"Other than Miss Priss? Oh, you'll see."

I peer down the hall to make sure Lionel is still secured in his office and then run toward the mud spa as fast as possible without causing alarm among the self-meditated.

By the time I make it across the property, I am breathless and sweaty. Halo and Sophie greet me outside a private room, where I can hear Wendy spewing complaints with some very colorful words.

"What happened?"

Halo starts in at a pace I can barely keep up with. "Wendy had her mud bath and then we asked her to sit in the sauna to keep the mud moist, you know...the usual. Well, Ms. Skies sneaks out for a cigarette break..."

"After Silk warned her not to go outside..." Sophie interrupts.

Halo's rant continues. "Well, three cigarettes later, on the veranda, in the sun..."

"Oh, no." I close my eyes in denial.

"Oh, yes. She looks like a giant overbaked chocolate cookie," Halo describes.

Sophie laughs. "Who are you kidding? She looks like a dried cowpie."

"Can't we just hose her down the way we normally would? It will just take longer."

"Tried that. She says it hurts. The spray pelts her, and it isn't penetrating the clay."

I cannot ignore the shrill yells coming from behind the closed door any longer. "I'll find a solution. Thanks, you two." I step forward with a false, but necessary, air of confidence.

As the door swings open, the cow dung image is indeed the more accurate description of our local celebrity. Wendy's petite frame is folded over from the weight of several inches of dried mud on her skin. I want to point out to her that some cultures actually make bricks out of this very formula, but I know she is not interested in a *National Geographic* moment. Silk is standing in a corner, frozen with fear. The hose is still in her hands, but only a drizzle flows from the nozzle.

"I'm here to resolve this, Wendy. Silk, you can go now. Thank you for following typical procedures. Unfortunately, our guest followed an atypical process and caused this difficulty." I refuse to let Wendy blame Silk or Halo or Sophie or me for her mistake.

Once Silk scurries out of the room, Wendy starts to cry. I hear sniffles, and then I see her shoulders shake beneath her crustation. I cannot help myself. I take pity. "We'll figure out a way, Wendy." A few heartbeats later I realize I have repeated Beau's comforting phrase.

"I just…I just…I wanted to relax, you know? Work has been stressful, and this weekend I walked this superhard trail all for a good cause. It was…" She goes silent while considering whether the person who just *had* to light up three cigarettes during her mud bath should confess to being the emcee of the breast cancer fund-raiser.

Kindly, I confess for her. "The Tucson Trot, for breast cancer. Yes, I know. I saw you nearing the finish line. At record pace, I might add."

Her startling blue eyes search my face for signs of betrayal.

"Don't worry, Wendy. I won't tell anyone. About the smoking or the golf cart."

"Oh!" She tries to flip her hair with indignation but just ends up clunking her torso against the wall.

With a hose the size of a WaterPik and a small scrubber brush with soft bristles, I begin to move my hand in circular motion across her back. She whimpers now and then but does not complain. The slow process allows for a lot of time to meditate about life, so I decide to use this in a positive way. "You know, I wouldn't do this for just anyone."

"Are you a fan?" She seems shocked, as she should be, to suggest this.

"Yes. But not of Wendy Skies. I'm a fan of Walter Simmons. Perhaps you remember him?"

The mud maven turns to look at me. Most of her face is visible by now and so is her surprised expression.

"I work at Golden Horizons...used to. And Walter is one of my favorite folks. He..." My throat is tight with emotion. "He loves you, Wendy. And misses you. Do you know that he watches your show every day and won't leave for lunch until you do that special sign-off. He thinks it is just for him..."

"Ow!"

"Sorry," I wipe her skin with a warm towel.

"It is for him. The sign-off." Wendy takes the towel from me and wraps it around her quite clean but red shoulders as if a sudden gust of cold wind had come into the room. "My childhood...it wasn't so great. Dad tried, but Mom was depressed and verbally abusive. As a kid I remember vowing to grow up as soon as possible and when I did," she wipes a tear from her eyes, "I would not look back, you know?"

"Yes, I know." Humbled again.

"So I climbed my way to the top...at least my version of the top, and pretty much stayed away from Mom. I wanted this new life to completely override the past. Unfortunately, that meant I didn't see Dad, either. When Mom passed away, I placed Dad in the best facility...which you know," Wendy gives me a quick smile. "But by then...by now...I felt so guilty about all the years he was alone with her and her illness. I really abandoned him."

Is this sympathy stirring in my gut? And understanding? Here I think I will shower Miss Skies with guilt and blame, and she's been doing that to herself. What she needs is exactly what Walter needs.

"Don't be so hard on yourself, Wendy. Your dad doesn't feel the same way. He just misses you terribly."

"Thanks. It's Ingrid, actually." She smiles at me shyly and extends a polished hand to me.

"It's Mari, actually." I laugh.

"Mari, you are good at this."

"Really? You aren't mad about the mud-bath-turned-terror?"

"No. This was my fault. But what I meant was...you are good at this." She motions the connection between us. "Why'd you leave Golden Horizons? I'll bet my dad and the others loved you."

My response could get back to Lionel, but so what. We're being honest with one another. "I'm really starting to wonder that very thing. I thought this was the good life and that was the life to leave behind. But now, I don't know."

"I understand exactly."

And right there, in the craziest of circumstances, we come clean with each other. And though it hurt to break through our mutually hardened exteriors, we walk out of that room purified and a bit closer to truth.

Something in Common

I have never admitted to my friends that I lied to an old lady at church just to save face for being single. I'd be too ashamed at letting down single women everywhere. We can fib about our weight, our shoe size, and our television viewing preferences…but never about our singleness.

So on this Sunday, even without their advice or better judgment to fall back on, I know instinctively that I need to lie again.

But only to correct the first lie. Today I will be straightforward during the time of greeting and tell Rose Waverly that I, Mari "Chanel" Hamilton, am now a widow. My husband's last photographic mission was, sadly, his last.

This puts me back in the honest position of being, once again, single.

For a moment I am unable to spot Rose. She has placed herself at the very far east end of the pew. There is still a large space about her, so I manage to make it there in time to prepare for my lie that will free me from past indiscretions.

"Please greet one another with the peace of the Lord."

On this far end of the seating arrangements, there are not many fellow worshipers to greet, so Rose and I face each other immediately.

"Hello…dear. I guess it's just us over here. I wanted to be able to get out if I didn't feel well. I haven't been doing so good lately."

Rose's eyes seem to wander about me rather than focus on my face. I'm second-guessing my plan. But I have to make it right.

"How is your husband?"

Okay, now we are back on schedule. "I wanted to tell you that…" I face this woman who, from the side reminds me a bit of Tess. Maybe because of this or because of my honesty exfoliation with Ingrid, I know what I need to say. "Rose, I lied before. I don't have a husband. I'm single. I always have been. I always…well, actually…" I realize that I do have a new story to tell my pew-sharer. "I am seeing a very nice guy. His name is Beau. He's really quite kind and amazingly he puts up with my very strange behavior. Speaking of which, I'm sorry about making up the photographer husband. I just got tired of saying I'm alone." I stop to take a breath.

Rose reaches out to my hand and holds it for the briefest moment. "I'm getting tired of being alone too, my dear."

Bordering on Crazy

In my dream I answer the phone late at night, my mind foggy with sleep. I expect to hear someone I know on the other end, but a man is yelling at me in Spanish. I can only guess at the meaning of a few words, but the tone of a stern and likely stout person is unmistakable. He is saying that I am in trouble. I hang up, slightly aware that perhaps the oddballs with flowers have found a way to hack into my dreams.

By the time the phone rings again, I have removed the pillow from over my head and slouched in a fetal position toward the nightstand. My close proximity turns the average ring tone into a shrill siren. I do not mistake this round for a dream. I push the night mask up with the back of my left hand, which is tingling with sleep, and grab the receiver.

"Hello?" I look at my alarm clock and see that it is 1:30 in the morning on a weeknight. I want to make sure my caller is aware of this fact, but he is focused on his message.

"Señora Hamilton? Don't hang up. We need to talk. We have Kate... no, excuse me, Señora, we have Señorita Caitlin."

I lean up on my elbow. My heart pounds and the web between my thumb and finger pulses with the force of adrenaline. Have I read anything about hostage situations lately?

"Don't hurt her. Don't hurt her," I say while my mind is praying a big ol' SOS prayer. Please, let her be okay. I'll do anything. Anything. With a voice that does not even sound familiar I speak with conviction. "I'll call everyone I know to gather ransom money. I'll get a nondescript vehicle and refuse to have police follow me to the drop-off. I'll take my night mask and go in to the hideout blindfolded so that I cannot recount the location to anyone, not even if I wanted to. I'll…"

"Just come take her from me. Okay?"

Oh. "Okay."

While I wedge the phone between my chin and shoulder and rush around to find my keys, officer Jim Rodriguez explains that my clever friend has passed out at the Nogales, Mexico/Nogales, Arizona border. This is his entire explanation, which leaves many details unanswered. Why would she be there at night? What caused her to collapse? Why is she being held at the police station? I drive the two hours south with blurry eyes and a lightning-fast heartbeat. There is little to do but drive straight ahead with my foot pressed on the gas pedal while my mind tries to think up reasons why Caitlin would be at the border at this hour.

The two-liter bottle of Mountain Dew I had grabbed on the way out the door is drained dry and my bladder is expressing its regrets. I reluctantly pull into a gas station. Each moment I spend off the road I envision Caitlin sitting in a sparse jail cell counting the seconds until I can rescue her. But the single girl's rule of the road to not stop at gas stations at night unless absolutely necessary does apply. Thankfully, the bathroom is one located inside a well-lit market attached to the station. I snag some jerky for me and a bag of Oreos for Caitlin but resist the urge to buy another bottle of soda.

After miles and miles of dark land and wide-open sky and lots of imagined scenarios, I reach the border town. During the day this area has lots of friendly foot traffic as tourists and townspeople go between the countries with ease to purchase handmade goods, bargain-down overpriced souvenirs, or eat at one of the many nearby authentic Mexican restaurants. But at night this place is eerie and definitely not a tourist pamphlet highlight. My dad will kill me if I don't get killed first.

This is one of those times when I wish I had a person in my life locally to call and say, "It's three-thirty A.M., and I'm in Mexico. Just thought you should know." Maybe there are lots of other benefits to living in the same town with your boyfriend. I tuck this aside for later contemplation and return my focus to my surroundings.

I use the minilight on the end of my key chain to read the final last two lines of directions on the back of my phone bill. My only handy writing utensil was eyeliner, so all the letters pretty much look like O's in the dim ray of light. While trying to figure out the last line, I realize I am just a block from what looks like a security station. A long, narrow stateside brick building is the only place where light shines from windows. I notice a large policeman standing near a corner window and consider this my likely destination. Only when I approach the gated door do I see the very small painted sign that reads "Police Station/Estación de Policiá."

Apparently, they do not care to be noticed.

The yellowed, cracked doorbell is loosely attached to wiring that hangs tangled from the doorway and seems to wind its way along the brick and through a small gap in the closest window. My finger presses in several times since I do not hear a noise from this side of the door. I'm praying it works and shudder as I look behind me, around me, and then finally back in front of me in time to see the same policeman I saw from my car fiddling with the lock on the gate.

The iron grates on the cement of the step as it swings wide and creates an opening through which I am to pass. The officer motions for me to come in and starts walking toward a hallway past a check-in desk without watching to see if I am following. It must be very obvious who I am because they do not even ask for my name or my ID. My first humorous thought of the evening…maybe they are eager to release Caitlin to my custody. She probably suggested that they add sequins or authentic Mexican braiding to their uniforms.

This image relaxes my muscles, which have had a death grip around my bones for nearly three hours. All of this is too surreal to take in. I just want to get to my friend. "Take me to Caitlin," I say, as if rehearsing lines for a part as an extra in an extraterrestrial flick. Though it is unnecessary to ask because the officer is already pointing toward a door near the end of the hall.

"Infirmary." His eyes are kind, not gruff as I expected them to be, and this setting is much warmer thanks to the Mexican cultural touches. Rooms painted with colors originating from rich natural pigments create a celebratory cell block. Draped, woven fabrics cover chairs, tables, walls, and counters. If one of those silver-and-turquoise seeking tourists were to stumble upon this place, they would think it a part of the market.

I receive a few nods and "holas" from a small grouping of officers and apparently their wives or girlfriends who have arrived with meals for their nocturnal lunchtime. Now, that is devotion. I can smell polenta and tamales from a nearby dish and realize that eating most of Caitlin's Oreos was not such a good idea on a queasy, shaken-from-being-awakened-in-the-wee-hours tummy. The fumes from a bowl of fresh salsa with lots of cilantro and peppers make my eyes water.

My pajama bottom legs slap against one another as I make my way past this makeshift dining area. In my haste I had only added a bra and a sweater to my nighttime attire. The drawstring, wide-legged cotton pants seemed good enough at the time, but I was really only thinking about my comfort during the drive. Now I felt a bit naked, knowing the kind-eyed officer was watching me. My Grocery Bag incident flashed in my mind. I slightly exaggerate the raising of each leg as I make my way down the dimly lit, pale green hall. No shuffle here…no, siree.

A first glance into the room reveals a village woman in colorful native clothing squatting on a cot. I stop my forward motion in order to look again at the sign outside the door. I glance once more at the officer down the hall and shrug my universal language question. He motions again and nods and points. I step back into the small room. There are two cots, one cabinet, and a wastebasket. There is no room to hide a human, except within the miles of fabric seemingly wound around this village woman.

"Mari?" A faint version of Caitlin's voice does indeed emerge from the folds of a woven poncho.

Either the woman is ventriloquist or…or…that hefty native woman is my friend.

"Caitlin?"

She starts crying, and even before the sombrero falls and the strap catches around her neck and strangles her voice for a moment, I know for sure it is she.

Her crying is loud enough to beckon a female officer from another one of the small rooms. The woman is young and pretty with a very full, round face and eyes that have endless, thick lashes that curl right at the very tip. A smile that holds warmth and not condescension invites me to lean closer toward her. The pile of clothing that sounds like Caitlin is rocking back and forth—either the back-to-the-womb movement of a shock victim or an effort to get up from the low military cot. While the blob is in action, the female officer pulls my sleeve toward her, motioning me to have a word alone. We step back into the hallway.

"Her friend?" she asks as she leans against the cement wall casually.

"Yes. I'm Mari." I reach out to shake her hand and her smile grows larger.

"Ah, our names are similar. I'm Maria. Officer Sanchez." Her petite hand offers a firm shake and then it returns to my sleeve. She is a person used to calming down victims or giving bad news to families.

Uh-oh. My heart races again. How bad is this? I mean, driving basically to Mexico in the dead of night is bad for me…but how bad is this for Caitlin? We all know she is quirky, but has she crossed over the border into the land of crazy?

"What happened? I don't know what is going on." My lips shake nervously as I talk.

She nods a few times and fails to keep in a small laugh. "Do not worry. She is fine. She passed out from the heat today, that is all."

"Passed out?" People park on the Arizona side and walk over to Mexico to shop all the time. I know Caitlin does this once in a while, but I still cannot quite put together the scene.

"Yes. She was overheated and passed out. This actually happens now and then, but with your friend and her…plentiful outfit…it was quite serious. The doctor came to check on her throughout the evening, but your friend refused medical attention."

"Why didn't she call me when she was starting to feel bad?" I think out loud. I'm getting a bit perturbed about the late-night hour and the risk Caitlin put me in to get here for her.

"Your friend was hallucinating a bit. Dehydration was the main culprit. That happens most often to women who are…" she pauses to choose her word carefully, "ample."

Ample? I laugh.

"Oh, the bulky clothes might make her look large, but she is really…" A sharp kick knocks my knees out from position. Apparently Caitlin is back among the living and gives me a not so subtle hint from her place in the doorway.

"…much larger. She gained even more weight lately. Ah, here's my ample friend." I turn around and look into Caitlin's face for the first time this evening…morning…whatever. Her usually flawless skin is red, bloated, and blotchy from heat rash. Wilted hair spikes have become sharp daggers of black etching into her forehead, plastered there by sweat. I give her a "that was so sweet of you to kick me" smile and turn back to Maria.

"Thank you for taking such good care of her, Maria." I want to pinch Caitlin, but I know I would have to drill for hours through fabric to find flesh.

"My pleasure." Maria now places her hand on Caitlin's shoulder…or in the vicinity of Caitlin's shoulder. "And you take care of yourself. Always bring water for a big day of shopping."

"Oh, you don't know how big," I say snidely and sidestep out of Caitlin's kicking range.

My friend is a waddling bag of rags who cannot get out of this place fast enough. We make our way down the hall in record time. Caitlin's path is a bit crooked, like a cartoon figure after being twirled around and around and then set loose to run. The tall officer stops us at the door and Caitlin's splotchy face grows pale beneath the rash marks. "Come on," she whispers to me while motioning toward the door in a spastic style.

I give her a dirty look. It isn't as if I plan to stay for dinner or volunteer for the night shift. But as desperately as I want to leave I am not about to ignore the policeman's request. "Yes, sir?" I ask in superpolite, solid-citizen mode. I am really saying "Despite my crazy friend's behavior, I am a responsible person of good standing and good sense."

"Your friend forgot her belongings, miss."

How sad that I am old enough to like being addressed as "miss."

"Oh, yes. Thank you." Caitlin approaches him and looks down at the floor, avoiding eye contact.

He removes a brown legal envelope from the drawer and unwinds the string around the metal brad. A few items tumble out of the container and onto the countertop. A piece of gum half out of its wrapper, a compact mirror, a slender watch, two rings, and a flattened chocolate bar that had obviously mutated through several forms of matter, from solid to liquid to something in-between.

I expect Caitlin to reach out and gather the items, but she motions with her eyes for me to take care of this small task. I actually haven't seen her hands, or any other body parts, for that matter, since I got here. She had better be able to explain why she is acting like a complete fruitcake and dressing for the Eskimo version of *Hello, Dolly*.

Our Laurel and Hardy frames walk toward my car when we realize the officer is saying something to us from the narrow doorway. His comment is meant to be discreet. A just-between-us courtesy. He says it softly and then winks, and I am so focused on his wink that I don't get what he is telling us.

"What?" I stand closer to the door, hoping to be able to read his lips should he repeat it again as a whisper. But he has already disappeared back into his warm, colorful world.

"Did you get that?" I ask Caitlin's back as she scurries to the car. Because her feet are hidden beneath the layers, she looks like an eccentric ghost hovering over the gravel.

"Just get in the car," she barks at me as if I have not just performed a divine act of friendship.

I follow her orders, not because she deserves control of my actions, but because it is now almost five o'clock in the morning, and I want desperately to be home and in bed.

Not until we are several minutes away from the *Twilight Zone* scene we just experienced does Caitlin begin to shed her clothing. Piece after piece after piece. This striptease goes on forever, and soon my backseat is piled up with rugs, belts, jewelry, vests, blouses, hats, and of course, the poncho. My incredulous stare goes unnoticed because she is frantic to get out of these hot, stifling garments.

"Did you steal these? Is that what the secrecy was all about?" Caitlin is odd, but she is moral and odd. And she is a proponent of higher wages and prices for Mexican craftsman, so I ask this shocking question not as a serious accusation but as a way to get her to spill the beans. Expect the worst so that the person can take responsibility for a lighter infraction. I may not be a police person, but I have had to wrangle the truth out of more than a few of our city's elderly.

Her response is a dirty look that fades to worry. "No. Oh, goodness. You don't think I would do that, do you? Please don't tell Sadie about this. Or Angelica. I get enough flak from everyone, you know?"

If Caitlin is my forgiving friend, I am hers. I hold up my little finger in honor of a pinky swear. But in case she has forgotten the situation, I remind her. "At an absurd hour this morning I was awakened by that tall policeman with kind eyes…in Spanish, mind you…*and* I drove all the way to another country to get you. So no, I will not tell Sadie or Angelica, but yes, you will tell me exactly what it is that I am not telling them. Go. Speak. Spill."

Her chest expands as she takes in air and courage. "You know how I am always looking for ideas from the Mexican artisans. Well, I had an idea to use parts of these things and incorporate them into more trendy fashion items. Like this..." She reaches back and grabs a rug that has a pattern of purple, navy, and a shocking pink. "If I alternate something like this with pieces of, say, gray suede or green silk, it could be fabulous."

"Yes..." Okay, so I wouldn't wear it, but I do appreciate her creativity. I do. "The point?" I motion for her to continue and then reach into the glove box for the remaining few Oreos. We both start crunching as Caitlin obliges.

"Well, you have to pay a tax if you bring more than four hundred dollars worth of stuff across the border. And I really need all these things now, so I had the idea to start wearing things as I bought them. Then at the border I just claimed these..." She holds up a dainty pair of silver earrings.

"Those? You only claimed those? They really believed you?"

"You heard Maria. She just thought I was ample."

We burst out laughing and sing a twisted version of the bo-bana song "ample ample bo-bample...ample" until our stomachs are sore.

Our cookie breath fogs up the windows and we each wipe a peephole on the glass so we can take in the rarely witnessed sight of early morning's arrival.

"I know!" Caitlin screams out of nowhere and shocks me back into adrenaline mode. She faces me for her personal epiphany. "Who does this kind of thing? I actually thought it was a smart idea at the time. Until about five o'clock. I tried to make my way to the bus station so I could catch the early evening return to Tucson. All of a sudden I was shaking and sweating and itching. Next thing I know, I am staring up at Jim. Officer Rodriguez...or as you call him, 'the tall policeman with kind eyes.'" She pauses to catch her breath and, I do believe, to also linger over the image of those eyes. As I change lanes and hit the middle road bumps she jolts back to the surface of her thoughts. In between hiccups she continues. "I swear, Mari, I need to come and live with you and your friends at the home. In a special wing of Golden Horizons." She pauses and then says, "I forgot you aren't there anymore." Her tone is solemn, as if this really saddens her. The thought gets to me a bit too. But just as quickly her eyes light up again and she is positive. "Oh, but you could probably still get me in without an initiation fee."

"Good grief. It isn't a gym, Caitlin." I have to laugh. "But don't worry. I'll get you in and set you up with a nice room by Wilson, the man who makes dresses out of the drapes when the staff isn't looking. You two might hit it off."

"Do you want to know what he said? The tall policeman with very kind eyes...?" I knew her thoughts would circle back to the handsome man.

"Of course."

Caitlin sits up and takes on his stoic demeanor. "Next time, just pay the tariff. Or better yet, make two trips and stop in to visit."

"So he knew!"

"Yes. He knew." She sighs and hiccups loudly. "He really did have nice eyes, didn't he?"

I exaggerate a Western drawl. "Nicest pair of eyes this side of the Mississippi." We both take a moment considering the man in uniform. "So maybe this was worth it after all." I wink at her the way Jim Rodriquez winked at her. And we laugh some more.

Surprisingly the drive north is quick. Our state of delirium is an easier accompaniment to travel than my upset stomach and visions of Caitlin's incarceration among killers had been. We are both hungry, our adrenaline burning through our junk food as quickly as we can inhale it.

Caitlin's escapade inspires me to practice something I am not very good at...spontaneity. That and trusting my instincts. When you ignore such urges and life compasses for too long, they get buried, just like Caitlin in her quest for Fab status. But this experience has allowed me to tap into an idea that seems perfect for this morning. Just a few minutes before our official turn, I take the exit to the San Xavier del bac Mission. Caitlin nods her approval, and we both hope that vendors are already preparing pastries and tamales at the stands by the mission's parking lot.

My hunch was a good one. We sit on top of my car, sipping warm sodas that were about to be placed on ice and savoring our treat. The biggest treat of all, a colorful and spectacular sunrise over the gentle hills leading to town. Deep pink and faint lavender splash against the white of the grand Spanish mission as though God has taken a paint brush to this church just for us and just for this moment.

"It's called the white dove of the desert," I say. Caitlin nods with understanding.

The mission, in a state of perpetual reconstruction and resurfacing, has a scaffold bracing its western half. The most recent efforts are to cover graffiti left by heartless people on the walls of a sacred place.

Huddled in Caitlin's purchases and sitting on one of the rugs, we must look like two passengers on a magic carpet headed for the mission and the city beyond. My field of vision places me smack-dab in the middle of the church…my legs straddling the pristine right half and the scaffold-gripped left. Once again, I am physically in line with my spiritual state. As much as I have strived to become shiny and acceptable to the world's eye, I am still very much in a place of limbo. I close my left eye to take in the perfect half only…but the urge to peek at the old side with scars is too strong. For the first time I am convicted, not by guilt or regret or selfish motives, but by the pure conviction of the Spirit that I am supposed to go home. I glance down at Tess' bracelet and the single, brass key and know for sure. I have unfinished business to resolve.

The sun rises in the sky. We begin to shed our layers as nature places a warm hand on our backs. This is how I will always remember this day. Not driving at night scared half out of my wits. Not even the comical state in which I found Caitlin. But this moment of sacred silence, friendship, and a feeling of flying in the right direction even if I'm not sure where it will lead.

"Thank you," whispers Caitlin, sharing my soulful mood.

"No, thank you, Caitlin." And I mean it.

Baggage Claim

Lady. Lady, let go."

Huh? I am in a total travel fog, the kind that feels as though your head has been stuffed with cotton. I slowly turn to face a waiflike woman dressed in Annie Hall-ish trousers, suspenders, and hat. "Huh?" I repeat aloud.

"That's my bag. Your hand is on my bag."

My luggage was given to me by my parents as a graduation present. They said they were just about to buy the sleek black-with-gray-trim set I had requested, but then they saw the vibrant fuchsia cases. "Nobody else will have these. You'll love that." They were wrong. I look down at the suitcase that has my hand attached to it. It's nearly identical to mine, except now I see a "Save Tibet" sticker on the side.

I release my hold but not before Annie beckons a nearby security officer to mediate.

"We're fine," I assure the man, who resembles Bill Murray. For a minute I think it must be him researching for a part. He asks Annie if we really are fine. She nods harshly, releasing him back to his post by the exit doors and the *Washington Post* dispensers.

"Sorry." I am sorry. Sorry that I thought traveling the day before Thanksgiving was a smart idea. Sorry that I am here in the Dulles airport, near enough to my childhood home to make me feel like I did as a child. In the way. Confused. Mistaken.

I spot my bag coming around the luggage racetrack one more time. A young Frenchman reaches for it when I fail to drag it off the belt. "*Merci pour l'aide,*" I say, making a mental note that I will have to tell Sophie that I used one of our few phrases…and with a very cute French boy, no less.

I check my watch one more time. Dad said he would be here at eleven. It is a quarter till noon. My parents are reliable but never punctual. The brass key clicks against my watch, and I am reminded of the letter from Tess. Glancing around for a place to sit, my eyes settle on a long empty bench by a magazine shop.

Unfolding the delicate linen sheet, I welcome Tess' handwriting with a smile. How she knew that she would be leaving me still requires too much thought and faith on my part. She writes as if in the middle of an ongoing conversation.

To my girl,

I told you. It is between me and God. Don't try to figure it all out. You have enough going on in your life to worry about how the end of life works. Mari, you are the one I hate to leave the most. I am thankful I was here to see you blossom…and see you dance with your love. I cannot wait to watch you move into the next stage of your life. Things need to settle down a bit…but then you will know exactly where you are going.

I digress. The key you have of course opens the bureau at Golden Horizons. But it also opens several other bureaus. My true love had the set made for me as a wedding gift. As you know, Gisele is my most trusted friend…so before I made the move to Golden Horizons, I entrusted her with these hand-crafted pieces and their contents. But now, as I make another move, a bigger move, it is you, Mari, who will watch over, dis-tribute, or use these items as you see fit. My faith tells me you will find a purpose for them very soon in your journey. But if not…think of them as good luck charms, never as burdens. Nobody needs extra baggage in their life, and in the end these are just things. Beautiful, yes. But still just things. You and I both know there is much more to life. Go live it, Mari. Live fully. Until we meet again, I will celebrate you and your joys to come from the Pearly Gates…the real deal this time.

Godspeed, Tess

After I spend a few days with Mom and Dad, I will fly to New York to help Gisele arrange for the shipment of these good luck charms. I'm more curious about this grand dame of New York than I am about my inheritance.

Inheritance. I have an inheritance from someone I met only five years ago. It's a miracle Tess could trust me so much in such a short time. Yet, in my childhood God showed me that the stranger I meet at breakfast is considered family before dinner. How many brothers and sisters had I welcomed into our home over eighteen years? I take a quick survey of my memory and figure more than a hundred. Could this be possible? A truth that used to bother me now makes me smile. In some ways it would be good to see…

"Marcus!" Front and center in my field of vision is the one I am not prepared to see. A stranger-turned-brother yes. But also my first love.

"Mari?" His dark eyes look me over and he speaks my name slowly. We are both amazed by the expanse of time that has passed. "You look wonderful! Up. Stand. I get a hug at least. I drove through lunch hour traffic to come fetch you. Ted got caught up with one of the food vendors donating to the big Thanksgiving feast."

I am amused and flattered that he is as nervous as I am. I figured that over time his good looks and quick wit would make him a bit jaded in the presence of women.

We embrace until I am uncomfortable. I swat the bill of his Cubs cap and point to my bag. He obliges after first bowing to me. We laugh and keep looking at each other as we make our way through the crowd, into the shuttle, and finally to the parking lot.

When I booked this ticket to D.C., I mentally prepared to face a lot of difficult memories, recycled emotions, former roles, and flashbacks of the childhood I still run from. My logic…the more I visualized what would take place during my three-day visit, the more I could troubleshoot the emotional pitfalls, the gaps between memory and reality, and the lapses in sanity that send my head spinning.

But in all that careful planning, plotting, and second-guessing, I had forgotten to consider exactly what I would do if my past love stood waiting for me in baggage claim.

As it turns out, I would sweat, vacillate between crimson red and ecru, and laugh uncontrollably and intermittently. Oh yeah, and I would ask to have the car pulled over to the side of a busy freeway so I could be sick.

As I'm doubled over in front of lunchtime commuters in this nation's fine capital, I can only pray that this is not a preview of things to come.

Old Familiar Places

Marcus and I enter quietly, with plans to surprise my folks in the midst of the commotion. But we could have used a bullhorn and come in riding cattle and never been noticed. Quick glances take in the large open kitchen with its ceiling fans above gigantic, purple cupboards, plank tables that seem to stretch for fifty feet, and multiple blackboards placed in random spots and at varying heights along the brick walls. Mom is a strong proponent for writing down expectations, events, ideas, lists, and the occasional inspirational quote when there is room.

At this very moment, she is crossing off "Wednesday: pick up 20 pumpkin pies from Georgetown Bakery" from the blackboard temporarily titled "Donated Food Items: What and When" located at the very top of the stairwell. She stands on a precarious ladder. Gospel music is blaring, people are running in and out of the back storeroom and delivery door, and a new generation of children tromp up and down the stairs on the way to their rooms.

After a few shouts at normal volumes to get her attention, Marcus and I shout at the top of our lungs, "Moooommmmmm!" and break up with laughter as she nearly topples from her high perch. The wiry woman scurries down the so-called ladder to greet me.

After a long hug she pushes me away for a look-see.

"Honey, you look all schmootzy." She is troubled by this.

"This is a term? Schmootzy?"

"Puffy here," she says, pointing to my eyes. "And flushed. Was it a bad flight? You didn't lose your luggage, did you?"

"Not her luggage…but her lunch," Marcus pats me on the back, smiling a knowing smile.

"You two are up to something," says Mom, pausing long enough to scan our expressions for proof of mischief. "Goodness, I knew it was trouble when Ted said he was sending Marcus to the airport. Will I have to keep my eyes on you?"

Without even thinking, I step a bit to the right to create some distance in case Mom is getting the wrong idea about me and Marcus or if she and Dad planned all along to send Marcus to fetch me. I promise myself that the minute I get a chance to speak to her alone, I will tell her all about Beau. Beau! I reach into my pocket and retrieve my phone. I turn it back on and watch for the little message icon. Two missed calls.

"Oh, no. She's one of those." Marcus digs his thumb into my side. This was cute when he was the object of my teen flirtations, but I'm… I'm…older, wiser, and I have an adult romance. There is no thumb jabbing, hair pulling, or ear tugging in adult love. I give him a look that says "stand back." He interprets the look but does not budge.

"Mari?" I hear my dad's voice near but do not see him. I think maybe he is suffocating beneath the piles of bread loaves and paper plates that overflow an old soda fountain counter my folks bought years ago when a local, old-fashioned drugstore went out of business.

Mom reaches past my right shoulder to a small black box. She presses the red button and hollers beside my ear, "Yes! She's here. Ted, take a break, would you? It isn't every day that your daughter comes home for a visit."

Or every year, I think, flooded with guilt. But I say, "An intercom system? Finally! How many years did I suggest that very thing?" I place my hands on my hips for a showing of strength and intelligence and due respect.

"Well, why do you think we got it, dear? All because of you." She pats my head in a silly fashion, emphasizing that she is indeed patronizing me.

"Woo-hoo. Why, there's my ma-Mari…back from sa-safari."

Dad comes bounding through the back delivery door with the very old and very tired line he created the year I went, against my will, to wilderness survival camp. They thought the experience would enlighten me. Instead, it frightened me into an extreme state of nature-phobia.

It's amazing I am even close to normal. I self-congratulate as Dad swoops me up in his arms with gusto. His smaller-than-I-recall frame can only lower me into a dance hall dip rather than lift me into the air. My silk beret drops to the floor and my honey-colored hair tumbles into view.

"Oh, my gosh! What on earth did you do with my daughter's hair?" Dad flips me upright and they all take in the look of Chanel. I hadn't had time to dye it back to normal. My fingers twirl the tips as I stand feeling naked and judged.

"I like it," Mom says, standing up for me. I smile at her and shake my head no.

"It was for work…just for a short while. I'm going back to the old look, don't worry." I fumble through an unnecessary apology.

"Golden Horizons did a performance of *Golden Girls*?" Dad laughs at his new bad joke.

"Ted, don't tease her. You know she works at that fancy resort now."

"Oo la la," Marcus says. He does not jab with his thumb, but I get the same sensation.

This is a scene I did manage to conjure up in advance. My tactical response: deep breathing and a change of subject. I am not ready to defend Majestic. Not because I plan to be invisible while here, but because I don't know what I would say.

"How can I help?" This trick has never failed.

"Blondie, come with me. We have corn to shuck." Dad does a country two-step dance and I roll my eyes. He lobs the van keys over my head to Marcus' sure catch. "The Capitol Deli has a bunch of salad that needs to be picked up. Do you mind?"

"Not at all. I'm there." He starts out but hesitates as his hand is about to leave the doorknob. "Mari, it's good to see you."

There are literally bushels of corn to shuck. Dad gives me a quick refresher for how to get the most corn from the cob into the big metal bowls. We speak in short spurts about current kids in the shelter, my job at Majestic, and the oddball house projects Dad has undertaken over the past four years.

Periodically, I try to shake off bits of husk and hull that gather like snowballs on my sweater sleeves. But really I use the moment to scan my dad's face. He looks a lot older. I used to see him as a blur of energy and motion. Now he is slow motion except for short bursts. I want to ask what happened, but the question only serves to point out my absence. The choices I made to avoid contact with this place now make their consequences known.

Evening is upon us as we evaluate the food prepared for tomorrow's big community feast. Dad and I go through a master checklist. This one is not on a blackboard but actually printed out from a computer (yet another technological advancement around here), so I have grid boxes to check off as Dad calls out the mounds of vegetables, bread, desserts, fresh turkeys, hams, and every side order imaginable, from sweet potatoes and mashed potatoes to stuffing and chickpea casserole. My stomach is about to state its case for dinner just as Mom opens up the walk-in freezer.

"Finish counting those frozen turkeys and then come and eat. Don't forget to add you two to your total. Ha." She closes the door and leaves Dad and me to fake laugh behind her back.

"Just like ol' times, eh, kid?" Dad leans his shoulder into mine.

"You got it." I lean back into him, wishing I knew all my feelings so I could express them right then and there. But I promised myself I'd enjoy moments as they happened rather than figure them out in relation to my past. To stay silent, leaning against my dad, seems like home.

For Whom the Bell Tolls

By ten o'clock in the morning there is a line wrapped around the neighborhood. Many diners have walked here from nearby areas, but some families or groups of neighbors have pooled their resources to take the Metro or a cab ride here from a distant part of the city. When I go outside to make an initial count, two local shelters pull up with their refurbished school buses and unload passengers.

"Is it my bad memory, or did Mom increase her marketing efforts this year?" I nudge my dad, who is karate chopping a head of lettuce with the vigor I recall. This visit has helped me understand one thing…my folks are extroverts, thriving under the pressure of being surrounded by people who need something from them. I am, however, an introvert…longing to pull up a chair in a corner with one of the guests or shelter kids, strike up a heart-to-heart, and observe the rest from a safe distance.

"Your mom, my dear, has at least half the city's politicians in her pocket these days."

I scrunch my face. "Isn't that a bad term? It sounds like she is making payoffs."

"It's the opposite. They are making the payoffs. Much of this food has come from organizations that boast having a politician or wealthy patron on their board." He looks up from his kung fu cabbage moves to look fondly at Mom. She is rerouting a new group of people to the covered outdoor porch, which we enclosed with particle board yesterday. "That woman wears the leaders down. At this point I think she could run for office and they'd all offer support just to keep her out of their hair."

Mom turns around and hollers at me. She can sniff an idle person from a mile away. "Mari! I need your help."

I trot over in obedient fashion. I know to not get smart with her on a day like this.

"Here are the van keys. Do you still have your fifteen-passenger-vehicle license?"

"Yep. From…Golden."

"That's my girl. I need you to go to this address and pick up a group of folks. They have no way to get here." Her eyes focus on the ceiling as she reaches for a thought. "The Morenos! They have been coming for years. Remember them? Robert Moreno wears that hunter's cap; he used to call you…what was that?"

"Mari Christmas," I offer, amazed that my memory is returning in full force.

"Yes! Well, they cannot get here, and we cannot do Thanksgiving without them. Go quickly. It's a ways. Don't get lost." I'm only a few feet away when she adds, "Take Marcus…Roberta is in a wheelchair now. You will need help."

It only takes us twenty minutes to get lost.

"I know we are close. There's the old arcade. Remember, we used to go there all the time."

"No. You went there. I was busy studying, remember?" Marcus smirks at me from the passenger seat.

"Oh yeah. I do remember…that you were the one who *had* to study." Chuckle. Chuckle. "Same ol' Marcus."

"Different Mari, though."

I grip the steering wheel and strain my neck to read the next street sign. I don't know if I really want to follow this conversational detour. But I take the bait anyway. "How am I different?" I give him a look. "Other than the hair. Or extra weight. No obvious statements."

"You seem comfortable here now. Maybe you are more so with yourself and that translates into handling this place better. You always belonged; don't get me wrong. You just resisted it."

"Can you blame me? Who would want to grow up that way…" I stop cold, realizing that I am being insensitive. This is the way we both grew up. At least I had parents. Sometimes my self-focus makes me ill.

"I would, Mari. You and I both grew up surrounded by love. Maybe we both had reasons to resent why we were there or why we had to share everything with everybody at a time in life when we were trying to be individuals. Or a couple…" he says this last part softly and doesn't look at me.

I'm growing more frustrated with my inability to decide whether to turn left or right. But more than that, I'm sorry for how I left things with him.

"What? Have you been taking psychology courses or something?"

"I'm here to work on my PhD at Georgetown, as a matter of fact."

"I'm impressed. With the degree…but even more with your coming back to the shelter to help Mom and Dad."

"Mari, I owe them my life. You do in a physical way, but I do in a spiritual and emotional way. I know you struggled, but what you didn't see was how jealous we were of you. All of us. We had families who couldn't or wouldn't take care of their own kin. You had a family that would take us all in…and never act like they were doing us a favor. I don't know how many times your mom came up to me and said, 'Marcus, you make our family so much richer.'" His strong voice wavers. He coughs and I do a quick wipe of my eye with my mitten.

"I do get it, Marcus. I do now, anyway."

"Your mom told me you have a beau…literally." He laughs at his obvious joke, but I'm not laughing with him.

"Why do I bother saying anything in private to them? I told her about him last night, in confidence. I don't miss that part of home. There are no secrets," I rant and slam my hand against the steering wheel in defiance.

"Maybe there is no need for secrets." He does a "huh" shrug. "Beside, she was probably telling me so I wouldn't get any ideas after all these years. But I am happy you have a good guy. You deserve it, Mari."

I stall at a stoplight so I can look into his eyes. "Thanks, Marcus. And…you deserve it too. A significant other," I say sincerely. "You deserved me to be a better person. I left without any closure…and you meant the world to me. You did." I look away shamed but glad to finally give him the overdue apology.

Marcus says with a bit of urgency, "Can't you stay longer? Why leave tomorrow? You just got here."

"I told you, I have an unexpected stop in New York to make tomorrow and then I fly immediately back to Tucson. I don't even have vacation benefits yet. My boss just gave me a couple extra days because of the holiday, which happens to be a busy time of year at the resort."

"All that busyness is pretty convenient, if you want to ask me."

"I don't. But thanks for your input," I say, acting very much like a bratty sibling to this man I apologized to just seconds before. "Hey, that's the house. I remember it." By divine direction we have pulled up directly in front of the old brick house. Robert pushes open the screen door for Roberta in her wheelchair and motions for the others to follow. Soon we are barreling down the freeway singing "Over the River and Through the Woods" in notes and harmonies that don't exist except in a vehicle filled with people who have never sung together but feel the urge to try.

The sound of forks banging against the tables greets us when we return to the house. This is the shelter tradition to bring any latecomers to a meal so everyone can begin.

A big cheer is let out as we cross the threshold and get the Morenos to their special table near Mom and Dad.

"Hush. Hush," say a few older folks as Dad approaches the makeshift podium with a small microphone.

"A little respect!" Shouts one of the older kids from the shelter, which makes everyone laugh.

"Well, we all know that being thankful is a year-round part of our lives. But it is a pleasure to take time on this day to really celebrate all that we are grateful for. I see…what? At least seventy people right here that top my list. I know you are hungry, but let's give one more moment to thank the Giver." All heads bow and a few hats come off as Dad leads us in a short but sincere prayer of thanksgiving. When he is done, he holds up his hand to motion that there is one more thing. "And for me and Sarah, we are especially thankful that we have our beautiful daughter here with us today. She is the pride and joy of our lives and has always been the spark that keeps our spirits lifted."

He points to me and I am, by now, crying. Marcus joins the others as they clap in celebration of my presence. I know how undeserved it is, but I am grateful just the same.

"So, Mari," continues Dad. "Will you do the honors?" He steps aside to reveal the dinner bell. With little grace or discretion, I wipe my nose with my sleeve and go forward thinking a million thoughts and feeling as many emotions. I realize that I always thought I could never be special if everyone was included. But now I feel it; I get it that love has room for everyone.

And that *is* what makes our lives special…not fancy jobs, apartments with full kitchens, vehicles with leather interior, blond hair, the perfect boyfriend, or even deadlines to "have it all" by thirty.

As I clang the bell in front of those people in my real family, adopted family, and those who will be family by dessert, a bell goes off in my mind, spirit, and heart. It reverberates with one pure thought.

I want my old life back.

New York, New Chance

On the flight to New York, sunglasses hide my sorry, swollen eyes. Saying goodbye to my family and to the kids was harder than I imagined. I did this to myself. My new vow is to make an annual trip home each year from now on. No excuses.

An envelope and package rest on my lap. I'm afraid to incite another round of tears by opening the contents, but our takeoff is delayed and I haven't brought any reading material. Opening the card and gift is the only activity on the menu, other than making faces at the little boy wearing a D.C. Hard Rock Café cap in front of me.

Instant camera images tumble from the card. These photos, a Thanksgiving tradition, end up posted along the blackboards and are featured in the shelter's monthly newsletter and on the annual thank-you cards for donors. The first cracks me up. Dad is standing in the walk-in freezer balancing a frozen turkey on his finger. Well, trying to. The next features Mom behind the long soda counter squirting whipped cream into the mouths of Carlos and Sam, twins that live at the shelter. Another shows Mom and Dad standing by the family portrait wall that showcases every child to ever live in the home. They are positioned one on each side of the large photo of me on my fifth birthday. Each holds an end of a sign that reads "We love you."

I'm crying again. I have got to get my act together. Who knew I was sitting on all these ridiculous tears? It really is amazing that I function at all. One last photo remains. It is of Marcus alone by that same photo of me. His sign says "Write home" followed by his email address. I tuck this photo into my jacket pocket and place the others in my purse. The birthday card is homemade with construction paper, string, and crayons. Dad's handwriting wishes me a year filled with happiness and tells me to report to him whether blondes really do have more fun. Yuk. Yuk. Mom's note is a bit more sentimental:

> Dear Mari, our girl is all grown up and we couldn't be more proud of you. Thanks for all of your help, but even more important...thanks for your presence. We couldn't be more thankful than when we see you walk through the door. I know this is eleven days early, but I wanted to give you a gift in person for once. (And your dad says, "Save postage too." Ha.) I sense that you are really figuring out your purpose in life. May this make the journey easier to understand, and may it serve as a reminder of God's faithfulness. You are a blessing to all who know you. We love you, Mom and Dad.

Within layers of tissue paper I find a beautiful leather journal with my name engraved on it. My fingers trace the lightly imprinted pattern of leaves on the cover. As I place the card in the front of the journal, I notice a photo of me tucked between the first pages. It was taken quite a few Thanksgivings ago. I am wearing a large chef's apron tied at the neck and flying behind me for a royal robe, a tinfoil tiara sits askew on my head, and I carry a wooden spoon ahead of me like a scepter. My delight is obvious as I lead a group of smiling people to their dining table for the

Thanksgiving meal. Beneath the photo Mom wrote, "Our nine-year-old princess is gone, but our thirty-year-old princess with a servant's heart is alive and well. Lead on."

My vision is so blurry from tears that I am gazing into the face of a short man dressed in a chauffeur's uniform before I realize that the sign he carries has my name on it.

"That's me!" I shout with sour travel breath. He is so professional he doesn't even wince.

"Yes, miss. Right this way. May I?" He reaches for my fuchsia bag which, with his uniform, is a bad fashion statement. Better him than me.

In the stretch limo I resist pushing all the little buttons on the center console and wonder what is in store for me if Gisele has a personal chauffer named Duke. Because of her devoted correspondence with Tess, I feel as if I know Gisele. At least, I know she is one fun-loving and interesting person.

Duke opens the car door and motions for me to go forward as he retrieves my bag. The wind blows from the direction of Central Park on my right as I make my way to the gold doors beneath an emerald green awning. Maximilian holds the building doors open for me and says that the elevator operator, Saul, will be sure I get to Madame Westwood's floor.

"Her floor?" I say, exposing my lack of exposure to affluence.

Maximilian laughs. "Yes. Her floor." He introduces me to Saul. At first I pity a person who lives out his eight to five job in an elevator. That is, until I enter the elevator. It is bigger than my living room and has a much nicer couch.

The button labeled 15 lights up. Ding. "Your destination, miss." Saul steps out and leads me through the small entry area to a large solid door. He rings a bell that is discreetly placed beneath a light sconce. Within moments Norah greets us with a hearty hello and a breathless reprimand. "Duke was supposed to call before he left the airport! Madame Westwood is still in the bath." She laughs at divulging this personal information.

"Come. Come." She grabs my sleeve and pulls me into the apartment. "Saul, you tell Duke he didn't call. Now poor Mademoiselle Mari will have to wait to be greeted by her hostess!"

I know to not mess with Norah, even though the twinkle in her eye gives away her big heart and sense of humor.

"Forgetful men. It isn't enough that I am a cook and mother for them all. Now I have to be their memory too! I'm too old for that. Now, Mari, come with me. I'll feed you lunch while you wait."

I don't argue and am grateful to be fed. My stomach had been too queasy when leaving home to eat the biscuits and gravy Mom and Dad had made for me. But somehow I feel refreshed and very excited for this part of my journey.

An informal tour of the apartment...house, really...takes place as Norah casually says room names and purposes as if I have a layout just like it at home. "There...the parlor. The library. The salon. That is where she will meet with you after you eat. My room...a mess only because I devote all my time to everyone else. Over there, that is her office. Next to it, her assistant's office. And on the other side, the room with the gold door, that is the guest room...where your treasures are."

"My treasures?"

"Oh, yes. Not that I have opened them, but," she pauses and leans her small face near to my ear, "I have heard it is quite a collection. Madame Westwood wouldn't use a room for storage unless it was for a treasure... and for such a dear friend." She shakes her round head in dismay. "It is a shame. Her friend. Your friend." Her fast, consecutive pats on my shoulder are meant for comfort, but they make me laugh.

We finally arrive at the kitchen, the kind you see in gourmet magazines. Spotless, it is colored by copper pans hanging from an elaborate rack and rich, mahogany cabinets. Beautiful crystal pieces line open shelves and contrast, yet complement, deep, ceramic bowls hand-painted in the sea blue and golden yellow hues of fine Italian ware.

"This kitchen is enough to make a girl want to learn to cook," I say, laughing.

This is no laughing matter to Norah. "You are kidding with me?" All of a sudden she speaks with a foreigner's mixed order of words.

I shake my head, "I work a lot. And my friends and I go out. It is sort of our form of entertainment." My words are a miniscule argument to what she is about to say.

"*Quel dommage!*" She throws up her stubby hands. "You go to the cinema or read a book for entertainment. But learning to cook is part of a lifestyle…or a way of living. Goodness. I was going to feed you leftover shrimp rolls, but now I see I need to cook a meal for you. You sit and watch. I might even have you help me, Miss Work a Lot." She points to a stool on the other side of the kitchen island. Her hands go to her cheeks as she counts off a recipe to herself and stares at cabinets and the refrigerator, sizing up whether she has the necessary ingredients.

"It must be quick. Unfortunately, you will not see a full meal prepared. But the next time you come I will show you what I mean by lifestyle."

"Oh, no…believe me, I'm understanding just by watching you prep those vegetables and that…whatever those are. At first I thought they were…"

"Frog legs! They cook up quick and delicious. And with fresh vegetables, they are beautiful. And fast enough for a working girl, I assure you."

This is when I start checking the doorway to see if Gisele will arrive in time to save me from this extreme culinary adventure.

But moments after the plate is in front of me, I am licking my fingers and digging into my second garlic-butter dripping leg and don't even notice when Tess' beloved friend enters the room. Instead of seeing her swirl in on a cloud of chiffon and satin and sit on the other side of the island, I am shoving asparagus into my mouth as though it is chocolate.

"Darling, you eat like a little stray cat. Didn't your family feed you for Thanksgiving?" Gisele's deep voice and throaty laugh fill the room and cause the copper pans to chime. Her tall and striking figure gracefully sashays around the counter to hug me.

"Gisele." We embrace for a few long seconds while Norah refills my plate.

"Mari, my dear friend loved you so. I should show you all the letters I have from recent years that just rave about you and your potential."

"Potential?" I'm a bit surprised by her choice of words.

"Yes, of course. She thought you had fabulous instincts with people. I would agree. Anyone who gets Norah to cook her frog legs is indeed good with people." Gisele looks at my full plate and then at her watch. "Finish up, and I will have Duke move the bureaus around so we can get into them with ease. You do have the…"

I raise my wrist to show her the key.

"Ah, good. This really is exciting. Leave it to Tess to create a bit of a surprise party after she leaves us. Oh, God…I miss her already. Don't you?"

"Yes. Very much."

"Eat up. I will see you in ten minutes." Gisele unclasps the bracelet from my wrist, fans the edge of her robe, and exits as poetically as she entered.

I hold up a pair of legs. "Don't you just want to pull these apart like a wishbone?"

Norah purses her lips. "Pwwuh. Maybe you should not be a cook after all." She stifles a laugh and rinses the sauté pan.

The room housing the treasures is long and narrow with large windows overlooking the park. Red and purple intermingle and present a color palate of royalty very fitting with the surrounding furnishings. The function of this space had, at some point in Gisele's history of residence, turned from sleeping and resting into storage. Stacked in corners are hat boxes, travel steamers, hope chests, and countless packages from Neiman Marcus, Saks Fifth Avenue, and Barneys. My curiosity wants to play here all day.

"Somewhat of a forgotten room, can you tell?" Gisele wipes a finger across a dusty windowsill and shakes her head. "Sad, but as you get older you tend to hibernate in smaller places. I have no need to roam like I did when I bought this place fifty years ago."

"You don't rent? You own this?"

"Correct, darling. In New York that is what people do. The lucky ones, anyway. And through the troubles and losses in my life, I have overall, been one of the lucky ones. Poor Tess had some rough years, yet I always envied how she found her own sense of self."

"She told me that she was a window dresser for Saks. That is so amazing."

Gisele let's out a sigh. "She's too humble. Silly woman. Tess was not a window dresser but a much sought after stylist. A mere window dresser does not become friends with the actual designers, my dear. A mere window dresser would not become the muse of so many that she would, over the years, amass a collection like this…" Her voice fades with awe as she reveals the contents of the first bureau, then the second, followed by the third.

Abundance. Color, texture, depth, richness, and style galore. The miracle closet I had been privy to at Golden Horizons was obviously a very slight sampling of this glorious collection.

"I hope you have big closets."

The meaning of her statement sinks in. These vintage wonders, these bits of fashion history, are mine. "What could I do with these? Other than sit and stare at them in reverence…and don't get me wrong. I think I could spend many hours devoted to just that. But why, Tess? Why me?"

Gisele circles around me as if sizing up whether I am up to the task of taking home such gifts. Will she close the doors and send me away? "I am only beginning to understand Tess' faith…and apparently your own. Can you believe I even gave up drinking for faith? You know all my stories. Let's leave my saga for another time. The answer to your question, as I understand it, is that all of this is between you and God. It is not 'Why, Tess?' that will lead you to the reason. It is 'Now what, God?'" She bites her lip and turns toward me. Her hair is piled up on her head and a few stray ringlets circle the dramatic cheekbones and broad lips. "I believe the answer will find you, Mari."

My phone rings and disrupts our personal moment. I look at the caller ID. Caitlin. Actually, this is perfect timing.

"I will leave you alone for this call. Time for me to put on some real clothes." She heads toward her room and I quickly connect with my friend.

"Caitlin!"

"Mari, how are you? That message you left me last night, about quitting your job or wanting to be old…I got worried. It was pretty garbled."

"No. I don't want to get old. I want to get my old life back, Caitlin."

"I never advised you to do the hair thing."

"Not just the hair. The job and the sense of purpose I had but didn't know I had at Golden Horizons. I don't want the fancy apartment with the private study or the convertible. I just want things the way they were."

"Quitting a new job is easy, but how will you get your old job back?"

"I don't know. I kinda left on bad terms with Rae. And from what I hear, they don't have the money to hire me. What a mess. The only chance I might have is to hold a successful fund-raiser in the next two weeks. Then Rae might listen to me."

"Does switching to your old life mean you don't want to give your relationship with Beau a serious try?"

"Just the opposite, actually. I'm not scared anymore."

"I have to admit that when you left Golden Horizons, I was sad. Happy about your cool new job, but I liked the idea of you helping those people."

"Speaking of which, I wish you were here. Caitlin, you'd freak out. You know Tess' collection of clothes?"

"Yes. Do you get to keep those? Don't kid me about something like that."

"I do…and about two hundred other pieces."

"Don't pull my leg, Mari. Just don't. Describe something!"

"I'll do better than that. I have the camera phone the spa gave me. I'll send you a couple images. Call me right back." We hang up and I snap several very interesting pieces: a sequined tank dress with little mirrors sewn all over it, three hats that resemble pieces of furniture, and a bizarre pair of shoes with very sixties psychedelic colors and a ridiculous heel.

Caitlin returns my call almost as soon as I send the images. "No way. Mari, do you know what these things are worth? Just the time period alone is so hip right now. The dress...I'm almost sure it is an original Chanel, the hats are made by a private company in London that only did designs for the royal family, and those shoes...Mari...those are Roger Vivier creations, they just have to be. He invented that heel shaped like a comma. And the stiletto heel! Nobody did art on shoes or art out of shoes like Vivier. I thought I was jealous of your boyfriend, but forget him. Just give me the clothes."

"Don't worry. I'll need you to advise me about what these amazing items are and how to care for them. We might need to contact some museum curators too. I think a few of these pieces should be under secured glass."

"Um, yeah. Try keeping me away. Call me tomorrow. You are still coming home tonight, right?"

"Yep. Tell the others hi for me. Bye."

"Perfect timing!" Gisele bursts in the room with a Japanese-style full-length dress made of brilliant blue silk with black-and-red embroidery. Stunning doesn't begin to describe her.

"It's a good thing I don't have to decide on one to wear right now. My mind is incapable of focusing."

"Sadly, a first decision is upon you. I wanted you here before we sent them off in case you wanted to select any for me to sell. Well, not me, of course. But I have a friend, Isabel Rossi, who works in the upscale vintage resale industry here in New York. She could certainly serve you well."

"Sell?" This hadn't been among my first thoughts. Would that betray Tess?

"That is, unless you plan on having a fashion show any time soon," Gisele says, laughing.

She is still amused by the thought when the idea whirls about my mind and kicks my creativity into gear with the force of a comma-shaped Roger Vivier heel.

"That's what I'll do!"

Tess has not only given me designer labels, she has inspired the design for my soon-to-be created, elaborate, detailed master plan to get my old life back in a matter of days. This task would normally be daunting—but that's before I discovered that I have potential.

Countdown: Day Ten

Saturday

A flight home can be quite productive when you stay up until dawn composing emails to send out the next, very important day in a ten-day plan. Racking my brain and straining single threads of connection to people of relative influence, I have a checklist in hand of those who will be instrumental in the dismantling of my new life and the resurrection of the old.

Before I even finish breakfast I have taken care of my first order of business: use my "change of financial circumstance" clause to free myself of the lease for Canyon Crest. This decision also means I will not have to pack up my belongings. I have saved myself endless hours of labor right there.

I give the remainder of my cereal milk to Elmo to make up for my three-day absence.

The landline rings and triggers my jet-lag shakes. "Hello?"

"Caitlin reporting for duty. I have Angelica here with me, and we are going to pick up Sadie. Should we meet you at the Sante Fe so you can tell us exactly what you are scheming?"

I wipe a Sugar Rice Puff crumb from my lip. "Sure. Meet you there."

"Do we get a hint? I mean, getting your old life back…does that really involve a master plan? Couldn't you just play Sweatin' to the Oldies and go back to calling bingo numbers?" Angelica shouts into Caitlin's phone.

"Believe me, a plan is needed. And why don't we meet at Freddy's for ol' times' sake?"

The girls are seated at our usual table by the time I arrive at the restaurant. From the enthusiastic reception I receive, an observer would assume I have been gone for weeks. Even Angelica seems joyful, and this is before coffee.

First, I insist that everybody else share what is going on. It seems like so long since we have talked to one another. Caitlin is eager to begin.

"Well, I started blending some of those Mexican textiles with more conventional fashion fabrics and have come up with some pieces I think could really take off. They aren't too out there, but just clever enough to get people's attention."

"Oh, I like that already," chimes in Angelica.

"Thanks." Caitlin pauses and actually blushes. When the hiccups start, I know she is holding out on some important information.

"What is it?" I give her my "divulge" look.

"I might…might…have a second date with officer Jim."

"Second?" Sadie says.

"I didn't tell you all about the first because, well, what are the odds I will like a police officer?"

"With great eyes," I add.

She smiles and bites her lower lip. "And the eyes have it…second-date motivation, that is. Why not, right?"

A busboy comes up to fill our coffee cups.

"Where's the waitress?" I inquire.

"She's running late. She had an early morning seminar at college."

This surprises me a bit. I had never thought about what Cruella did when she didn't serve tables. I tug on the guy's apron. "Do you happen to know what class she is taking?"

"Something tied into her master's degree, I assume. Samantha's a real brain. I think it's psychology, but there is a more specific term," the teenager scratches his red ear, seemingly embarrassed by the attention of a table full of women. "Oh, yeah. It's behaviorial science. I remember because she took this job so she'd have material for her thesis on patterned social behaviors. Anyone need decaf?"

A big round of no's follows this question.

Sadie looks around at each of us. "Can you believe it? We are all dating. This has never happened."

"Wow."

"True. That is strange," I say, still thinking a bit about being a test subject for Cruella…or Samantha.

Angelica holds up her hand in protest. "I'm not dating Peyton."

"Isn't that just semantics, really?"

"No. I like the guy a lot. A lot. But…I've decided not to date for six months at least. I need to get my focus straight again; dating always throws me off-kilter. You all tease me about my breakup dramas, but living that way really isn't all that fun or funny. It's tiring. Peyton says he'll wait, but I'm not asking him to. I don't want any pressure to have to date until I'm ready." Her eyes peer over her coffee cup as she drinks in our first responses.

Out of surprise and respect, we give her a round of applause.

"Miss Verity? The table is yours." Angelica volleys the conversation back to her friend.

Sadie looks across at me. "Our talk…it really helped. I needed to clear my head and stop focusing on the baggage." She turns slightly to look at the others. "Carson has a former wife and a ten-year-old son. I was doubting everything. His past. Our future." She waves away the air in front of her face as if clearing out cobwebs. "Anyway, I'm better. We're better. I'm not going to second-guess him or where this is going. I plan to enjoy it for what it is right now."

"Good for you." Caitlin pats her friend on the shoulder.

"No more stalling, Mari. What are you up to?" Angelica taps her fork in my direction.

After a few stories about my trip home and about the amazing inheritance, I summarize my theory about how one good fund-raiser could be my ticket back to the slow-track life. They all nod in agreement and start to offer some long-term ideas.

I destroy their mundane suggestions one by one. "No wrapping paper campaigns or walkathons or monthly bingoathons. I have the most fabulous solution, and it will happen in ten days."

"Ten days!" Sadie grimaces. "I get testy with a fund-raiser every six months at the Botanical Society."

"No frowns. Golden Horizons would have to have the money before the end of the year, so ten days will have to do. Besides, it's a fabulous idea." I lean in toward the center of the table and they all follow the secrecy gesture. "It's a fashion show and auction."

Caitlin squeals as she did when we discussed the London royal hats.

"That is fabulous. And very trendy right now," Angelica encourages.

"So you'd part with your inheritance?" Sadie looks at the big picture.

"Only a few select items. If these pieces are worth what Caitlin and Gisele say…it won't take many. And you know, that last day I saw Tess, she was wishing she had a way to save Golden Horizons from their financial troubles. This event will support and create awareness for the recreational program's ongoing needs."

Sadie's concern turns to support. "She'd be very happy. So let's get busy." She counts off on her fingers. "With such short notice the key factors might be tough, Mari. Just be prepared. You need a location. Immediate promotion. An emcee. A caterer. Maybe even cosponsors, if that is at all possible."

"Wait a minute. Ten days…that's your birthday." Caitlin is also counting on her fingers.

"I thought that would be appropriate since I've been carrying around this crazy, but perhaps conceivable, notion that I would have it all…or at least a large stake in the life I want…by the time I am thirty. Of course, now that life looks different than I imagined."

"Isn't that the way it goes," says Sadie, sighing.

"Hold it. Ten days would be a Monday. You don't hold trendy fundraisers on a Monday. It has to be the Saturday before."

The blood rushes from my face to my heart, which is racing. "So only eight days to plan the show? Lord, help me." There's that prayer again. This time, I mean it. "Well, it's a good thing I have taken care of one very important piece of this ambitious plan."

"What's that?" Sadie has a pen poised over the napkin she is using for notes.

"I have three fabulous models who are willing to work the runway for the mere price of a Saturday breakfast."

"That is, if we ever will get breakfast!" Angelica raises her voice and shows a bit of her old self.

Samantha approaches us in a shuffle. It is the fastest I have seen her move. "Orders?" she says, still tying her apron.

The others order their recent usuals, but she pauses when she gets to me. "Blueberry crepes?"

"You remembered. I'm touched. But no…I want the Senior Sunrise Delight, thank you very much. There, that wasn't so hard to say."

"Coming right up." She is surprised by my sunny disposition today; I see her scribble some extra notes on her order pad.

"Can I ask you a question about your thesis?"

Samantha looks around her and directs her ballpoint pen in the busboy's direction. "Did Willy tell you?"

"Yes, but don't be mad. We find it fascinating. I'm just curious. Did I make your thesis?" I bat my eyelashes.

"Are you kidding? You're one of the main subjects. But don't worry. Names have been changed to protect the guilty."

If only she knew I am the diner formerly known as Chanel.

Countdown: Day Nine

Sunday

I'm sorry I couldn't be in town to meet you at the airport," Beau says sincerely. "It's just such a long drive."

I wonder if he says this to address the same-city relationship I have not yet agreed to. "You know, going home really helped me see things clearly. Want to know something funny? I think I was afraid of you…or us. I didn't want to end up like my parents."

"Which is…?"

I laugh. "Uh, boring, poor, too busy to love me, always sacrificing and never receiving. At least, that was my childhood view."

"And now?"

"I see it for what it is. They are happy, in love, committed, overflowing with gratitude and blessings, and they have boundless love for everyone. I always thought there was a limit…like the well of love would run dry and I would be left out because they were always giving."

"I'm glad you figured that out, Mari. That gives me hope that maybe we will be able to date like normal people in the future."

"Future. Meaning…not soon?"

"Well, work has been crazy lately, but I promise that I will be more available down the road. Maybe it is good that we decided to hold off on the move thing."

Wait—I didn't say hold off. I was just indicating we could move forward.

I become a bit defensive. "It's okay. I have a bit of a busy schedule ahead of me as well." I proceed to tell him of my plan. I leave out that my deadline is at all birthday related. I don't want the guy to think I am desperate. He picks up on it anyway. The deadline part.

"Seems that a special someone's birthday is coming up."

"Hmm?"

"Go ahead and be coy. I assume you will want the present I have for you?"

"Of course! Do I get a hint? I don't like surprises."

"Gosh, I wish I had known that sooner. Too late."

He continues to tease me until I can no longer take the not knowing. Before we hang up, he promises to attend the big show and maybe give me a hint then.

Angelica joins me after church to turn my living room into event headquarters.

"Let's move the couch against the wall and then put the dining table in front of it," she suggests. In seconds we have an ideal master plan desk.

"Perfect. That gives Yvette and Zane two outlets. They'll need them for the computers."

"What are they doing again?"

"Believe it or not, I decided to resurrect my old site. But this time it will be all about the fashion show. Yvette designs retail sites, so we will be able to accept bids online."

"Genius!"

"It's amazing that something I thought was so bad will be a tool for good." I laugh as I realize that this is a theme for my life now. "We'll send e-vites to the entire mailing list. A global fashion auction. Can you believe it?"

"Not really. But I'm just learning to have faith again, so bear with me," Angelica says, revealing her recent struggle.

"Maybe we both are." I join the confession.

Zane and Yvette arrive on time with armloads of equipment.

"Welcome home, honeymooners!" I greet them with genuine affection. They look so happy that Angelica and I share a glance of envy between us. I'm dating…but they're…they're like the perfect couple after knowing each other only a few months.

"Believe it or not, it feels good to be back, though we had a splendid time. It helped us plan for the future too. With Zane's business taking off, and our plan to sell mostly online within a year, we've considered living overseas for a while."

Second look of envy with a sigh added on.

"Set up over there. Meanwhile, we'll go out and grab lunch for everyone. It will be a long day."

I watch the married team dance about each other with perfect co-ordination and flow. The singles team, Angelica and I, bump heads and trip on each other's shoes before we are out the door and on our way to the deli.

Five hours later, the site is up and running. Sadie and Caitlin have arrived to design the online e-vites and the snail mail versions that will have to be hand delivered. They have taped three different designs up on the wall and we all vote on our favorite.

Yvette raises her hand as though she is in third grade. "Mari, I spoke with your Golden Horizons webmasters a few times today to get this set up. But I think I will also need them to help me actually reestablish the original list of emails."

"Could you send out an email flash? It'd have to be to a real select group of people. We wouldn't want random invitations sent," Angelica suggests.

"Great idea. Could we? We'll ask them to bring donations instead of Pez dispensers." I give Angelica a cheesy smile.

"We could do something like that. It just wouldn't be anonymous." Yvette nods and starts to click away at the keyboard.

"Mari, I almost forgot. I brought my printout from the original site. It has the proof you wanted that Rae did bet on your love life." Angelica digs in her dark brown leather bag.

"How humiliating," I say.

Zane looks up from his HTML code and speaks his first words of the day. "Why do you want that?"

"I need a little leverage to get my old job back, if you know what I mean. Though I'm hoping that my fund-raiser idea will be the real selling point."

"If not, you have a lot more than her online gambling," Yvette says as she prints a few pages. "Rae did more than bet on your love life."

"What do you mean?" I skim the pages and try to make sense of it. There is a listing of images...prints. My eyes catch on a Chagall. "I love this print. We used to have it at..." It is all coming together. "You mean she..."

"She sold the art online from your site. If anyone else had figured this out, they would have suspected that you were stealing from Golden Horizons, not her."

"Do you really want to work for this woman again, Mari?" Sadie asks a very good question.

"I'd prefer it if she moved on, but I know Golden Horizons is where I need to be. I consider her an inconvenience."

Caitlin holds up the winning invitation design. "Inconvenient...like not having a location yet for our event."

Countdown: Day Eight

Monday

And to think that I was about to make your travel arrangements to Mexico, kid." Lionel points to my employee file on his desk.

"I know. I'm so sorry. You've been so great to me…giving me this job when I never even interviewed with you." And you carried my limp body to the massage room.

"Well, my mother has great instincts about people." His smile is kind. "I like to think that I had something to do with the choice too. I saw your potential. The fact that your potential is going to be used to help the elderly again…how can I complain about that? It wouldn't be a very good community service statement, now would it?"

"So you like to do your part?"

He peers at me over arty reading glasses.

"Can I interest you in joining me to help the elderly?"

"What do you have in mind? I'm already giving them back their top person."

"As kind as that is, I won't have a job unless I can pull off a very important event." I start my spiel about my amazing inheritance and the fund-raiser idea. When I start to see his eyes wander to the golf course just yards away from his office window, I redirect my information as to how he can help me. "Now I just need a spectacular location that could attract the affluent, big-hearted people I know Tucson has. The kind who would lay down decent amounts of money for original designer dresses, hats, shoes, and…" I pause, recalling Lionel's outfit the night of Sadie's gala, "ascots. Plenty of those too. Did I mention these are original designs? This level of the auction could attract a lot of publicity."

Lionel's fingers go to his collar and then to his heart. He taps a few beats before standing up to look out the window. "How many people?"

"Well, I'm praying for one hundred people who are in the buying mode. We could draw a much bigger crowd except that our promotion is, regrettably, short notice. With Majestic Vista's membership list, I imagine we could get at least fifty or a hundred more."

I notice him considering what he might look like walking the runway at the end as two hundred people applaud his humanitarian efforts.

"And there will be worldwide exposure. We are allowing international online bids. Just think of the promotion you…Majestic Vista…will get from this. I could add a link to your site." I'm getting to him. He now taps his toe.

"How short is short notice?"

"I need the space this Saturday. I know how…" I'm about to apologize before he interrupts.

"The space we have, but I happen to know that our chef is gone. He's teaching a holiday cooking class in Phoenix this weekend. This is why the ballroom is available."

"What if I told you Jace Burch was going to be the chef of honor? Could Majestic's sous-chef and waitstaff be utilized?" This piques his attention. "Donated, I mean. We would need all of this donated. You'd receive very generous credit, of course."

"Jace, you say? Is he signed on?"

What is this, the pro football draft? "My team is this close to signing him." I pinch my fingers together to show how close Jace is to donating his time and stretch the truth.

"Deal," he says, reaching out a tanned hand to shake my pale one. I knock over his gold desk clock in the process.

"Thank you so much, Lionel. For everything. I hope that my leaving doesn't leave you in a bind." Why do I bring up the negative part of this meeting when the man just agreed to donate more than a thousand dollars' worth of services?

"We'll manage, but we'll miss you. You started our Scrabble tournament and the very popular Yoga to the Oldies class. Do tell me you will come back for the staff bingo tournament. You're our only caller."

"I'd love to come back. Who knows, if my meeting tomorrow with my future boss doesn't go well, I might ask you to forget that this quitting thing ever happened."

"Can I ask why you left Golden Horizons? I understand the attraction of this place, but your heart is clearly there."

"Sometimes you have to detour through your fantasy to get to your reality."

This makes him laugh. "I have never had my resort described as a drive-through, but I'll take that as a compliment."

"Oh, that reminds me. Can I post this in the employee lounge?" I hold up a handwritten "car for sale...like new" sign.

"No! Not that too?"

"It goes with the fantasy." I shrug.

"Of course," he says with a slight bow of his head. "You may post the sign." Lionel starts to close my folder but notices something inside. "Oh, I almost forgot. Your test subject sent you a thank-you note."

"Wendy? Are you sure it is a thank-you?"

"She also sent me a very complimentary letter about your professionalism. In fact, it was her satisfaction that guaranteed your ticket to Mexico."

"I'll get to your resort someday, Lionel. I will just enjoy it as a guest."

"Well, let me know when you do, and I'll be sure you are taken care of. Thanks, Chanel…Mari…for your work here. I wish you well."

Lionel pushes the tiny reading glasses back to the bridge of his nose and begins to read his schedule for the day. I exit quietly and find a secluded place beside an indoor pond to read Wendy's note. It starts out very proper and professional, but eventually she sounds like the person I got to know by the end of our shared time in the mud room.

> *Dear Mari,*
>
> *You went above and beyond the call of Majestic Vista service during my visit last week. Not only were you courteous and professional, but you were also incredibly kind and understanding.*
>
> *On a more personal note, you reminded me to return to the piece of my life that has been missing…my relationship with my dad. You helped me see that my guilt from the past was keeping me from a future with him. I wish, for my dad's sake, that you were still at Golden Horizons. But for my sake, I am glad you were at Majestic Vista to save the day.*
>
> *If you ever need a favor from a person some consider a local celebrity, call me. God bless ya, Wendy Skies…a.k.a. Ingrid.*

Although it was hard to see a bigger purpose while picking mud flakes off of this woman's back, it now is clear that she needed a private shoulder to lean on…just as I will need a very public face to bank on.

Countdown: Day Seven

Tuesday

I have good news," I say to my cohorts, who are all piled into my car for one last luxury joyride. I asked them to join me for a planning meeting at a surprise location.

"You are unemployed again?" Angelica asks without sarcasm.

Hmm. "Well, yes. Yes, I am. But that's not the best part. I have secured three important pieces of our invitation."

"What?"

"Who? Or where?"

"Wendy Skies agreed to be the host for the show and for the auction."

"How on earth did you get Wendy Skies?" squeaked Caitlin. She is overjoyed.

Angelica looks at me suspiciously. "I thought you didn't like her."

"I got to know her and she's really quite nice. And…" I draw out this last part for effect, "she sort of owes me a favor." I pretend to turn a key and lock my lips.

"What else should we add to the invitation?" Angelica has her Black-Berry out and ready.

"Majestic Vista's ballroom is ours for Saturday night. Free of charge."

"Perfect!" cries Sadie.

"Okay, you quit your job and they give you a perk like that? Are you more valuable to them gone or something?" Angelica tries to figure out the angle.

"In a manner of speaking. I sort of promised Lionel that I'd bring in a famous chef." My arm reaches across Sadie in the passenger's seat; I point to the burgundy awning as I pull up to the curb.

"Jace agreed to cook for this?" Sadie'e eyebrows rise with surprise when she sees where we are.

"Not yet," I smile as the others get the picture. We are here to turn on the charm and secure our chef.

"Welcome to Lily's," Pierce greets us and then gives a thumbs-up when he sees that it is me driving this nice vehicle.

I hand him the keys. "I'm sort of borrowing it from a future owner, so take good care of it for me. Is Jace here? I have a little business proposition for him."

Pierce looks at his sports watch; I notice it has Zane's company logo on it. "Jace will be making his rounds with the guests very soon, if that is helpful information. Have a nice dinner, ladies."

When Jace sees us, he first takes in that we are a group of nicely dressed women and bows. But within seconds he notices me and comes over to greet us. We are immediately whisked away to a beautiful table in a prime location and served the first course within minutes.

"Carson always requests this very table," Sadie says, nodding in approval.

"Things are still going well for you two?" Angelica inquires.

"Yes. Very well. I'm taking things one day at a time so I don't get ahead of myself."

"Or hurt," offers Caitlin.

We all nod knowingly.

Sadie fidgets a little in her seat. "Now, about the event. Carson said he wanted to talk with you about getting involved somehow. I don't know if he wants to be a sponsor or what. I decided to step out of the way for this so he can talk to you directly. I don't want him to feel obligated because of me."

I grab a roll and lace it with honey. "If the boy's sense of obligation leads to a donation, bring it on."

"Do we even know what Carson does? Other than stare at Sadie and the stars?" Angelica brings up a mystery.

"I read people pretty well. My guess is that he is a broker," I say, reaching for another roll.

Angelica takes it from me and begins to eat. "I guess real estate."

Caitlin bobs her head to her right and then left shoulder a few times to keep pace with her thoughts. "Carson strikes me as an investor for himself. I think he has lots of money that just keeps breeding money."

Sadie nods at each of our guesses. "Are you ready for this? He is all three and then some. Carson works for his dad, who owns Oasis Jewelry."

We all know this means classy, high-level, high-fashion jewelry. But apparently Angelica know it means something else as well. "As in…he is the heir to this fortune. You do realize his dad owns a lot more than just that chain of stores?"

Sadie gives her a "now why did you bring that up" look.

"He has to be wealthy to keep this group in balance. I decide to go back to poverty level…Sadie decides to go the way of American royalty." I use my hands as scales to show how this levels us out.

Sadie gives a half-sigh, half-laugh. "Just give him a call. Please. Here is his card."

Even Carson's business card is edged in gold.

"How are my most beautiful guests?" As Jace turns on his charm, I prepare to make my move.

"Jace, the meal has been spectacular. You really are a genius. No wonder Kevin Milano asked if you were going to be my chef for the biggest fashion event of the year. I told him that this would be too short notice for someone of your fame." I raise my glass high before taking a sip so that Jace's line of sight would follow. Just above us is the framed Kevin Milano photo of Jace and me.

The bait is taken. Jace pulls up a chair and places his darling chin in his hand. "And which event is Milano speaking of?"

My mind is racing. I realize I have not thought of a name for it. "The...the Hip to Be Square fashion show. It's a benefit for the Golden Horizons Retirement Center. Didn't you mention once that you are considering having your mom live there?"

"I like that. It's playful." Jace scratches his stubble.

"The only problem is...it is this Saturday at Majestic Vista. I know how you like to prepare and perfect your cuisine far in advance. Too bad..." I stare at the photo one more time.

"I'm in. Yes, I'm in. I'll have my sous-chef cover that night."

We can all see that this decision worries him a bit.

Sadie adds her professional tone to my efforts. "That's a fine idea. Besides, anybody who is anyone will be at the fashion show. Your usual dining clientele will all expect to see you there donating right alongside them."

We can see that Jace's mind is already sifting through menu possibilities as he rushes back to the kitchen, hands flailing as if adding seasonings to the imagined main course.

"Is Kevin going to cover the event?" Caitlin asks.

"How could he not? The Majestic, Wendy Skies, and now Jace. Like Sadie said, it's where anybody who is anyone will be."

"I never thought I would say this...and mean it...but you are a better networker than I am. Cheers." Angelica toasts me with her diet soda.

I raise my glass but hold up my other hand in protest. "You guys, this is not about me networking. I'm just gathering up all the bizarre pieces God gave me over this past, crazy year."

"Here's to trusting God to put together the bizarre puzzle of our lives," says Angelica without any hesitation.

"Amen!" we all say.

Countdown: Day Six

Wednesday

I think you'll find that the evidence points directly to you, Rae. All we would have to do is access security tapes from last year to see which paintings have gone missing. You might be the star of a few of those tapes. Ever think of that?"

Rae does not offer me candy, a seat, or a response.

I hug my arms around myself to keep warm in her icebox of an office. "Look, I'm not here to ruin your life. I'm here to get mine back."

Her eyes show that she is considering this as a possibility, weighing whether I am being truthful. "There is no funding for your position. I explained this."

"I will exchange this portfolio of evidence for the chance to hold an end-of-year fund-raiser on Saturday and to earn enough to cover my position until Golden Horizons gets back up to financial speed. If the fashion show brings in enough to fund me, Sonya, and the recreational program for two years, you will make sure that I am hired back and that my record is cleared. I can only imagine what terrible lies you have written in my file or submitted to the state."

"Three years. Funding for three years."

I wave the paperwork in front of her. "Do the right thing, Rae."

"I could say I was selling old pieces to buy new ones...to offer a variety of visual beauty to the residents. You don't have much leverage here."

My mouth starts to protest, but I realize this argument might work.

"Okay, three years. I want it in writing and notarized."

Rae fans herself and looks, for the fifth time, just beyond me to the right corner by the door. When I catch her eye, she looks away quickly. "That would take this matter out of house. I won't go for that."

"Lysa!" I call out to her. She is listening on the other side of the office door.

"Rae, if you knew anything about your employees, you would know Lysa used to have a career in banking before she decided to become a nurse."

"Let me draft the letter," Rae stalls. She is starting to log on to her computer.

"Not necessary. I have it right here. We'll just fill in the details of three years coverage and that estimated amount." I pull from my briefcase the document Angelica helped me create. I had forgotten that Angelica had been pre-law when we met in college.

"Mind if I have a piece of candy?" Lysa asks boldly.

No answer.

"I don't recommend the red hots," I say, extending the dish to Lysa while Rae signs on her line. A moment later I sign on mine.

On our way out, I look to the right and see a stack of flat banker boxes.

"Lysa, be sure a copy of this stays in my file. As a matter of fact, could you sit on my personnel file until next Monday?"

"I have a lockbox tucked away in a place she'd never go."

"Where?"

"A resident's room."

We laugh at this unfortunate truth.

"Do you think she might be planning her escape?" I ask.

"Would we care?" Lysa deadpans while grabbing her coat and locking up her file drawer.

"Only if it ruined my plan to start back here on Monday."

"Keep your perspective, Mari. What if she did leave on the first plane to Nepal tomorrow? Do you think some new director is going to reject a big, fat check and a fantastic person, like yourself, who is willing to work here for peanuts because you care? She'd be nuts."

I consider this. "Why Nepal?"

"Just a random location."

"Very random." She's right that I shouldn't worry.

"Let's walk out and grab a coffee at the corner? I can't wait to have my office buddy back." Lysa's arm goes around my shoulders for a quick squeeze.

"Sure." My eyes take in the hallways that used to seem so drab and sorry. Now I notice the small things that make them personal and warm. The scattered decorations. A master list of every resident's birthday. Embroidered nameplates on each door. Photos of family members and days gone by pinned to bulletin boards and door frames. "Can you believe I miss this?"

"I wouldn't have believed it my first week here…but yeah, now I can."

Count Down: Day Five

Thursday

The man of our dreams stands in my doorway. The man we have been waiting for all of our lives—well, our past week—fills the frame and is bowed on one knee. I hold my breath and twirl my hair in anticipation.

"Whichever of you is Mari Hamilton, sign here."

I bow down beside him and accept his muscular knee as a more-than-adequate desk. "You don't know how happy you have made me." I feign tears, but the sight of five large clothing cartons leaning on the stoop is enough to incite real ones.

"Okay. I must state the rules," I say to the women gathered in my small apartment. "I love you all, but no food or drink until after we have looked through the clothes."

Nobody argues. Lysa, Caitlin, Sadie, and Angelica are joined by my Majestic friends and future models Sophie, Sonya, Amie, and Halo—who want their spa names for the runway. All stare past me and focus on the boxes with excitement. Tess' clothes from Golden Horizons are also displayed in all their glory.

"No fights. Something fabulous will be found for each of my models to showcase. Caitlin will help us create looks that add the hip factor, and then I'll use this printout from Isabel in New York to asses the value." I merely glance at the numbers on the suggested starting-bid list and my heart races. "Okay, I did mention no food or drink by these incredible clothes, right?"

"We got it, dear. Let the show begin." Angelica rolls her eyes, pries the paper from my hands, and also notices the prices. In a daze she adds, "No kidding about Mari's food rule. Oh, my gosh. We will literally be dressed like royalty."

I thought there would be screams and shouts as I opened up box after box of incredible fashion creations, but everyone stands in a circle of awe around me. For nearly two hours we evaluate the designs and compare their size, color, and style to the model lineup. Caitlin literally swoons every few minutes as she recognizes the work of famous designers.

"Mari, this is an original Edith Head gown. She was the most sought after designer for films. She dressed Grace Kelly, Audrey Hepburn...everyone." Caitlin starts to embrace the floor-length, off-the-shoulder number but pulls back before the fabric can get near her lipstick.

"It is incredible. You should be the one to wear that. It even has bright colors. Who else could pull that off?" I ask.

"Sadie...and you know it. This is so elegant. Sadie should wear something as famous as an Edith Head design." Caitlin, as always, puts Sadie above herself.

"I disagree. Strongly. This is you. You are our designer, our theatrical kind of gal. Besides, I already set aside a whopper for Sadie." I motion her over to the hallway. Hanging from my closet door is a breathtaking bridal gown.

"Oh, yes! This is perfect." Caitlin claps and laughs with delight, beckoning the others to peek around the corner from the living room into the hallway.

"That is amazing!" cries Halo, who pushes her way to stand in front of the dress. Gingerly she touches the beaded bodice.

"It's for Sadie to wear," I say, turning to watch my friend's expression.

Sadie shakes her head back and forth. A bit in disbelief, I think, but also in protest. "Mari, you should wear this. It's the pearl of the show." She says this but her eyes say more.

"I am the director, not a mere model. Besides, I have the dress I'm going to wear." From where I stand, I can see the clean lines and gentle sweep of the gray Christian Dior. Or "my finale" as Tess called it. "The one I plan to wear is not for sale."

"Yet you plan to sell *this?*" Halo tries to phrase her next question sensitively. "What if…I mean…what about when you get married someday, wouldn't you love to have this?"

"Like you said, 'someday.' I've lived with my head in the future for too long. You can get lost that way. Besides, this dress will go for a good price and help me reach the goal for this event." I shake my head slightly. "I need to sell it. Friends, can I chat with Ms. Verity alone?"

The gathering of women have primped and sashayed long enough. They head for the kitchen and soon are more than making up for missing their dinner.

"Mari, I agree with Halo. This should either be your keepsake or at least worn by you."

"You, Sadie, are the one closest to wearing one of these for real." I drape the accompanying veil over her immaculate hair.

"I'm not so sure about that. Carson's been kind of distant recently. I think my period of odd behavior might have made him rethink the forever after part of our potential. He'd probably think this was my idea as a way to bring him around or something."

"I will make it very clear to Carson that this was my doing. He is going to contribute to the show, by the way. You were right."

She looks relieved. "I was hoping he would. How much?"

"I think he'll be writing a check, but his big contribution will be to loan to us diamonds and jewels for the show. The look will be complete. I thought I'd save that little extra as a surprise for the others. He even showed me the jewelry he plans to bring. Incredible stuff. The guy has taste."

"Obviously," she says, laughing. "Hey…wait. That's not fair. You get to go look at jewelry with *my* boyfriend. What's wrong with this picture?" She takes a glove from the mesh bag draping from the dress hanger and slaps me with it.

"Ha, ha. Very funny. Now try this on." I place the bridal gown in Sadie's hands and attempt to keep my lips from forming a large, obvious smile.

Countdown: Day Four

Friday

Where are you?" Angelica whispers over the phone to match my own tone.

"I'm in the restaurant bathroom. Beau's waiting for me, so I don't have much time. What do you think?"

"Okay. Let me get this straight. The question is…do I think you should ask Beau to move here for the sole purpose of giving the relationship more time or do I think you should *not* ask Beau because when he asked you were noncommittal."

"Right. That's it."

A loud flush fills the cavernous room.

"Wait, Angelica. I couldn't hear your answer."

"I think you should not," she shouts.

Doesn't she know that I called her specifically because I thought she would support such a courageous and strong-woman move? "Don't tell me you think only the guy can suggest this for it to work!"

"Hey, lady. Are you ever going to get out of there?" A young girl's hand points under the door of my stall with urgency.

"One more minute," I tell her and Angelica at the same time.

"The guy did suggest this Mari. And you weren't ready."

I protest, "But I am now. This is the point of this mid-dinner conversation."

"I believe you should let this bizarre piece of the puzzle also work itself out. You said it. You're trusting God's hand in this. Maybe you will be the one to introduce the idea again. But Mari, in a matter of days you will have everything you've been hoping for. Let a few details wait. I know more than any of us that rushing into relationships is usually about settling, not about believing in something real."

Dang. I forgot that Angelica has undergone a metamorphosis. I should have called Caitlin. She would encourage anything romantic. But I know Angelica is right.

The child bangs on the door with the palm of her hand.

"Okay!" I shout from my impromptu phone booth. "Bye, Angelica. Thanks. See you tomorrow."

I exit my stall and face off with the girl who is crossing her legs. "I'm sorry I made you wait, but this is a dire case of life or death."

"'Dire case of life or death' is redundant for one thing. Secondly, get real. Dating is hardly a matter of life or death." She pushes past me and shuts the door in my face.

I look heavenward and grimace. Now that Tess is gone, God is apparently giving me life lessons from a ten-year-old.

Count Down: Day Three

Saturday

◆

Places, everyone!" I stomp my very feminine shoes in a very nondainty way to bring order to the backstage chaos. Just an hour before, Halo and I had everything organized. Each model has her own rack with four outfits, one for every season, and all the accessories. Pinned to each outfit is a description and price card the models will hand Wendy Skies as they start out on the runway. Thanks to Isabel and a few brainstorming calls with Gisele, this is one streamlined, short-notice fashion show.

Well, was. "Get in order. Remember the order. Does everyone have their winter outfits on first?" I quickly scan the lineup to be sure that my friends are clad in muffs, furs, winter whites, and silver snowflake necklaces courtesy of Carson.

I peek out from the velvet curtains and see that nearly every seat is filled. Lionel had arranged the tables in long rows all facing the stage. So the feel is more Vegas show than banquet. I love it.

Life-sized color photos of the various items in the fashion show dangle from fishing line attached to the ceiling. White tabs outline the images to look like paper doll clothes. Cool handbags with polka-dots, alligator shoes, thigh-high boots with sequins, minidresses with turtle-necks, hats in styles ranging from exotic to refined, and graceful gowns dance about our heads.

This fantastic display is Caitlin's vision, but it reminds me of Tess.

I give Beau, who graciously agreed to be my backstage manager, a thumbs-up. He cues Yvette to lower the house lights, focus the spotlights, and start filming for the online bidders. Zane is right on the heels of the mood change and starts playing a CD. "Baby, It's Cold Outside" by Dean Martin fills the room.

I make sure each girl has her information card to hand to Wendy, who is dressed head to toe in Chanel. The blue silk gown with honey-colored trim and a lace-up back I gave her as a thank-you reveals the apparent benefits to an extended mud bath…a rosy back, smooth shoulders, and glistening arms.

"Go, Angelica." I direct my friend forward with a gentle push.

One by one my wonderful friends strut along the runway that runs parallel to the guest tables. When we realized that our ministage was used up by our makeshift backstage, Beau and Carson put together a runway out of long banquet tables, press board, and a plush pink carpet that Lionel uses when Majestic hosts their annual Mother's Day spa weekend.

"Mari, you could sell a few of these, live off of the money, and then volunteer at Golden Horizons. Why the bigger goal?" Halo asks while wriggling out of a Diane von Furstenberg wrap dress.

"It's what I am supposed do. I feel it. And it's about more than my security. It's about what these people need now and down the road. Besides, this event will bring more attention to Golden Horizons than any promotional campaign ever could."

"Uh-oh, watch out." Halo feigns fear.

"What?"

"You're starting to sound like a politician."

I laugh. "Actually, I sound like my mother."

"Is this too short? I didn't think about walking a bit above the guests." Caitlin walks with a stride that gives the illusion she has hips. This is her last dress to model and she wants it to be a showstopper.

"Wait, let me try this." I sit on the ground and pretend to applaud and raise my bid paddle. She repeats her walk beside me.

I get up and go over to a chest of extras I brought just in case. An oversized purse in a color similar to the stripes on her fall outfit should do the trick. "Hold this close to your body and keep it on the side of the audience when you turn."

"Yes! That's it. Can you believe this is almost over? Do you know how we are doing?"

"Every outfit has had several rounds of competing bids, so I think we did more than okay. And there is still the finale."

"Sadie will look so pretty."

"You and the others can go out into the audience after this last round. I want us all to be able to see Sadie. Now, go make that tall policeman smile."

"Can you believe he came to a fashion show? What a good sport."

"Your amethyst brooch is crooked...there." I adjust my friend's pin and send her on out. I hear a round of applause as Wendy announces the dress.

"It doesn't get any more hip than this ladies and gentleman. This is an original Mary Quant design. In fact, this very dress was featured in her first New York show. Don't be shy...this is the last piece before tonight's finale." I watch the paddles rise in every row. Caitlin strategically places the bag between her hemline and Kevin Milano's zoom lens.

While Caitlin holds center stage, I go in search of my closing act. Behind the row of clothing racks, Sadie is turning slowly in front of the full-length mirror.

"Do I have time to present her with this?" Carson approaches me holding a beautiful pearl necklace in a satin box.

I wave him through the narrow space between me and the curtain.

Sadie notices she has an audience and turns to face us just in time to see the necklace. Her slender hand goes to her neck.

Carson looks at her with deep affection. "I thought diamonds might be too much. I hope this is okay."

"It's beautiful. Thank you. Mari, isn't this the perfect choice?" Sadie models the whole look.

"A-hem," Lionel clears his throat to get our attention.

"Heavenly. And your lucky escort just arrived." I step aside to introduce Lionel to Carson and Sadie.

The two walk toward the opening in the curtain. Sadie glances back at Carson one more time before stepping onto the runway. Once they are out of earshot, I break out with a laugh and nudge him. "You thought diamonds would be too much...nice line. Do you have it?"

The nervous man beside me pats the breast pocket of his tuxedo.

"Showtime," I say, grabbing his hand and leading him to the masking tape X on the floor. "I will let you know when she and Lionel are at the very end of the runway...then you can step out." My breathing is quick with anticipation, but my mind is moving in slow motion. I think about the day I met Sadie, and how after college we were so glad to hook up again because most of our mutual friends, other than Angelica, had moved out of town as soon as they had diplomas in their hands. My eyes mist up as I prepare to watch this dress rehearsal for a future, real wedding.

One of us is getting married. It is a startling thought. As much as we all secretly hope or boldly assume this step will be a part of our lives, it is still a shock to me when it becomes reality for someone.

I see Lionel stop at the edge of the runway and step aside so Sadie gets all of the attention. The crowd adores the dress. As Dean Martin's "Amore" plays overhead, the event is transformed from a fund-raiser into a night of romance. Even Jace is down front blowing kisses at Sadie. "Get ready," I say to Carson. "She'll be turning around to return down the runway any second."

Carson moves forward with an appearance of confidence his shaking hands betray. I appreciate him all the more for coming up with such a romantic surprise. Sadie in the dress and him waiting for her at the end of the aisle, ready to propose.

The audience's growing understanding of what is about to happen leads them to "ahh" and "ooh" loud enough to pull me out of my thoughts and into the moment.

Sadie looks around her, at the audience, and finally at Carson. Her inquisitive look seems to be asking him whether he knows he is visible on the stage. But as she approaches him, her expression softens and tears form in her eyes. Carson moves to one knee and removes the small box from his pocket.

I watch my beautiful friend receive the ring and the hand of the one who will walk with her into the future. My heart is so full that for the first time in days…in years…my mind is not on my personal deadline but on the joy of the moment.

And thanks to Kevin Milano, this scene of my friend saying "I will" to a future "I do" will trump Jace's soufflé, Wendy's smile, the models' gowns, and Majetic's elegance to make the cover of tomorrow's Style section.

Countdown: Day Two

Sunday

Beep.

"Mari? Hey, this is Sal. Remember me...the lavender guy? I watched your fashion show yesterday. I bought a rhinestone brooch for my girl-friend online. We met in one of the chat rooms off your old site, so I guess I owe you a big thanks for never returning my call for a first date...I got me a real soul mate. Well, best of luck with everything. (Pause) Guess that's it. Okay...Bye now."

Beep.

I hit the replay button one more time so Beau can hear all of the message.

"Should I be worried?"

"Sal is hardly my type."

"No, I meant the..."

"Oh, the scary factor. Don't worry," I reassure him.

"I'd worry less if I lived nearby. Someday..."

Now he is rubbing it in…my earlier lack of courage. I heed Angelica's advice and do not say I changed my mind. Instead, I change the subject. "I'm glad I indirectly helped Sal find true love." I spend a few moments looking at Beau and wondering…have I met my soul mate? Then wondering…do I even believe in such things?

I mentally shrug my shoulders and shake off the big, vague question I might never be able to answer with complete faith.

"Shall we head to church?" he asks.

I look at my watch. "Yes, just right. We should be five minutes late."

He raises his eyebrows but only smiles. He knows better than to try and figure out my logic all the time.

"Don't worry. I have someone who holds my seat for me."

The service is nearing its end and there is no sign of Rose. I'm disappointed. Now that I have confessed my sin of being single to her, I wanted to introduce her to my *real* boyfriend. Our usual usher, Linda, shares between songs that she thinks Rose has been ill.

As I look around the congregation and realize there are quite a few people in my age range, I wish that I knew a few of them so I could introduce Beau. He notices how quickly I grab my rolled-up bulletin and march for the doors.

"Don't you do the fellowship hour after service?"

"I would…but we hardly have any time before you have to drive back to Phoenix."

"True. Maybe next time. I could start coming here every weekend."

I give him a look. That's a lot of driving. "You would do that?"

"Yes. Maybe I'm old-fashioned, Mari, but this every other weekend dating thing feels a bit too much like a Hollywood arrangement to me." He walks me over to the passenger side of his Honda.

"I should be making the drive your way too," I say, realizing I have not invested a lot of my time meeting him halfway in this relationship.

"Not with your old car, you won't. I still can't belive you kept that thing. Besides, I haven't plugged in very well to the church in Phoenix. If I come here, we can try to build a connection…as a couple."

This is sounding good. Angelica was wise. Beau and I are still moving in the right direction without my worrying about it.

"So what do you have planned for your birthday?" He asks as we step into a festive Mexican restaurant.

"Apparently everyone is busy with something. It's okay. After all, they made my birthday by helping with the show. The girls and I will try to get together next weekend to celebrate. Oh…the girls and you, I mean." This every weekend schedule will take some getting used to. "Hey, weren't you supposed to give me a hint about my surprise?"

"I changed my mind. Maybe I will give you a hint tomorrow."

"But that is my birthday."

"Oh, right. I keep thinking Tuesday for some reason. I sure wish you had a way to celebrate on your actual day."

"I do. Tomorrow morning when I walk into Golden Horizons, show Rae the amount of money the show raised, and start my new, old job…that will be the ultimate celebration."

"Ultimate, huh? That doesn't leave much hope for the rest of us to get you something great. I hope you like my surprise, but it will seem quite small in comparison to getting your low-paying, lots of hours, barely-any-benefits job."

We both laugh at the reality of my choice. "You helped make it happen for me. The time you spent working on the show this weekend…you made my dreams come true. Anything that needed to be done, you just did it. And my friends…everyone loves you."

Beau reaches across the table to feed me a loaded nacho chip. I fill my mouth with guacamole, salsa, and sour cream rather than admit that I happen to be a someone who is part of that everyone.

Countdown: Day One

Monday, Thirtieth Birthday

Caitlin talks a mile a minute. I switch my cell phone to the other ear. "Gisele's contact, Isabel, was so fabulous. It turns out that we have a lot of the same fashion interests. Her ideas are just the expensive version of mine. Did you notice that my parents bought the Mary Quant dress I modeled? They said it was an early Christmas gift."

The connection is breaking up as I get into my old car to head to Golden Horizons. "I did. That is so sweet. I'm glad they participated."

"Halo told me that she bought your car. Now you can guzzle gas and break down just like old times," Caitlin teases affectionately. "Well, happy birthday, my friend. We'll all get together this coming weekend. Sorry that we flaked out today."

"Quite all right," I say. "Beau says he has a surprise for me. I'm wondering if he might come back tonight to take me out. If not, I don't mind a night of reflection."

"I hope Beau does surprise you. I hate for you to be alone. Let me know how work goes."

As soon as I hang up Angelica's name pops up on my phone's screen.

"Happy birthday, Mari!" She singsongs to me from her cell phone. There is a lot of background noise.

"Are you at the coffee shop?"

"Sure. I'm at the coffee shop, Mari," she says like a remedial reader in a loud voice. "Sounds like the plan for this coming weekend will work for everyone. We will celebrate really big. Maybe golf?" She laughs loudly; I hold the phone away from my ear. I can see the Golden Horizons sign up ahead and am getting excited.

"Very funny. Never again. Okay, get back to your muffin and triple espresso."

Click.

Ring. It's Angelica's name again. "Did you think of another bad way to celebrate my birthday?"

"What?" Sadie's unmistakable voice responds.

"Sadie? What are you doing calling from Angelica's phone?"

"What?"

"Caller ID. You are on Angelica's phone. Are you having coffee with her?" This would be a first.

"Yes. I am having coffee with Angelica and borrowed her phone." Sadie also borrowed Angelica's remedial reader voice. "I just wanted to wish you a happy birthday too. We hope today goes really well. Rae is crazy and in for trouble if she says no."

"Thank you, Future Mrs. Curtis. Did you round up extra copies of the Style section?"

"Are you kidding? I bought out three different street stands of the paper and the Fast Mart by my house. Thanks for helping Carson carry out the best proposal a girl ever had. I heard that the wedding dress was purchased by an online bidder. I know you said you didn't mind, but I was really hoping you would keep it. For someday."

"You just have marriage on the brain now. As you should…you got yourself one great guy, Sadie." I want to enter into the soul mate conversation, but there isn't time. "I'll let you know how today turns out. Bye, friend."

I hang up with my circle of three just as I am about to arrive at Golden Horizons. I tap the gas gauge on my dash a few times to get the needle to work. It raises just a hair, but enough to get me back home tonight. My old parking place is still marked by a makeshift sign made by a resident: "Mari's Cari."

I smile, sip my coffee, and take in each moment of my approach. There is no sign of Lysa. I kind of thought she'd be waiting at the door for me today. But I let the building itself greet me with familiar smells, sounds, and sights. Most residents have their doors closed this morning. They're probably too scared to come out and run into Rae.

When I turn the corner near my cubicle, Lysa is there to give me a hug. Her rushed words in my ear don't make sense. "Sheila who?" I ask.

"No. I said 'she left.' Rae left. I just found out a few minutes ago. Mari, there is a new director."

My knees buckle beneath me. "No! I had a plan. A perfect plan. What if she doesn't accept my proposal?"

"You do come bearing cash, Mari." Lysa reminds me of the envelope in my hand as she adjusts my shirt collar as if I am going in for school pictures.

"That's right. And…and I'm good. I'm talented. Giving. Kind. And it's my birthday, dang it!"

"That's the spirit." Now she rubs my shoulders in the manner of a prizefighter's coach. It's working. There is a confidence building in my gut.

We both stare at the closed door in front of us. Rae's nameplate is gone.

"What do we know about the new director?"

"Seems okay. More professional than Rae. And a tad nicer. I did indicate that you were coming in."

"And?"

"I didn't explain the situation, dear. That's up to you. I just got you in the door. Let me check and be sure now is a good time." Lysa disappears into the office. I strain my neck to try and look beyond the potted palm just inside the door, but I can only see the top third of the barren bookshelves.

This place is dead. I check my watch. The morning newspaper club should be gathering by now.

Lysa walks quietly backward out the door, as if afraid to stir a sleeping giant. This quickens my heartbeat. The new director said no.

"Go ahead, Ms. Hamilton." She curtseys and swipes her finger across her neck. This was our signal for Rae's bad mood days.

"Great," I mutter before quickly putting on a warm smile. "Knock. Knock." I enter with a stupid line.

"I know that joke." A familiar voice comes from the left corner of the room, behind a set of stacked file drawers.

I walk toward the voice until I stand face-to-face with Beau. I look about me, waiting for others to jump out and yell surprise or happy birthday. But it is just me and him. "What?" I say, still waiting for the farce to play out.

"Welcome, Ms. Hamilton. I was just reviewing your personnel file. Quite impressive." He leans over and pecks me on the cheek.

Now I see that the boxes lining the wall have his name on them. This is not a surprise party…this is Beau's surprise.

"You are the…my boss?"

"Rae's recent bad state review was the last straw. Our shared board had been watching her for months, actually. I had already told my supervisor that I was open to a move here, to be closer to you, by the time the verdict was in about Rae's position being open." He watches my face for a reaction.

I try to process all that he is telling me. My emotions are trying to catch up.

"I didn't know that you would ever want to return to Golden Horizons…or I would have asked how you felt before I accepted the transfer." Beau is trying not to state his worry, but his rambling says it for him.

"Shhh," I say with my finger to my lips.

"And God seemed to work out the details because that great place…Canyon Crest…they called and said they had a last-minute cancellation. I got the last condo available. Remember that place? You mentioned it once…"

"Be quiet." I step back to put a few feet between us.

After a moment of silence Beau adds, "But then you were so uncertain about us living in the same town…*and* you made it clear that you hate surprises…"

I just look at him and consider all of this. The package of having my job, having him here in town, working with someone who actually cares for the residents.

"What, Mari? Say something." Beads of sweat are forming on his forehead.

"Be quiet," I say at barely a whisper. "I'm trying to enjoy the most incredible birthday gift I have ever received."

When Beau realizes I have just said something positive he rushes forward and hugs me so tight that my feet are lifted off the linoleum the color of oatmeal.

While Beau still holds me above floor level, he grabs a party favor horn from his desk and blows into it. The door opens and everybody I care about floods into the office. Caitlin, Sadie, and Angelica enter with sheepish grins and are followed by droves of residents who hold "Welcome home, Mari" and "Happy Birthday" signs with letters made out of macaroni.

I realize, looking at all of their smiling faces, that my circle of three might be my core group…but they've never been my entire support system of love, kindness, and joy. My circle is much, much bigger.

About six months later
Golden Horizons
A Monday

A toast to Lysa…for graduating top of her class at nursing school," says Beau as he salutes our friend and coworker with a paper cup's worth of watery punch.

"To Golden Horizons, for adding me to their nursing staff," cries Lysa, with a bit of a yodel afterward.

"To Mari, for raising enough money for Golden Horizons so Beau could hire me on full-time," toasts Sonya—whose real name turns out to be Claire—on her first day as a permanent member of the recreational program crew.

"Oh, my," I say. "Aren't we a self-congratulatory bunch."

"Yeah. Especially for such a group of slackers. It's nearly 8:30. Work, work, work." Beau scrunches his paper cup as a sign of great power.

"We wondered how long it would take for the real Beau to surface." Lysa laughs and looks at her watch.

I look at mine in jest. "That would be one hundred and eighty-eight days, to be exact."

"You," Beau shouts like a corporate sergeant in my direction, "you have a new resident to welcome." He looks at his watch and mimics, "in seventeen seconds, to be exact." Then he adds, "And after that, you have to choose a new book for Wendy Skies to read for this week's story hour. And…"

Lysa and I both toss our empty cups at him and exchange looks of gratitude. Dreading Mondays is so a thing of the past.

As we leave, he calls out his parting words. "Mari, just give some more thought to the wheelchair version of rugby, would you? I think it could be perfect for the residents' Friday game night."

"I'll do that, boss. Right away, boss." I walk backward and offer him little bows of consolation. I will never introduce that game to the residents. Nevertheless, I love the guy for trying.

Love the guy. It has taken me a long time to admit this. Love and the whole "our, we, us" lingo is still new to me. But I'm getting the hang of it better every day. "We will never play wheelchair rugby or it will be the end of us," I call out between snorts of laughter.

Still walking backward, I don't notice that I am about to run into our new resident. Lysa pulls me forward by the sleeve of my stylish new uniform designed by Caitlin and spins me to face…a face I know. It is more worn, scared, and pale than I recall, but it is unmistakably Rose Waverly.

It takes a moment for her to recognize me, but when she does she steps toward me for an embrace. Her heart is racing, but for once she seems glad to see me. I hold her and begin to tell her how great this place is and how much it means to us that she will join our family.

"And I can introduce you to my real boyfriend. He works here," I say to trigger memories of our old conversation topic. It works. I see her eyes flash with recognition and happiness. I recall what she said the last time I saw her at church and hug her tightly as I whisper, "You won't be alone anymore, Rose."

A year ago I would have wanted to be anywhere but here next to this woman who used to intimidate me. But now I recognize I am in the right place at the right moment to help Rose…because this is the way of faith.

And if I've learned anything over the past year, it's that there is a lot of faith to be gained when a woman finally figures out that it was in her old life that God was doing a new and very hip thing.

About the Author

Hope Lyda has worked in publishing for eight years and is the author of the One-Minute Prayers series in addition to several gift books, including *Everything I Know I Learned from Home Improvement*.

When not journaling or aspiring to write and travel, Hope enjoys her work as an editor helping others reach for and achieve their dreams.

Hope can be reached in care of:

Harvest House Publishers
990 Owen Loop North
Eugene, OR 97402

Or by email at:

HopeLyda@yahoo.com